DEATH

of the

GRINDERFISH

"People of fear will never rise up. People of truth will never remain slaves."
~ King Gaal

Epertase Publishing
First American Edition

ISBN: 978-0-9899917-8-0

Visit Douglas R. Brown at his author Web site
www.epertasepublishing.com
Email Douglas R. Brown at epertase@gmail.com.
Follow Douglas R. Brown on Twitter using @Douglasrbrown22 or Facebook at
https://www.facebook.com/pages/Epertase/212541268758981

DEDICATION

To my late Aunt Beth. Throughout our adult lives we've had our differences, but they were just that—differences. I had always planned to sit with you one day and put our squabbles behind us. I never thought you could possibly leave us so suddenly and so young. I've always loved you and hope you're in a better place. Your whole family misses you.

ACKNOWLEDGEMENTS

I've been gone for a few years. After Rhemalda Publishing closed their doors, I lost a little of my love of writing. It was never the writing that I didn't enjoy anymore, but the other publishing and marketing garbage. Writing with no real guarantee that anyone will ever read what I've written after having a publishing company behind me for a few years was, well let's just say it, soul-crushing. Cue the tiny violins.

Since that happened in around 2014, I've started two new manuscripts during occasional bursts of renewed excitement. Then, 2020 hit everyone in the face. Though I was fortunate to have a career as a firefighter where I never stopped working, my days off on house arrest like the rest of you had me looking at my writing career more seriously again. So, I picked up the figurative pen. And I love it. I hope you enjoy reading this as much as I have enjoyed writing it.

Following are some of the people who made my return possible.

I want to thank my gorgeous, smart, out-of-my-league wife, Angie for all her support and being my sounding board. You and my smart, handsome jiu-jitsu prodigy of a son, Aiden, are my everything. I love you both.

To my always supportive mother, Lillian Dove: You have always been there for me and I am the person I am today because of how you raised me.

To my talented Aunt Bobbe Ecleberry: I am only a writer because of your help and constant encouragement. I can never thank you enough.

To my grandma, Lona Davis: I miss you every day. You were my biggest fan and I'm so sad that you left us.

To my cousins, Greg Ecleberry and Sarah Capitano and your whole families for always supporting my writing.

To Becca Brown for your talent and hard work in making my work so much better. You are as talented as they come. I hope I didn't mangle or decimate this acknowledgement page too much.

To Steve Murphy: What can I say? You are the most talented artist I've ever met, and this cover ranks with the best of them. I could never present my work in a better way than it is with your covers. Thank you. And thank you for being such a great friend.

Thank you also to my jiu-jitsu crews, Elmann Cabotage, James Guynn, Clinton Hewitt, Steven Friedman, Oscar Valle, Brian Baltz, Tana Lantry, and my instructors, Dale Ullom and Tracy Hopkins for all their support and the frequent bruises. Everyone at Station 22 and Columbus Fire (except John Galloway).

A special thanks to Jeff Stanforth, Sean Wooten, Bobbe Ecleberry, my wife, and Cindy Busi for proofreading this story. Every critique you gave made this book better.

I'd also like to thank my friends Brent and Janelle Rudolf and Shannon Prior for cramming by books down your customers' throats, Mike and Rochelle DeNoble (Denotice the difference), Kevin and Sara Stevenson, Bryan and Kara Young, The amazing Mattman McNemar, Cory and Aimee Knight, and Darby and Hazel Blackstone.

Now dig in. Let me know what you think. The best way to help an author is to review his/her work and share it with your friends. I no longer have a marketing department behind me, so if you like this book, try my other works and share a link or two on social media. Or don't. I'll still love ya.

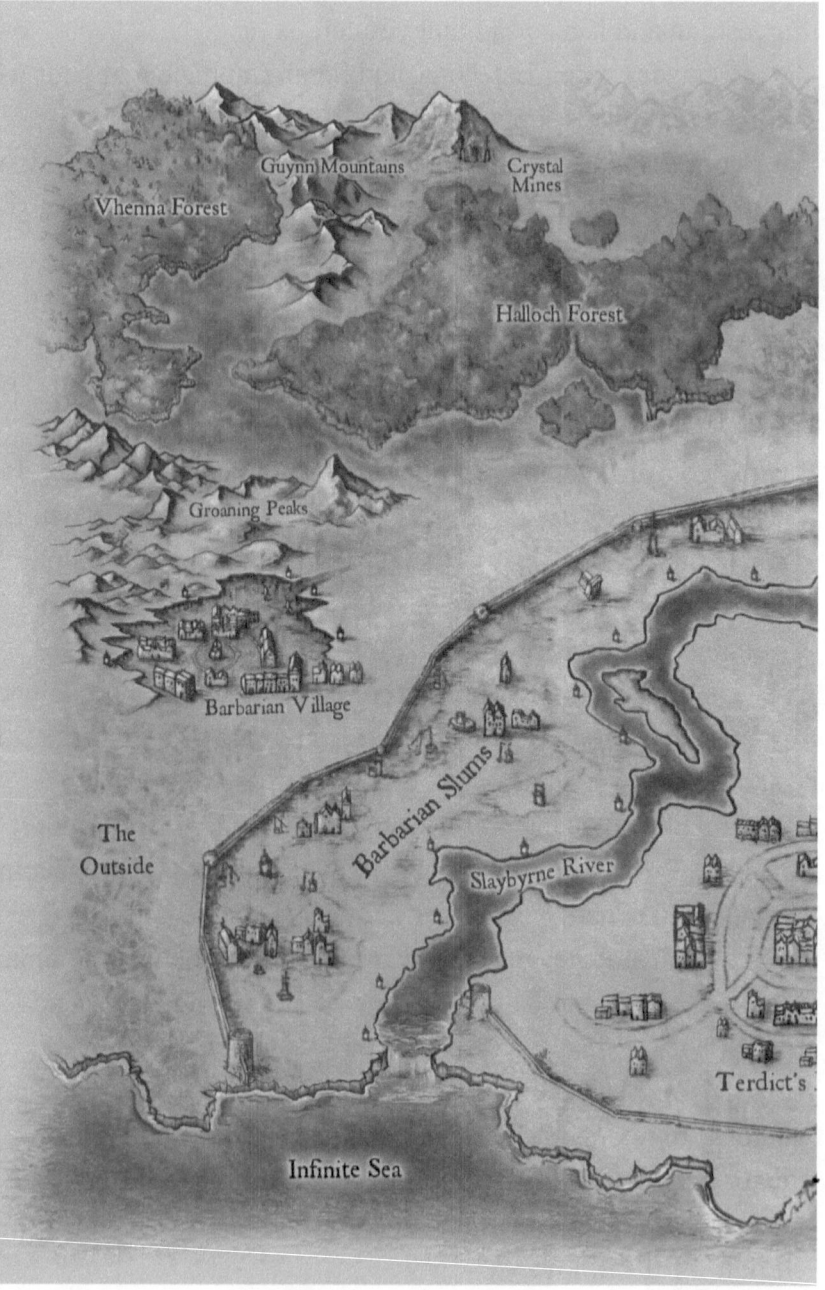

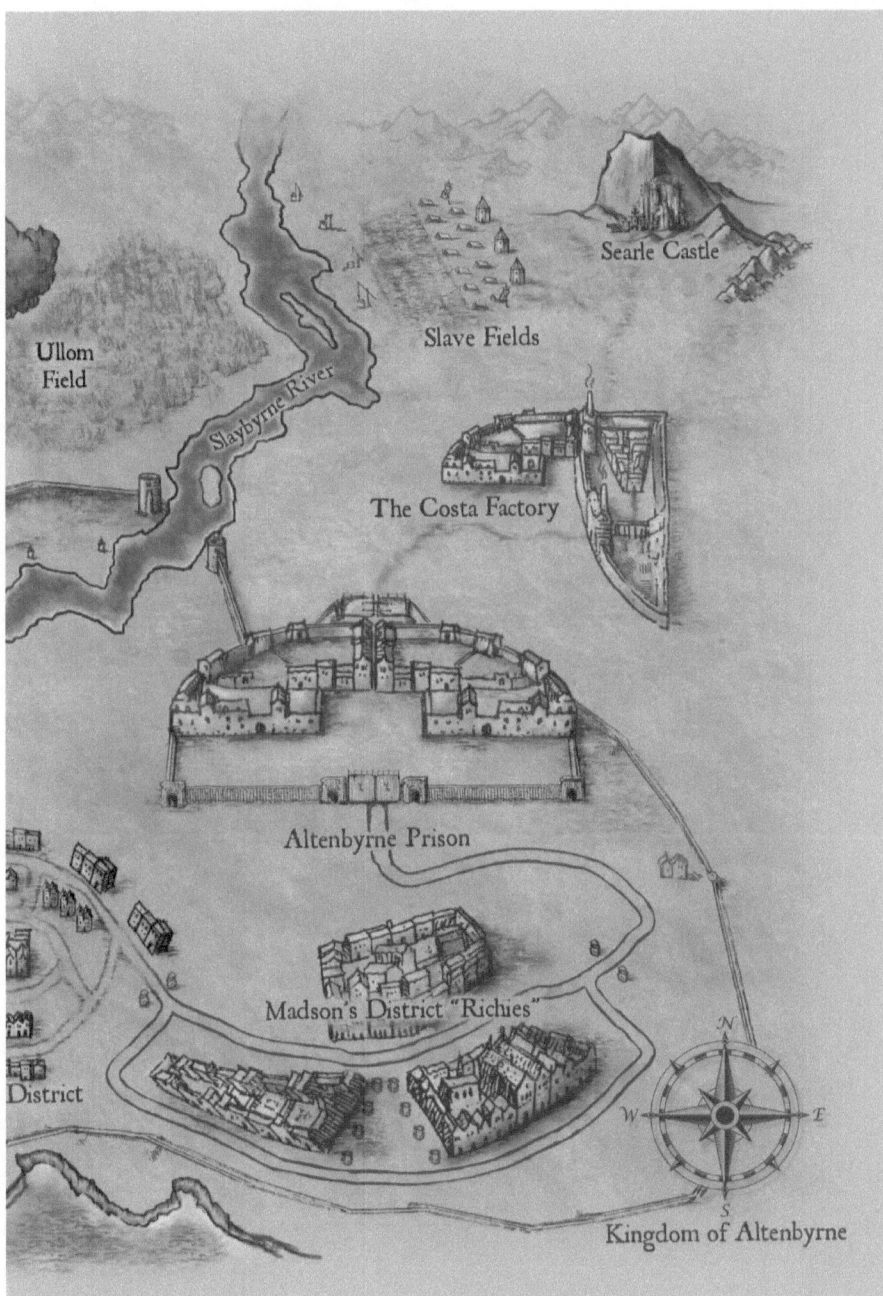

Searle Castle

Ullom
Field

Slave Fields

Slaybyrne River

The Costa Factory

Altenbyrne Prison

Madson's District "Richies"

District

N
W   E
S

Kingdom of Altenbyrne

EPERTASE

DEATH OF THE
GRINDERFISH
BY
DOUGLAS R. BROWN
4

Prologue

A Legend is Born

The green haze that had settled on the kingdom of Altenbyrne during the second month of the siege moved sluggishly in the breeze. It was just before dawn. The foreign army stirred outside the city wall in anticipation of the poisonous fog doing their dirty work.

Keenan shifted nervously, waiting for his summons. He was Altenbyrne's gatekeeper, like his father before him, and only he could open the magical Gates of Exilium that allowed passage through the city wall. His services would be needed soon, as King Searle couldn't put off an offensive for much longer. The Altenbyrne army had been pent up for weeks and was itching for a fight, despite being vastly outnumbered. Tension hung in the air almost thicker than the fog.

Sitting astride his steed at the head of his army, King Searle beckoned Keenan forward. Keenan took a deep breath and immediately regretted it. The chalky film that coated his tongue tasted of rot. For some, like Keenan, the more serious effects of the toxic air hadn't yet taken hold. But for others, like his young son, simply breathing was becoming a chore.

King Searle met Keenan at the wall. He was an older man, though still fit, with tough, leathery skin. "It is time, gatekeeper," he said.

Keenan stepped up to the stone and mortar. His eyes rolled back, and his lips moved as if they had their own free will. He spoke foreign words even he did not understand, perhaps sent by the gods themselves. A thin ribbon of light shaped like a great gateway wide enough for ten men riding abreast to pass through formed in the face of the Wall. The last words he spoke were the only ones in his native tongue: "Open the Gates of Exilium." The stones within the light shimmered out of existence. With a nod to the king, he passed through the magical gate.

The darkness of predawn combined with the green haze to severely limit visibility. But while he couldn't see the enemy camp he knew was crowding the riverbank, the enemy also couldn't see the force creeping out to meet them. Surprise was the key. Keenan's unit of one hundred men headed for the edge of the camp. As the gatekeeper, Keenan wouldn't usually march out to battle, but if Altenbyrne didn't win the day there would be no more use for gates anyway.

Keenan glanced back to see Altenbyrne's barbarian allies from the kingdom's western edge pour through the gates next. With each barbarian soldier standing several heads taller than a man and three times as thick, the disadvantage of numbers would hopefully be minimized. Keenan only wished there were more than a couple hundred of them. Even with the rest of King Searle's army following the barbarians through Exilium, the numbers were still more lopsided than expected.

But now was not the time for idle wishes; they had reached the camp. Keenan's heart beat frantically against his sternum. An enemy guard stumbled upon them, releasing a high-pitched whistle that sent the camp into a flurry before Keenan could strike him down. The early morning silence erupted into deafening chaos.

The enemy quickly regained their composure. Men fell with injuries so horrific that Keenan couldn't process what he was seeing. One soldier wandered past looking for his severed hand, heedless of the battle raging around him. An enemy cut him down before Keenan could help. As Keenan fought forward, he tried desperately to shut out the wails of the dying and focus on where his blade would next land. There were too many of them. Most of Keenan's unit fell within minutes.

An enemy soldier swung a sword at his head. Keenan parried, spun, and skewered his attacker. Another sword came from his right, and he batted it away. The onslaught was relentless. His arms seemed made of lead. His lungs felt bound in leather straps.

The enemy snorted like pigs as they fought. Locked in close combat, Keenan got his first look at their distorted faces. They lacked noses and lips, and their ears were mere slits on the sides of their heads. When they opened their mouths, black mesh stretched between their front teeth. They were the same creatures who had attacked Altenbyrne over a century ago. They had no name and had never tried to communicate, only conquer. After their defeat, the wall was built for protection against future invaders. Now to defeat the wall, the invaders brought the fog to which they seemed immune.

A battle ax whirled at his head. He arched backward and the ax barely missed his nose. Before he could straighten, his right side below his ribs erupted in fire. He dropped his sword and clutched at his side.

He felt the rough wooden shaft of a spear and his eyes fell on the snarling invader who held the other end. Keenan fell to his knees, suddenly cold and nauseous. The creature ripped his weapon free and turned to a new opponent. His carelessness told Keenan what he already knew: it was a mortal wound.

Blood gushing between his fingers, Keenan fell to his side. Another fallen warrior landed on top of him. And then another. And another, until he was buried beneath the dead and dying. He thought of his wife and son.

The pain slowly faded, as did his consciousness. The violent sounds of war grew muffled. As the warm blood of those piled above him flowed down his face, his eyes drifted shut. He couldn't fight sleep any longer.

It was over.

Keenan's eyes blasted open. The weight of the dead bodies pinning him down was no longer crushing. A euphoric wave exploded through his chest. As he thrashed to free himself, the bodies tumbled and fell away. He reached for his wound and found a nasty purple scar in its place.

He breathed deep and looked around. The fighting had drifted toward the wall with Altenbyrne's forces on the defensive. The barbarians fought to the north, plowing through the enemy and tossing their bodies aside like discarded trash. But even they were overwhelmed by the numbers. Before Keenan could move, a twisting, simmering sensation grabbed his gut and spread to his heart. His blood suddenly warmed. He collected a discarded sword and helmet and raced toward the melee. To protect Altenbyrne, he whispered the words that closed the Gates of Exilium.

Keenan's arms felt strong and refreshed. With unnatural speed, he closed the distance. Some of the invaders turned to head him off, but Keenan wasn't the same man they had tried to kill. He ducked and bobbed and spun almost without thought. His every thrust, his every swipe, was perfect and lethal. Not a single blade could get by his defenses, nor defend against him.

More and more invaders peeled away to meet him. He slaughtered them at will. Some of Searle's men even stopped to watch. He didn't acknowledge them as he charged headlong into the enemy, killing without mercy. He didn't hear, or feel, or even tire.

The budding massacre shifted the other way. Keenan howled with delight. Even the barbarians paused to watch. He must have killed a hundred more invaders before he slowed just to soak in his triumph. His success grew contagious, sending King Searle's men back into battle with renewed vigor.

Realizing the odds had drastically changed, the invaders swarmed over each other to retreat. King Searle lifted his sword, his face covered in blood. He thrust his weapon forward and cried, "Chaaaarge," and his men gave chase.

Before Keenan could join them, King Searle waved him over. Keenan jammed his sword into the ground and knelt with bowed head.

"Rise up, gatekeeper," King Searle ordered, his voice deep and authoritative.

Keenan rose with his head still bowed. "Your Majesty."

"I am beyond impressed with your skills in battle."

"Thank you, Your Majesty."

"Where did you come by them?"

Keenan tilted his head and thought hard before answering. "I do not know, Your Majesty. They just seemed to … come to me."

"You have given us a great victory today. According to the histories, the last time these same invaders attacked the fighting reached the city and did extensive damage. I'd say my ancestors' investment in building the wall was a worthy one, wouldn't you?"

"I would. Even with their new fog weapon, they still failed."

"Because of you, gatekeeper."

Keenan shied away from the praise. "With the enemy defeated, the green fog should clear up soon, no?"

The king did not answer right away. He was gazing pensively at a green bulb with a twisting root lying in the dirt. It was called a costa fruit, a common weed and the bane of Altenbyrne farmers and gardeners. The invaders had brought them in by the wagonload. Keenan knew not what they wanted with the foul things. Since they were able to breathe poison, perhaps they could eat it too.

"Your Majesty?"

The king shook his head slowly. "I'm afraid it's not that easy. This fog was created by their damned wizard."

"A wizard? I hadn't heard that. Then we must find him."

"It's no use. He sacrificed his life to create the fog in a foul ritual. The curse is irreversible."

A thousand possibilities raced through Keenan's mind, most of them bad. "Then we should flee to where the fog doesn't reach. I will help you evacuate the cit—"

The king cut him off. "No. That will not work either. In the early days of the fog, we sent scouts past the enemy lines in search of clean air. Only one of them survived. He said there is no end to the fog, and deadly creatures hunt within it. There is nowhere to flee to."

Keenan's shoulders slouched. "But we have to do something. I hear of people already starting to succumb to the poison."

"I have heard that as well." King Searle put his hand on Keenan's shoulder. "I will gather our best doctors and scientists and together we will find a cure. I will do anything to keep my people safe in the city. *Anything*."

Keenan nodded. "How can I help?"

King Searle gave him a grim smile. "First, you can finish off the invaders."

Keenan hesitated. "But … they're already broken and fleeing. They're no longer a threat."

"That's what our ancestors thought. I don't want them coming back a third time."

Keenan nodded. "Very well, Your Majesty."

"Godspeed to you, Keenan. Once you have finished annihilating them, you may return to your family. I will come for you soon."

"Oh?"

"I believe I can make further use of your skills."

"Anything you wish, Your Majesty."

Keenan led King Searle's army to slaughter hundreds—if not thousands—more that day.

During the weeks after the war, the poisonous fog started taking lives. First, nearly all the animals of the kingdom died. Then some of the young and elderly. Keenan's ten-year-old son, Crighton, was one of the victims. The day after his only child's death, his grief-stricken wife took her own life when Keenan left her alone briefly to arrange Crighton's funeral.

Within a week of their funeral, King Searle announced the development of a "miracle lifemask" that would stave off the effects of the poison fog. Keenan was too racked with sorrow to attend the announcement.

While staring at the wall and wondering what he had done to deserve such pain, two soldiers arrived on his front stoop. A royal carriage waited in the street, one of the few remaining horses in the kingdom wheezing slightly in the harness.

"What is it?" Keenan asked.

"The king would like to have a few words," one of them answered.

"I am in mourning. I'm not fit to meet with the king today."

"It's not a request, sir," the soldier replied.

Keenan sighed, pulled the door shut behind him, and followed them to the king's carriage. A dozen or more soldiers were surrounding it. The door was already open, so Keenan climbed in.

King Searle sat in a plush seat with his arms crossed.

"To what do I owe this great honor, Your Majesty?"

"I wondered if you'd heard about the lifemasks I've created?"

"I did."

"I'm sorry I didn't get them done soon enough to save your son."

Keenan stared down at his hands and said nothing.

"We developed them as quickly as we could. It pains me deeply that we lost so many before …"

"I know. I understand."

"I am truly sorry for your loss, Keenan."

"Thank you, Your Majesty. I fear I may never fully recover."

The king gripped Keenan's shoulder in sympathy.

"Is this all you came to tell me, Your Majesty?"

King Searle's forehead creased slightly. "Right to the point, eh? Very well. As we no longer have much use for gatekeepers, I have a proposition for you."

"Oh?"

The king smiled. "I've chosen you to enforce my laws within Altenbyrne. Your word will become the final judgement on all crimes committed within the kingdom. This is a good opportunity for you, Keenan. It'll help you move past your tragedy."

Keenan didn't know how to answer, so he sat quietly.

"My army will become your peacekeeping force. You will use them to police the districts."

Keenan lifted his eyes. "Why me?"

"I think you know. I will never forget the sight of you descending on the invaders like an avenging angel. You have a talent no man has ever displayed before. We need that talent to impose law and order. Besides, you can't just sit around and mourn for the rest of your life."

"It's only been a week, Your Majesty."

"I understand that. But I'm leaving for a while and I need you."

"Leaving? Where are you going?"

"My family will be taking up residence in the north beyond the prison."

"Outside the wall?"

The king nodded. "That is where we found the resources to make the lifemasks. The fog creatures don't venture there. My castle is being built into the face of a mountain where I may monitor the lifemask factory I'm having constructed. That is where my family will dedicate our lives to finding a permanent solution to the deadly fog, no matter how many generations it takes."

Keenan looked down and picked absently at his thumbnail. Finally, he raised his head to meet the king's gaze. "If this is what you command, Your Majesty."

"It is."

"Then I cannot refuse." Keenan had nothing else to live for anyway. "I will not fail you, Your Majesty."

"I know you won't, Keenan." King Searle opened the carriage door and waved for Keenan to step outside. Once he did, King Searle followed, groaning and hobbling on stiff, tired knees. "Don't ever get old," he said as he straightened. The soldiers formed parallel lines on either side of Keenan and King Searle. The king unsheathed his sword. "Kneel before me, Keenan."

Keenan did as commanded.

King Searle touched his blade to Keenan's left shoulder. "Keenan, son of Toriac the gatekeeper." He lifted the blade and touched his right shoulder. "From this day forward, you will be known as …" He paused and then smiled. "As the Angel of Justice." His words hung heavy in the green haze. "Now, rise up, my Angel."

Keenan stood tall and proud. He felt invincible.

King Searle regarded him for a moment and nodded approvingly. "As my Angel of Justice, you will have only two rules to govern you. First, you will enforce every law my family puts forward without question."

"I can do that."

"And second, you will never allow anyone, yourself included, to travel north of the prison walls or leave Altenbyrne under any circumstances, except by orders from me or my family. We must not be disturbed in our research. Is that understood?"

Keenan nodded. He had no interest in traveling outside the wall anyway. He looked back to his home and felt another wave of sadness.

The king followed his eyes. "Listen to me, Keenan. Justice never grieves. Is that understood?"

Keenan bowed his head in assent.

King Searle patted his shoulder and then climbed back into the carriage. He looked out before closing the door. "Do my work well, Keenan."

A deep, lingering anger painted a scowl across Keenan's face. He had spent weeks feeling helpless and impotent as the fog worked its vile curse. Though he had defeated the enemy, they had still succeeded in destroying nearly everything he loved. He would never forgive them, and he would never forget how hard King Searle was working to save his people. He used his rage to smother his grief. Then he locked eyes with the king.

"Is there something else, Keenan?"

Keenan's mouth twisted with resolve. "There is no more Keenan. I am the Angel of Justice."

Part One
Building the Slums

Chapter 1

God of Speed

Tristin burst across the finish line with his arms raised above his head in victory. The gasps and grunts of his six pursuing classmates was the only evidence that he was in a race. It wasn't even close. But then again, it never was. Even the thick green fog that saturated the air couldn't slow him down.

"It's not fair, Tristin," one of the boys complained.

"You always win," another one groaned.

"They're right, you know." Tristin's twin sister, Makenna, approached him once everyone else had started for home. Her lips were pursed in annoyance. "Why don't you let them win once in a while?"

Tristin scowled. "Why would I ever do that?"

"I don't know. Maybe so no one figures out you have a god?"

"How would they ever figure that out? You know I'm a lot faster than what I show them."

"I'm just saying. You. Always. Win."

"And I always will." To Tristin, it didn't make sense to ever lose a race when he had such a talent.

Makenna looked around nervously. "It's getting late, Tristin. Mom's waiting for us."

"Yeah, yeah." Though their mother had strict rules about them finishing their schoolwork before dinner, Tristin knew that wasn't what had been making Makenna so anxious to get home lately. His gaze drifted past her toward Main Street where a crowd had started to gather. "Hey, Makenna. What do you think's going on over there?"

She glanced toward the growing crowd. "I don't know, and I don't care." She touched the side of her face like she did whenever she was nervous. "I have a lot of work to do still. We need to get home."

"All right. You go. I wanna see what's going on first."

Her eyes widened. "You're not coming?"

He shook his head as he took a step toward the crowd.

"Tristin," she snapped.

"I'll be home in a few minutes, sis. I just wanna see." He looked back with a mischievous grin. "I'll probably still beat you there."

"Well, I'm not waiting for you."

Tristin waved and rolled his eyes. Though it had been a few hours since the last time his lifemask had gone off, its shrill chirp still caught him off guard. As he approached the back of the crowd, he unfastened the mask from the metal clasp at his waist, pressed it over his mouth and nose, and took a blood-cleansing breath.

"What's going on?" he asked a man at the rear.

The man regarded him. "Aren't you a little young to still be out? Don't you have lessons to work on?"

Tristin gave him a sour look. What business was it of his anyway? "I'll get 'em done. What's going on over there?"

"Some guy was caught stealing a mask."

Tristin's eyes widened. "He stole one?"

"That's what they're saying."

"Why?"

"Who knows? Maybe his is failing."

Tristin thought of his sick mother at home.

"Did you know that if you live in Madson's District you can get all the masks you want?" the stranger added. "Not like us Terdicts. One for life, however short that is."

Tristin knew that all too well. Why the king wouldn't give a new one to everyone if theirs failed, Tristin would never understand. He stood up on tiptoe trying to see past the crowd. "What's going to happen to him?"

"Nothing good, I'm afraid. The soldiers will take him to the Angel of Justice to be sentenced."

"And then what?"

"He'll be banished beyond the wall, most likely."

"To the Outside?"

"Yeah. Without his lifemask, too."

"But … he'll die."

The man cocked an eyebrow but didn't say anything.

Tristin felt foolish. "Oh. Right. Of course."

The man turned back to the spectacle and Tristin finally caught a glimpse of the soldiers at the front of the crowd. A man wearing worn-out, hand-me-down shirt, trousers, and shoes with the soles barely hanging on knelt between them. He was obviously from Terdict's District like Tristin. It wasn't fair that none of the Richies ever seemed to meet the Angel. "Richies" was the derogatory nickname Tristin and his friends used for the wealthier people from Madson's District. Tristin often wished the kingdom of Altenbyrne had never seen a nobleman named Lord Madson back when Altenbyrne still had lords. It was Lord Madson who first separated the two districts according to wealth. And it was Lord Terdict who died trying to keep the kingdom united. Tristin had always been taught that Lord Terdict was a villain, but secretly he believed he was a hero.

"Should we help him somehow?" Tristin asked.

"What did you say?" He shoved a first finger to his lips and looked around. "Don't let anyone hear you talk like that, kid. You know there's nothing we can do." He gave Tristin a firm shove. "Go home. And keep your rebellious thoughts to yourself before you get into big trouble."

Tristin slowly backed away.

"Go on," the man ordered with a jerk of his head.

Tristin turned and jogged away from the crowd. As he ran, his thoughts drifted like they often did. To get his mind off the poor mask thief and his imminent death sentence, he fantasized about living in a world where lifemasks never failed. Or better yet, where they weren't even needed at all. Once he was in the alleys where no one was watching, he called upon his God of Speed and zipped the rest of the way home. From the front stoop, he could hear his mother wheeze inside. He squeezed past the leaning front door, careful not to knock it over. The hinges had long ago rusted and fallen off.

Makenna was already sitting at the table with their mother, Emma.

"Hi, Mom," Tristin said.

Emma sat with her chin in her hands. Seeing her son always made her smile, but even her smile was weaker than usual. Her hair was a ratted mess, but that was normal lately. Her loud, shallow breaths combined with the breeze whistling through the holes in the sagging walls to sing songs of despair. Tristin sometimes listened to her wheezing from his bedroom and wondered if her sickness would have been cured had his family lived east with the Richies.

"My special little boy," she said.

Tristin rolled his eyes. He wasn't a little boy anymore, and he was tired of everyone thinking he was so special just because he was a twin. A complete set of twins surviving was extremely rare, and even having them in the first place was so unlikely and unexpected that his parents never suspected they had two babies on the way. They had only requisitioned a single lifemask, and Tristin had almost died in the Mask Exchange while his father frantically petitioned for a second one. Maybe that was part of the reason his mother's gaze always lingered on him. And why she squeezed him an extra few seconds when she tucked him in at night. Though he usually told her to stop it, he secretly hoped she never would.

Despite what she said, he didn't feel so special when his stomach rumbled, or his fingers were numb from the cold. Or when he and Makenna were gawked at by strangers whenever they went out in public together. In fact, he felt the opposite. That's why he didn't like her calling him that.

His father, Rhett, had said he'd be late returning home from work, which gave Tristin extra time for his lessons. He sat across from his mother and opened his tattered history book. His belly grumbled, so he shifted in his seat in hopes his mother wouldn't hear.

An old, battered but warm blanket that his mother had knitted was draped over the back of his chair. He wrapped it around his shoulders. An icy breeze howled through the room, sending a shiver up his neck. The blanket couldn't be pulled much tighter, but he gave it a good yank just to be sure.

Emma's lifemask let out a sick, muffled chirp that had become so familiar in recent months. It sounded like someone was smothering it with a wet cloth. Tristin slowly lifted his eyes from his lessons. Makenna held the mask to Emma's face and helped her take a feeble breath. Even the pulsating blue glow from the vent appeared to have lost its brilliance over the last few weeks.

Makenna finished her schoolwork first because history came easier to her. She had a better memory than Tristin. With a side-eye to him, she said, "Looks like I beat Tristin again, Mom."

Emma shook her head. "Now, honey, it's not a race."

Searching for any rebuttal, Tristin settled on, "If it was a race, I'd win. I beat the kids racing again today." It wasn't a good retort, but it was the best he could come up with in a hurry.

Makenna rolled her eyes.

Emma smiled. "You always seem to win. You must be pretty fast."

If she only knew.

Makenna crinkled her nose at him and turned the subject back to their history lesson, knowing it would annoy him. "Why does King Searle still punish us for what Lord Terdict did?"

Emma shook her head. "He must not feel we've learned our lesson yet. We must strive to be better so he will return from his castle one day and lift the taxes that keep your father working so late with so little to show."

Tristin thought her explanation was nonsense and couldn't hold his tongue. "What lesson are we supposed to be learning? How to be taxed into oblivion? Maybe Lord Terdict had it right and King Searle's not so perfect."

Emma stared at him in horror. "Don't ever say that again. If a soldier hears you …"

"There're no soldiers in here, Mom."

"Just the same. You keep those thoughts to yourself."

Tristin looked disgustedly at the last page of his assignment. "Why do I even have to still go to school? I'm just going to take Dad's place at the blacksmith's shop."

"If you're lucky you'll take his place. That job isn't guaranteed. If an opportunity ever arises for you to move east with the Madsons, you need to be well-educated."

"Yeah, right. That never happens for people like us."

"What do you mean? Just two years ago, Talik's boy became a soldier. He and his family moved there."

"He became friends with a Madson. That's how he did it. It wasn't hard work. I knew him. He's lazy."

"Well, maybe *you'll* become friends with a Madson."

Under his breath, he mumbled, "Not likely."

Once he finished and closed his book, Makenna gave him the same crooked grin she often gave before trying to tweak him. "Can we do some extra math problems for practice?" She was also better at math.

Emma knew what her daughter was doing. "If you want."

Tristin's shoulders slumped. It frustrated him when Makenna got her way because he could never be sure she wasn't using her own secret god to sway their mother.

Emma smiled weakly. "You can quit now, Tristin." Her voice was soft and caring, though gravelly from frequent coughing spells.

Rhett's heavy footsteps sounded on the front stoop. Instead of squeezing through the gap like Tristin had done, he lifted the front door from the frame and set it aside. Once through, he propped it back over the opening.

Rhett was a strong man with a tired slump to his posture. He set a burlap sack on the table and touched Emma's shoulder. "How are you today?" he asked.

Emma shook her weary head, held up by one frail arm still propped on the tabletop. Her face was tired, waxy, and strained. "Why are you so late tonight?"

"The soldiers ordered us to the town square for another sentencing and some news."

"Death in the Outside again?"

Rhett nodded.

"What was the news?"

He rubbed the cropped hair on the back of his head. "Just the same nonsense as always. They threatened another tax increase."

Emma covered her mouth. "We can't bear that."

"Don't worry. They make those same threats all the time. What are they going to do? They can't get water from a rock."

"They can take you to the prison."

Rhett brushed off her concern with a wave. "They're not going to do that. It's just talk. Don't concern yourself. We'll be fine."

Inside the burlap bag were a few pieces of fruit and some green beans in a pail to go with their usual porridge. Though it was a smaller than usual haul, Tristin knew not to say anything. That would have been disrespectful to his father's hard work.

Emma waved off her portion. "I'm not very hungry tonight," she whispered.

Rhett set a jar of porridge in front of her anyway. "You must eat. You're too thin as it is." He opened the lid.

She pushed the jar to Tristin.

Everyone in the house knew why she really refused her food. She always thought of her kids first. If guilt had a taste, it would be bitter like the apple Tristin reluctantly ate.

"I think I'm going to lie down," she said. The two suns still hadn't set.

Rhett nodded and helped her to their bedroom. He returned and plopped into the chair where she had been sitting. He watched Tristin chew on the apple. "Savor that, boy. A day's work doesn't buy as much food nowadays," he said.

Makenna asked, "Dad, can't you ask the blacksmith to pay you more? He's got the money."

Tristin snorted, already knowing the answer.

Rhett gave him a hard look. Then he answered, "I'm afraid not, honey. There're plenty of others who would work for less. I'm just thankful to have a job." His eyes were heavy and weary.

After sharing a piece of bread, two apples, porridge, and some beans, Makenna asked, "Dad, what's wrong with Mom's lifemask? Why's it failing?"

Rhett reached across the table and rested his hand on hers. "I don't know."

"But it means she'll ..."

He squeezed her hand. "I'm afraid so, honey."

Tristin turned away. It wasn't that they didn't already know what was happening, it was just something they didn't talk about in hopes that everything would simply work out.

Makenna started crying.

It made Tristin angry. "I hate the fog, Dad."

"I know, son. We all do."

Tristin looked into his father's heavy eyes and wanted to be strong like him, but despite his anger tears blurred his sight. "How soon will she die?"

Rhett bowed his head and wiped the corner of his eye with a handkerchief. There was no use softening his words anymore. "Days, if not hours."

Makenna stood up and ran into the bedroom to be with Emma.

Tristin found the hopelessness hard to accept. His thoughts churned. "Why can't we get her a new one? Another mask, I mean?"

Rhett sadly shook his head. "I have been saving all the silver I could to buy her a new mask on the black market. I just couldn't get—"

Though Tristin knew not to interrupt, he couldn't help himself. "What about my mask? The next time it chirps, I'll let Mom use it."

"You know that wouldn't work. Many have died trying to do just that. Your mask is made for you and it won't work for anyone else."

"I don't understand, though. How's it made for me? How does it know?"

"It just does. I'm sure King Searle knows why, but that's not for us to know."

"What if I breathed into mine to trick it and then let Mom have my breath? Would it know then?"

"Maybe not. But your blood would turn toxic before it allowed you another breath. You wouldn't survive. Your mask is made for you and you alone." He lifted his mask and examined it. "Whatever it is that makes these masks special, that's what has failed inside your mother's. And soon she will die because of it."

Tristin's mind raced. "What can Makenna and I do? We're sixteen now. We can work. We'll help you save the money to buy another one."

Rhett shook his head.

"Maybe the king will give us a new one. We can ask. Maybe he would trade us for something. I'm a hard worker."

Rhett reached over and massaged the back of Tristin's neck. "I've done all I can."

"And if my mask fails, I just die too?"

"We don't need to worry about that. It's not gonna happen."

"You don't know that. What about the Angel of Justice? What could be more just than saving Mom's life?"

Rhett sadly shook his head again. "The Angel will be of no help either. He only distributes justice for crimes committed. He doesn't intervene in the hardships of the people."

"You mean we just have to watch her die then?"

Rhett nodded.

"No. I can get her a new mask, Dad. I'll ... I'll ..."

Rhett shook his head again. "No. You must accept that there's nothing more we can do except show her love. You must stay strong for Makenna. The next few days are going to be very difficult for us."

"The Richies get new masks, don't they?"

Rhett's face fell stern. "What have I told you about using that name? I don't like it."

"I'm sorry. Do the Madsons get new masks when theirs fail? Or do they even fail?"

Rhett dropped his mask back to his side. "Money buys a lot of things, son."

Well, if they can make new masks work when theirs go bad, then it can be done."

Rhett shrugged. "Not for us."

"It's not fair."

Rhett's stern face softened. "Life isn't always fair. But jealousy has no place in this world. We don't concern ourselves with what others have. Is that understood?"

Tristin picked at a knothole in the table and nodded.

"We have love in this house. Gold doesn't buy what we have. There are plenty of people in those fancier houses who don't have as much as we do."

Tristin listened as Rhett explained how good their family supposedly had it while his mother wheezed in the back room. His broken heart didn't feel so "good."

"I've been thinking, Dad. There's got to be some other place Outside where there's no King Searle. Or Angel of Justice. Or lifemasks that fail."

"I'm afraid there are no magic utopias, son. There are only fog creatures, barren land, and death. You've heard the stories."

Up until then, Tristin and his sister had vowed to never tell anyone, not even their parents, about their gods. But with the situation so dire, surely Makenna would understand if he told their father now. In fact, he was convinced she would want him to if it meant saving their mother's life. Mentally, he played out how he would tell him. *I have a secret, Dad. Makenna and I both do. We have gods that give us gifts. I'm really fast. I mean, reeaally fast. I think I can run faster than the soldiers' horses, even. And Makenna can make a person do what she wants simply with a suggestion.*

But even as he rehearsed what he wanted to say, he knew his revelation would end in his father asking what he planned to do with that gift. And knowing how Rhett felt about stealing, Tristin's answer wouldn't go over well. The more he thought about revealing his secret, the more he realized it wasn't the time.

Tristin went to Rhett and hugged him before going to say goodnight to Emma. Makenna had already gone to bed. Tristin sat next to his mother and gently touched her forehead. She opened her eyes slightly. "Tristin, my baby," she whispered.

Tristin wiped his eyes. "I love you, Mom."

The corners of her mouth lifted. She coughed. "I'm so proud of you," she whispered.

"Why? I did nothing to be proud of."

It seemed to take all her strength to touch his hand. "For being you." Her eyes closed again. Tristin lay beside her and hugged her. He couldn't accept that she was going to die. Lying beside her reminded him of all the times she'd read bedtime stories to him and Makenna and lain next to him until he fell asleep. He wished he could comfort her like she had comforted him so many times before.

When Rhett finally came in, Tristin kissed Emma's cheek and went to the tiny room he shared with Makenna.

As he crawled onto his pallet on the dirt floor, Makenna rolled over and said, "Your face is red."

It might have been red because he had been crying, but it could have been because he was angry. Cursing, fighting angry. He didn't answer and rolled to his side, his back to her.

As he waited for her to doze off, he heard Emma wheezing in the other room. It only fueled his resolve. Maybe Rhett had given up, but not Tristin. He wouldn't give up as long as his mother still drew breath. He thought about the man who'd stolen the mask in town and wondered if he was dead in the Outside yet. He wondered how he had gotten caught.

The moon was high. Tristin drew in a deep breath of puke-green air in preparation of the coming run. Hidden behind the crumbling remains of a garden wall, he watched two soldiers from the Angel of Justice's army march toward him on patrol, oblivious to the boy breaking curfew a few feet away.

The soldiers continued past, their complacent patterns easily learned. Tristin hugged the wall until they were out of sight, and then zipped across the narrow alley to the back of his neighbor's house. A peek around the front revealed the two soldiers standing on the corner a few houses away. Their conversation seemed to take precedence over doing their job.

Tristin darted behind an old bronze statue of some previous king on the opposite side of the street. His stomach tightened and his hands trembled.

Kids in Tristin's neighborhood often talked about how nice it was in Madson's District, though Tristin wasn't convinced any of them had actually been there. As he sneaked from alley to alley, covering the few miles to Madson's District, the conditions of the houses dramatically improved. Though they weren't made of gold like some of his classmates claimed, they were far from being rotted shitholes like where he lived. He used the slight sting of jealousy to push him forward.

Tristin didn't see a single boarded-up window or broken front door after he entered the district. Most of the houses even had cloth curtains on the inside that matched the brightly painted front doors. Who had time to worry about curtains matching doors? Most Terdicts were too busy working themselves to death to feed their families.

As complacent as the guards had become on his side of town, they were even more so in the wide, clean streets he prowled now. They probably didn't think the "filthy Terdicts" would venture so far east without a work permit. And definitely not after dark.

The farther Tristin ran unnoticed, the bolder he grew. Along one alleyway, he heard voices from the main road. He slowed and made his way along the side of a grocer's store. From the street, torch lights flickered and the voices grew louder. He crept around the front corner for a better look.

To his shock, Madsons were outside, talking and laughing and drinking from oversized tankards. A few of them even talked with the patrolling soldiers, which was something Tristin couldn't imagine doing voluntarily.

Watching the lax administration of curfew only further convinced him that what he was doing was right. Even angrier than before, he retraced his steps to the back of the grocer's. As he passed a window, movement caught his eye from inside. He dropped to his knees. With his fingertips on the sill, he pulled himself up enough to look between the slight gap in the curtains.

Two men unloaded boxes of bread and fruits and vegetables onto shelves already packed with supplies. He'd never seen so much food. He nearly drooled at the sight and his stomach grumbled. In one corner, neatly cut pieces of wood were bundled together for sale.

Tristin imagined they were for Madson fireplaces. Burning perfectly good wood like that was unthinkable for a Terdict. He could only imagine how warm the bitter winters would be with the benefit of fire.

He hurried from the main part of town to the less populated outskirts where the wealthy houses were increasingly farther apart. For no other reason than it seemed like the right house to pick, he chose a blue one. A flag dangled from a pole alongside one of the windows. Since it wasn't windy, he couldn't see the flag in its extended glory, but enough lavender showed to surmise it bore the king's crest—not that any other flags were permitted. A neat path sliced through the meticulously raked gravel yard to the front door.

Tristin raced toward the back of the house, mindful of his footing on the gravel. A stone-lined pit behind the house held a pile of refuse that the garbage gatherers hadn't collected yet. Tristin hid behind the pit.

So far, so good.

He studied the house, his heart beating through his chest. With his leg muscles tensed to sprint to the house, a familiar smell wafted past his nose and held him rooted to the spot. It was food. But not just any food. It was the smell of the most glorious food he'd ever tasted. It was the rich aroma of a cooked sugar beet, and it was coming from a discarded crate. Sugar beets were rare and very expensive. He only knew what they smelled like because his father had given his mother one for her birthday a few years back. Those few bites Emma had shared with him and his sister had really set his taste buds aflutter, and the smell had secured a spot in his senses for the rest of his life.

Hopeful yet wary, he looked inside the crate. It seemed impossible, yet there it was: a half-eaten sugar beet like the one he had dreamed of so many nights. He was stunned. How could anyone discard something that tasted so wonderful?

The temptation was too much to resist. After a nervous look around, he snatched the beet and crammed it into his mouth. His taste buds danced. His eyes rolled back and his shoulders slumped. His knees weakened. If that was how the Richies treated their food, no one in Tristin's family would ever have to go hungry again. With his eyes closed, he swallowed the magnificent beet, licked his sticky fingers, and then turned his focus back to the house.

Realizing his lifemask hadn't chirped since he'd left home, he decided to wait. It wasn't long before a bright blue glow pulsated from the nosecone and rewarded his patience. He muffled the accompanying chirp with his hand, shoved the mask over his mouth and nose, and exhaled. A whine preceded a louder whistle from the nose cone with his next breath in. He felt instantly refreshed. Late-night lifemask chirps were nothing out of the ordinary, so he wasn't surprised when no one came to investigate.

Tristin crept to the side of the house and peeked through a window with burgundy curtains. Seeing no movement inside, he gently pushed up on the frame. He couldn't believe his luck. The window wasn't locked. From what he could see, Richies didn't have many worries.

Pushing the curtains aside, he poked his head through. The moonlight shone on a bed nestled against the farthest wall. Tristin wondered what it would be like to sleep in a bed instead of on the floor. He climbed into the room making all the sound of a shadow. The floor was soft and cushy and warm beneath his bare feet, the whole thing covered by the kind of rug Emma used to weave for Richies at her old job in the textile mill. Maybe she'd even made this rug before she'd been fired for getting sick.

A little boy no more than five or six years old slept on the bed, surrounded by blankets that swallowed him so deeply Tristin almost didn't see him. The boy's thumb was jammed into his mouth, a tattered scrap of fabric clutched in his slobbery fingers.

Curious, Tristin reached out a hand to touch the bed, but his better judgment yanked it back. Waking the boy would be disastrous. The little boy's mask dangled from a hook screwed into the wall next to his head. Tristin barely gave it a glance before he turned away to the open door. He'd never steal a mask from a kid.

Before he reached the doorway, a blue glow pulsated in the room. Tristin froze. Behind him, the boy's lifemask chirped and Tristin nearly wet himself. As he saw it, he had two options: run into the unfamiliar hall with his god's help, or keep quiet and pray the boy didn't fully wake. Tristin chose the latter. He looked over his shoulder, expecting to see two frightened, innocent eyes meeting his gaze. The boy fumbled for his mask, took a whistling breath from it, and then hung it back up, all without opening his eyes. The mask swung slightly on its hook, the pulsating blue glow dimming until it was mostly hidden behind the vents. The boy rolled over with his back to Tristin and shoved his thumb back into his mouth.

Tristin sighed and crept through the doorway. He saw a room at the end of the hall that looked like another bedroom, but he couldn't pass up what might be his only chance to explore a Madson house. There were more rooms in it than he could imagine anyone ever needing, including separate rooms just for cooking and eating.

He went looking for the front door in case things went south and he needed another exit. He found it next to a living room that could have fit his whole house inside. Beside the door was the mandatory portrait of King Searle that hung in every house in the kingdom. Tristin had the urge to put his fist right through it, but settled on lifting his middle finger instead. He wouldn't dare to do that at home. His father would skin him if he saw.

He made his way back to the second bedroom and peered inside. It was much larger than the boy's room. The moonlight coming through the open curtains highlighted two people sleeping in a huge bed. This was it. Time to do what he came for. Tristin wished he could momentarily trade his God of Speed for a God of Bravery because he was scared out of his mind. His hands trembled at his sides.

The man slept on his belly with one leg poking out of the covers and dangling over the edge of the mattress. A woman slept with her back to him. A breeze blew down the hall from the little boy's open window and tickled the back of Tristin's neck. He rubbed the shiver away with a cringe. The breeze grew into a small gust that caught the boy's door and slammed it shut with a bang. Tristin jerked his hand down, his knuckles colliding with a waist-high dresser. He grabbed his hand with a muffled yelp.

The man in the bed grunted and rolled over, almost falling out. He smacked his lips, farted, and started to snore. Tristin couldn't believe how soundly Richies slept. A noise like that in his house would have brought Rhett from his sleep like a ball of fire.

After Tristin's heart started beating again and he was confident that neither the man nor the woman was any wiser, he glared at the dresser that had almost given him away. A gold coin as large as his palm sat on top next to several smaller gold coins. Staring in awe, he imagined how much better his life would be if he had even one of the small coins. He could probably buy a whole box of sugar beets. He picked up the larger coin and examined it, having never seen one like it before. Stamped on one side was the fat face of King Searle. Tristin tilted the coin so he could better see it in the moonlight. On the flip side was a single lifemask beneath the word "Obey."

He held his fist to his mouth and squeezed the coin until it hurt and left indentations in the creases of his fingers. Everything Rhett had taught him about the evils of stealing battled against the urge to put the coin in his waistband. By the looks of the house, the family wouldn't miss it. He lowered it from his mouth and pressed it against his chest. With his eyes closed, he pictured the food his family could buy with such wealth. Or maybe firewood for the winter.

With a frown, he set the coin back on the dresser. It was bad enough that he was about to steal someone's mask, but that was to save a life. Stealing gold was just plain thievery.

He tiptoed around the bed to where the woman slept. Her mask hung from a hook in the wooden post of the headboard. Staring at her plump, healthy face he grew even angrier, knowing she would be able to replace her stolen mask at the Mask Exchange. What made her more worthy of being saved than his mother? He reached for her mask, which seemed a mile away. He had never been so scared in his life. When his quivering finger touched it, an image of Emma's loving smile gave him courage. The leather strap of the mask felt even better within his grip than the gold coin had. Quietly, he lifted the mask from its hook. The woman didn't move.

Success.

With his prize in hand, he backed toward the door, giddy with excitement at how easily he'd succeeded. As he passed the foot of the bed, he briefly considered taking the man's mask as well just for the sport of it. He imagined returning home with two new masks. He would be doubly the hero.

No, he told himself. *One mask is enough.* Greed ranked up there with jealousy on the list of things his father hated.

Before his foot touched the hallway floor, his thoughts drifted to returning home. While Rhett would undoubtedly be furious at first, once they figured out how to fix the mask to work for Emma and she got better, he would surely forget how angry he had been. Especially since the Richie could simply get a new one. No harm done.

He pictured the scene in his mind as he walked toward the little boy's room, triumphantly twirling the mask at his side. As he reached for the doorknob, he caught a glimpse of a pulsating blue glow in the twirling mask's vents growing in intensity.

Oh no. His hand hovered inches from the knob; the mask twisted on its strap at his hip. A single chirp echoed through the quiet hallway. Tristin's eyes widened. He slowly turned back toward the parents' room.

In his eagerness to get the woman's mask, he had been foolish. Instead of waiting for her to use it and thereby giving himself hours before anyone would have noticed it was missing, he had rushed. Now he held a mask that needed to be used.

Don't panic. Maybe it wasn't too late. If he returned the mask before she noticed it was gone, it would chirp again, she would use it, and she would be back asleep within seconds. He summoned his God of Speed and tore back toward the open bedroom door. Then he slammed into something solid as a wall and fell to his rear with a grunt.

"Oof, careful, Liam." The man stood in the doorway, rubbing his eyes with both palms. "Are you thirsty, too?" he asked.

Tristin froze, staring up at the giant of a man. Looking past the man's legs, he saw the woman blindly reach for the empty hook. Tristin shoved her mask behind his back as though hiding it would save him. The man stopped rubbing his eyes and looked down. "You're not Liam. Who are you?" he asked in a tone that strangely lacked anger or fear.

Tristin scrambled to his feet and backed into the hall, his voice strangled with fear.

The man calmly followed him. "Hey, kid." His voice carried a gentle warmth. "Are you all right?" He reached out a kind hand. "What are you doing in my house?"

"Henry?" the woman called from the bedroom. "Who's there?" After a moment of terrifying silence, she added, "Where's my mask?"

Tristin's panic boiled over. He backed through the hallway while the man slowly followed. The man put his hands in front of his chest. "Wait a minute, kid. Don't run."

The word "run" was all Tristin needed to hear. He turned and darted back into the little boy's room, the stolen lifemask firmly in his grip. He was through the window and around the house in a flash. The man appeared at the front door and shouted at two soldiers patrolling on horseback down the street. He pointed frantically at Tristin. "That boy. He stole my wife's mask."

The soldiers turned their horses and kicked them into a trot. "Get her to the exchange," one shouted back. "We'll take care of the kid."

Tristin wanted to cry. He wanted his dad.

Chapter 2

Regret

Tristin used his god to the fullest to race toward the main drag, the pursuing soldiers growing more distant with each quickened step. They would have done just as well chasing dust in the dark as trying to keep eyes on him once he really got going. An empty alley gave him a moment to rest and figure out how to get home. Clutched in his fist, the stolen mask's shrill chirp shot through him with a jolt. This wasn't the sort of place where a chirping mask would go unnoticed at this time of night.

"You there," someone shouted from behind.

Tristin turned to find a lone soldier who had ducked into the alley for a piss. "I'm so sorry. I didn't mean to do it."

The soldier adjusted his pants and tied the string in the front. "What are you doing out here so late, kid? Come 'ere for a minute."

Rhett was going to be so angry. Summoning his god, Tristin turned and ran toward home again. He blazed past three more soldiers who stood oblivious at the border between the districts.

By the time he got home, he had lost the soldiers again. The stolen lifemask no longer chirped but wailed constantly, loud enough to wake the entire town. Tristin ignored it, his only concern getting inside where Rhett could make everything all right.

As he squeezed past his front door, he took a last look at the street and saw three more soldiers watching him from the south. He had been too sloppy. The wailing mask had gotten their attention, and his suspicious behavior while being out past curfew had kept it.

"Dad, Dad, Dad," he screamed as he shoved the door back into the frame in hopes of shutting out the world. The wail drowned out his voice, so he shouted louder.

Rhett stumbled into the room, groggy and confused. "Tristin, take a breath from your mask already. It's going to wake the entire neighborhood."

"It's not mine, Dad."

Rhett rubbed his red, puffy eyes. "What do you mean it's not yours?" Makenna stepped into the hall behind him as he lit a lantern to better see.

Tristin couldn't find the right words, so he simply held out the screaming mask.

Pronounced lines across Rhett's forehead punctuated his confused squint. He snatched the stolen mask from Tristin's hands. "Where did you get this? What did you do?" His tone was sadder than it was angry.

"I stole it. Hurry, give it to Mom."

The look in Rhett's eyes changed from confusion to instant terror. "Stole it? No, son, I've told you it won't work. It wasn't made for your mother."

"We can fix it so that it works for her. Take it apart. That's what they must do for the rich people. I don't know how, but ..."

Rhett calmly walked to the table and slammed the mask against it as hard as he could. He drew back and did it a second time before the screeching stopped. Then he left it setting in pieces on the table as he set the lantern next to it and took a calming breath. "What have you done, son?"

"I wanted to help Mom, but I think I messed up." Tristin thought of the doomed mask thief he'd seen earlier and panic gripped his chest in a vise.

"Oh, Tristin. Come here, boy." Rhett grabbed the nape of Tristin's neck and pulled his head against his chest. "I wish I could fix it to work for your mom, but I don't know how." He lifted Tristin's chin so he could look into his wet eyes. "We have to hide this. If anyone finds out that you stole a mask, the Angel's soldiers will—" He broke off as he looked past Tristin through the gap between the front door and the frame. Transfixed, he whispered, "Did they see you?"

Tristin didn't answer—he didn't have to. He slowly turned his head toward the gap. On the opposite side of the street, the three other soldiers who had seen him spoke with the two soldiers on horseback from Madson's District.

"Did they see you, son?" Rhett asked again without taking his eyes from the intense meeting outside.

Tristin's eyes filled with tears. "I'm so sorry." Like knives to his heart, two of soldiers pointed to the front door.

Rhett grabbed Tristin's shoulders, his expression now dark and serious. "Take Makenna to my room and stay with your mom. Do not come out no matter what you hear." Tristin started to look to the door again, but Rhett snapped his attention back with a shake. "Listen to me. They're going to take me away. You must take care of your sister now. Your mom is too sick."

The two Madson's District soldiers dismounted and walked toward the house.

Tristin watched them until Rhett snapped his attention back yet again. "Do you hear me? You are a man today. From here on out, you must protect Makenna no matter what. Do you understand?"

Tristin nodded, though he hadn't completely processed what Rhett meant.

"Now, go," Rhett ordered, and gave him a hard shove into the hallway.

Tristin met Makenna in the hall. Fear painted her face white. She nervously touched her cheek. Rhett walked to the doorway, slid the door aside, and waited on the stoop for the soldiers. Tristin led Makenna to their parents' room. Emma lay motionless on the sleeping pallet. Her mask clunked beside her.

Tristin gave Makenna a slight shake. "Help Mom take a lifebreath."

Makenna's eyes widened. "What's going on out there?"

"I've caused some trouble. Just stay with Mom. I'll be right back." He sneaked back into the hall to listen.

Though he couldn't see the soldiers past Rhett's wide back, he could hear everything they said.

"Sir, what is your name?"

"Rhett."

"Very well, Rhett. We need you to step out here and speak with us."

Rhett stepped down from the stoop. Tristin moved quietly into the room and hid so he could keep listening in.

"Sir, we have evidence that someone in your family has stolen a lifemask. Have you anything to say?"

Rhett rubbed his forehead and bit his lower lip. "I know better than to lie. Your evidence is correct."

"Your honesty is appreciated. Bring out the criminal and we will leave you be."

"I cannot do that."

"Excuse me?"

"It's just that … well … it was my young son. It was just a foolish mistake."

"Crime has no age limit, sir. Punishment must be dealt. Bring out your son to face the Angel or be guilty of harboring."

"Wait, wait, wait. Calm down for a second and let me explain."

"You have thirty seconds."

"I'm not harboring my son. The reason I don't call him out here is because he only committed the crime after I asked him to. My wife is sick, and I thought my son could steal a mask for her before she died. He's just a boy. Please don't punish him for what I ordered him to do."

"What kind of coward are you that you would send your son to commit a crime while you waited in the safety of your home?"

"The worst kind."

"Very well. Hands behind your back."

Tristin couldn't bear listening anymore. He stepped into the doorway. "Don't take my dad," he said, attracting all eyes his way. "He didn't steal the mask. I did."

The soldier who seemed to be in charge stepped forward while his companions bound Rhett's hands and forced him to his knees. "Boy, you committed the crime at the behest of your father."

Tristin shook his head.

"You must learn never to steal, regardless of the reason. Stealing masks is among the worst crimes of all. I have sympathy for your sick mother, but stealing is stealing." He waved the other soldiers toward Tristin. "This situation is too convoluted for me. Go in and bring out everyone in the house. We will take them all to the Angel and let him decide who's innocent and who needs punishing."

"No," Rhett shouted, locking eyes with Tristin. "Be silent, son." He looked back to the soldier. "I did this. No one else is at fault. He was only doing what I ordered."

The other soldiers pushed past Tristin into the house. They quickly returned with a tearful Makenna and the broken mask. One of them said coldly, "The woman in there is dead. This girl is the only one left in the house."

Rhett bowed his head and moaned.

Tristin's stomach turned. *Dead? No, no, no.* "Makenna? Is it true?"

"I tried to help her take a lifebreath," Makenna sobbed. "But she wouldn't wake up."

Tristin started back into the house, but the soldiers blocked the doorway. The one who had spoken before said, "There's no point. You can't help her. It's time for you to face the Angel for your crimes."

The lead soldier studied Tristin's face and then looked at Makenna's. "Well, I'll be." He turned to the others. "Have any of you ever seen twins before?"

The other soldiers shook their heads and stared curiously.

The lead soldier smirked. "Maybe if King Searle finds out, he'll pardon you both and put you on display somewhere."

His men started laughing.

He turned to them. "All right. All right. That's enough. Grab him."

The soldier closest to Tristin reached out a hand, but Tristin stepped back. The soldier reached for him again. "Now, kid, don't do anything crazy. It'll only add to your punishment."

Tristin knew several Terdicts who had been accused of crimes over the years. Some of them had never returned after meeting the Angel. He looked to Rhett for guidance, but the grim determination in his father's eyes scared him. Tristin turned to Makenna with wide eyes.

Makenna gave him the slightest of nods. Then she looked up at one of the soldiers tightly holding her arms. Her lips moved as she called upon her god. The man released her arm and punched his partner hard in the face, sending the man sprawling. He dove onto him and the two men started wrestling.

With the other soldiers distracted by the bizarre turn of events, Rhett bounded to his feet, hands still tied behind his back, and plowed another soldier to the ground.

Makenna ran without looking back.

Rhett didn't stand a chance, and the soldiers quickly pinned him down, splitting his chin on the broken cobblestones. But he had given Makenna the time she needed.

The soldier standing in front of Tristin screamed at the men wrestling on the ground to stop and get it together. He turned back to Tristin. "Kid, you're just going to make things worse. Come with me and we'll see about finding your sister."

Tristin backed away from the man's outstretched hand until his back met the wall of his house. He wanted to stall as long as possible to give Makenna a good start. Then it would be his turn to use his god. He locked eyes with Rhett, who lay with a soldier's knee pressed down on his back. "I'm sorry, Dad."

"Just run," Rhett answered.

With his back against the wall and the soldier about to grab his arm, Tristin called upon his God of Speed. There was an opening to the soldier's right, and Tristin sprang past him like a blur. He didn't look back to see if anyone gave chase. Within seconds, Tristin caught up to Makenna, slowing enough to grab her hand and lead her down a maze of side streets. They knew the district better than their pursuers.

Once they'd stopped to catch their breath in an alley, Makenna pulled her hand away and slapped Tristin's face. "What did you do?"

He resisted the urge to rub his stinging cheek and reached for her arm again. "I was trying to help."

She recoiled from his touch. "Help? You did the opposite. You made it worse." Barefoot and shivering in her nightdress, she could hardly look at him. "Why did you do that?"

"I was trying to save Mom."

"Well, you didn't." She buried her head in her hands and sat with her back to the wall. "Mom's dead and Dad's on his way to prison."

"I know."

"We'll never see them again." Makenna tried to muffle her sobs with her hands, still conscious that they weren't completely in the clear yet.

Tristin turned away. He could hardly breathe. She was right. It was all his fault. He didn't know what to do. Nothing would ever be the same again.

Tristin reached down and touched her shoulder. "I'm so sorry, Makenna."

She shrugged his hand away. He stepped back. He knew she needed time, but he also knew they needed to keep moving. He waited as long as he could. Then he knelt before her. Gently, he lifted her chin. "We have to keep moving, sis."

She looked into his eyes and reluctantly nodded. It took everything he had to keep it together long enough to find somewhere safe. He led her from alley to alley, eventually finding an abandoned cobbler's shop with an unlocked back door.

Inside, Tristin paced near the window, watching for soldiers. He didn't see any. Makenna didn't say anything for a while as she sat and cried in the corner. Tristin wanted to cry too, but his need to be strong for her kept the tears away.

For a while.

Hours passed before Tristin sensed Makenna approach. He turned to her. Seeing her sad eyes again drained more of his strength.

His eyes blurred. "I killed Dad, didn't I?" He hoped she would tell him that he hadn't, even if it was a lie, but she didn't answer.

Instead, she reached for his hand and pulled him closer. Her sympathetic side broke through her grief and anger. He let the tears flow as she hugged him. "I love you, Tristin."

"I know. I love you, too."

"We have to be careful from now on. If the Angel finds you ..." She covered her mouth and her wet eyes widened as though it was the first time she had thought about the consequences of what Tristin had done.

At that moment, Tristin didn't care what the Angel was going to do to him. Whatever it was, he probably deserved it. He'd really thought he could just sneak into some Richie house and steal a mask, Rhett would fix it so Emma could live, and the Richie would get a replacement. It had seemed so easy. How could he have made things so much worse?

"You can't be so careless anymore, Tristin. I know you were only trying to help Mom, but you can't just react and do what feels right." She tapped the side of his head with her finger. "You have to think. You can't be so stupid."

He nodded and she hugged him again. Together, they cried until he eventually pulled back and wiped his eyes. A sick feeling grew in his gut, and he thought it would probably never leave. Makenna's lifemask pulsated and chirped. She let go of him to take a whistling breath from it. At least the soldiers had let her take it when they'd dragged her out of the house. He'd have to figure out how to get her some clothes later.

Tristin looked into her eyes, searching past the tears for that special something Makenna always seemed to have. It was a warmth that said "everything will be all right" even when Tristin knew it wouldn't. She'd had it whenever they'd talked about their mother's sickness or how hungry they all were, and he needed to see it now. And there it was. He'd never told her how much her innocent hope meant to him, and he never would for fear he might take it from her. It might be what he most loved about her.

"We're going to be okay," he said, echoing what he saw in her eyes.

She nodded.

Cold and scared, Tristin held his sister close. After she cried herself to sleep, he let his own tears flow again.

Chapter 3

Stealth and Killing

The abandoned cobbler's shop made a good place to hide for a few nights, but Tristin couldn't get any real sleep for fear of soldiers barging in. They were known to randomly search abandoned buildings so they could catch any squatters.

By the second night, Makenna was getting frustrated. "We have to eat something soon, Tristin."

"I know." He'd been able to sneak back into the house to get Makenna's clothes earlier, but their meagre store of porridge jars had already been looted. He hoped it was his hungry neighbors who had taken the food and not the smug soldiers. He couldn't stand the thought of the last of his family's food feeding soldiers for even a single meal. He had been thinking about the sugar beet, which was the last thing he had eaten, and it gave him an idea. "I know where I can get food. But it's too dangerous for both of us to go."

"Well, what are you waiting for? I'm starving."

"I can't just leave you here alone again. What if a soldier stops in?"

"Then I'll hide."

"What if he finds you?"

"He won't. I'll be all right. At this point, I'm more likely to starve than be found in here."

"I don't know." Tristin rubbed the back of his neck.

"Just go. I'll be fine."

After a little more nudging, he reluctantly agreed and slipped out into the night. It didn't take long to find a half-eaten, browning apple and a broken clay bowl full of green beans in a Richie's trash heap.

When he returned to the cobbler's shop, he gave her the green beans. He couldn't understand why she liked beans so much—they were pretty bland to him—but he was happy to not have to share his apple. They took turns sleeping and keeping watch through the rest of the night.

Being alone together in such tight quarters wore on their nerves over the next few days. At one point they tried to play a guessing game to pass the time, but couldn't get past the rules without arguing. Then Makenna told Tristin to stop looking at her. He hadn't been, but he made it a point to stare at her intently after that. They even stopped speaking to each other for a few hours over a perfectly innocent comment about her annoying habit of humming songs when she was bored.

By that evening, he was ready to turn himself in to avoid any more bickering. His only break from Makenna's company was his nightly scavenges for food. He was starting to look forward to them despite the danger.

While they ate a midnight dinner of stale bread and wilted vegetables, he said, "I've been thinking lately."

"That's a first."

He rolled his eyes. "I'm serious. We can't stay here much longer."

"Why not?"

"Well, first because you're driving me crazy."

"Ha-ha. No, really."

"Because it's only a matter of time before the soldiers find us. I can't sleep even when you're on watch because I'm always worried they'll pop in. I'm exhausted."

"Where would we go?"

"I have an idea, but you'll have to trust me."

She cocked her head. "What is it?"

He hesitated.

She nudged him. "Well?"

"The Barbarian Slums," he finally answered.

"On the other side of Slaybyrne River?"

"Yes."

"What about them?"

"We should go there."

"Are you crazy? There's no way to get there. The grinderfish will kill us before we take two steps into the water."

"You've never heard the rumors of people living over there?"

"Uh. No."

"Well, I have."

"That's impossible. How would anyone get over there in the first place? No one can cross the river. The grinderfish eat everything that touches the water. Including skin and bones, I might remind you."

"There's a man who can take us."

"What? Are you losing your mind?"

"I'm serious. That's what my friend Clinton told me once."

"Clinton? You mean red-haired Clinton from school? His lips run faster than you." She rolled her eyes. "You do know Clinton also says that there's life other than the fog creatures outside the walls, don't you?"

"Maybe there is."

She snorted. "Oh, Tristin. You can be so gullible sometimes. Without the king's masks, no one can live out there."

"But what if it's true?"

She shook her head.

"No, really. What if?"

"I don't know, Tristin."

"I'll tell you what. I went to the riverbank and found a place where we could hide for a few nights. We can watch and see if anyone crosses the river. If no one comes, at least we can get some real sleep for once."

She scowled.

"What else are we doing?"

"It's just … Ugh. You're killing me, Tristin."

He tilted his head forward and looked up with begging eyes. She tried to look away but he followed her.

She groaned. "All right, I'll play along. What is this place you found?

"It's an islet in the river. There's a tall rock that we can hide behind where no one can see us from the bank."

"Let's pretend I'm even considering this. How do we get to this islet?"

"Remember that game we used to play with the rocks?"

"You know I hated that game."

"I think it'll work. We just have to distract the grinderfish. Pleeease."

"I hate it when you beg, Tristin."

"Just come with me before the suns rise and let me show you. If you don't want to try it, I'll bring you right back."

Her mouth went crooked and her nose crinkled. "Promise we'll come back?"

"If you give it a chance, I promise."

She reluctantly nodded.

He took her hand and led her from the shop, through the dark alleys, and onto the bank of the Slaybyrne. The two suns hadn't risen yet, but the muted pre-dawn light brightened the green fog. Tristin pointed to the islet in the water. "The other side of that rock juts out and gives cover. It's the perfect place to watch the river."

She looked cross at him. "Wait. How do you know what the other side looks like?"

He cringed.

Her jaw dropped. "You went out into the water already?"

He nodded, unable to look into her brown eyes.

She brushed a strand of her long, dark hair from her eyes and crossed her arms. "Tristin. Are you crazy?"

I had to be sure it would work, didn't I?"

He glanced over his shoulder for patrolling soldiers or garbage gatherers. Then he stepped to the edge and picked up a rock. A large, yellowish glow from a school of grinderfish crowded the bank in hopes of him being foolish enough to step into the water.

"Stupid grinderfish," he said as he heaved the rock. When it plunked into the water, the school of bright, fist-sized creatures swarmed it, devouring it in a frenzied flash. As soon as the creatures were finished with the rock, they hurried back to the bank. There were hundreds of them now. He'd never understood how the grinderfish not only survived in the murky green muck of the Slaybyrne, but seemed to thrive when nothing else could.

Makenna leaned close to the water for a better look. "Hey, Tristin, what do you think they eat?"

"Everything."

"I know that. I mean, how do they survive if nobody throws anything into the water?"

"That's where the garbage goes at night. That's what they eat."

"So why don't they stop feeding them? Won't they die?"

"I asked Dad and he said they feed on their own babies sometimes."

Makenna covered her mouth. "That's awful."

Tristin jabbed her side. "Sometimes the babies feed on them first, though."

She swatted his hand away. "Stop it."

The twins stared across the river to where the rising suns highlighted the opposite bank. "Can you see anything?" he asked.

"Some shadows of old barbarian buildings, is all."

"Well, I can see *them*. I mean, anything else."

"You mean like strange magic men swimming across?"

He scrunched his nose at her. He hated when she talked down to him.

"No, I don't see anything out of the ordinary. Maybe there's still barbarians over there. Do you think?"

"Not since they took war to the Angel a hundred years ago. You know that. You read the same history books as I do."

"I know. But it didn't say they were *all* gone. Do you think our great-great-grandpa ever met one?"

"Probably."

"Really?"

"I don't know. I guess."

"Do you think they survived after the Angel banished them to live beyond the wall?"

"The Angel let them keep their lifemasks, so I guess it's possible. Clinton's not so dumb after all, is he?"

She surprised him when she said, "I think I'd like to meet a barbarian one day."

"Really? You know, they'd probably crush your bones and drink the dust if you did."

She swatted his shoulder. "Stop it. You're just trying to scare me."

Tristin couldn't hide his grin. It felt good to really smile again. "We should get going. I'll draw them away so you can get to the islet. Are you ready?"

She nodded, but it wasn't a confident nod.

He gathered a few rocks for the trip over and for the trip back. When he heaved the first rock into the river, the grinderfish swarmed the splash. Tristin jumped into the water. "Go."

As he ran, the grinderfish followed. He looked back to see Makenna reach the islet and hide behind the large rock. Tristin circled back to the bank as the grinderfish closed in. After another rock throw, he joined Makenna.

"Well?" he said.

"It's not bad, I suppose."

"It'll cover us from the rain, too."

There was more than enough room for him to sit next to her. He set his mask out to dry and tried to wring out his wet pants. The itching on his legs had already started. He couldn't understand why the mucky water irritated his skin so much but not Makenna's.

Makenna sighed. "Three days, Tristin. That's all I'm giving you. Three."

He smiled triumphantly at her as he scratched.

She brushed his hand from his leg. "Stop it. You're just going to make it worse." She took in their surroundings. "You know, I kind of like it out here. The sound of the water is nice. Peaceful."

"I knew you would."

"Liar."

He returned to Madson's District for food each night. On the third night, Tristin kept watch while Makenna slept. He was starting to doze when he heard something splash in the water in the distance. It could have just been a grinderfish fight too close to the surface, but it could also be what he was waiting for. He stood up and strained for a better view. There was another splash. It was definitely something bigger than a grinderfish. He tapped Makenna, waking her.

"What?" she snapped. She sat up and stretched.

Tristin lifted his finger and pointed. "Something's coming across."

"What?" She stood up next to him and followed his gaze.

"I can't see it clear enough through the fog. Can you?" he asked.

She squinted. "I can't believe it."

"What?"

"I can't believe I'm saying this. It's … It's a man swimming."

Tristin pumped his fist. "I knew it."

The twins watched in disbelief as the man reached the shallows, stood up, and climbed up the bank.

"How is that possible?" Makenna asked.

"He must have a god like us." He gave her an I-told-you-so look.

"Don't even say it," she snapped.

Tristin's grin spoke for him. He hefted a rock. "Are you ready?" She nodded.

The rock game got them both safely to the bank. "Wait here," he said.

The stranger was already sprinting toward town. Tristin gave chase, using his god to close the distance between them in a flash. The man had just reached the edge of town when Tristin caught up to him.

"Mister?" Tristin whispered.

The man jumped, spun around, and grabbed his chest. He looked Tristin over with wide eyes. "You scared me to death, kid." He held up his hand while he caught his breath. "Who are you?"

"My name's Tristin."

"Tristin, huh? How'd you sneak up on me so quickly?"

Tristin decided honesty was the best way to gain the man's trust. "I can run faster than most people," he answered.

"Oh. You have a god, too?"

Tristin bobbed his head.

The man was probably in his mid-twenties, with short-cropped chestnut hair and a serious round face. He was Tristin's height, though a bit more solidly built. Tristin stared at his mustache, having never seen one quite like it before. It extended beyond the edges of his mouth and curled upward into tight points.

"Why are you out so late? Are you hiding from the Angel?" His voice was kind behind its raspy gruffness.

Tristin felt almost relieved being able to tell someone besides Makenna what had happened. "Yes. I stole a mask."

"Really. I'm assuming you had a pretty good reason?"

Tristin nodded. "My mom was dying."

"Ahh. I'd say that's a pretty good reason."

"What do you call your god?"

"The God of Stealth. He keeps the grinderfish from knowing when I'm in the water."

"Stealth? But I saw you."

He chuckled. "Yeah. I guess stealth isn't the right word for it. But absent of anything better, it'll have to do. My name's Ian, by the way." He extended his hand.

Tristin shook it firmly and confidently like Rhett had always taught him.

Ian playfully twisted the tip of his mustache. "Do you live out here?"

"Sort of."

"You're too young to be living out here alone."

"Well, my sister and I didn't have anywhere else to go."

Ian's lifemask chirped inside a leather pouch at his hip. Tristin had never seen that much leather on a Terdict. Ian took a breath from his mask before replacing it in his pouch. Tristin's mask chirped soon after, but it was covered with river gunk. He wiped it away as best he could.

Ian looked over his shoulder toward town as though he was expecting someone. "Kid, I don't have much time. Do you want somewhere safe to stay for a while?"

Tristin silently thanked Clinton for being such a gossip. "Are there others with you over there?"

"A few."

"Is it safe?"

"As safe as anywhere else, I suppose. At least you won't have to deal with the Angel of Justice anymore. Tell you what, kid. Come with me. If you don't like it there, I'll bring you right back. Promise."

Tristin agreed with an enthusiastic nod.

"Great. Is your sister here somewhere?"

Tristin pointed back toward the riverbank.

"Go get her and meet me back where I came out of the river. You must hurry, though. My friend Samuel will return soon and sometimes he brings unwanted company."

Without another word, Tristin ran to Makenna. It took everything he had not to gloat, but he restrained himself. Maybe he was growing up after all. Instead of staying by the bank, they picked a spot where they could watch for Ian and his friend. Before long, Ian exploded from a side street, waving his hands above his head. "Get to the water," he screamed.

Tristin stuttered back a step, though he didn't retreat. He nudged Makenna. "Go. Wait for me there."

"I don't know about this, Tristin."

"Just go. It's all right."

She reluctantly did as he asked.

Ian shouted as he sprinted past Tristin, "Samuel's coming, kid. Run."

But Tristin didn't want to run, not until he saw who Samuel was and what kind of company he was bringing.

"Stop," someone shouted from the alley seconds before a single man exploded onto the main street. He wore a black covering over his mouth and nose. Two soldiers chased him.

Tristin cringed as the man he presumed to be Samuel stumbled on the broken cobblestones and almost fell. The faster of the two soldiers tackled him from behind. Samuel rolled onto the soldier's chest and rained punches until the soldier was unconscious. Then Samuel stood in time for the other pursuer to slam into his midsection. He quickly ended that fight as well. He faced the town as if wanting more. A half-dozen soldiers poured from the side street.

Part of Tristin wanted to help Ian's friend, but he was no good in a street fight.

Ian shouted, "Come on, Samuel. Not today."

Samuel glanced over his shoulder as if Ian was squashing his fun. His eyes met Tristin's.

Tristin whispered, "Run."

Samuel looked back to the soldiers with disappointment, and then started running toward the river.

As Samuel approached Tristin, he shouted, "You'd better run, too, boy."

Tristin's legs wouldn't work at first. He was paralyzed by seeing so many soldiers running directly at him. Makenna shouted, snapping his attention back. He blazed past Samuel to where Ian and Makenna stood.

Ian stepped into the water. The grinderfish scattered away from his feet.

"Now what?" Tristin asked.

Ian glanced at the charging soldiers as several more joined the chase. He calmly answered, "We cross the river, of course."

Tristin smiled.

Makenna glared back. "I don't know about this."

Ian gave her a warm, comforting smile. "Don't worry. My god casts a wide net and will protect us. Have faith."

Samuel ran toward them, two dozen soldiers on his heels. Ian held his hand out to Makenna. "It's all right. Trust me."

Makenna hesitantly took his hand.

The bright yellow grinderfish circled them. Tristin's heart pumped nearly out of his chest. Makenna shivered as her eyes darted back and forth. Once they were in the chilly water, Ian stopped and waited for Samuel. The grinderfish surrounded them, but the deadly creatures seemed confused, as though they couldn't find their prey only feet away. Makenna flinched each time one of them brushed against her legs.

"Can the two of you swim?" Ian asked.

They shook their heads. They'd never had the need.

"That's all right. The water isn't very deep, but it's deeper than the two of you stand. When Samuel gets here, he'll help you ..." He pointed to Makenna and raised his eyebrows at her.

"Makenna," she answered, her voice squeaking with nerves.

"Right. Makenna. Samuel will help you, and I'll help your brother."

Makenna looked nervously at Tristin.

Tristin took her hand. "We'll be fine, sis. I won't let anything happen to you."

At the water's edge, Samuel splashed into the Slaybyrne without fear. Once in the safety of the river, he turned back to the soldiers who'd stopped abruptly on the bank. He dared them to come forward with a raised middle finger. Tristin wondered if the soldiers would be protected by Ian's god since they were so close. Fearfully, he realized they probably would. He only hoped they didn't realize it.

"Come on," Ian shouted.

The soldiers stared with acid in their eyes, itching for their foe to step back out of the water. Though Samuel eventually backed away from them, Tristin got the sense he did so grudgingly. The unlikely foursome waded deeper into the Slaybyrne while watching the helpless soldiers pace on the bank. Luckily, archers weren't within their ranks.

Tristin looked Samuel over. The warrior was thick and intimidating, his arms nearly the size of Tristin's thighs. He wore scars like the Richies wore jewelry—all over. Makenna nudged closer to Tristin and Ian. "Who is he?" she whispered as if Samuel wasn't within earshot.

Ian smirked. "His name is Samuel. He has the God of Killing on his side."

Samuel regarded Tristin out of the corner of his eye. "You're pretty fast, kid." His voice was deep and as intimidating as his muscular arms.

"Yeah, thanks. Uh ... You're pretty good at ... well ... fighting, I suppose."

Samuel nodded. "That I am. One of these days I will test my god against the Angel himself. As soon as I convince this one that it's a good idea." He jammed his elbow into Ian's side.

"Well, it's not," Ian snapped as he rubbed his ribs. He continued on in silence until the water reached Makenna's chest. "Samuel, these kids can't swim. You're going to have to help her."

Samuel lowered the cloth from his face. A bulging purplish scar ran from the corner of his left eye to his jawline and his nose was slightly crooked. Long, black, curly hair was matted to the sides of his rough, sweaty face. His chin hid behind a dark, neatly trimmed beard. He squatted enough for Makenna to climb onto his back and wrap her arms around his neck. Tristin climbed onto Ian's back.

Makenna squeezed for dear life, causing Samuel to cough and gently pull her arm away from his throat. "Not so tight, girlie," he said with a strained voice. Then, in a lighter tone that didn't match his brawn, he added, "Relax. You'll be fine."

Makenna apologized and loosened her grip.

Tristin felt his lifemask bounce against his thigh beneath the water. "What if we need to take a lifebreath?"

Ian shook his head. "Don't worry about that. We won't be in the water long enough for it to matter."

That was good to hear since Tristin's skin was already itching like mad.

The four slowly crossed the Slaybyrne, escorted by the glowing grinderfish. When the water was shallow enough for Tristin and Makenna to touch the bottom, they climbed down.

"We're going to have to teach you two how to swim in this stuff," Ian said. "Especially if you want to go back and forth like Samuel."

By the time they reached the banks of the Barbarian Slums, the water around them was more yellow with grinderfish than green with muck. Tristin even stepped on one by accident. It didn't react at all and he wondered if he was dreaming.

As they walked up the bank, Tristin dug at his irritated skin. Samuel walked off on his own, soon disappearing over a slight hill. The others continued past an abandoned house to a small town hidden from the river by the hill. The appearance of houses always told Tristin a lot about what kind of people he was dealing with. The better the house, the snootier the owner seemed to be. By the looks of those dilapidated homes, he figured they would be treated pretty well.

The houses were huge. Not in the sense that they had a lot of rooms but in their overall size. The doorframes were wider and taller than any he'd ever seen. Even standing on his father's shoulders he'd be lucky to reach the eaves.

As they walked, Makenna gazed at the houses with wide eyes. "Barbarian houses, Tristin."

Tristin chuckled. "I know."

"Are there barbarians here now?" she asked.

Ian shook his head.

Tristin looked around for any signs of food. Seeing none, he asked, "What do you eat over here if you can't buy food?"

Ian smiled. "Have you ever eaten japsy weed?"

Tristin had never even heard of japsy weed. He shook his head.

Ian retrieved a green sprig of some sort from his pouch and handed it to him. Tristin held it in front of his mouth, reluctant to put it in. Ian guided Tristin's hand to his lips. "It's all right. It won't hurt you. It's nutritious, actually. And surprisingly filling."

Tristin put the weed in his mouth and chewed.

"What's it taste like?" Makenna asked, eyes full of hope.

Tristin swallowed with a sour face. "It tastes like … dirt."

Ian smirked. "You shouldn't eat for taste, anyway. Also, if you rub two leaves together fast enough and long enough, it'll start a fire."

A fire? Tristin couldn't imagine why anyone would choose to eat something that tasted like dirt *and* could start a fire.

Ian pointed to one of the houses. "That one will be yours."

Makenna's face contorted. "We get a whole house?"

"Where did you want to sleep?"

"Well, I don't know. But that's ours now?"

"For as long as you choose to stay."

With the prospect of forever eating japsy weed still fresh in Tristin's mind, he thought "as long as you choose to stay" might as well be another way of saying, "it was nice meeting you and we'll see you later." But this had been Tristin's idea in the first place and he had to give it a chance.

There wasn't anyone outside at that hour and the angry clouds growing overhead assured it would stay that way. Ian said, "We should probably get inside until the storm passes."

Tristin nodded. The house's front door was still fastened to its frame, which was a new luxury for the twins. Tristin grabbed the oversized brass handle with both hands.

The door opened into a room with ceilings Tristin probably couldn't touch on a ladder. The warped wooden floor was gray with age and rippled like frozen waves. All he could think was at least it wasn't dirt. A crack of thunder pushed the three inside. The four walls were peppered with holes of various sizes, including some large enough for Tristin to stick his fist through.

A table as tall as Tristin stood in the center of the room on wooden legs as thick as his waist. Each of the four chairs were wide enough that he and Makenna could comfortably sit side-by-side, and tall enough that they'd probably need a boost just to climb up.

Ian passed him a handful of japsy weed from his pouch. "Eat the leaves first and then the stem. It's the best way to enjoy them."

Enjoy them?

Tristin looked through the opening that had once been a window as the rain started to fall. He hated rain almost as much as the river. As it fell, it soaked in the green fog and turned the drops into slime the consistency of snot. And it itched his skin terribly. The first steady drips started to fall from the holes in the ceiling.

Ian walked over to a pile of buckets. "We need to collect water whenever it rains, just like you did over there."

Tristin finished chewing another japsy weed, surprised at how filling even a couple of stems were, and joined Ian at the buckets. "Is japsy weed really all we get to eat over here?" His tone sounded whinier than he intended.

Ian dropped his bucket and cocked his head. He took a deep breath. Tristin already regretted his question. "I don't know what you're accustomed to eating, but you're welcome to go back anytime you'd like. I'll be happy to escort you."

More drops fell from different holes in the ceiling.

Tristin shrank from the mild rebuke like he often did when his father was displeased. "No, no, no. I'm sorry, sir. I didn't mean to be rude. We're lucky to have them." He didn't have the courage just then to tell Ian how good he could eat by stealing trash in the wealthier parts of the kingdom.

Makenna quietly positioned a bucket under one of the holes, careful to not become part of the conversation.

Ian bent over his bucket and removed a rag from inside. "You should be thankful we have japsy weed at all. If it wasn't for them, no one could live here, including you, and everyone would still be living under King Searle's rule. Many of those here, like you, would still be hiding in fear of the Angel."

"I didn't mean to sound ungrateful, Ian."

"Well, you did." Ian stretched the rag over the top of the bucket and Makenna did the same with her pail. Ian sighed and took a deep breath. "I'm sorry to be so curt, Tristin. I'm doing the best I can over here. I shouldn't get so worked up."

"I didn't mean to offend you. We're eternally grateful for your hospitality. I was only wondering about other kinds of foods like fruits or vegetables. They must grow somewhere in the kingdom, so I thought maybe …?"

Ian set the covered pail under a steady drip. "No. Nothing grows in the green fog except japsy weed."

"I don't understand. Where do they come from, then?"

"You've never gone to the road east of Madson's District and seen the early morning wagon parade?"

Tristin shook his head.

"That's where the supplies are brought into town. They come throughout the night. The Madsons get the good stuff, and the Terdicts get whatever's left."

"I know, but where's the food *come* from?"

"King Searle's mountain. The fog is thinner there. His royal servants grow the food and make raw goods, and he distributes the supplies by way of those wagons."

"How do you know so much?"

"I keep my ears open. Or used to, at least."

Makenna whispered into Tristin's ear as Ian turned to look out the window, "He sounds a little like Clinton."

"I'll show you around a bit in the morning. Hopefully, it'll be done raining."

Makenna joined him at the window. "I'd like that. Thank you."

Ian turned back to Tristin. "Make sure you two always fill your pails when it rains so you don't have to drink from the river. There are no clean water deliveries over here."

Tristin shuddered at the thought of drinking river water. It was always bitter no matter how many filters it went through. Just then his stomach rumbled slightly. He had a hard time looking at Ian when he asked for more japsy weed.

Ian grinned but didn't comment. He simply retrieved another handful from his bag and passed it over. He said, "See you in the morning." He covered his head with his shirt and then ran into the rain.

Tristin watched Makenna tend to the pails, wondering if he had made the right choice by taking her to the Slums.

Though they dozed on and off on the hard floor throughout the night, they didn't sleep much. When Ian showed up early in the morning, Makenna was ready and waiting. Tristin wasn't so eager.

"Can't we wait until the suns burn some of the slime away?" The slick ground terrified him because trying to run on it was like finding traction on a polished floor covered in porridge. It was reason number seven thousand why he hated the rain.

Ian studied him with crooked eyes as if trying to figure out a puzzle.

Makenna cleared her throat. "You won't need your speed, Tristin. There's nothing we need to run from over here."

Tristin's shoulders relaxed.

Ian escorted the twins through the Slums, introducing them to everyone who crossed their path. There weren't a lot of people out that early, but the ones they met seemed plenty friendly. Like Maddy, a bubbly girl just a little older than the twins. She was a Madson who had been sent to what she called a "behavior correction school" after she'd befriended her family's Terdict servants and started demanding they be treated better. When she'd escaped, she met Ian.

Or Leannan, who was barely twenty. He was wanted for punching a Madson.

"Why'd you punch him?" Tristin asked.

Leannan shrugged. "Ah, you know. My mom cleaned his house for fifteen years and he called her grinderfish food after she died."

Tristin contorted his face. Terdict funerals involved pushing the bodies into the river. *All* dead Terdicts were literally grinderfish food.

Leannan huffed and snapped, "I know what you're thinking, but that's not the point. I didn't want *him* saying it."

A few older boys ran by chasing a ball. One of them almost plowed into Makenna and apologized profusely before catching up to his friends.

Ian said, "That was Jackson. You'll hear plenty of him while you're over here. He's a bit too curious for his own good, but he's basically a nice kid."

Tristin already knew who Jackson was. They'd grown up in the same neighborhood, though Jackson was a couple of years older. He'd just disappeared one day, and his family feared he had been taken to the labor fields beyond the prison for some thoughtless transgression.

"Where'd they get the ball," Tristin asked, already looking forward to getting in on a game.

"Jackson brought it over. He begged me to let him get it before he'd come with me. He plays with it every day."

Makenna constantly scanned every group they met, seemingly in search of someone, which Tristin found strange since everyone the twins knew were already standing beside them. And by everyone, he meant Ian.

Eventually, she asked, "Can we go see where Samuel lives?"

Ah, yes. Tristin had already forgotten about Samuel. He lifted an eyebrow. "Why would you want to see him? Did you see something pleasant about him that I didn't?"

"Yes, actually. He was really gentle with me in the river, and I didn't get the chance to thank him."

"Gentle? Really? He looks dangerous."

Ian scoffed. "He's not dangerous, Tristin." After a pause, he added, "Well, not to us. Probably. Come on. I'll show you where he lives." Ian led the twins beyond the outskirts of the Slums until they'd walked a full mile or more without seeing another house. When they finally did, Ian said it was Samuel's.

"Doesn't he like neighbors?" Makenna asked.

Ian chuckled and shook his head. "Not really."

Samuel's home appeared solid and clean like a Richie's house, minus the fresh paint. Tristin wasn't surprised that the supposed rival of the Angel lived in the nicest house he'd seen so far. After all, who would challenge him for it?

Samuel was outside, practicing with a sword. His strikes were deadly and quick, his movements flawless. Though he didn't slow his training when the three visitors stopped on the road, he nodded to let them know he had seen them. He was glistening with sweat and green slime, revealing he'd been at it for quite some time. His long, dark curls whipped past his face with each thrust of his sword only to settle back onto his shoulders as he retracted his blade. His face was partially hidden by strands that stuck to his sweaty cheeks.

Makenna shyly said her thank-yous and asked if there was anything she could do to return the favor. Samuel grunted and resumed his blade work.

Annoyed that they were being ignored after coming all that way, Tristin said, "Kinda messy out here to be training, eh, Samuel?"

Samuel lowered his sword to his side and glared at him. "What do you need, young one?"

"I just said it's awfully messy out here to be training, don't you think?"

Samuel's voice was much deeper than Tristin's and carried farther with less effort. "No."

Ian said, "Samuel believes a good warrior needs to be proficient in every type of environment. He always trains during and after the rain."

Samuel rested his hand on his hip. "Is there anything else, kid?"

Ian smirked.

Tristin started to ask another inane question about whether it was as slippery there as it was where he stood, but Makenna yanked his arm. "Leave him be. He's obviously busy."

Embarrassed, Tristin mumbled some feeble apology under his breath.

Samuel lifted his blade again and continued his training.

As they walked away, Tristin asked, "Ian? Why didn't you tell me he can't take a joke?"

"Oh, it was far more entertaining how it actually played out."

Makenna giggled and Tristin shot her a glare.

Ian patted his back. "Don't fret. Samuel's always a little grumpy when he trains. Just be sure to never startle him while he's sleeping, and you'll be just fine. Oh, and he sleeps with his eyes open, so good luck."

Chapter 4

Samuel

S amuel sat at the bar inside his favorite tavern in the center of Madson's District. At least twice a month, he had Ian take him across the river so he could enjoy a few drinks with the barkeep, an old friend named Robert. They had been friends since Samuel had stumbled upon a robbery attempt years earlier and helped Robert out of a pinch. Though he'd never admit it, he hadn't even known he was interrupting a robbery when he stumbled into that fight.

Samuel took a swig. "You believe that kid? He's as optimistic as anyone I've met. Always talking about some fantasy where everyone has better lives. A bunch of nonsense."

"Why's that nonsense?"

"Because there isn't a better life for a Terdict. Not here and not over where I stay. Especially not when you're wanted by the Angel."

"Maybe you should take him over your knee and knock some of that enthusiasm out of him before he gets himself in even more trouble."

Samuel slid the empty tankard across the bar and Robert replaced it with a fresh one. "Nah. He seems like a good kid. Just naïve."

"You said he's only sixteen?"

"Yeah. Him and his sister both. Twins, I guess."

"Really? I've never seen twins before. Heard of a pair once, but one died. Is that the sister you were talking about earlier? The one who's been coming by your place in the mornings?"

"As sure as the suns rising. She's a sweet enough girl. Reminds me of my daughter."

"You're turning into a real softy, Sam. I never took you for someone who liked visitors."

"I don't … Usually. But she's always trying to get me to smile. It's a little endearing. What is it about smiles that give people the warm and fuzzies?"

"I don't know. Being human, maybe."

Someone called Robert away, leaving Samuel alone to sip at his new tankard. Terdicts didn't fit in on the Madson side of town, but Samuel had a way around that. When he'd fled to the slums with Ian after his wife and daughter were murdered, he'd taken some of his possessions. One of those possessions was a nice suit befitting a Madson. It turned out the best disguise was hiding right out in the open.

Other than Robert, no one else much talked to him while he drank. His square jaw and deep set-eyes seemed to speak for him. The other patrons' eyes burned through his back. They might not have been able to decide what it was about him that didn't fit in, but they could tell there was something. The well-dressed man beside him had been side-eying him all evening.

He didn't have many loves in life other than fighting and ale. He was about done drinking, and a good scrap would be the perfect topper. But he knew it would piss Ian off something fierce if he brought soldiers to the riverbank again. He was still hearing about it from the last time. That damn nervous Ian never wanted anyone to have any fun.

"What are you looking at?" Samuel demanded. His scowl warned the man that he wasn't seeking an answer.

The man tossed a few coins on the bar and left in a huff. One by one, the other patrons drifted out as curfew closed in, leaving Samuel the last man standing.

"Curfew's coming, Sam," Robert said as he leaned on the bar. "You wanna stay upstairs tonight in the extra room?"

Samuel plopped his empty tankard on the bar next to the others. "Nah. I'm good. Thanks, though." He pushed to his wobbly feet.

Robert cleared the empty tankards. "See you next time, friend."

"You headed home? I'll walk with ya."

"Nah. I'm going to stay here tonight. Early start tomorrow." Robert reached across the bar and shook Samuel's hand.

Samuel stepped back and covered his mouth with his fist. His cheeks puffed with a wet belch. He tossed a silver bit on the bar for his friend's time and stepped outside so Robert could lock the door behind him.

He stretched, groaned, and smacked his lips, still tasting his bitter belch. A lantern lit the upstairs window as Robert got ready for bed. Samuel pulled his suit jacket tighter across his chest and shivered. It was a lot chillier than when he'd arrived.

A look around at the empty streets made him realize that he might have waited a bit too long to head back to the Slums. Ian was probably getting antsy at the river. His mask chirped, so he took a lifebreath. Before he started the long walk to the Slaybyrne, he decided a piss would be a good idea. Though he considered dropping his pants right where he stood, he respected Robert's tavern too much to pee on the front walk. The rear, on the other hand …

He lifted a black handkerchief over his mouth and nose in case someone saw him and walked to the rear. It was just his luck that a soldier had had the same idea. It was too late to hide.

"What are you doing still out?" the soldier asked.

Shit.

Breaking curfew could earn him a meeting with the Angel if the soldier wanted to press the issue. But since he was a Madson for all intents and purposes that night, he figured he'd get by with a warning. Smooth and calm was the way to handle it.

"I was just having a couple drinks and time got away from me. Surely, you can understand."

"I don't drink, sir. You think your thirst is more important than the king's laws?"

Samuel was already getting peeved with the conversation. "Listen. This isn't a big deal. Just go about your business and let me get home before it gets any later."

"I don't think it's that easy."

Great. Samuel had gotten one of *those* guys. Just as he was thinking about putting the young soldier to sleep, a scuffle broke out in front of the tavern. The soldier nudged Samuel toward it. Two soldiers dragged a flailing man out of a shop across the way. They were having trouble controlling him.

Samuel smirked. "I guess you should go help your friends."

The soldier shook his head. "I don't think so. They've got it under control."

Of course they do. The two soldiers pinned their prisoner to the street, gasping for air like they'd been in a chase.

"Hey, Charlie," one of them shouted. "What's your guy's deal?"

"He was out past curfew." Charlie pointed to their prisoner. "And him?"

"We caught him breaking into that store."

Charlie's eyes brightened as if this was the most excitement he'd had all night. "Oh. Good catch."

Samuel took a sly step backward. "I think I'll be getting home, now," he said.

Charlie cleared his throat. "Ah, no. You wait right here."

It was worth a try.

But then the burglar made eye contact with Samuel and Samuel saw his brain working frantically. *Don't do it.* He had seen plenty of criminals try to lessen their punishment by pulling someone else into their scheme. It never worked, but they always tried. And if that guy succeeded, it would complicate Samuel's situation something fierce.

The burglar's eyes lit up. "It was him. He forced me to do it. He said he'd kill me if I didn't steal for him."

Samuel's shoulders drooped. He knew the routine now. "I don't know this man at all. He's lying."

The burglar persisted. "He made me. It was him."

Samuel gritted his teeth. As he glared at the burglar, he recognized him as someone who frequented Robert's tavern. "Shut up, man." He looked to the soldiers. "You guys don't believe him, do you?"

Charlie said, "It's not for us to say. You can have your words with the Angel. He'll decide if you're guilty."

Samuel wasn't meeting the Angel until he wanted to meet the Angel.

"Come with us, sir." Charlie reached for Samuel's wrist.

Damn it. Samuel took a frustrated breath. Before he struck his first blow, he silently asked his God of Killing to let him take it easy on them. Sometimes he didn't feel in control when the fighting started, and he didn't want to hurt the soldiers too terribly. There was no reason to kill three blokes just for making a living.

Samuel's fist shot out. Charlie dropped with a grunt. The two other soldiers stumbled back and grabbed for their swords. Samuel pounced. They were sloppy, probably not used to someone resisting them so violently. Samuel slammed their heads together and they dropped like Charlie.

When he spun toward the burglar to dish out some much-deserved payback, the man was already running away. He burned the thief's face into his memory. As Charlie started to stir, Samuel melted into the darkness. It took him twice as long as usual to get back to Ian once the alarm was raised and a lot more soldiers joined the search. They didn't take kindly to an assault on three of their own.

Before Ian could open his mouth, Samuel snapped, "Don't say a word, stealth boy. I'm in no mood." The swim across the river was quiet.

Chapter 5

A New Calling

L ife in the Slums would have been perfect if not for the damn japsy weed diet. Tristin had quickly grown to hate the leafy plant. Just over a week into his new life and his taste buds were begging for something different.

He decided to go to Ian with a proposition. After yet another boring japsy weed in water dinner, or "soup," as Ian called it, Tristin excused himself from the table and headed for the door.

"Where are you going?" Makenna asked.

"For a walk. I'll be back soon."

Makenna clanged his empty bowl into hers with a huff. "Don't worry about cleaning up. I'll do it. I looove cleaning up after you." Sometimes Tristin wondered if Makenna would have anything to say at all if she didn't have sarcasm. Ignoring her was his best defense. He strained to open the heavy front door enough to squeeze through. Knowing how much it would further annoy her, he left the door ajar. She cursed him from inside as he ran laughing down the street.

The suns were nearing the horizon when he knocked on Ian's door. No one answered. Ian's neighbor, an older man named

William, sat on his porch working a japsy weed stem from one side of his mouth to the other. William was solid and strong like Samuel, though not nearly as spry, as was evidenced by his slow, plodding movements accompanied by winces and groans.

"Hey, William?" Tristin called out. William's ears perked. "Have you seen Ian?"

"He's probably on the banks. He goes there in the evenings to relax."

Tristin thanked him and zipped to the Slaybyrne, where he found Ian wading in the knee-high water. It was amazing how relaxed his friend could be while surrounded by so much instant death. Tristin stopped on the bank.

Without looking at him, Ian asked, "What's on your mind tonight, Tristin?"

Tristin started to step into the Slaybyrne, but Ian held up his hand, halting Tristin's foot just above the surface. Grinderfish swarmed beneath. "Don't ever assume I have you protected."

Tristin withdrew his foot and the grinderfish swam away.

"What do you need? You didn't come out here just to have your foot eaten."

"My sister and I are hungry."

"Heh. That's all? You'll get used to that feeling. The Slums aren't paradise, after all. If you'd like to go to paradise instead, well, you'll just have to stop using your mask for a while. For now, hunger is the price we pay for our freedom." Ian playfully pinched and twisted one side of his pointy mustache. He squinted. "Just the same, I'll see if we can't get you and your sister a better ration of japsy from here on out. We have to be careful, though, at least until the fields are more mature."

"No, no, that's not what I mean. Japsy weed tastes like dirt."

"And?"

"And I can't stand it anymore."

"You've just gotten here."

"I know, but it's making me crazy."

Ian glared at him. "What kind of privileged life do you think you deserve?" He stepped out of the river and retrieved a towel to wipe his bare feet. With a hand on Tristin's shoulder for balance, he slipped into his worn-out shoes.

Tristin toiled with how to say what he wanted to say without being immediately turned down. "How many people would you say live here in the Slums?"

Ian stepped away. "I'll tell you exactly. Thirty-seven, including you and your sister. Why?"

Tristin quickly calculated the numbers and whether his idea would even work. After concluding that it might be plausible, he nodded toward the Slaybyrne. "Did you know there are people over there who never want for food?"

"Of course I know that. I lived most of my life over there, just like you."

"Well, I was just thinking, what if we went over there and gathered some food and brought it back as a treat? They just throw the stuff away like garbage. I've seen it myself."

Ian stepped closer to the water and the gathering cluster of grinderfish swam away. He rubbed the back of his neck. "It's too risky. The more chances we give the Angel's men to see us, the more chances the Angel will focus on finding a way over here." Ian shook his head and walked up the bank. "It's bad enough I have to take Samuel over there so he can have a few drinks of the king's fancy ale."

"Ale?"

"It's a beverage the rich people drink that makes them feel funny if they drink enough of it. Samuel loves it."

"Why do you take Samuel over there if you don't want the Angel's men looking for you? *That* sounds risky. Especially just for a drink."

"Would you like to tell Samuel no when there's something he wants?"

His point was well made.

"I simply try to keep him happy. It serves us well here in the Slums to have the greatest warrior ever born on our side." Ian's eyes drifted to the sky where the green fog had thinned. He pointed. "Look, Tristin."

Tristin squinted upward. "What am I looking at?"

"The stars."

"I see them."

"Can you see the shape of them?"

"Yes."

"Do you see how they form a fish?"

If Tristin looked just right and strained hard enough, he could see an outline that might resemble a fish. It even had an eye that was brighter than the others.

"Pretty interesting, huh?"

Before Tristin could answer, the green fog drifted in front of the stars, obscuring them again.

"Every once in a while, you get a chance to see how amazing the sky can be. I suggest you always take it. So, is there anything else you want?"

"I want you to take me across tonight."

Ian paused. "Did you not hear anything I said?"

"I did. And I don't accept it."

Ian laughed. "Unless you're planning an ill-conceived swim, I guess you'll have to."

"Maybe I will swim across," Tristin snapped, his mouth outrunning his brain.

Ian stepped to the side and flicked his wrist toward the river. "Enjoy."

Tristin's mouth had cornered him. He could waiver and never be taken seriously again, or he could dive in and hope Ian relented.

Ian scoffed. "You're just a kid. You should leave the food gathering to the grown-ups."

Just a kid? Just a kid? Tristin's pride overrode his reason. He found himself marching toward the river before sanity could kick in. Ian watched with a smirk. Once Tristin reached the water's edge, he had gone too far to wilt. If Ian thought Tristin wouldn't call his bluff, he was about to be surprised. Tristin stepped into the muck with a wince. The grinderfish swarmed. Before the nearest grinderfish took its first bite, they all swam away. Tristin slowly turned back to the shore.

Ian stood in the water behind him. "Thanks for making me get my shoes wet, kid."

Tristin started walking, hopeful his friend would follow.

Whether out of curiosity, or the appetite for something adventurous, or respect for Tristin's gall, Ian followed. "You're one brave kid, I'll give you that."

They crossed the Slaybyrne together and Tristin couldn't stop smiling. When they reached the deeper water, Ian gave Tristin a brief swimming lesson. It was a disaster. Tristin choked on the muck and sank below the surface repeatedly. Ian pulled him up by his shirt collar and towed him the rest of the way across.

Once on the opposite bank, Tristin wiped away the irritating slime and slung it into the dirt while Ian tried to salvage his shoes. Tristin raced to Madson's District in record time, and it wasn't long before he found a treasure trove in the rubbish pile behind an eatery. By the back door was a discarded empty crate with a cloth liner. *Perfect.* He carried it to the pile of rubbish and started shoveling anything edible he could find into the crate. After mentally rationing the food to each of the thirty-six other Slummers, he determined one trip wasn't enough.

Preoccupied with gathering his loot, he didn't hear two soldiers approach the front of the store until one of them spoke to the other. Tristin's heart nearly stopped. He stood motionless, afraid of making too much noise if he tried to hide, and terrified of losing Ian's shaky confidence in him if he fled without his loot. There couldn't be a worse time for him to be spotted.

The soldiers hadn't yet noticed him. Chatty in their complacency, they stood joking about their wives spending their money almost before they made it. Tristin waited like a stone in the shadows barely ten feet away.

Nearly an hour passed while they griped about their lives. Tristin mentally calculated how long it had been since he'd last used his mask. He was okay for now, but he didn't have much longer. As he listened to the monotony of the soldiers' drivel, he shifted his weight and leaned slightly forward by accident. His shoulder brushed the rubbish pile and a box tumbled to the street with a thud. His lungs froze and he nearly lost control of his bladder.

"Did you hear that?" one of the soldiers asked.

Tristin had no choice but to crouch behind the rubbish. The soldiers had just blocked one of his two escape routes. He planted his back foot, ready to run.

"Who's there?"

It wasn't clear whether they had seen him. Though Tristin couldn't see them, he could hear their breathing.

"Eh, forget it, Frank. Let's go. There ain't anyone back there, just like there wasn't anyone behind Murphy's last week. Look." He kicked the tumbled box. "It was just a box that fell off the pile. Put it back and let's get outta here. It's time to check in, anyway."

"Hmph. I suppose," Frank answered, though he didn't sound so convinced. He leaned into view as he reached for the fallen box. Tristin's eyes widened and he held his breath as he stared at the dark, curly sideburns of the soldier less than an arm-length away.

Don't turn you head. Don't turn your head.

The soldier tossed the box back on the pile and returned to his partner. Tristin held his hand over his heart, leaned his head against the wall, and sighed. Maybe it hadn't been his God of Speed who helped him that time, but he thanked him anyway.

He decided the incident wasn't something Ian ever needed to know about. He grabbed his box of goodies, tore off down the alley, and didn't slow until he reached a spot in Terdict's District where he knew he could hide his loot while he went back for more. It was the same abandoned cobbler's shop where he and his sister had hidden after their father was arrested.

Though caution made Tristin take most of the night to gather a second crate of food, eventually he made his way back to the Slaybyrne unnoticed. Ian nodded proudly when Tristin arrived carrying a crate under each arm. He peered into one.

"Well, I'll be." He lifted a half-eaten apple with brown edges. "You did well, boy. Looks like you've got some good stuff in there." He patted Tristin's back.

Tristin played it cool even as he danced inside. A slight smile might have even cracked the corners of his lips. They made it across the Slaybyrne with one crate, and then Ian went back by himself for the other.

Once Ian returned and both boxes were safe on the Slums-side bank, he said, "We're definitely going to have to teach you to swim soon. I can see how I'll quickly grow tired of carrying you back and forth." Tristin grinned, knowing it meant he had proven himself and future trips were likely.

An early-rising couple on a morning stroll happened past Tristin and Ian on the bank. "Good morning," the older lady said.

Tristin nodded.

Ian waved. "Good morning, Lillian."

"Playing in the water again, Ian?"

"Aren't I always?"

She chuckled.

"Lillian, would the two of you be so kind as to gather everyone and meet me outside my home? I wish to address them this morning."

"Oh. Of course." Her companion grunted, though an accepting nod accompanied it.

Within an hour, everyone except Samuel had made their way to Ian's, curiously waiting to see what the big news was. Tristin saw Makenna standing near the back.

"I need everyone to form a line," Ian shouted. "I think most of you have met Tristin by now. Well, this young man has taken it upon himself to acquire a special treat for each of you this morning." He bowed and stepped aside. "Show them what you have, Tristin."

Tristin was ecstatic to distribute the literal fruits of his labor. Each man, woman, and child eagerly awaited their turn in line. When that turn came, they grabbed whatever food was offered and personally thanked Tristin. Some of the women hugged him, and the men shook his hand as if he were a grown-up. He heard more thank-yous that night than in his entire life combined. Helping people other than his sister for a change felt good. In that moment, Tristin was a child king among men, and he lavished in the Slummers' unending praise.

An older man Tristin hadn't met before reached the front of the line. The top of his head was bald with a ring of shoulder-length, delicate gray hair wrapping the sides like a crown. A black mole as large as Tristin's pinky nail sat beside his thick nose just above his bushy mustache. Tristin handed him a half-eaten apple. The man cocked his head, examined the apple, and smiled, revealing a missing front tooth. Most Terdicts were missing at least one tooth, with many of them missing quite a few. While holding up the line, he took a bite and savored it with his eyes closed.

Still chewing, he said in a raspy voice, "Kid, you're definitely something special. This might be the best apple I've ever had." He tapped Tristin's back with enough force that Tristin lunged forward with each painful blow. The old man tore into his apple again. He stood and ate the entire thing—seeds, core, and all—while the remaining Slummers waited patiently behind him.

"Is there something else I can help you with, sir?" Tristin asked, knowing there wasn't enough food to give him seconds.

After swallowing his last bite, the man licked his dirty fingers and then wiped his hands on his pants. He reached into a leather pouch tied around his waist and held out his closed fist.

Tristin stared at it before looking up curiously. "Go ahead," the man said. "It's a trade for the apple."

Tristin glanced at Ian and Ian nodded. He held out his hand. The older man opened his fingers and dropped a gold trinket into Tristin's palm. Its small size belied how heavy it was. Tristin held it up, examining it. One side was smooth gold, nearly flawless. The other side was white, protected by a rare glass covering, and decorated with twelve numbers spread within a circle around the border. Tristin couldn't take his eyes away.

"It's a watch," the old man grumbled. "You've seen a watch before, haven't you?"

Tristin shook his head, eyes still fixated on the treasure. He'd seen the watches that rich men carried from a distance, but he'd never expected to see one up close, let alone hold one in his hand.

"What's your name, son?"

"Tristin?" he answered, unsure for a moment.

"Well, Tristin, it's nice to meet you. My name is Jakodi. Go ahead. Have a gander at it."

Tristin's father had once said, "If ever you get the chance to hold a watch in your hand, press it against your ear. It'll sound like a faint heartbeat." Tristin lifted the gold trinket to his ear and held his breath. As Rhett had promised, he heard the faint "tick, tick, tick." His lips curled upward.

"Well, of course it works," Jakodi huffed. "You think me a fool to hand you a watch that doesn't work?" He sounded almost put out.

Tristin could see why the rich people sought to own such magnificent pieces. "How did you get it?"

"I was a fixer when I lived over there. A man I once worked for gave it to me. What I didn't know at the time was that it was stolen and he'd set me up to take the blame. The Angel sent soldiers. I figured I had little chance of the Angel believing my side of the story, so I fled to the banks of Slaybyrne that night."

"To meet Ian?"

He winced as if someone had stepped on his foot. "Never heard of Ian before then. I went to Slaybyrne because I wasn't going to the prison, no matter what."

Without looking up from the watch, Tristin asked, "Why would you go where there is nothing but grinderfish?" Jakodi didn't answer, instead giving Tristin a chance to figure it out on his own. "Oh," Tristin finally said, lifting his eyes from the watch.

"Anyway, that's where I met Ian, and he brought me here."

Tristin didn't want to offend Jakodi by holding the watch for too long. He offered it back, but Jakodi rebuffed him with a wave. "No, no, no. I want you to have it."

Have it? "But I don't understand. Why me?"

"Look what you've brought me ... brought us."

"But I didn't do it to get something in return."

"I know you didn't, kid. That's why it's yours. Since I don't have many more years left on this world, I figure this watch will give you far more enjoyment than it could ever give me. I've just been waiting for the right person to give it to."

Tristin was speechless. Other than his parents, no one had ever given him anything of value. The gold of the casing alone was probably worth more than his life in most circles. He was hesitant to take the treasure, but he didn't want to offend either. In a timid whisper, he said, "I'll cherish this forever, sir."

Jakodi mussed Tristin's hair and chuckled. "No need to cherish it, kid. It's just a watch." Jakodi winked limped down the street.

Tristin made a mental note to find out where the fixer lived and to visit him soon and often.

In a cloud of euphoria, he continued serving his neighbors. Whether it was a half-eaten apple or a heel of bread, for the Slummers it was worth more than gold. It had likely been a long time since any of them had tasted such delights, if they ever had. Jackson sifted through the crate until he found a squishy tomato. He smiled, thanked Tristin, and hurried off, kicking his ball along the way.

Makenna was the last person in line. She stood, beaming with joy and pride. Tristin had held some green beans back just for her. He presented them to her and she ate them one at a time while they watched everyone head back to their homes. Seeing her savoring the bland little things, he decided she didn't need to know how it had taken him an extra hour of avoiding the soldiers just to find them for her.

Ian shook Tristin's hand and turned to go inside.

Tristin stopped him. "Where's Samuel? I saved him some food."

"Eat it yourself. Unless you have ale somewhere in that box, I don't think Samuel cares."

Ian winked and disappeared into his home. Tristin and Makenna were left standing alone, two empty boxes beside them. Makenna's grin nearly split her face in two.

"Why do you smile?" Tristin asked.

She stood a little taller. "Don't you see how much the Slummers appreciate you?"

Tristin shrugged. "Yeah, well, I was just hungry."

"I don't believe that." She patted his shoulder. "You should get some sleep. You look ready to drop."

She was right.

Chapter 6

Broken Masks

Tristin's expedition into Madson's District had been such a stirring success that he and Ian made biweekly trips for food over the next six months. As long as they only stole from rubbish piles, they hoped no one would be the wiser. One early morning when Tristin returned to the bank, his one-time schoolmate Clinton was waiting. He saw Tristin before Tristin saw him.

"I knew it," Clinton shouted, nearly sending Tristin out of his shoes. He pumped his fist.

"What are you doing out here, Clinton?"

"You're going across Slaybyrne, aren't you? I knew I'd find you one day."

Tristin shook his head and opened his mouth to protest, but Clinton interrupted. "That's where you've been hiding, isn't it? I can't believe I was right."

Tristin sighed. "How did you figure it out?"

"My crazy gran swore she saw someone swimming in the river before she died. I've been sneaking out here whenever I could for the last two years, hoping to see him. I never dreamed it would be you."

"It's not me."

"How do you keep the grinderfish away?" Before Tristin could answer, Clinton pried at the crate under Tristin's arm to see inside. Tristin pulled it away.

"You're going over there now, aren't you?" Clinton asked.

"Don't worry about that. Just go back home before you get caught out here." Tristin scanned the edge of the city for patrols.

"Take me with you. I wanna see the other side of Slaybyrne. I wanna see the Barbarian Slums."

"I can't, Clinton. You don't want that life. Just stay with your family."

"Are there other people over there with you? Is your sister with you?"

"Yeah. We're all people wanted by the Angel. We're just trying to keep quiet and safe."

Clinton shook his head. "I told you people were over there, didn't I?" A puzzled look crossed his face. "So ... You're saving people from the Angel?"

Tristin shook his head and waved his free hand. "No, no, no. It's not like that."

Tristin looked past Clinton's shoulder to where Ian was cautiously climbing onto the bank. "I gotta go, Clinton. It was good seeing you. Don't tell anyone. All right?"

Clinton pinched his lips together with his fingers. "I won't tell a soul."

Tristin doubted Clinton's secret-keeping abilities, but there was nothing he could do about it. He left Clinton behind and returned to the Slums with his single crate of food.

When he returned with Ian to the Terdict-side bank two weeks later, a young man and woman were waiting.

Ian shot Tristin a look. "I guess your friend's been running his mouth."

Tristin heaved a sigh.

"Let's just go back before they see us. We can come back tomorrow night."

Tristin glared at him. "What if they need help?"

"That's not our place."

"I can't just ignore them. They took a chance to come here. At least let me see what they want."

Ian rolled his head with an annoyed groan. Tristin smiled. He hurried to the couple, startling them when he whispered, "Hello."

"Are you the boy who can give freedom to those wanted by the Angel?"

Tristin looked over his shoulder at Ian still standing in the muck. Ian shook his head.

Tristin grinned. "That I am. Why are you fleeing?"

The man answered, "I work for a Madson clothes maker. She reduced my salary until I couldn't pay the king's taxes and eat anymore. I'm more than a month overdue. I know the soldiers will come for us soon."

Tristin puffed out his chest. "I understand. And if I take you to the Slums, will you promise to be productive?"

"I can make clothes and mend them. That is, if you can acquire fabric and needles and thread."

Tristin bobbed his head, a new idea forming. "Very well. You may come with us."

Ian threw his hands in the air and turned away.

And that was all it took for Tristin's motivations to change. Over the next six months, Clinton's big mouth spread the word of Tristin's deeds like a spark igniting the Slaybyrne. Soon, bringing "criminals" to the Slums became Tristin's top priority. He brought over ditch diggers, handymen, and even a teacher, all of whom were behind on their taxes or accused of petty crimes. With Ian's leadership, the Slums were becoming their own little thriving kingdom with nearly seventy productive inhabitants and growing. The japsy fields were already twice as large.

Tristin still gathered food when he could, but it was never enough, and the adulation of the Slummers had dwindled. Though he knew deep down that the Slummers appreciated him, he was lucky to hear a passing "thank you" when he returned. Except for Jakodi, who was always grateful and always received an apple, even if it wasn't a food gathering trip. Tristin had almost been caught twice, as his newest endeavor had resulted in an increase in patrols along the banks. He wondered if gathering food was even worth the risk anymore.

But Tristin wanted to do more than just bring people to the Slums and be the town scavenger. After a growth spurt, he was able to stand eye-to-eye with Ian and he felt it was time to stop acting like a child. He knew he could handle more responsibility. Makenna thought so, too. She kept saying she saw their father in him more and more each passing day. He liked hearing that.

The Slummers looked at him differently, too. They didn't speak to him like he was a child anymore and didn't patronize him when he had differing opinions. He was even occasionally invited to meetings of the unofficial Slums council, though they usually just wanted to give him a list of supplies they wanted him to scavenge.

Tristin took his next trip across the Slaybyrne closer to dawn than dusk—a change-up he and Ian sometimes used to lessen the risk of soldiers catching them. Tristin had become so familiar with the soldiers' routines that he rarely had to use his speed anymore. The only real threats to him now were the occasional soldiers on horseback because they took their jobs more seriously and rarely followed routines. But patience and a keen eye easily nullified their advantage.

As Ian and Tristin reached the bank, Tristin noticed a small gathering to the south. A Terdict funeral was in progress. "Ian?" he whispered.

"I saw."

"Let's go pay our respects."

Ian shook his head.

Tristan blinked in surprise. "But it's tradition."

"I lost interest in that tradition long ago. I've attended too many funerals."

Tristin left Ian behind and went to stand on the outskirts of the small crowd. He was relieved to see it wasn't anyone he knew being lowered into the water. Giving the bereaved family plenty of space, he bore silent witness until the grinderfish finished their grim task and swam away.

Having paid his respects, Tristin began his mission with a heavier heart than usual. He found himself thinking of his mother, wishing she had gotten the funeral she deserved. Who knew what the soldiers had done with her body? It was yet another reason to hate King Searle and his twisted laws.

When time was tight, Tristin had a favorite spot where he could get the most reward with the least amount of hassle. It was a row of seven two-story houses in the middle of nowhere, all identical in shape and size and painted the same shade of taupe. They were unique in that they were the only houses Tristin had seen that had covered porches protruding from their doors like horse snouts. The people living in those houses were particularly generous in what they threw away and equally careless in their security.

Getting across town to those houses was the trickiest part of the trip. While hiding next to a little-used horse trough outside of a blacksmith shop, he waited for the patrolling soldiers to finish their shift. He idly wondered if it was the same blacksmith shop where his father had worked.

On schedule, a fire-haired soldier arrived at the general store across the street. The store had a large picture window through which he could see the proprietor setting up a table and a deck of cards. As expected, the fire-haired soldier removed his helmet and waited for his two friends. Once the other two men arrived, the redhead knocked three times on the door, paused, and then knocked twice more. The proprietor invited them in and lowered blinds in the window.

Perfect. They would be busy for the next two hours at a minimum. Tristin brazenly marched down the middle of the street. Maybe he was getting a little too cocky.

Nah. He was just that good.

The rest of his trek was uneventful. When he reached the houses, he tried to remember which one he had looted on his last trip. He was always careful not to steal from the same place more than a few times a month. Had it been the third house last time or the fourth? He figured he'd better go to the fifth just to be safe. After all, rifle through someone's rubbish once and they might not be the wiser. Do it again and they might start watching with a closer eye. Do it a third time and they might be waiting. While his concern was probably unwarranted, it helped to keep him sharp when the monotony of his excursions threatened to make him lazy.

The only real danger with that row of houses was in how close the owners kept their trash piles to their back doors. Quietly and methodically, he dug through the trash pile behind the fifth house with one eye on the back door. As always, it was a jackpot. He dumped a box of garbage, wiped the inside clean with his hand, and filled it with anything edible he could find. Fruit, beans, corn. There was even a part of what Ian called a blueberry muffin, which Tristin confiscated for himself. With the box full of goodies, he looked around for witnesses. There were none. There never were.

He was home free.

As he stepped away from the pile, glass shattered inside the house, freezing him in his tracks. The crash was followed by a man cursing. "Damn it, Shelly, not this again."

Candlelight illuminated the window closest to the rubbish pile. Tristin dropped his box and pressed himself to the wall.

"I can't believe this," the man continued. "You should have been more careful."

The woman, Shelly, answered with a quivering voice, "But it's not my fault. I don't know why it doesn't work anymore."

The candlelight darkened as a figure paced to the window and then turned away. Tristin pressed tighter against the wall and held his breath. The man sighed. "It's because it's from the black market. I told you a new mask might not work. And I spent a fortune to get it for you, too."

"I know, but you have plenty of money. Maybe the next one will work. Maybe there was something wrong with this one."

"It's not the money as much as the favors I had to call in just to keep the Angel's soldiers outta my hair. It's not the same as if my mask went bad. You might live here as my nanny, Shelly, but you're still a Terdict. The king won't let you have a new one. I'm sorry. The black market was your only chance. Are you sure this one won't get you through?"

Shelly sobbed. "I don't know what's wrong, but it's already broken. Maybe the guy you bought it from will replace it for free. I'm getting worse faster this time."

"That's not how it works. It's not his fault that the new mask is failing. It must be you. You must be sick or something."

"What do you want me to do? I can't help it that the mask only lasted a few months. It had scuffs all over it. It wasn't really new."

"Of course it wasn't *really* new. You're a Terdict."

"Maybe if you paid me more, I wouldn't still be one."

The man fell silent for a moment. Then he said coldly, "I gave you shelter and everything you needed to live. Do you know how many Terdict women would love the life you've had?"

"I'm sorry, I didn't mean that. I know you've been good to me. I just don't want to die."

"I can't help that. You knew there was a risk. Black market masks are unreliable." The man moved away from the window. "Shelly, I'm sorry. I can't get you another mask. It's over. Maybe you should pack your things and go before the kids wake up."

The silence that followed was like a great wind had sucked the life from the room. "G-g-go somewhere else? What do you mean?"

"The kids shouldn't have to see you die. It's not fair to them."

"You'd rather I just not be here when they wake up? No good-byes? Nothing?"

"You're not their mother, Shelly. She died giving birth to Jacob. You just filled a void."

"You bastard."

Something else shattered on the floor.

"Curse all you wish and break all the dishes you want, but you need to leave before I call the Angel's soldiers and show them how you destroy my property." His voice was even colder than before.

"Where will I go?"

"I don't know. That's not my problem anymore." The man's tone changed again, sharp and irritated. "You know, Shelly, you really are ungrateful. After everything I've done for you, you just want more and more. I'm going upstairs to make sure you didn't wake the kids. I want you gone before I return."

Tristin stood motionless. Ice melting would have made more noise. And then he heard a subtle but definite wheeze from inside. He hadn't noticed it when the two had been arguing, but in the silence it was hard to miss. The sound hurt his heart. Images of his dying mother flashed through his mind and turned his stomach.

A faint sob followed the wheeze. Though Tristin's every urge was to run, guilt held him against the wall. He wanted to do something for Shelly, though he didn't know what. He supposed he could bring Samuel back to teach the man a lesson, but Samuel might just as easily kill the guy, and what would that do to help her or the kids?

Lost in his thoughts, he didn't hear Shelly approach the back door until the handle rattled. He should have run—she would have never seen him if he did—but his feet were fixed to the ground. The door swung open. A young woman with dark, curly, shoulder-length hair stumbled out. Her frail hand was pressed to her face with her fingers spread apart just enough for her to see where she was going.

With tears flowing, she ran past Tristin's box of stolen garbage before dropping to her knees. She took a stuttering, wheezy breath. Tristin quietly peeled himself away from the wall, afraid of startling her.

He stood within an arm's length of her and waited for the right time to say something. The right time never came. He looked around, nervous that someone else would hear her sobbing and come to investigate. Knowing he couldn't stand there forever, he finally whispered, "Miss?"

She jerked around like someone had dumped freezing water down her back. Tristin held up his hands with his palms out. "I won't hurt you."

She stood up and backed away. Her high cheekbones accentuated the thinness of her face. She looked tired, not like she needed a nap, but worn out to her very soul, just like his mother had looked in her last days. "Who are you?" she asked.

Her red, swollen eyes fixated on him. Her lifemask gave off the same muffled chirp that Emma's had before she'd died. Tristin timidly retrieved it from her waist and helped her take a breath.

"My name's Tristin. I'm from the Slums."

"The Slums? That's impossible."

"I wouldn't lie."

"You dress like a Terdict. Are you looking for work?"

"No, ma'am. I'm just here looking for food."

She wiped her eyes with the back of her hand. Glancing down at Tristin's box, she asked, "Is this what you came for?"

He nodded.

"Well, take it, then. I'm not going to stop you. Not that I could if I wanted."

Tristin had an incredible urge to comfort her, but didn't know what to say. Telling her she would be all right would be a lie. She struggled to her feet, ignoring his offer of assistance.

"Your name's Shelly, right?"

Her forehead creased. "How'd you know?"

"I heard that man say it when you were arguing."

"Oh."

The rising suns reminded Tristin how dangerous it was about to get for a scavenger in Madson's District. He needed to get moving, but he couldn't leave without helping her somehow. "Come with me," he blurted with no idea of what he would do if she accepted. "I'll help you."

She searched his face for any hint of a trick. He didn't waver.

She turned away. "You can't help me."

"Maybe not. But I can try."

Her eyes widened slightly. "Unless you have a lot of money ...," she paused to look him up and down, "... which it doesn't appear that you do."

"No, I don't. But I'd like to try just the same."

She sighed. "Why do you want to help me?"

Tristin pictured his mother again, but he held his tongue. He didn't trust her enough for that story. "I just think I can help."

She looked at the house and then back at Tristin. Pain and sadness lined her tired face. Her eyes lingered. Timidly, she nodded.

Tristin gently touched her wrist. "Lean on me." He lifted her arm over his shoulders. "I have a friend who might be able to help us. Will you trust me?"

"I have no other choice."

Tristin lifted the box of food under his other arm and helped Shelly around the side of the house. Out front, two men pulled a wheeled rubbish cart along the sidewalk. One of them went behind the houses on the south side of the street while the other went north.

Soon, they both returned with armfuls of garbage and tossed it into the cart. They would feed the grinderfish later in the morning. Once they moved on, Tristin helped Shelly all the way to the Slaybyrne's bank. Between the patrolling soldiers, Shelly's slow pace, and the garbage gatherers, it took him three times as long to get there.

By the time Tristin and Shelly approached the river, he had abandoned his crate and was practically carrying her. Ian was waiting with a stranger—a man with a swollen lip, holding his injured arm.

Ian raced up the bank to meet them. "What are you doing? Who's this?"

"Her name's Shelly. She needs our help."

"Help? She needs more than help. She looks like she's dying."

Shelly wheezed. Panic brightened Ian's eyes. "Is her mask failing?"

"Yes. But hear me out. She has nowhere else to go. I thought maybe Jakodi could fix her mask."

"And why would you think that?"

"Because he's a fixer. He fixes things."

"But not masks." Ian bowed his head, avoiding eye contact with Shelly. "Damn it, Tristin. We can't fix masks. No one can. You should know that by now. You have to be smarter than this." He eventually found the courage to look at Shelly. Her head rested on Tristin's shoulder. She was barely conscious and too winded to speak. She didn't look up when Ian spoke to her. "I'm sorry, my dear. Forgive my young friend if he's given you the impression we could help you, but—"

"The king fixes masks," Tristin interrupted.

Ian sighed. "Yes. Are you a Madson now?"

"Don't you get it? If *he* can fix them, then they *can* be fixed."

The look Ian leveled at Tristin didn't lack compassion, but it did lack hope, which was even more devastating.

"What would you have us do, Ian? Lay her here on this bank and let her die?"

Ian sighed. "Of course not. But you're giving her false hope, and I will not be party to it."

"Ian. Please."

"I don't know," he mumbled. He bit his lip and cursed under his breath.

"This isn't her first mask," Tristin blurted.

"What do you mean?"

"She was a nanny for a Madson family. They got her this mask a few months ago."

"You mean from the black market?"

"Yes."

"You can't trust the black market, Tristin. They're all a bunch of thieves preying on desperate people."

"Yes, and I know that's probably why she ended up with another bad mask. But if they can make masks work for other people, then it means others can do it besides the king."

"If this isn't her original mask, that means you would need to have a working mask and someone to alter it, which we have neither."

"What if I got her another mask? Jakodi could fix it."

It appeared to kill Ian to concede, even slightly. "I suppose it's possible."

Tristin started to smile.

"*Theoretically*. But where are you going to find a working mask?"

Tristin had already thought of that. "The Madsons get new masks, don't they?" He couldn't hide his mischievous grin.

Ian's eyes narrowed. "Yeeees."

Tristin's grin widened. "And the soldiers are Madsons, aren't they?"

"Tristin. No. I'm not even entertaining this idea."

"How long do I have until we absolutely must go back across Slaybyrne?"

Ian groaned. "I'll wait as long as I can. If I'm gone before you return, you'll have to hide until I come back for you tonight." Ian looked at Shelly as her head slouched forward. "You'd better just get back quickly. She's pretty sick." He turned away and shook his head. "You're going to get us a lot more attention than we want if you steal a soldier's mask. You're going to anger the Angel something fierce."

"But we'll be saving someone's life. That must count for something. We can't live our entire lives playing it safe."

Ian shook his head again. "This is a bad idea."

Tristin looked to the town. "Be ready to go when I get back. We may be leaving in a hurry."

Ian and the injured man took Shelly so Tristin could pull away. Tristin whispered into her ear, "I'm going to get you a mask, Shelly. I promise."

His lifemask chirped just in time to freshen him for his run. He took a breath and checked the positions of the rising suns. "I'll hurry." With that he turned, called upon his god, and raced into the city again.

Chapter 7

The Birth of a New Agenda

Tristin waited beside a Terdict house not far from the river as the streets filled with men and women heading to work and children going to their morning lessons. He joined the Terdicts in the street, blending in as though he'd never left. He didn't know if the Angel knew who he was or if anyone might recognize him, but saving a life was worth the risk. And he didn't have time to play it safe.

By accident, Tristin made eye contact with an old friend of his father's, Rudolf, as the older man exited his home. Tristin tried to turn away, but he was too slow.

"Tristin?"

Damn it. Tristin lowered his head, hoping Rudolf would think he was mistaken and move on. No such luck. Rudolf hurried to him. "Oh my, it is you."

Tristin looked up. "Hi, Rudolf."

Rudolf grabbed his shoulders. "My goodness. You're the spitting image of your dad when he was younger. Where have you been?"

"Around." Tristin had always liked Rudolf, but right now he wished the man would shut up and leave.

"We heard about your mom and dad. We've been so worried. Please tell me Makenna is doing well."

"Yes, sir."

Rudolf sighed and pulled him in for a hug. "You are so skinny, son. Can you come in for something to eat? We don't have much, but my wife would make you something. She'd love to see you."

"I'm sorry, I don't have time to stay. You shouldn't even be seen with me. It's dangerous."

"Dangerous?"

Tristin nodded.

Rudolf stepped back. His eyes squinted and crossed.

Tristin saw two soldiers strolling along the opposite walkway. "Rudolf, it was great seeing you. Now get away from me and pretend you don't know me. You've always been good to me and Makenna, but things are about to get really bad."

Tristin stepped back, took a last look at his father's old friend, and then turned away as if he'd never met the man before.

Tristin called upon his god, took a deep breath, and charged at the two soldiers. As he ran, he focused on the mask hanging from the belt of the soldier on the right. Dust lifted from the ground in his wake as he wove in and out of the commuters.

The two soldiers laughed and talked, oblivious to being stalked. Tristin positioned his left hand waist-high. His timing had to be perfect. Though he closed the distance in a flash, when he used his god it seemed like the world slowed for him.

The soldier extended his right leg for another step. Tristin lunged, slowing just enough to grab the mask. His concentration was at its peak. Resistance from the soldier's mask nearly yanked Tristin's elbow out of its socket. The soldier lurched forward. The clasp snapped, flinging two pieces of metal into the air. The mask gave way. Tristin stumbled, caught himself, and regained his footing. As he ran, he chuckled at the idea of the soldier rushing to the Exchange for a replacement mask and explaining himself to his superiors. The other soldier was probably giving chase, but it would do him little good. Tristin didn't slow until he reached the riverbank.

When Ian saw him coming, he lifted Shelly's arm over his shoulder and helped her into the river. Trusting Ian completely,

Tristin splashed into the water behind them without fear of the grinderfish. His swimming was getting good enough that he could help the injured man while Ian helped Shelly. Once free of the water, Ian lowered her to the ground for a breather.

Tristin ran past him. "Ian, bring Shelly to Jakodi's. I'll be there waiting." He zipped through the Slums. When he reached Jakodi's, he pounded on the door like he was being chased by the Angel himself.

"Hold on," the old man grumbled from inside. Tristin continued pounding until Jakodi finally opened the door. "All right, already." Jakodi groaned, rubbing his bloodshot eyes. "Tristin? Where's the fire, son?" He opened the door wider and Tristin followed him into the house.

The old man had done a remarkable job of patching over the many holes in his roof and walls with various mismatched scraps of whatever wood he could find.

Rudimentary hand-crafted tools of every shape, size, and function littered the room and Tristin wondered where he had gotten them. A three-legged table propped up by a stack of flat rocks sat in the center. On the table, next to a bundle of japsy weed set out for Jakodi's breakfast, was an unrolled cloth on a strap with pockets holding smaller tools. Tristin hoped they'd work on masks.

Jakodi noticed his interest in the tools and said, "Those were my watch fixing tools on the other side. But that's not why you're here so early this morning, is it?"

"No. I mean, yes. I need your help."

Jakodi's eyes drifted to Tristin's waist pouch. "Is that an apple?"

Tristin looked down. He'd completely forgotten stowing the apple for Jakodi before abandoning the crate of food.

"Is it for me?" Jakodi licked his lips.

Tristin fished it out and tossed it to him. Then he tossed the stolen mask on the table with a thud. "I need you to fix this so it works with a different owner."

Jakodi loudly chewed a bite of his apple and rubbed the back of his neck. With a hard swallow, he shook his head. "Boy, I thank you for the apple, but I can't fix that mask. You know that. I wouldn't even know where to begin." He took another bite.

"You have to try. It can't be much different than the workings of a watch. They're both mechanical, right?"

"No idea." Jakodi picked up the mask and examined it. "I've never taken one apart. It's prohibited by King Searle."

"The king's laws don't reach the Slums. Just tell me: can it be done?"

"Hmph." In slow, repeated movements, Jakodi stroked his mustache with a finger and thumb.

Tristin's lifemask chirped, but he ignored it, too busy burning a hole through Jakodi with an intense stare.

Jakodi turned the mask over and held it closer for a better view. "There are two issues that would need to be solved, as I see it. First, something inside the mask has to fail. Finding and replacing whatever that is would be one thing. The second issue is a bit more puzzling."

"What is it?"

"Somehow, these masks are dedicated to a single person for their lives." He scratched his head. "Some people think it's witchcraft."

"And you? What do you think?"

Jakodi rubbed his forehead. "I don't tend to believe much in witchcraft. I have always wanted to tear into a mask, but if I ruin this one, then what would you do?"

"It's not my mask. Will you try?"

Jakodi paused before setting the mask back down on the table. He shook his head. "No, I don't think I can. These aren't watches. I'm sorry, Tristin."

Tristin's lifemask chirped again. He ripped it from the clasp on his waist and took an annoyed breath. "Jakodi, I need you to try. Tell me what you need, and I'll get it."

"Why are you so obsessed with fixing masks all of a sudden?"

Three heavy-handed knocks on the door came in answer. Jakodi looked to the door and then to Tristin.

"Expecting someone?"

Tristin nodded. Jakodi opened the door. Ian cradled Shelly in his arms. Her wheezing had gotten even worse.

"She's why," Tristin said. He rushed to Ian and helped Shelly to Jakodi's sleeping pallet where she could lie down. Her lifemask clunked instead of chirped.

Jakodi's face paled and his voice turned serious. "Ian, grab a pail of rainwater. I'll do what I can." He pointed toward his washstand where the pail was.

Tristin had never seen someone's condition deteriorate so rapidly from their mask failing. Even at the end, his mother's health had taken weeks to worsen so badly.

Jakodi dug through his tool pouch until he found what he needed. It was a long, narrow tool with a flat end that fit snugly into a hole in the nosecone of the soldier's mask. He spun the tool in three separate holes until the cover loosened. With the cover off, Jakodi stopped and stared in awe at the guts of the mask as if time wasn't a concern.

"Hurry, Jakodi," Tristin snapped, breaking the old man's fascination with the mask's workings.

"Yes. Right." Tristin handed him Shelly's mask and then sat on the floor next to her. Jakodi got to work on her mask. As he pulled away the cover, he mumbled to himself, "Interesting."

Tristin dabbed Shelly's forehead with the wet cloth Ian handed him.

She whispered barely loud enough for him to hear, "Thank you, Tristin. You're so kind."

He gently touched her cheek, thoughts of a grinderfish funeral turning his stomach. He stood up. "Save your strength, Shelly. I'll be right back." He covered her with a blanket and went to the table where Jakodi and Ian were sitting.

Jakodi mumbled to himself some more as he carefully removed a black, shriveled, cloth-like material from inside Shelly's mask. The stuff disintegrated between his fingers and floated away like ashes above a fire. The only thing left in the nosecone was a porous, dark-blue crystal. A slight blue glow, duller than any glow Tristin had seen from a mask before, pulsated from its center.

Jakodi held out the soldier's open mask. "Look, Tristin. See the difference?" The cloth in the soldier's mask was as white as new teeth with just a hint of yellow staining the top ruffled edge.

Tristin leaned closer. "Sooo? Just take out that white cloth and put it into Shelly's mask." He reached for it.

Jakodi pulled the mask out of reach and swatted Tristin's hand away. "No. Did you not see what just happened when I touched the black one? It fell into nothingness."

"It was probably because it was from a bad mask. Trade them out. That's all you have time to do." He reached for it again, and again Jakodi pulled the mask out of his reach.

"Tristin," Jakodi snapped in a voice louder and more intense than Tristin had ever heard him use. The old man calmed himself with a deep breath. "If the cloth falls apart, there's no getting another one in time."

"What if you touched it with something else besides your fingers? Like that metal tool?" He pointed to an odd, curvy tool in the shape of an "s."

"Maybe. But it's too risky. We only have one to experiment with and we can't ruin it by being hasty."

Tristin had already determined he'd go back across the river for another one if that's what was needed to save Shelly. Hell, he'd go back and get fifty more if that's what Jakodi asked.

Jakodi tilted his head, looked over at Shelly, and then looked back to the pulsating blue glow of the crystal in her mask. "See that?" he said.

"What?"

"Watch her breaths."

Tristin watched Shelly. "What about them?"

"Look how they match up perfectly with this pulsating light?"

"So?" Everyone knew the blue light pulsating from their mask matched their breathing. That was how it had always been.

"Are you sure he's up to this?" Ian muttered.

"The crystal is the key to adapting the masks to our bodies. If only we could figure out how." Jakodi's tongue poked from the corner of his mouth as he squinted and stuffed his fingers into the soldier's mask. He was careful not to touch the white cloth as he tugged at the crystal. It was wedged tight, but after a determined wiggle it broke free.

Once the crystal was out of the soldier's mask, Jakodi dropped it on the table with a start. "Ouch," he shouted. The crystal rolled to a stop near the bundle of japsy weed. He rubbed his fingers together and examined them.

"What happened?" Tristin asked.

"It stung me like I pinched my finger in the door."

The crystal's pulsating light grew steadily brighter as Ian, Tristin, and Jakodi watched. Shelly's wheeze was the only sound that broke the silence until Tristin asked, "What's it doing?"

"I think it's ready to chirp."

After the pulsating blue glow had encompassed the entire crystal, it hissed and a puff of bluish mist sprayed into the air. The japsy weed instantly curled, blackened, and died. No one moved, their eyes transfixed on what they had just witnessed.

"Why did it kill the japsy weed?" Ian asked.

Jakodi studied Shelly's mask again. "Hm. I wonder …"

"What?"

"The white cloth must be a filter. When the cloth in Shelly's mask blackened, the off-gas of the crystal became too toxic for her. The crystal is the key. The crystal is what's linked to her … to all of us."

Tristin rubbed his head. "I don't understand."

"Look at the mask." Jakodi held up Shelly's open nosecone so Tristin could see inside. "Look at how the air moves in a direct route from the outside vents, through the porous crystal and the cloth filter, and then into your lungs. When Shelly's filter went bad, the crystal sickened her."

"That's all fine and good, but how do you fix it?"

As Jakodi searched his kit for the right tool, he explained, "Since we can't trade out the filters without risking ruining them, we trade out the crystals. Shelly's crystal goes into the mask with the clean filter."

It sounded like a solid enough plan. "Do it, then."

Just as Jakodi pulled the crystal from Shelly's mask with his tool, it started to brighten and pulsate and threaten to off-gas. He jammed the crystal into the soldier's mask as quickly and carefully as he could.

Tristin waited on the edge of a blade. Shelly wheezed another worthless breath and seemed to shrink under the blanket. Jakodi slid the nosecone cover back over the mask and fastened it with Shelly's crystal inside. "Now, with her crystal and the new cloth filter, it might work."

The mask immediately chirped. Tristin snatched it from Jakodi and rushed it to Shelly. "Take as deep a breath as you can," he said as he pressed the mask against her face. She inhaled a shallow, labored breath and the mask whistled slightly.

"Well?" Tristin asked. "Did it work?"

Jakodi shrugged. "I don't know yet. I would guess that it'll take more lifebreaths before she starts to improve, if she improves at all. It could take all night."

Tristin sat beside Shelly and she nodded off with her head on his lap. Ian paced the room, pausing by a bucket near the door. He looked in. "Hey, Jakodi. You have grinderfish here? How the hell did you catch them?"

Jakodi looked up from further examining Shelly's old mask with a mischievous grin. "There's ways. As long as you're careful."

"But why?"

"I'm fascinated by the creatures. I'd like to know if there's anything they won't eat besides river mud. And I've been known to eat one or two of 'em on occasion." He rubbed his belly. "They're not very tasty, but they fill an empty gut and are a welcome change from japsy weed."

"Don't they give you the shits?"

"Sometimes they do, sometimes they don't."

Ian furrowed his brow and looked to Tristin.

Tristin shrugged.

Jakodi continued his inspection. "Now this is interesting," he mumbled. He motioned Ian over. "Come look at this."

Ian huffed to Jakodi and peered over his shoulder. "What?"

Jakodi held the stripped-out mask to his mouth and lightly blew into it. The mask whistled. "Very clever."

"What is?" Ian asked.

"The crystal's off-gassing sends tiny bursts of mist through a whistle which causes the chirp. It's ingenious."

Ian examined the mask. "So, any idea yet why the soldier's mask couldn't work for Shelly? Why did you need to swap the crystals?"

"That I don't know. Plenty of people have died trying to use other people's masks over the years. Somehow, the crystal knows its owner. I suspect the crystal in the soldier's mask would be poisonous to her, even through a healthy filter. At least, that's my guess."

Tristin's lips moved as he quietly prayed to his God of Speed just in case it was also the God of Luck or even the God of Answered Prayers. Shelly's chest continued to rise and fall. She still had a chance.

The soldier's crystal was now hissing relentlessly as if it were screaming. "What's it doing?" Ian asked.

Jakodi leaned closer to it. "I think it needs to be used." His eyes bulged. He scooped up the crystal and juggled it from hand to hand. He handed it to Ian. "Take it and bury it outside. Hurry."

Ian grabbed the crystal and shuffled it from hand to hand as he raced outside.

Tristin cocked his head. "Why are you burying it?"

"If it keeps off-gassing without a filter, it could make the air in here toxic."

Ian soon returned and asked the same question Tristin had asked. Jakodi repeated his theory and then returned to his study of Shelly's mask for the next few hours. By the time he finished, he had disassembled the entire mask and set the pieces in a row. Tristin dozed off next to Shelly while Ian paced.

Soon, Shelly's new mask pulsated blue light before releasing a chirp that woke Tristin. He smiled and whispered into her ear, "Shelly?" Her eyelids twitched. "Can you hear me? It's time for another lifebreath. Can you do it?"

She nodded. Tristin held the mask to her face. "Try as big a breath as you can."

Shelly exhaled and then took a deep breath, far eclipsing her first lifebreath with the new mask.

After a few seconds, she opened her eyes and looked around.

Tristin captured her confused gaze. "It's all right. You don't have to talk. Just rest."

As some of the color returned to her face, Tristin noticed for the first time the light freckles that peppered her nose. Shelly touched his cheek. "I feel better. You saved my life." Her voice was hoarse and tired, but her wheeze was gone. "I'm forever in your debt."

"No, you're not." It was sad that the right thing to do seemed so foreign to people. As he saw it, they'd had no other choice once they knew she needed help. "I would do it a hundred times again, Shelly. It's only right. Now get some sleep. You need your rest."

She smiled and closed her eyes again. After she was asleep, Tristin stepped outside where Ian was standing on the porch. Jakodi joined them.

Ian shook his head. "Unbelievable, kid. You actually did it. You and Jakodi actually saved her life."

To Tristin, it wasn't just about saving Shelly's life; it had ramifications that would reach the whole kingdom from one outer wall to the other. In knowing what could truly be done, there was no way Tristin could sit idly by while people died from failing masks. "Do you know what this means, Ian?"

"It means you were actually right for once. Congratulations."

Tristin shook his head. "No. Not just that. It means no one else in the kingdom will ever have to die from their masks failing simply because they don't have the gold or influence to get another. We can help them all."

"Whoa, Tristin. Slow down. If we start stealing masks like we do garbage, the Angel will definitely take notice, if he hasn't already."

"We have a responsibility now, Ian. If we can prevent even one person from dying, we have an obligation to do it. It's only right. The Angel can't get to us here, so the Slummers will remain safe. We'll continue bringing people over like we have been, only now we'll bring people with failing masks as well. I'll get word to Clinton. We'll save them. All you have to do is get me over there and I'll take all the risk." He backed from the stoop. "Thank you, Jakodi. Thank you, Ian. I need to go see my sister now."

Going across the Slaybyrne for food no longer seemed as important as it once had. In fact, Tristin didn't care if he only ate japsy weed for the rest of his life as long as it meant he could stop people from suffering like his mother had.

Ian shook Tristin's hand and followed Jakodi into his house. Before he closed the door, Tristin heard him say, "I'm afraid we've opened a dangerous door with this."

Tristin understood his friend's concern, but Ian would have to banish him and his sister from the Slums to stop him from doing what he knew in his heart needed to be done. As he walked, he closed his eyes and pictured his mother's pretty smile before the mask had made her sick. *Never again, Mom. Not if there's anything I can do about it.* Full of emotion, he raced home to Makenna. He had so much to tell her.

The next morning, Shelly was up and about by the time Tristin returned to Jakodi's home. Her cheeks were flush with color and she wore what seemed to be a permanent smile. "There's my special friend," she said when Tristin walked in.

Tristin opened his mouth to protest being called special, but stopped short when he realized it was the first time anyone had called him that since his mother. He hid a smile. "Where's Jakodi?"

"He's still sleeping."

Tristin offered his arm. "Go for a walk?"

"I'd love to."

He escorted Shelly through the Slums, introducing her to everyone they passed. When they reached his and Makenna's house, he retrieved a couple of apples that he had tucked away and gave her one. Her mask chirped and she took a lifebreath. Even the mask could barely hide her smile. They continued to stroll while finishing their apples. Tristin stopped at an empty house. Before he could say anything, she giggled.

"What is it?" he asked.

She reached out, stopping short of his face. "May I?"

Tristin shrugged, unsure of what he was giving her permission to do.

She gently picked a seed from his chin and then wiped the spot clean with her sleeve. Tristin cringed.

"Don't be embarrassed. I'm used to cleaning faces. I was a nanny just yesterday, remember?" She looked up at the house. "What are we doing here?"

Tristin smiled. "It's yours. Ian said you can stay here for as long as you'd like."

She touched her chest, a bit startled by the offer. "Oh."

"You don't like it?"

"Well, no … I mean, it's fine. I just haven't thought that far ahead. I don't even know anyone over here."

"You know me."

"Barely."

"You don't have to take it, Shelly. You're free. Ian will take you back across if you'd like."

"I don't know if I want that either."

Tristin grinned. "I know it's a lot to take in. You don't have to decide today. Give it a few days."

Shelly gave it more than a few days. Over the next three months, she settled in nicely, spending more time at Tristin and Makenna's house than at her own. Tristin enjoyed having her there. As much as he tried to portray himself as a confident young man, in the quiet moments when no one was around he found himself longing for someone to confide in who wasn't named Makenna. Shelly was perfect for the role because she had a motherly quality and a sympathetic ear. It was obvious why Richies would hire her as a nanny.

One evening when she was scolding him for his lack of manners at the dinner table, he couldn't contain his smile. She sounded like Emma.

With her hands on her hips, she snapped, "What are you smiling about?"

He shook his head. "Nothing. You just remind me of someone, that's all."

"Well I hope that someone would also tell you not to belch at the dinner table. It's quite rude."

Makenna lowered her head to hide a grin. She loved it when Tristin got scolded. Tristin stuck out his tongue and she returned the gesture.

Shelly gave him a glare. "Do not start up with her just because you got in trouble."

"Yeah," Makenna added.

Shelly's glare shifted. "You either, young lady. I won't have you two bickering tonight. I've already got a headache."

They ate their japsy soup in silence. Makenna finished hers in record time and washed her bowl at the sink. Then she started for the front door.

"Where are you going?" Shelly asked.

"Samuel's," she said as she rushed out.

"Again?" Shelly shouted after her, but she was already out the door.

Shelly turned to Tristin. "I guess it's just you and me this evening. Maybe we can play a game."

Tristin carried his bowl to the sink. "Can't tonight, Shelly. I'm going across for supplies. Hopefully, I can score some fabric this time." He started for his room, but noticed how Shelly seemed to droop slightly. He stopped and tilted his head. "What is it?"

She shook her head. "Nothing. I just have something to talk to you about."

"All right. Go ahead. I'm listening."

She waved her hand. "No, no. Not tonight. You go do what you need to, and I'll see you when you get back."

"Are you sure? I might be gone for a few days, maybe even a week this time."

"It's fine. It can wait."

"Positive?"

She nodded.

Tristin gathered his things, said, "Goodbye," and raced to meet Ian at the Slaybyrne.

Chapter 8

A Richie Life

As she did every morning, Makenna headed to Samuel's house not long after sunrise. She knew right when he finished his morning training and timed her arrival accordingly. She knew some people wondered what a young girl saw in a hardened warrior old enough to be her father, but they'd likely never seen his softer side. Few people had. She liked his company and he seemed to like hers, and she didn't care what anyone thought about their friendship.

"Hi, Samuel," she shouted as soon as he came into view in his practice yard.

He wiped his brow with a rag and waved from a chair on his porch. She watched for a smile, as she did each morning, but didn't get one. She never had. She'd made it her life's mission to crack his taciturn shell.

"Good morning, Makenna. How are you today?"

Makenna sat on a second chair that hadn't been there the day before. "Did you put this out for me?" she asked.

He nodded and wiped his sweat again. "What are we going to talk about today?"

"You."

He groaned. "Why do you always want to talk about me?"

"I don't know. Maybe because you hate it so much." She smiled.

"Well, it's gonna have to wait a bit. I have a special surprise for you today."

"A surprise? What could you have for me?" She wondered if it was a sugar beet.

"You'll see. If you'll excuse me, I'm going to go in and get cleaned up a bit first. You don't have plans today, do you?"

"Nope."

Makenna sat back in the chair while Samuel disappeared inside. She tapped her feet and hummed her favorite song. It was one her father used to sing about clear skies and refreshing air. Though she knew the words, she preferred to hum it. Samuel was gone for about an hour before he returned. His long, black hair was pulled tight into a tail. His beard was neatly trimmed, and he carried a bag over his shoulder.

"Samuel. You look ... nice."

"Of course. Don't I always?"

"So, what's my surprise? Is it in that bag?" She reached for it, hoping to sneak a peek.

He swatted her hand away. "Patience. You'll see in due time. Are you ready to go?"

"Go where? I can't have it here?"

He shook his head.

"Do I need to clean up, too?

He shook his head again. "Come on."

They walked through town to the riverbank where Ian was sitting with his feet in the water. When Ian saw them coming, he stood up. "Ready to go?"

Samuel nodded.

Makenna asked, "Ian, will you please tell me where we're going?"

"And face Samuel's wrath? No thank you."

Makenna followed Ian into the Slaybyrne with Samuel behind them. Once they reached the opposite bank, Ian said, "I'll be back for you this evening."

Makenna crossed her arms and gave Samuel a sour look. "I'm not going any farther until you tell me where we're going."

"Suit yourself." He started up the bank toward town.

"Damn it," she grumbled. Then she raced up the bank to Samuel. "You were really going to leave me," she said.

He looked slyly at her. "I knew you'd come." As they joined the flow of foot traffic in Terdict's District, Makenna realized she was touching her face again. She had been trying hard to break that nervous habit. She told herself she had nothing to be nervous about. If anyone could protect her from soldiers, it was Samuel.

He leaned in and whispered, "Just keep your head down and don't make eye contact with anyone. Especially soldiers. We'll be fine. Nobody's looking for you today."

Makenna lowered her head, but her hand still itched to touch her cheek.

While they walked east through town, Samuel asked, "So, what do you want to know about me?"

Her eyes lit up. "Really?"

"Sure."

"All right. Let me think." Though she wanted to know a thousand things about him, she never truly thought he'd open up to her. She blurted out the first thing that broke through the dam of many questions. "Were you ever married?"

Samuel nodded. "Once. A long time ago."

"Did you have any children?"

"A daughter. You remind me of her."

"I do?"

"Yes. She was also full of questions."

She scrunched her nose at him. "What happened to her and your wife?"

Samuel frowned. "I'd rather not talk about that, if it's all right."

"Oh, I'm sorry."

"Don't be sorry."

When they passed into Madson's District, Samuel's demeanor grew a little more serious. "We need to be more careful now. You look a bit young to be working, so a lot of people are going to stare at you. Just ignore them. We need to keep out of any soldiers' sights." He took her down less populated side streets, constantly peering around corners before continuing.

Makenna scrambled for another topic to keep the conversation going. "What did you do for work before you lived in the Slums?"

"I was a soldier."

Makenna nearly choked on her own spit. "You were?"

He tilted his head. "Yes. Is that so hard to believe?"

"No. I mean, you were a Rich—I mean, a Madson?"

"Sure."

"I thought you were a Terdict like me and Tristin."

"I *am* a Terdict. I just wasn't always one. It's very difficult to gain wealth in the kingdom, but fairly easy to lose it. Just lose a job or cross the Angel, and there you are. Do both and, well ..."

"How did you lose your job?"

"I'd rather not talk about that either."

Makenna sighed, wondering what she could ask that wouldn't be off limits. "Why can't Terdicts become soldiers. Or doctors. Why is it so hard to become a Madson?"

His tone was gentler than she'd ever heard it. "They do sometimes. Usually, it's by a favor or luck, though. I was a soldier only because my father was one. That, and I had a natural talent for it."

Makenna gave him a sneaky glance. "You were rich."

"I wasn't rich."

She poked his side. "Yes, you were."

"Okay, stop it."

She looked for that elusive smile. He didn't give her one.

"We're here." He stopped in front of a Madson house.

Makenna looked up. The house had glass windows and frilly curtains and even a fancy bronze door knocker. "Where are we?"

"A friend's house. He's not home. He said we could get ready here."

"Get ready for what?"

"You'll see." Samuel opened the door and they slipped inside. Portraits of people Makenna didn't recognize adorned the walls in the immaculate entryway. They were beautiful. She wondered if

Samuel's friend had painted them. They were far superior in quality to the ugly portrait of King Searle that glared at her beside the door.

"Will you tell me what we're doing now?"

Samuel sighed. "I'm going show you what it's like to be a young Madson lady for an afternoon."

Makenna's hand lifted to her mouth. "What? Really?" Her eyes welled up.

He brushed her chin with his knuckle. "Hey. There's no crying here. Everyone deserves such a life. I wish I could give it to you permanently, but a day is all I'm able to do."

Makenna didn't fully understand what being a Madson meant, but she knew they led a better life than she'd ever experienced.

He pointed to a door at the back of the room. "I want you to go into that room. There should be a wash sink with warm water in it. I want you to wash and put your hair up. My friend Robert has a daughter about your size. He said he'd leave one of her dresses out for you to borrow. Once you're ready, I'm going to take you to my daughter's favorite place."

"Oh, Samuel. Thank you, thank you, thank you." She rushed over and hugged him. She couldn't remember ever being so excited as she ran into the back room. As promised, a powder-blue dress with white ruffles around the collar was laid out for her, along with underthings and completely impractical shoes. It took her the better part of an hour to get completely ready. She wanted to be perfect.

When she finally stepped from the room, Samuel was half asleep on a chair with his head hanging awkwardly to the side. He wore a dark blue suit and looked so much like a Madson that his scars almost seemed to disappear.

She cleared her throat.

He lifted his eyes. "You look very nice, Makenna."

She tried to fight her happy tears, but one escaped.

"I said no crying."

She nodded.

"Are we ready?"

She nodded again.

"A few rules first. You must walk with a confident posture. You greet anyone who greets you with sir or ma'am. And if I say it's all over, you follow my orders exactly. We don't want to draw undue attention, but if we do, I won't let you get caught no matter what. You understand?"

"I just don't know what to say."

"Just say you understand."

"I do."

"I do, what?"

"Sir."

"Perfect, ma'am."

Makenna felt like royalty as she stepped outside. Something about the fancy dress and shiny black shoes made her straighten her spine without thought. She felt a strange, undeserved confidence. They walked from a side street into a bustling town square. Everyone looked so proper and clean. Some men carried walking sticks despite appearing not to need them.

"Does everyone dress like this over here?"

"Mostly just when they make a day at the town center. It's kind of a tradition."

If anyone passed by, the women nodded and the men tipped their hats. Makenna grabbed Samuel's arm and squeezed. She whispered, "This is amazing. I've never seen so many stores. They probably make everything here." She couldn't believe people lived in such luxury so close to where she'd slept on a dirt floor and prayed her father would bring home food.

Two soldiers strolled toward them through the crowd. Makenna automatically dropped her gaze. Samuel gave her a subtle nudge and whispered, "Posture."

She straightened again. A nervous tickle formed in her stomach. She caught herself reaching for her face and snapped her hand back to her side.

When one of the soldiers made eye contact with Samuel, Samuel nodded and said, "Good day, sir."

The soldier nodded back and returned the pleasantry. Then the soldiers continued past as if Makenna and Samuel belonged there.

Samuel led her to an eatery called Renoble's Treats. "We're here," he said. He opened the door and held it for her.

She played along. "Thank you, kind sir." The store had an odd, tangy smell. It wasn't a bad smell, just strong, and one she'd never experienced before. They waited their turn in line. When the person in front of Samuel received his order and walked away, Samuel stepped up to the counter.

A woman waited behind it. "How many custards would you like today?"

"Just two, thank you."

She did something behind the counter and then passed two bowls to Samuel. He set two bits on the counter. She thanked him.

Samuel handed one of the bowls to Makenna and led her to an empty table. They sat across from each other.

"Did you just give her two gold bits?" Makenna asked, eyes wide. She'd never even seen that much money before.

He nodded. "Custard is expensive. This is the only place in the world that I know of where you can get it. Go ahead. Take a bite."

Makenna lifted the wooden spoon and sniffed the custard.

Samuel encouraged her with a slight nod.

She shoved the spoon into her mouth. The most exquisite flavor exploded over her taste buds. "Oh my, Samuel." Her eyes closed in bliss. "This is amaaaazing."

"I know."

"I can see why your daughter liked it so much. It might be my new favorite thing in the whole world. How do they make it?"

"Have you ever tasted a sugar beet?"

"Once."

"Almond milk?"

She shook her head.

"Right. Probably not. That's the rarest part of the custard."

Makenna ate slowly, savoring the way each spoonful dazzled her senses. If she'd been standing, her knees would probably have given out. As she scraped the bottom of the bowl, she dreamed of a second, but didn't dare ask.

Samuel rubbed his belly and said, "You know. I'm quite full. Would you like the rest of mine?"

She blurted, "Yes … er … I mean, if you insist, kind sir."

He passed his bowl to her and she devoured it.

Instead of leaving right away, Samuel said, "Why don't we sit and savor it for a bit?"

Eating for pleasure was a foreign concept to Makenna, and sitting to savor it when finished seemed a waste of time. But Samuel was the expert. Makenna concentrated on the taste still mixed in her saliva and hoped it would never go away.

After a while, Samuel said, "I think we should go now. We don't want to be late."

Late? She couldn't wait to see what was next.

Samuel escorted her to where a crowd was forming around a stage. He said a "show" was about to start. A man approached them carrying a large bowl. Samuel tossed a silver bit into it. She wondered how many bits Samuel actually had. He led her through the crowd until she could see the stage.

The "show" was two people pretending to be people they weren't. They must have been pretty good at it because Makenna kept forgetting that they were pretending. Though she found it strange that anyone would want to be watched by so many people, she also found it intriguing. They were telling the story of a clumsy man who fell in love with a graceful woman. She couldn't stop thinking about how much Tristin would enjoy the show. He'd especially like the clumsy parts.

After the show finished, the audience clapped. Makenna joined in. The two pretenders bowed to the crowd as if they were all kings and queens. "Why are they bowing to us?" she asked Samuel.

"They're thanking us for our gratitude."

Makenna cocked her head. *Thanking us for thanking them?*

With the show over, the crowd slowly dispersed. As Samuel and Makenna turned to go, they stepped into the path of two soldiers.

"Excuse us," one of them said.

Samuel nodded. Though he quickly looked away, it wasn't before the other soldier got a look at him. The man cocked his head, squinting slightly. His partner had kept walking and glanced back. "Come on, Charlie. Let's get back. I'm off soon."

Charlie said to Samuel, "Have we met, sir?"

Samuel shook his head. He whispered, "It's over, Makenna." He made a fist at his side.

Makenna looked around, seeing at least a dozen other soldiers patrolling the area. Charlie's eyes brightened with sudden recognition. His mouth dropped open, but he seemed to momentarily forget how to talk.

Samuel tensed beside her, ready to spring. Makenna touched his rock-hard forearm. "Wait." Looking Charlie in the eyes, she said, "You don't know this man."

"I don't?" His eyes seemed to cloud over.

Samuel's arm relaxed slightly.

"Catch up to your friend and forget about us," Makenna said.

Charlie's gaze grew even more distant and his mouth opened slightly. "Yeah, that's probably a good idea. Good day, sir." Charlie bowed and then hurried to catch the other soldier.

Samuel looked to Makenna. "What did you just do?"

She smiled and shrugged.

The suns had started their descent. As they walked away from the town center, Samuel looked at her sadly. "I'm afraid we should head back. That was a bit too risky."

She didn't ever want to go back, but she knew it was time. Makenna tried to savor every moment of the walk back to Robert's house. She decided she loved dressing up and eating custard. She enjoyed being looked at as an equal instead of being seen as an inferior. But as good as all of that was, the show was even better. Her day as a Richie had showed her how much she enjoyed pretending to be someone she wasn't, just like those people on stage. She thought how lucky they were to have a job that allowed them to pretend all the time. And for people to applaud them for it seemed like the best reward possible. If she could choose anything in the kingdom to be when she was older, she would like to be a pretender. She couldn't wait to tell Tristin all about it.

Alone once more in Robert's back room, she danced to imaginary music in front of the mirror. She didn't want the perfect day to end.

Samuel knocked on the door. "Hey, Makenna. We need to get going soon."

"I'll be right out." She bit her lower lip and looked into the mirror at the dress she wished she could keep. Her lifemask started to pulsate. She studied it as she waited for the inevitable chirp.

Something wasn't right. *Shouldn't the light be brighter than that?* She cocked her head, wondering if something in the Madson's District had somehow affected her mask, though that didn't seem plausible. The fog wasn't any different there than where she lived. Despite expecting the chirp, she flinched when it actually happened. Her lifebreath was just as refreshing as it usually was. She shrugged, hooked it back to her hip, and rejoined Samuel in the front room. Hopefully, once she returned to the Slums her mask would return to normal.

Chapter 9

The Failed End

Tristin had been gone for over a week searching for fabric.
Though it had been a longer trip than intended, it had paid
off. Not only was his belly full, but he had finally secured a
roll of discarded fabric from the back of a seamstress's shop. In an
even bigger success, Tristin and Ian helped another man across the
Slaybyrne who was as close to death as anyone since Shelly.

Finding people in need was the easy part. Getting new masks was
where it got tricky. The Angel's men had stepped up patrols in
Madson's District. With the soldiers taking their jobs more
seriously, it was getting harder to steal from Richies. Sometimes he
would hear of someone dying and he could slip in and take the
deceased's mask before someone from the Exchange or the black
market arrived to claim it, but those instances were rare. Tristin
simply had to up his game.

Jakodi switched out the crystals and gave their new friend a fresh
chance at life. While they waited to make sure the new mask was
working, Tristin left the sick man sleeping and approached Jakodi.
"Can I ask you something?"

"I'm all ears." He flicked one of his big ears and grinned.

Tristin dutifully chuckled at the joke and then grew pensive. "Do you think there are places far away from here where masks never go bad?"

"Oh, I doubt it. Sounds a little far-fetched to me."

"Well, I think there must be. And I think there are places where no one is richer than anyone else, and the food is free, too."

Jakodi smirked and leaned over to pat Tristin's cheek. "You have a wild imagination, kid. Just wanting things don't make them so."

"What if the Slums could be a place like that someday?"

Jakodi snorted. "The Slums? Have you looked around? I'm not going to tell you not to have big dreams, but I'm not going to encourage insanity."

Tristin was disappointed that his wise, older friend didn't share his optimism, but he let it drop so as to not get into a debate. He would just keep his dreams to himself, Shelly, and Makenna from now on, even if Makenna often rolled her eyes at them.

"Are you going to the celebration tonight?" Jakodi asked.

"Didn't know about it."

"Well, there is one at the usual place."

The "usual place" was a cavernous building the Slummers guessed had been used as a barbarian town hall. "Yeah, I suppose I'll go. After I get cleaned up a bit. What are we celebrating?"

"I'm not supposed to say."

"Jakooodi."

"Really, I can't."

"Come on, Jakodi. Just tell me. You know you want to."

Jakodi shook his head and looked away.

"You know I'm not going to stop until you tell me."

Jakodi stood his ground for a bit, but Tristin persisted. Finally, Jakodi snapped, "All right. Just don't tell anyone I told you. It's for you, you little shit. The people you've rescued wanted to do something nice for you."

Tristin cocked his head. He couldn't wrap his mind around people throwing him a party. "Are you sure?"

"Of course I'm sure. Now get home and get cleaned up. I'll keep an eye on our new friend."

Tristin was speechless as Jakodi escorted him to the door and pushed him outside. When Tristin turned back, Jakodi shut the door in his face. Tristin sauntered home, trying to wrap his mind around the idea that he was going to be honored with a celebration. How should he act? He practiced a surprised look. If anyone was watching, they'd think he'd lost his mind.

Neither Shelly nor Makenna were at the house when he arrived. He figured he'd see them both at the hall.

At the party, two of the older ladies taught Tristin how to dance while their husbands made improvised music, humming and whistling and beating out a rhythm on overturned pots. Ian gave a nice speech and called Tristin to the front. Tristin politely declined.

About twenty times.

Ian finally let it rest.

As the night passed, Tristin kept watching the door for Makenna or Shelly. He was getting a touch worried.

During a lull in the dancing, Maddy asked, "Where's your sister? She said she wanted me to teach her some Madson dances, but I haven't seen her all night."

"I haven't seen her since I got back. I haven't seen Shelly, either. Have you?"

Maddy shook her head. "Not lately." Unbothered, she left Tristin and pulled Jackson onto the dance floor.

Tristin made his way over to where Samuel sat by himself. "Hi," he said.

Samuel mumbled, "Evening, Tristin."

Tristin stood beside him and leaned back against the wall. "I was wondering if you've seen Makenna tonight."

Samuel shook his head. "She's probably sleeping. She's been working too hard in the japsy fields lately."

"She wasn't at home when I left."

"She sometimes sleeps in my extra room when she's tired. It's closer to the fields. She's probably there now."

He was probably right. Where else could she go? Tristin picked nervously at a fingernail. "Can I ask you something else?"

Samuel shrugged.

"Do you think the Angel is evil?"

"Doesn't matter what I think."

"I think it does."

Samuel lifted an eye and then looked back to his tankard. "I don't think he's evil, kid. He's just naïve."

Tristin had never heard anyone accuse the Angel of being naïve. "What do you mean? Isn't he over a hundred years old?"

"Old doesn't mean wise. I mean, he's so fixated on enforcing the laws handed down by the king that he can't see the bigger picture, that the laws themselves aren't just." He stopped and took a drink. "You know, I don't much feel like talking about the Angel tonight."

Tristin got the message. "Is that ale?" he asked.

Samuel's eyebrow lifted. "What do you know about ale?"

"Oh, nothing really. Ian said you liked it, is all."

"I do. I brought some back the other night. Would you like a taste?"

Tristin regarded the tankard for a few seconds. "Sure."

Samuel passed it to him. "The best way to enjoy it is to take a big swig."

Tristin nodded. He tilted the tankard to his mouth and filled his cheeks. With a single gulp, his eyes teared up and his throat cursed him. The harsh, face-distorting taste made him cough and gag and wonder why anyone would drink such a thing. It burned going down and left a fire in his mouth that an entire cup of water couldn't douse. When offered a second swig, he considered vomiting as an answer. He waved his hands frantically, shaking his head. From his seat nearby, Jakodi saluted him with his own tankard and chuckled.

Tristin wiped his mouth with his sleeve. "That was horrible, Samuel. I'd rather you pull out one of my teeth than pour that liquid fire down my throat again."

"Suit yourself." Samuel chugged the rest of the tankard, got up, and walked away.

The night drifted into dawn before Tristin dragged himself home and fell asleep. Makenna still wasn't home. When he finally woke in the afternoon, he stretched and staggered to the piss bucket to relieve the pressure ten hours of sleep had put on his bladder. He was surprised Shelly hadn't woken him up. Maybe she didn't know he had returned.

After emptying the bucket, he went to the pail of clean water and splashed some into his sleepy face. His stomach rumbled. Staring at him from across the room was a bundle of japsy weed, and he wrinkled his nose at the idea of another tasteless breakfast. He sat down and pulled the bundle toward him. Before he could eat a single leaf, someone pounded on his door in a panic. "Come in," he shouted. Jackson pushed open the door.

Jackson spent most of his days investigating the most mundane things like rocks and grinderfish. He often tossed the rocks into the water just to watch the feeding frenzy that followed. Tristin jokingly referred to Jackson's trait as his God of Curiosity. Jackson really hated when he did that, but Tristin had never seen him as upset as he was now.

"Tristin," Jackson shouted. His long, skinny face was as pale as paper and his squinty eyes as wide as silver coins. He wore only one shoe and Tristin wondered if his panic had something to do with losing the other.

"What is it, Jack? What's going on?"

Jackson doubled over, trying to catch his breath. Tristin waited patiently. Between gasps, Jackson blurted, "Shelly … Come quick."

Sudden dread dropped like a stone in Tristin's stomach. "What's wrong with Shelly?"

"It's …"—two more winded breaths—"… her mask."

Tristin tore off through the open door toward Shelly's home. Before he reached her door, he heard the all-too-familiar heartbreaking wheeze. He burst inside without knocking. "Shelly?"

She was sitting on the floor against the farthest wall, her head too heavy to hold up on her own. He knelt beside her. "Shelly? When did this start?"

He lifted her head gently so he could see her eyes. Her lips were tinted blue.

She whispered barely loud enough for him to hear, "A little over a week ago."

"I don't understand. How did you get so sick so quickly?" He pressed his forehead against her temple, struggling to stay calm. Then he realized something horrible. "Is that what you wanted to tell me before I left?"

She didn't answer.

"You should have said it was important. I would have gotten you another mask while I was over there."

Her mask clunked as if on cue.

He lifted it to her face, and she inhaled a miserable breath. "Don't you see, Tristin? Another mask won't work for me."

Tristin refused to accept it. He grabbed her hand. "Come on. We'll go to Jakodi. He'll fix it." He started to pull her to her feet.

She winced and weakly pushed him away. "No, Tristin. There's nothing he can do. It's too late."

"Why didn't you make me listen? I could have ..."

She smiled sadly. "I didn't think it would get so bad so fast. I thought I had time."

"Oh, Shelly, I'll never forgive myself for leaving when you needed me. I've been so busy lately."

"Don't do that, Tristin. I'm the one who encouraged you to go. You have nothing to feel guilty about. You've given me a longer life ..." She struggled to catch her breath again. "... than I could have hoped for before you found me. You gave me a family again."

Images of Tristin's mother threatened to break into his thoughts, but he fought to keep them out. He didn't think he could handle the pain. "I don't understand. The mask should have worked."

She shook her head. "Don't you see? Jakodi's fix ... isn't permanent. Just like the mask my employer bought ... on the black market. There's something else wrong ... Something wrong with me, maybe."

A dagger pierced Tristin's heart. His horrified thoughts went to all the others he had brought to the Slums and given replacement masks.

"I can't lose you, Shelly." His stomach turned as his mind raced.

She touched his cheek. "There's nothing you can do, Tristin ... Not anymore ... You need to tell Jakodi ... so you can help the others."

As much as Tristin wanted to deny it, he knew from her wheezing how far her sickness had progressed. He pulled her against his chest and tried to take her mind somewhere more pleasant. "Were you ever happy, Shelly?"

Her smile wasn't sad this time. "I'm happy now ... You and your sister have given me that."

"No, I mean before all this."

"Sure I was." Her voice was a gravelly whisper between gasps for air. "When I was younger ... my parents ... I really loved ... my dad."

"Tell me about him."

She told him about her father's smile and how much he had loved his family. She spoke of his warmth and his mischievous side, laughing as she recounted some of his practical jokes. The laughter triggered a coughing fit, but she simply waited for it to pass and kept going. Her sentences slowly grew more labored and broken.

"I feel ... my arms ... tingling. It doesn't hurt." She smiled again.

"What can I do for you?"

"You've done ... so much. Just sit with me ... for a while."

"Of course. I'll stay as long as you need me."

"Promise ... me something."

"Anything."

"I don't want ... to be fed ... to the fish ... I'd like ... to be ashes ... in the wind ... beyond the wall."

It was rare for someone to be burned after their death instead of buried because wood was so hard to come by, but Tristin promised to do as she asked. If he had to tear down his own house to get enough wood, he'd do it.

As they sat together her breaths grew weaker. There was no more talking. Her wheezing had replaced words. The weight on Shelly's eyelids grew too heavy for her to keep them open. Tristin closed his eyes as well, not because he was tired, but to keep his tears from pouring out. It wasn't long before her breathing slowed and her last breath gurgled from her lungs. Tristin ground his teeth as she stiffened and then relaxed in his arms. It wasn't fair. He held her for what felt like a god's lifetime while the tears streaked his cheeks. "I'm so sorry, Shelly."

Sometime after his arm went numb beneath her weight, his mask chirped and jolted him back to reality. Painful memories of Emma rose to the surface. In the mad scramble to survive, he had never properly grieved for his mother. Because of that, Shelly's death felt even more overwhelming. He wanted to hold her forever. If he never let go, maybe he wouldn't have to face the pain that she was really gone. Maybe, in some way, his mother wouldn't be gone either.

Shelly's door swung open. Makenna stood in the doorway with red, puffy eyes. "Jackson said Shelly's dying. What happened?"

Tristin couldn't look at his sister, afraid he would see what a failure he was in her eyes. "Her mask failed again. Our fixes aren't permanent."

Makenna knelt beside him and put her forehead on his shoulder. She caressed Shelly's cheek. "Is she already gone?"

Tristin nodded.

Makenna's face twisted and she dropped to her rear. "This is my fault," she sobbed.

"No, it's not. Why would you say that?"

"I haven't been around much the past few days. I knew something was bothering her, but I was too busy to be there when she needed me."

"We were both busy. You can't blame yourself."

Makenna looked up with crushing sadness. "Why does everyone we love die?"

Tristin pulled her into a hug. Heaviness weighed on his chest like he'd been buried alive. It was a familiar pain. As he'd done far too often in his young life, he found a way to mask some of the sadness with anger. Through clenched teeth, he whispered, "It's because of King Searle. Him and his Angel."

He gently moved Makenna to the side and stood up.

"What are you doing?" she asked.

He wiped his eyes. "We need to take care of Shelly." He cradled her close and picked her up. Her head lolled back over his arm with her mouth gaping open. He grabbed her mask and carried her outside.

Makenna followed. Shelly's neighbors were chatting across the street. Seeing Tristin emerge carrying Shelly's lifeless body, they rushed over. "Tristin?" one of the men, Frederick, shouted. "What happened?"

Tristin choked on the words. "Her mask failed again."

Frederick reached out. "Let me help you."

Tristin didn't want to let Shelly go at first, but Frederick insisted, adding, "We'll take good care of her, Tristin. We'll send her to the fish at dawn."

"No," Tristin snapped. "Not the fish."

Frederick reached for Shelly's body. "Come on, Tristin, let us help."

Tristin didn't pass her over to Frederick as much as Frederick took her from him. "Do you think you could find enough wood to burn her body? It's what she wanted."

"I think we can do that. Do you want to be there?"

Tristin looked away. Watching her burn would be too painful. He shook his head. "Will you bring her ashes to me when you're done so I can take them to the wall?"

"Of course."

Frederick started to turn away.

Tristin called him back. "Will you be sure to speak nice words about her before you light the flames?"

"Yes, I liked Shelly very much. I'll speak well of her."

With the help of the other man, Frederick carried Shelly away. Once Frederick was out of sight, Tristin turned his attention back to Shelly's mask clutched in his fist. "I have to go to Jakodi's. I have to tell him what happened so he can figure out how to fix this."

"Right now? Shouldn't we take some time to grieve for our friend first?"

"Our other friends don't have time. You go home. I'll be there soon." He kissed her cheek and took off with a burst of speed. A trail of dust followed him to Jakodi's.

Jakodi was stripping the last of the meat from the bones of a grinderfish when Tristin burst through his door. Jakodi jumped and clutched his chest. Tristin tossed Shelly's mask onto the table with a thud.

"You got me another mask?" Jakodi asked with a smile. "I didn't even know you were going over today."

"No."

The wrinkles at the corners of Jakodi's eyes deepened.

"This was Shelly's mask. It failed again."

"Oh my. And where's Shelly now?"

Tristin couldn't speak the words, so he solemnly shook his head instead. After a few seconds he said, "Putting Shelly's crystal into the soldier's mask didn't work. I need you to find out why."

"I'll look into it right away." Jakodi grabbed his tools and immediately dug into Shelly's mask. After he opened the cover, his shoulders slouched. Tristin leaned over for a look. The cloth-like filter, once soft and white, was now brittle and black like Shelly's old one had been. "Oh no," Jakodi said under his breath.

"What does that mean?" Tristin asked.

"It means the filters aren't the problem."

"If not the filters, what then?"

"It must be the crystals. It has to be."

"But ..."

"Don't you see? The crystal killed the filter, not the other way around. Some flaw in the crystals must make them grow too potent."

Tristin spoke before he fully grasped the enormity of the new problem. "Then we need new crystals."

Jakodi shook his head. "I have never seen such crystals in all my years until I opened Shelly's mask. Have you?"

Not only had Tristin never seen the crystals before, he had never even heard of them. But then he had a thought. "What about the Mask Exchange?"

"What about it?"

"Do you think they have crystals in there?"

Jakodi's eyes widened. "No, Tristin. You can't go there."

"Why not?"

"The Exchange is manned at all hours. It'll be locked up tight and guarded. You can't sneak in there like a Madson house."

Tristin didn't say a word, only smiled with grim determination.

"It's a terrible idea. There's no way Ian will go for it."

"You let me worry about Ian."

Jakodi shook his head again. "They'll kill you for sure."

"They'd have to catch me first." Tristin turned to leave, but Jakodi stopped him.

"What's your endgame, Tristin?"

"What do you mean?"

"This is getting too dangerous. You can't steal masks forever. At some point, your luck will run out."

Tristin hesitated at the door. With his eyes on the handle, he answered, "I know that, Jakodi. But I have to try. I can't just do nothing and let people die." He glanced back at his friend through wet eyes. "You wanna know what I really want? I want a world where masks don't kill people ... A world where we don't need to steal trash just to eat." He lowered his head and whispered, "I want my mother and father back. And Shelly." Then he opened the door and stepped outside. Making his way to an uninhabited part of the Slums, he sat with his back against the wall of an empty house. There he quietly sobbed, feeling an enormous sadness and weight on his shoulders.

Part Two
The Prison

Chapter 10

Close to Home

Makenna had done everything she could to keep others from hearing her mask chirp for several weeks, including working extra shifts in the japsy fields. Whenever she visited Samuel or Tristin, she never stayed for more than a few hours. She only returned home at night after Tristin was asleep, and she made sure she was gone each morning before he woke up.

She was already exhausted when she reached the japsy fields for another day of work. It was the worst day yet and she hadn't even started. As she worked, she had to stop often to catch her breath, looking around to make sure nobody noticed. She couldn't believe she was getting winded so quickly. It took twice as long as usual to fill her basket.

Samuel arrived at the edge of the field to check on her. She'd started skipping her morning visits when the state of her mask got more obvious. She hadn't been to see him for several days. As he marched toward her, she calculated when her mask's next chirp should come. It could be any time. Once he was halfway across the field, she waved and shouted, "I don't have time to talk right now, Samuel."

He stopped and stared.

"I'll come see you later." Then she turned away and pretended to focus on the japsy weeds. She sneaked a peek as he turned away and started back toward his home. She hoped he didn't think she was mad at him.

Maddy was working the fields that day, too. She and Makenna had become friends. Makenna was so preoccupied watching Samuel out of the corner of her eye that she didn't see Maddy approach. Samuel was just out of sight when Makenna's mask gave a sickly muffled chirp.

Maddy gasped. "Makenna," she said, her eyes filling with concern.

"It's nothing, Maddy. It'll be fine." Makenna took a lifebreath. She knew her lungs weren't filling as much as they should. She wouldn't be able to hide it much longer. Especially now that Maddy knew.

Maddy set her own basket of japsy weed down. "It doesn't sound fine. What's going on?"

Makenna scanned the field to make sure none of the other workers were close enough to hear. "You can't say anything to anyone, Maddy. You have to promise."

"Is your mask failing?"

Makenna shoved her finger over her mouth and looked around again. "Shhh. Promise."

"All right, I promise. What's Tristin say?"

Makenna's eyes widened. "I haven't told him. And you can't either. You promised."

"But he has to know. How could he not hear it?"

"I've been very careful to not be around him when I'm getting close to needing a lifebreath."

"I don't think you can hide it for long. It's pretty obvious. You should at least tell Samuel. Or Ian."

Makenna picked a handful of japsy weeds and put them in her basket. "I know. I'm trying to figure out what to do."

"Tell Tristin. He'll get you a new mask."

Makenna snapped, "No. No one can know. Not yet."

"But why?"

"Because I don't want him to panic and do something crazy like he did when our mother's mask failed."

Maddy shook her head. "I can't just sit on this until you waste away and it's too late."

"You won't have to. Tristin's due to go back across soon. When he does, I'm going with him."

"He'll never let you. It's too dangerous."

"I know. I'm working on that."

Maddy gently took Makenna's basket from her. "You look so tired. Why don't you quit for the day and go talk to your brother? You've waited long enough."

Maddy was probably right, and even if she wasn't, Makenna wasn't up to arguing. "Thank you."

Maddy smiled warmly. Makenna started the long, tiring walk home, still not convinced she was going to tell her brother anything yet.

At home, Tristin was gathering a bag of supplies, which probably meant he was going across the Slaybyrne that night. He filled a small bag with a waterskin of strained rainwater and some extra japsy bundles in case he was stranded by patrols for a few days.

"Hey, sis," he said as he hurried past her. "In a rush. I'm meeting Ian to head to the Richies' District."

"Why so early today? Don't you usually only go at night?"

"Yeah. But I got big plans tonight. I'm going all the way to the Mask Exchange." His eyes practically glowed with excitement. "I'm hunting crystals tonight."

"What? That's insane."

"I've got no other choice."

"And Ian is letting you do this?"

"It took some convincing."

Though she was careful not to let on, his trip couldn't have come at a better time and his idea to get crystals couldn't have been more perfect. "How do you plan to get the crystals from the Exchange? Even if you get past the guards, they'll be locked up tight."

"I'll think of something."

"You don't have a plan? That's a pretty big detail."

"I'll figure it out when I get there."

"That's the worst plan I've ever heard."

"It's all I've got. Without crystals, everyone I've brought here is going to die, just like Shelly."

Makenna saw her chance. "What if I helped you?"

Tristin's eyes narrowed.

"Take me with you."

He shook his head. "No way. It's too dangerous."

"You don't have a choice. You need my god. I can make the guard let you in and open the locks."

"There's no way I could ever put you in danger. I'll come up with something."

"You know I'm right, Tristin. Quit treating me like a little kid. I'm older than you, you know."

"Yeah. Like, three whole minutes."

She was done playing games. She locked eyes with him and called on her god. "I'm going with you today. You need me, and you'll tell Ian the same." She felt a wave of guilt, but convinced herself using her god was necessary.

Tristin made a funny face. She let her Influence marinate. He slowly nodded his head. "You're probably right. Are you ready?"

"I am."

Tristin grabbed his bag, and he and Makenna left for the river.

Ian wasn't keen on the idea of Makenna joining them, but Tristin sold him on it with a lot of heart. And a little push from Makenna's god. The swim across the river was uneventful. Ian left them on the opposite bank and said he'd be back when the moon was high. Tristin agreed and then led Makenna through the safest and least traveled route to Madson's District.

"So, why did you wanna come along today?" he asked as they walked.

Makenna felt a stab of panic. Was her Influence wearing off? "I want to help. Besides, you can't do this without me, and you know it."

Her words hung heavy in the air. He didn't say anything. She hoped it was because deep down he knew she was right.

As they slunk deeper into Madson's District, he showed her little tricks he'd learned to keep from getting caught. Like the patrol patterns of the soldiers and how to hide in the shadows behind trash pits. At one point, they stopped at one of his favorite trash pits and he gave her part of a corn cob and a carrot. She savored the treat while quietly catching her breath, careful not to let on how winded she already was.

The suns had started to set by the time Tristin and Makenna reached the part of town where the Mask Exchange was located. They coincidentally hid beside Renoble's Treats. The lingering aroma of custard tempted Makenna to abandon the current mission and break into the shop instead. She'd really love to see Tristin's face when he took his first bite. He deserved it. But she knew better.

They sneaked to the back of the building where they could see the Mask Exchange. Two soldiers patrolled outside while a third sat behind a counter at the front. The door behind him had three keyholes and reinforced metal latches.

Tristin tapped Makenna's shoulder. "The crystals will be behind that door."

"Yeah. No kidding." She couldn't tell if the dancing in her stomach was from fear or excitement. "Get me to that soldier and I'll get him to open the locks."

"You know, I still don't like this."

"I know you don't. But how else are you going to get in? Now, let's do this before more soldiers show up."

Tristin hugged her and whispered, "You be deadly careful. If he doesn't give in to your Influence right away, you run. If someone sees you, you run. If anything at all goes wrong—"

"I know, I know. I'll run."

He smiled. "Sorry. I'm just nervous. There's a reason I've never asked you to help with getting masks. Though I could have used your god many times, I couldn't live with myself if you were arrested. If I can't get back here before you're done, sneak back to the riverbank and I'll meet you there."

She kissed his cheek. "I'll be fine."

He winked and backed deeper into the alley until he disappeared around the front. Makenna watched the soldiers pace. When they stopped for a smoke out of sight of the man behind the counter, Tristin approached from behind. Her stomach knotted and her hands trembled. She whispered a prayer that he would be safe.

Tristin's eyes met hers. She mouthed, "Be careful."

He grinned. And then he blazed toward the soldiers. He ripped the mask from one soldier's hip. Before the soldier realized what had happened, Tristin stopped and turned toward them. He gave a "come and get me" wave. The two soldiers gave chase.

Makenna hurried to the side of the Exchange unnoticed. She took a deep breath before stepping around to the counter.

The soldier lifted his eyes from the paper he was reading. "And what are you doing out here, young lady? Mask emergency?"

"I want you to open the locks on that door and let me in."

Even as the soldier scoffed and asked if she was crazy, he unlocked the first of the three locks.

"After the door is open, you will walk away and forget I was ever here."

"There's no way I'll leave my post," he grumbled even as he unlocked the second lock.

Makenna brushed off his protest, knowing there was nothing he could do about it. She scanned the streets along both sides. "Come on, come on," she whispered.

The soldier unlocked the third lock and reached for the handle.

Makenna shuffled from foot to foot, on high alert. "Hurry up," she snapped as she looked behind her.

The soldier opened the door. The world seemed to move in slow motion as Makenna turned back toward him. Her heart skipped and she lost her breath. "How?" she whispered.

Three soldiers poured through the door. Makenna staggered backward. The second soldier in line blew a whistle. In the dead of night the sound was deafening.

The first soldier out the door sneered at her. "The Angel knew you thieves would show up here one day. You just couldn't resist, could you? Don't move." He started to climb over the counter.

Makenna's knees weakened. She cried, "Stop where you are," pushing her god at him. Her gift didn't work on more than one person at a time, and the others crowded past their frozen comrade. It gave her a slight head start. She didn't have Tristin's speed, but she was fast in her own right. She cut into the closest alley as more soldiers filled the street in response to the whistle. They would be everywhere soon.

Makenna didn't slow as shouts filled the street behind her. She was already winded because of her damn mask failing. With miles upon miles to go just to reach Terdict's District, her only chance was to lose them and hide for a while. She ducked into another alley. And then another. She used every trick Tristin had taught her, but could still hear their pounding feet behind her. She raced across a street seconds before two more soldiers appeared at the intersection. She ducked behind some trash as they raced by.

Makenna sat hidden in the shadows, shivering with her knees pulled to her chest. She hadn't been so scared since the soldiers took her father. "Tristin, where are you?" she whispered.

Chapter 11

The Angel

A glance over Tristin's shoulder assured him he had put enough distance between him and the soldiers to take a breather. There were at least a dozen chasing him now. He ducked into an alley behind some rubbish and empty crates.

A distant whistle in the direction of the Exchange gave him a sinking feeling in his stomach. It was too far away to be the soldiers chasing him; their whistles were much closer. There was only one reasonable answer: Makenna had been spotted. Why had he let her join him?

As he peeked between two slats of a crate, he saw some of the soldiers searching farther down the street. "Stay with me," he whispered.

Tristin sucked in poisonous breaths of the puke-green air. "Just a little closer," he whispered.

The soldiers continued searching, oblivious to how close they were getting to their prize. His thighs tightened in preparation for another sprint. Then he knocked over the crates to get their attention. All the soldiers looked up at once. Tristin smiled. Then he tore west along the street. They renewed their futile chase.

He prayed Makenna would make it to Ian at the bank. With fear churning in the cellar of his gut, he knew it was a long shot.

He slowed to a jog, remembering Makenna's pleas to join him on his hunt. The memory was a little foggy. Why had he given in when he never had before? What was different that time? Even as he quietly cursed himself, he knew she was at fault. She'd used her god on him, damn her. She'd broken her promise never to do so.

Tristin's lifemask bounced against his hip with each step of his blistering pace. *If she's not on the bank ... No.* He shook his head as if trying to jar the nagging doubt out through his ears. *Stop thinking like that. She'll be there.*

Satisfied that he'd led the soldiers far enough away for Makenna to have a chance, he decided it was time to lose them completely and then check the riverbank for her. He poured on the speed until he couldn't hear them any longer.

Winded again, he rested behind the same abandoned cobbler's shop where he and Makenna had hidden so long ago. After catching his breath, he listened closely for any sign that the soldiers had rediscovered his trail. All was quiet. The only way they would find him was by luck.

Damn luck.

He wiped the sweat from his forehead and started to step away from the store when a single rider on a magnificent, ghost-white steed appeared at the end of the street between Tristin and freedom. In that instant, all hope drained from his every pore. *No, no, no. It can't be. Why would they send* him *this time?*

The rider looked south and away from Tristin. Tristin scurried behind another rubbish pile. A fresh bead of sweat formed above his brow, but he was too terrified to wipe it away. The bead trickled past his temple, traced the outer edge of his eye, and followed the contour of his cheek to where it grew into a drop along his jawline. When the drop fell to the cobblestones, it sounded like thunder to his petrified ears. He held his breath, afraid even that would make too much noise.

By luck—damn luck—the rider turned toward him. Tristin had a good view of his polished silver helmet with golden filigree decorating the sides. Along the rider's right hip hung an intricate, gold-encrusted lifemask unlike any in the world. The stallion snorted through its own specially fitted lifemask. It was truly Tristin's most feared nightmare. His hands began to shake.

The soldiers had called in the Angel of Justice.

Tristin waited for his best opportunity to flee. He was about to embark on the run of his life.

Praying that the Angel would continue his search elsewhere, Tristin realized how long it had been since he had last used his lifemask. He looked to his mask nervously. A slight bluish glow throbbed from the tiny vents in the nosecone.

Keep moving, he mentally urged the Angel.

Then, as though the gods wanted him to be captured, his lifemask released a single high-pitched chirp that echoed through the alley as well as his mind. He shoved his hand over the nosecone a split second too late.

Wide-eyed, he stared at the Angel from the dark alley, convinced the world had just ended. The greenish air grew thicker with tension.

The Angel didn't act as though he'd heard the mask chirp. Maybe it was louder to Tristin's ears, like the drop of sweat had been. His blood grew more toxic with every second that passed. Another chirp was imminent. Tristin struggled with what to do. While taking a lifebreath would cleanse his blood, the accompanying whistle would bring the same end to his deadly game of hide-and-seek as another chirp might. His palms grew clammy as his heart fluttered within his chest. His only chance now was patience.

Patience and luck.

Damn luck.

The Angel guided his horse a few steps toward Tristin's hiding place. Small chains stretching from the Angel's hardened leather shoulder pads to hoops along the sides of his metal chest plate jingled with each of his movements. The racket they made was intentional, for it showed any potential foes that the Angel had no need for stealth, that he had no rivals. Tristin wished he had brought Samuel.

The Angel looked once again toward the shadows that were Tristin's cover. If his stare were a blade's edge, it would have opened Tristin's flesh. The Angel dismounted, his feet sending a puff of dust into the greenish air as they met the ground. His lifemask chirped. He unclipped it from his waist and pressed it against his face, releasing the high-pitched whistle that accompanied his blood-cleansing breath.

At the same time, Tristin's mask chirped again. And again, the Angel didn't react. Maybe he was simply baiting his prey.

The Angel stood eye-to-eye with his magnificent steed. His long, blond hair peeked from beneath his helmet and framed his soft, clean-shaven face. He had no visible scars despite his penchant for violence. He was almost pretty, if such a word could be used for a man. Tristin recognized the king's crest of a curved sword across a purple lifemask upon the Angel's polished silver chest plate. The Angel removed his helmet and fastened it to his saddle. He turned back toward the alley.

Why was he waiting so long if he knew Tristin was there?

A lifetime seemed to pass while Tristin watched. If the Angel moved any closer, he would be forced to test his speed against the Angel's horse. It wasn't a prospect he particularly favored. And then, Tristin's lifemask chirped beneath his palm again.

The Angel smirked and tilted his head slightly. Was this it? Was this the moment when everything ended?

Tristin's next breath burned his windpipe. The Angel walked closer to the alley and then stopped as Tristin tensed.

Chirp.

The Angel's smirk widened, his laugh lines creasing his perfect golden skin. "I know you're there, young one. I have known for some time." His voice was deep and scratchy with the weight of power behind it.

A chill ran the length of Tristin's spine.

"Whoever you are, you are due for a lifebreath. I suggest you take it and then show yourself and accept your judgment. There can be no escape." He reached over his head and slid a long blade from the sheath that was fastened to his back. The shrill screech of the blade sliding free could pierce the ears of a god. The blade was etched with gold in thin, seemingly random twirls.

Tristin slowly unfastened his lifemask from the thin metal clasp that held it to his hip. He quietly prayed to his God of Speed. "Please, make me faster than the Angel's horse. Faster than the Angel himself."

He pressed his lifemask against his face, closed his eyes, and exhaled. But before he inhaled a cleansing breath, the Angel jerked his head toward where his horse still stood. His chains rattled with his sudden movements, sounding like hail against tin.

Curious, Tristin lowered his mask and leaned closer for a better view, his lifebreath suddenly far from his thoughts. He counted the fog-shrouded outlines of seven soldiers approaching in formation from the opposite end of the street. A smaller person walked in their center.

The Angel said in a booming voice, "Now you will see why I waited to draw you out, boy. I am well aware of your unnatural speed."

Tristin swallowed hard. Though he was growing dizzy from the lack of a lifebreath, he was more concerned with who walked within the soldiers' circle than cleansing his blood. He already knew who it was, but he had to see to be sure. As if feeling Tristin's stare, the Angel glanced over his shoulder and locked eyes with him. The air died between them. The deaths of hundreds, maybe thousands, swirled within the Angel's cold glower. Tristin's knees weakened.

The Angel shook his hair from his eyes. "I will deal with you in a moment, criminal. Do not try to flee. You will only make it worse for your companion."

Tristin looked toward the seven soldiers. They stopped in the street next to the Angel's horse and waited for their orders. The Angel approached them.

A burning sensation rose into Tristin's throat, but he swallowed it back with a bitter gulp.

The Angel pointed to where Tristin hid. "The other troublemaker—the fast one—hides in that alley." All eyes turned Tristin's way. The Angel then flicked his hand to the side and the soldiers parted, allowing Tristin to finally see their prisoner.

To his horror, it was indeed Makenna. Her hands were bound in front of her. Her scared blue eyes met Tristin's. His heart nearly stopped. The soldiers shoved her to her knees.

Tristin's mask chirped again, no longer muffled by his hand, reminding him why the world swayed at his feet. He pressed his mask against his face, exhaled the angry air from his lungs, and drew in a deep breath. The whistle screamed. He refastened his mask to his hip and stepped out into the open as if bravery pushed him from behind. Standing straight and defiant, he held his chin high and his jaw firm. Not more than twenty feet away stood his judge, jury, and, quite likely, executioner. But worse than his own fate was the knowledge that the Angel had Makenna.

The Angel climbed onto his stallion again and looked down at her. She wilted under his gaze. After studying her face, he looked back to Tristin with a curious squint. "How old are you, boy?"

Barely above a whisper, Tristin answered, "Seventeen."

"Hm. You share a remarkable likeness to this girl."

Tristin bowed his head. He had no words.

"You are twins, yes?"

Tristin hesitated before nodding a single time.

"Interesting. I've been looking for you for some time."

And then Makenna's mask let out a muffled chirp. Tristin's stomach dropped. "Makenna? Your mask is dying?"

Makenna locked eyes with him.

"No. It can't be. Not yours, too." As a million thoughts and worries raced through his mind, he suddenly understood why she had been staying away so often lately. He'd thought it was because she was so busy with Samuel and the japsy fields, but it was obvious now. She didn't want him to hear her mask's sickly chirp.

Tristin knew even a prison sentence meant death if her mask was failing. He couldn't hold his tongue. "What will be her punishment, Angel?"

The Angel tilted his head as if not accustomed to hearing raised voices directed at him.

One of the soldiers moved toward Tristin, but the Angel motioned for him to stand down. Makenna's lips moved.

The soldier tilted his head and said, "Sir, I think maybe we should let her and her brother go free." The others looked at him like he had gone crazy.

The Angel groaned and rubbed his forehead as though it had been a long night. "You fool. She's using a god on you. Move away from her before she convinces you that she's your best friend."

The soldier shook away his confusion and backed away.

Makenna sobbed into her hands.

Tristin slipped his hand to the small of his back and clutched the hilt of the small knife that he carried on his missions. Though he wasn't foolish enough to attack the Angel, or to flee before Makenna's judgment was handed down, he wasn't going to accept a death sentence without a fight.

He had to be perfect in his timing. He would only have seconds to sacrifice himself and try to free her. All he could do was wait and hope for mercy while preparing for blood.

He clenched the knife in his fist. The Angel's judgment would be final; he never changed his mind. *Please don't say death,* Tristin prayed. Though prison would be an unimaginable horror for Makenna, it would mean she was still alive for the moment. And if she was alive, Tristin and Ian could find a way to come back for her. He slid the knife from his waistband, careful to keep it concealed behind his back.

But instead of handing down his judgment on Makenna, the Angel addressed Tristin yet again. "Young man, stealing masks is the greatest sin you can commit. You are hereby sentenced to death by banishment to the Outside without your mask for your crimes against the civilized."

Tristin stood stunned. Not because the Angel had sentenced him to death—he expected as much—but because the Angel had sentenced him before having him in custody. He shouted, "I don't care what judgment you have for me. I want to know your plans for my sister." Tristin squeezed his knife and prayed harder.

The Angel turned back to the others and regarded Makenna. She looked up from her hands with a sour expression. Tristin's stomach crawled into his throat. *Just do it already.*

Finally, after much deliberation, the Angel said, "What is your name, child?"

"M-M-Makenna, sir."

"Makenna, I do not know of any previous crimes that you may have committed before tonight. I do, however, know what you were doing at the Mask Exchange, but since you did not succeed, I cannot give you death. However, you must be punished for the attempt."

Tristin took an angry step forward. "She did nothing wrong. I was the one trying to steal masks. I steal them all the time. Sometimes from right under your nose."

The Angel waited for Tristin to finish before continuing. "Makenna, I sentence you to ten years in the prison for attempted theft of the Mask Exchange and for aiding your brother."

With her failing mask, Tristin knew even a year was a death sentence. She had months at best.

The Angel turned back to Tristin. "Now, boy. It is time for you to submit willingly to your sentence. Though you can run, there is nowhere to go. There is no ultimate escape from me."

Tristin was preparing to spring into the alley when the Angel froze him with his next words. "I'm coming for the Slums, boy."

Tristin lost his breath. "What? No. Wait. What do you mean?"

The Angel turned his back. "Apprehend him." Glancing over his shoulder, he added, "If you can."

Tristin staggered. In six simple words the Angel had drained him of all hope. He backed away while three of the Angel's soldiers stepped toward him. Makenna screamed, "Run, Tristin," but it was as if he'd suddenly forgotten how.

With an eye on the cautiously approaching soldiers, Tristin shouted, "Angel, if I surrender to you now, will you leave the Slums be?"

The Angel didn't answer, not that Tristin expected him to. His judgments were final, no matter what.

Tristin stumbled backward. His legs didn't obey his brain. He concentrated on each clumsy step, desperately trying to push the Angel's words from his mind so he could flee. He looked to Makenna and tears blurred his vision. She mouthed a single word: "Go."

Tristin's heart broke. With no other choice and drowning in an ocean of guilt, he turned and ran. His mission couldn't have been more of a failure. The Angel didn't give chase, though a few of his soldiers did. Tristin cut through alleys, ran behind shops and houses, and headed toward the Slaybyrne.

When he reached the western edge of town, he saw Ian ahead, waiting as usual. He slowed to a jog, trying to find the words to tell Ian everything that had happened. Ian shouted, "Tristin, where's Makenna?"

Before Tristin could answer, half a dozen soldiers poured from a side street between them. More soldiers filled other streets and moved to surround him. The Angel had laid a trap. Even with his speed, he couldn't get around them in time.

Tristin shouted, "The Angel's sending her to the prison."

Stunned and helpless, Ian staggered backward. "Run, Tristin," he shouted as half the soldiers started for him.

Tristin shouted, "The Angel's coming for the Slums," but the charging soldiers were too noisy, and Ian was already too far away to hear.

The other soldiers started for Tristin. His only chance for escape was back the way he had come, which meant he'd be stuck on the Terdict side of the Slaybyrne for the foreseeable future. At least Ian had enough of a head start to make it to the river. All Tristin needed was somewhere to hide until it was safe for Ian to come back for him. The abandoned cobbler's shop where he and Makenna had taken refuge seemed the best option.

With the soldiers getting close, he broke for an empty street, using his god to lose them. There was no one around when he reached the shop, so he ducked inside and sat with his back against the wall beneath the front window. Thoughts of Makenna in the prison with a dying mask tortured him. He wondered if barbarians were still alive in there and if Makenna's Influence was strong enough to hold them off.

And the Slums, oh gods, the Slums. How could they fight off the whole army? And could Samuel really defeat the Angel? He needed to get back as soon as possible. Every second they didn't know the Angel was coming was a second they didn't have to prepare.

Each painful realization of what his exuberance had caused sent daggers into his heart. It was all his fault—every bit of it. If he had never started stealing masks, none of the rest would have happened.

Somehow, he needed to make things right. Like his sister had once said, he needed to stop being stupid. He buried his face in his hands and sobbed.

Chapter 12

The Long Walk

Through all Makenna had endured over the years, the rising suns had never carried as much fear of the unknown as they did that morning. Every step of her march to the prison drained her of more and more hope. She repeatedly looked over her shoulder for Samuel or Tristin, but only a deserted road trailed them.

The rope around her wrists burrowed into her flesh. Another rope tethered her wrists to the waist of a fat, sweaty man ahead of her who wore silk nightwear with dirt stains on the knees. Despite her attempts to be strong, she had shed her share of tears. The man in silk sobbed even more. When she wasn't stealing glances over her shoulder, she walked with her head bowed.

Her mask chirped. The nearest soldier held it to her face. He was a young man, not much older than she, and he seemed a little more compassionate than the others. "Mister?" she whispered.

"What is it?"

Her bladder ached terribly. "I have to … I mean … I need to pass water."

The soldier nodded and shouted for the line to halt. With a sharp nudge to the whimpering man in front of Makenna, he said, "What about you?"

A yellow stain had already appeared on the inside leg of his nightwear, but the man sniffled and bobbed his head anyway.

The soldier grimaced when he caught a whiff of what Makenna had been smelling for the last mile. "Very well. I think it's time for a break." He untethered Makenna from the others and led her away from the group. The other prisoners—all men—relieved themselves where they stood.

Showing Makenna a modicum of decency, her escort stood with his arms crossed and his back to her, shielding her from the group. Once she finished, he led her back to the line, gave her a drink of water, and secured her to the fat man again for the rest of the long walk.

Eventually, the prison appeared in the distance, looming in the fog. One look at the dreary stone fortress changed Makenna's fear into downright terror. It was a sprawling three-story compound, settled behind a winding, twenty-foot-high stone wall that stretched as far as Makenna could see in both directions. The closer to the prison they walked, the thicker the green fog grew and the more often they needed to use their masks.

Makenna tried to appear calm and brave on the outside, while on the inside she panicked like she was being thrown to the grinderfish. Another hopeful glance at the road behind her netted the same heartbreak as before, only this time it seemed more final.

Little was known about life inside the prison or behind it. Even the luckier prisoners who returned home were forbidden to speak of it. As far as Makenna knew, no one had ever broken their silence. Most prisoners never returned at all.

From the view through the open front gates, the prison was colder and lonelier than she could have imagined. The stone walls were cracked and water-stained. Many barred windows on the second and third floors had pairs of arms poking through and dangling over the sills. Makenna wondered how the prisoners kept warm in the brutal winters, and then, horrified, she realized they didn't. Another awful thought immediately followed that one.

"Sir?" she asked the soldier who had helped her before. "When do you separate the men from the women?"

His narrow lips pressed together and he shook his head. "I'm sorry. If it's any consolation, you won't be going to the most dangerous part of the prison. You'll be housed with the less violent offenders."

Her lower lip quivered. She hoped he wasn't lying to ease her fears. The line stopped at the gate. A prison guard waited to receive the prisoners. He was a big, solid-looking man, like Samuel, but with a bit of a vacant look to his slack-jawed face. His fat head sat directly upon his shoulders with no neck to speak of. His bloated cheeks were covered with deep pockmarks like divots kicked into the dirt. He held a blood-stained club across his chest.

Makenna listened closely as one of the soldiers rattled off a list of everyone's crimes along with their sentences. When he spoke of her, he mentioned her god.

Once the soldier finished, the prison guard answered, "Um-hm. You come far enough. Neeter you nor da Angel is welcome past 'ere. By orders a King Searle, you no more da boss of dese pritiners. Gimme da records and bugger off." He snatched the papers the soldier had been reading from and twitched his crooked nose like he might sneeze, though he didn't.

The friendly soldier leaned in and whispered, "I'm sorry, young one. I hope the guards aren't too hard on you in there. Find one who can help you and use your god on him."

Before the soldier walked away, Makenna whispered, "It doesn't seem fair. The Angel sentenced me to prison, not death. How can he let the guards hurt the prisoners?"

"Like the man said, the Angel has no reach in there. King's orders."

The other soldiers headed back toward the road. "Let's go, Curtis," one of them shouted.

Curtis gave her one last sip from his waterskin and whispered, "Good luck. Try to be strong." He hurried to the others. The big guard at the gate ordered the prisoners forward.

Makenna's hands trembled. Two more guards exited from within the prison and led the line of prisoners through the gate.

Before she passed through, the large gatekeeper shoved his bloody club against her chest. It stank like feces. He leaned in and his eyes traced her from head to toe. "You has a god, yes?" He picked his nose and examined his finger before rolling his findings into a ball and wiping it on his leg.

Makenna nodded. She looked away, afraid of being accused of staring.

"What'um you do?" he asked.

Makenna was too afraid to lie. "I can make people do what I ask them to do."

His forehead creased. "Does ya want ta dead?"

"No, sir."

"If your god touches me or dose utters, I chucks you wit da lowlifes in A-wing. Does you understand?" His knuckles cracked as he gripped his club tighter.

"Yes, sir."

He withdrew his club and shoved her through the gate with the others.

Prisoners shouted hateful words she'd never heard before from the windows above as she walked from the gate to the prison entrance. The shouts were slowly joined by more and more until the voices melded into an unintelligible cacophony.

The guards held tarps over their heads and Makenna wondered why. Then something green-tinged and thick splattered on the ground next to her. Another glob landed on the tarp above the guard beside her. Did everyone have lung disease in there? She hid beneath her arms as a gooey wad landed in her hair. Her stomach turned.

The guards opened the door and stood beside it, motioning for the prisoners to hurry through. Makenna crowded the fat man in front of her and they ran as spit and piss rained down around them.

The first room inside the prison was empty except for a lop-sided table in the center, a wheeled bin, and a clothesline stretched taut from one dank wall to the opposite. A row of gray rags hung from the line. The guards untethered the prisoners one by one and ordered them to strip down, gave them a holey one-piece garment from the clothesline, and then sent them through another door into the next room. Makenna thanked her god that they'd saved her for last.

"Put your clothes in the bin," the portlier of the two guards said. The other guard watched her with a menacing smirk.

"Don't look at me," she whispered, pushing her god at him without thinking. She found a small stain on the wall and stared at it, blocking out her surroundings while she disrobed. She felt the portly guard ogling her from behind. With teeth chattering and hands trembling, she slipped the smelly gown over her head. By luck, they had given her one without gaping holes in the wrong places. She gagged on the musty, sweaty stink and nearly threw up. A red blotch in the shape of a bib stained the front below the collar and she wondered if it was blood.

The portly guard handed her a cloth belt and a blanket. He had already attached her mask to the belt. Then he pointed to the next door where the other prisoners had gone. When he noticed his partner staring at the wall, he gave Makenna a dark look and went back the way they had come. Makenna hurried to catch the others.

In the next room waited a tall, skinny man who wore crooked glasses and a leather apron over his bare chest. Dirty gray hair topped his long, narrow face and wrinkles around his eyes highlighted the callousness of his glare. He stood next to a table and an empty metal chair.

"Sit," he ordered, his voice strained and crackly.

A small container full of black liquid and several metal tools with needles protruding from their ends waited on the table.

"What are y—" she started to ask.

"Shut up," he answered with an open-handed smack to the back of her head.

Makenna sat and watched with wide, terrified eyes as a guard grabbed her left wrist and pinned her arm to the cold metal armrest. The man in the apron picked up one of the tools, dipped the needle into the black liquid, and pricked the soft underside of her forearm. Her skin turned to fire as he repeatedly stabbed the needle into her flesh.

As the man worked, the large oafish guard from the gate burst through the entrance with the portly guard close behind him. His chest rose and fell in deep, angry breaths. "Wait," he shouted.

The man stopped with the needle still pressed into her arm.

"Used ya god, idn't ya?"

Makenna shook her head frantically. "You believe me," she whispered, pushing with her god.

His jaw went more slack than usual for a moment. The portly guard quickly grabbed his shoulder and gave it a shake. "See? She just did it again."

The large guard took a moment to digest that information. Then his dull eyes brightened.

Oh no.

"Ya just can't eben stop, can't ya?" He looked to the guard holding Makenna's arm. "A-wing fer dis un."

Makenna shook her head even more frantically. "Please. I won't survive in there."

The guard spoke over her. "A-wing? Are you sure? I thought her crime was nonviolent."

"I told er nottin be usin' er god." Then he stormed from the room.

Makenna nearly choked on her terror. She considered trying her god on the man with the needles to change her sentence, but the guard would see. He'd call the big one back and he'd kill her on the spot. Using her god in front of a witness was what had gotten her in trouble in the first place. She silently cursed herself. How stupid could she be? She was worse than Tristin. She was panicking—that was the only way to explain it.

The man removed his needle from her arm and dabbed her skin with a damp rag. "Good luck," was all he said before he started stabbing her flesh again.

Her eyes pleaded with him to stop, but he met her gaze with a stoic one of his own and kept going. Makenna squeezed her eyes closed, bit her lip, and tried not to move. When the man was finally finished, he ordered her to inspect his work as though he was proud of what he had done. Her wrist was red and swollen. "Theft. 10" was etched into her flesh in bold lines of black ink. The man dabbed at it, cleaning away the oozing blood.

In his crackly voice, he said, "You'll come back each year on your anniversary and I will give you a new number reduced by one. Once you get to zero, you'll be free."

With her wrist throbbing, the guard jerked her to her feet and led her into the next room where the other prisoners from her line sat in a row of chairs. The floor around them hid beneath piles of hair of every color and shade. She sat in the last empty chair as ordered.

At the far end of the room, a guard grasped a handful of one man's long, greasy hair and sawed at it with a knife. The man winced with each rough swipe of the blade.

The fat man who had been in front of Makenna sat next to her with his head bowed. He looked like a man who had already given up. Under an older tattoo she couldn't make out, his seeping arm read "Repeat offender. Life." Makenna waited for the butcher of a barber to make his way down the line. He finished with the man beside her, leaving a few straggly strands and small trickles of blood on the man's scalp.

He stepped behind Makenna next. She closed her eyes, praying it would be over fast.

He grabbed a handful of her hair. "I wish I could say this won't hurt, but I'd be lying." Though she couldn't see him, she could hear the smile in his bubbly tone. He liked his job.

He yanked her hair back and sawed away her locks. When her head jerked backward for the third time, he grabbed her chin and snapped, "Hold still, girlie."

She was *trying* to hold still. More than anything, she wanted to do as he ordered, but his tugs were too strong and painful. After having enough of her fidgeting, the barber braced her head with his elbow until he finished. More hair had been ripped from her head than had actually been cut.

Once he was done, he stepped back, admired his work, and said, "Perfect." Warm blood dribbled down her cold scalp behind her ear.

He smacked the back of her head with his palm and the slap echoed through the room. "Don't worry, it'll heal." Then he shoved a damp towel against the wound, and she cringed at the thought of what infections might be festering on it. Whatever *was* on the rag stung terribly, but she was careful not to pull away since doing so would likely encourage more torture.

"They're all yours," he shouted to the guard. With a nudge to the back of her head, he added, "I don't know why you had me waste my time on this one, though. She won't make it a week in A-wing."

"A week?" the guard scoffed. He grabbed her arm and led her into the line of prisoners. "I give her a few hours, tops."

Makenna waited with a roiling stomach as the guards split her line into two groups. One went left while hers continued into what could only be described as a coliseum with a roof. Instead of bleachers surrounding the wide stone floor, there were cells stacked three floors high. When she passed from the hall into the open floor, the air seemed to still, heavy and thick and darker green than anywhere else she had ever been. She coughed and choked and wheezed. The stink of unwashed bodies and human waste burned her nostrils. She covered her mouth and nose with her hand. When her lifemask chirped, she nearly gagged trying to take a lifebreath.

Other masks were going off in an almost constant chorus of chirps. Makenna wondered how long it would be before the noise drove her mad. Blaring over the chirps and shouting prisoners, someone's mask wailed from the cells to her right. She shuddered. The last time she had heard that sound was the night her family had been torn apart.

The guards steered the line of new prisoners across the floor to the opposite side where a set of stairs led to the next floor. Prisoners, mostly men but a few women as well, chanted "fresh meat" as the group climbed the metal stairs.

"Put her in with me."

"No. With me."

Makenna looked around in terrified silence. Her feet tried to stop after each step, but she willed them forward for fear of a beating. She had no more tears left or else she would have cried. Some of the men pointed at her with malicious grins and lusting eyes.

Stopping at one cell, the guards opened the barred door and shoved the first prisoner into it. Then they opened the next cell and the next prisoner in line entered. When the fat man's turn came, panic filled his face. He dug his heels in as the guards pushed him toward the cell.

As if his terror gave him strength, he struck one of the guards on the side of the head. The other guards momentarily froze in disbelief. The prisoner, realizing what he had just done, fell to his knees and pleaded for his life. He kissed the feet of the guard he had struck. The guard looked to his coworkers in embarrassment and rubbed the red blotch on his cheek. With a scowl, he grabbed the prisoner's collar.

"Please. I'm so sorry," the man cried.

Another guard swung his metal truncheon at the back of the prisoner's head. The clunk echoed through the prison. Makenna winced and turned away. When she turned back, they were dragging the twitching body to the rail. It took a few of them working together, but eventually they heaved the fat man over the rail. Makenna would never forget the sound of his body hitting the stone floor below.

The man's death meant Makenna got his cell. One look inside explained his dread.

The guard pointed the bloody truncheon to the open cell door. "Thanks to your fat friend, you'll be living with a barbarian now." He pushed her inside. Death itself seemed less terrifying than what awaited her. The cell door slammed closed behind her. She choked on her own spit, forgetting how to swallow.

Inside, a man leaned against the side wall, staring intently at Makenna. A chill went up her spine. He stood partially in the shadow, his exaggerated cheekbones catching the light and making his eyes look like dark pits. He wore his ratty prison gown wrapped tightly around his emaciated waist and his ribs pressed against his pale, paper-thin skin.

The light of the setting suns shone through the barred window to highlight the knee of a monstrous man who sat mostly hidden in shadow. His leg was as tall and thick as her entire body. He was probably seven feet tall.

As she tried to get a better look at his face, she saw him grimace and realized he was shitting into a hole in the floor. She gagged and swallowed the bile back with a hard gulp. She whispered to herself, "Face the bars. It'll be over soon." She turned back to the bars and stared past the railing to the open floor below.

The guards clustered in the center where another man was waiting. The other man addressed the prisoners, holding a large cone to his mouth. "Excuse me," he shouted through the amplifying cone.

Every inmate in the prison silenced. Two guards dragged the dead man across the floor, leaving a crimson streak.

"As most of you know, I am Warden Davis. A new group of citizens have joined us tonight." He let his words hang in the air while he scanned the cells. "As it turns out, one of them is a young girl."

Makenna wished he had left that out in case there was at least one prisoner who hadn't yet noticed.

"This girl is not to be touched under penalty of blah, blah, blah. You know the rules." He paused, letting his words marinate again. Then he added with a sickening chuckle, "Enjoy," before marching out through the main entrance. The clang of the door behind him wasn't especially loud, but it was deafening to Makenna.

Chapter 13

Ugh

Hatred permeated the moist green air of the prison, oozing from every pore of the stone walls. The bars were ice against Makenna's forehead as she stared helplessly through them, convinced she was about to die whether she faced her new cellmates or not. Standing on the precipice of death, there was one thing she still didn't understand. Why wasn't the barbarian killing her already?

The skinny man's sour breath reached her from across the cell; its stench could crumble stone. Every muscle in Makenna's body tensed as she felt him approach. "Hey, pretty girl," he said in a crusty, tired voice that lifted an army of tiny bumps on her arms. The back of her neck caved beneath his warm breath. He sniffed her stubbly scalp and then let out a sigh. "Ahh. You smell nice, yes?"

She crowded the cold bars.

He backed a step away. "I ain't gonna hurt you, pretty girl."

She didn't believe him.

"I just want to meet you. I ain't never been this close to a girl as pretty as you before. Not since my mama, that is."

Makenna closed her eyes and breathed in courage. She slowly turned, pressing her back against the bars. There was nowhere she could hide. "What's going to happen to me?" she asked, surprised her voice escaped the strangling fear.

The skinny man tilted his head and looked her up and down. "Well, if you're like the other girlies that come to the prison, you won't be pretty for long." His words weren't what sickened her so much as the inevitability of them.

"Who are you?" she asked barely louder than a slight breeze.

"I'm Feeble. Who are you?"

"Makenna. Are you sure you won't hurt me, Feeble?" She hoped using his name would make her seem more like a friend. His forearm read "Manslaughter. Life."

"What about him?" she whispered with a subtle nod toward the barbarian still sitting in the dark against the back wall. "Is *he* going to hurt me?"

Feeble glanced over his shoulder as though he had forgotten they weren't alone in the cell. "Oh, Ugh?" He scratched his head. "To be quite honest, I don't know what he'll do." His words were daggers.

"Why are you here if you killed somebody? Shouldn't you have been banished?"

"Da Angel said I ain't too bright and it might not have been completely my fault."

The barbarian grunted and stood up, his enormous back and head blocking out what was left of the dying light coming through the barred window. Makenna followed him with wide eyes as he rose. Panic doubled her heartbeats. Somehow Feeble had survived in there with a barbarian. She needed to know how he had done it, and she needed to know fast.

She pushed her Influence at Feeble. "Please, don't let the barbarian hurt me." Though she couldn't imagine the frail man doing much to stop him. The barbarian groaned again and stretched, his hands brushing the stone ceiling. He hunched over and massaged his right knee.

"Is he going to hurt me?" she whispered. She nervously touched the side of her face.

As if unconcerned, Feeble answered, "I don't know. I'd say you could ask him, but he don't talk. Everyone calls him Ugh because that's the noise he makes when he stands up."

The beast hobbled toward her, his footsteps making the stone floor quake. She crowded behind Feeble. Despite her Influence, he shuffled away, fear of the barbarian apparently stronger than her god.

Makenna froze. A trickle of snot leaked from Ugh's nose and he clumsily wiped it on his forearm. He leaned his massive head near her. She pressed her cheek against the bars. His nostrils flared and his nose crinkled as he sniffed her like Feeble had done. She couldn't breathe. Ugh sniffed her cheek, down her neck, and over her shoulder.

Please, God of Influence, make him like me. Make him like me.

Ugh snorted, nearly scaring the life out of her. He straightened. He was shirtless with his prison garb tied around his waist like Feeble's. His exposed chest was as wide as two men standing side-by-side and covered with dark, curly hair peppered with gray. Makenna came up to the bottom of his ribcage and stared up at his equally furry, gray-peppered chin. He slowly lifted his tree-trunk arm toward her. She cringed and squeezed her eyes shut.

Showing unexpected gentleness, he brushed her cheek with the back of his hand. And then, as if satisfied, he returned to the back of the cell and sat on the floor with a groan.

Feeble's eyes crossed. "You lucky. He likes you."

Her heart fluttered in her chest. "Where are the guards?"

Feeble chuckled. "Guards? They're around. They stays in a compound nearby."

For the first time since she arrived, she didn't feel Feeble's eyes studying her. He retrieved a burlap bag from the corner of the cell and removed his lifemask. Its chirp had been so muffled that Makenna hadn't heard it through the bag. He pressed the mask against his face, breathed into it, and then inhaled. It gurgled instead of whistling. "Ahhh," he sighed, even though she knew it couldn't have helped much.

"Feeble?" She stepped away from the bars for the first time. "How long have you been sick?"

He grinned, though she could tell it was forced. "For a while now. I ain't got much more time in dis world, I don't imagine." His words carried a deeper sadness than his cheery tone portrayed.

"Your mask has gone bad."

He nodded.

Though she barely knew him, she felt an incredible urge to comfort him. "Can I tell you a secret?"

"No one ever told me a secret before."

"My mask is going bad, too."

His eyes widened and he tilted his head. He had no reason to care about her in the least, yet he sounded sincere when he said, "Oh no."

"But do you know what? I'm not going to give up, and neither should you."

He lowered his head. "Once the masks die, they don't get alive again."

"I know. But I've seen a man fix them."

"Well, I wish I could get you to that man."

Makenna touched his bony chin. "I wish we could both get to that man."

A slight reddish hue colored his pale cheeks. "You can sleep near us if you want. It'll take some of the coldness away."

"Thank you."

"For what?"

"For not hurting me."

"Ah, Makenna. I don't wants to hurt anyone. I just wants to do my time."

"But your time says life."

"I stills gotta do it."

"If you don't mind my asking, what did you do to get here?"

He looked at her sideways for a moment. Finally, he said, "When I was nears your age, my older brother was pickin' at me somethin' fierce. He was always pickin' at me. One night while he were slappin' me good, I gives him a hug around his neck." Feeble giggled and covered his mouth. "When I lets go, he doesn't pickin' at me no more."

Makenna touched her cheek. "Oh."

Feeble winced like he knew he'd done something wrong, but wasn't quite sure what it was. "He doesn't pickin' at me anymore," he repeated. He sat next to Ugh. "Come. Have a seat."

Makenna stayed where she was. It wasn't long before Ugh was snoring like thunder and Feeble was writhing and moaning in the throes of a nightmare.

Makenna gently shook him. "Feeble?"

His eyes shot open. "What? What's happening? Mama?"

"No. It's me, Makenna. You were dreaming."

"Oh. Hi, Makenna. I does that sometimes. I'm terribly sorry."

She touched his back. "It's all right."

He closed his eyes and rolled over.

Makenna lay next to him and rested her head on the unforgiving floor. She shivered until her muscles were stiff and sore. The dim prospects of the next day weighed heavily on her thoughts. What ate away the most at any hope she still had were the haunting moans that echoed from nearly every corner of the prison. Like the chirping lifemasks, they didn't let up for the entire night. People were miserable and nobody seemed to care.

The first hint of light through the barred windows landed directly across Feeble's feet. He squinted and stretched and then smacked his lips like he'd eaten something sour. He sat up and smiled. "You're really here. I thought yous was a dream."

Makenna's bladder reminded her with a sharp poke of how long it had been since last she went. "Feeble? I need to pee."

He pointed toward where Ugh had voided the night before and then turned toward the wall so she could have some privacy. A half-full bucket sat in the hole. She held her breath, squatted, and did her business. Once finished, she went to Feeble and whispered, "Thank you."

He grinned.

She looked back to the rank bucket. "What do we do with it?"

"We take it with us."

"Where?"

"To breakfast." He went over and pissed into the bucket. Makenna turned away. Once he finished, he grabbed the metal handle and yanked it from the hole. It splashed onto his leg and foot. He didn't seem to mind.

Ugh gasped and snorted like he had choked on his own tongue. He sat up.

"Good morning," Makenna whispered, hoping the giant really did like her as Feeble said. He grunted, stretching away the kinks from the hard floor. Ugh was a good name for him. It took him plenty of effort and grimaces to stand up, and his knees creaked like old hinges, but once he was up he was more intimidating than any man she had ever met save Samuel. Her mask was the first to chirp that morning, followed soon by Ugh's.

All the cell doors clanged and then swung open as if tied together on a string. A fresh wave of dread washed over her. She grabbed Feeble's arm. He winced from her overzealous grip. "They'll kill me out there," she cried.

He pulled his arm away, splashing more filth from the bucket onto his leg. That time he seemed slightly annoyed as he looked at the speckles on his foot. He wiped them away with his free hand. His yellow fingernails were long and curled.

Calling on the full strength of her Influence, she blurted, "You have to protect me."

He squinted and thought for a moment. "I'll try, but you should stay close to Ugh, not me. That's what I do." He sauntered from the cell into the crowded walkway. Ugh followed, ducking to fit through the door.

Makenna, not about to be left alone in the cell, quickly caught up and crowded Ugh. To test her god on him, she whispered simple commands. Ugh continued walking. She tried again. Nothing. With no other choice but to hope Feeble could somehow protect her, she used her Influence on him again. "Keep everyone else away from me."

He squinted at her. "I feel funny sometimes when you're nears me. It's like I want to help you, but I don't know whats to do."

The walkway was packed with prisoners, some of whom were barbarians like Ugh, standing head and shoulders above the rest. No one acknowledged each other, not even the barbarians. Makenna had thought they would stick together. The metal landing rattled and creaked as more and more prisoners left their cells and headed toward the stairs. Each time someone bumped into her, she flinched and grabbed Ugh's firm, bulbous arm. It wasn't clear whether he even felt her grip.

They filed down the staircase. A line of wheeled carts with guards standing next to them waited in the center of the open floor. Countless stacks of clay bowls sat beside them. Despite Makenna's fear, the other prisoners didn't come near her. In fact, they went out of their way to give her and her barbarian cellmate a wide berth.

Feeble dumped the bucket into a large trough then carried the bucket back and got behind Ugh.

The line of prisoners at the food carts parted when Ugh approached. Feeble, acting as though he was the reason for their parting, ambled past them to the front of the line. Ugh followed, and Makenna clung to him like she was part of his garb. Some of the men in line glared at her as she passed, but shockingly that was all they did. Her stomach twisted.

Ugh went to the first cart. The other prisoners kept their distance while the rest of the barbarians filed in behind him. Makenna counted fifteen others besides Ugh. Everyone else stood back and waited for Feeble and the barbarians to finish collecting their food. No one made a sound.

The bowl was about the size of Ugh's fist. One of the guards slung a thick, pasty glob of shit-brown goop into Ugh's bowl, an equally stinky spoonful into Feeble's, and then one into hers. Makenna and Feeble followed Ugh to an empty space on the floor near the wall. Once the other barbarians had collected their food and scattered to various spots, the other prisoners got back in line.

Ugh leaned against the wall with a grimace. The way he shuffled from leg to leg told Makenna how sore his creaky knees were. At first she wondered why he wouldn't sit down to relieve them, but eventually concluded getting back up wasn't worth the rest. Makenna quickly sat beside him, while Feeble sat farther away. She worried she might be too close for Ugh's liking, but when he didn't react, she figured the risk was worth the protection.

Most of the prisoners ignored her and Ugh, but as Makenna choked down the nasty paste from her bowl, she noticed a particular group staring from across the floor. The man at the head of the group licked his lips in an exaggerated suggestive manner. The man next to him excitedly shuffled from foot to foot as though he was either excited or needed to piss.

Ugh must have noticed them, too, because he turned and faced the wall to finish his slop. Holding the bowl to his face, he lapped up what was left of its contents.

To Makenna, the paste tasted like sulfurous mud. Each bite stuck to the roof of her mouth and she spent more time fighting it with her tongue than she did eating it. One particularly potent bite turned her stomach and she nearly vomited.

"Ugh?" she whispered and tapped his leg.

He ignored her. She gently tapped his leg again. He rested his left forearm on the wall and peered beneath his armpit at her. She couldn't tell whether he was angry, annoyed, or both. Before he grew too angry, she offered her bowl. He glared at it suspiciously, looked back at her, and then back at the bowl.

"Take it. I don't want it."

Ugh took the bowl. Though she couldn't be sure, she thought she saw the slightest of smiles dent his broad, cracked lips. With a loud slurp, he devoured her paste in a hurry. She knew she should've tried to eat more, but it was worth giving her food away if it endeared her to her barbarian cellmate. She turned to see if Feeble had seen what she'd done. But instead of Feeble sitting behind her, the lip-licking man from across the room stood there.

She scooted back. "Oh, excuse me."

His left eye traced the outline of her body. His right eye was a soulless glass orb filling an empty socket. His lips formed a chilling leer. He looked past her to Ugh's back. The man's leer grew, revealing three rotted teeth. He was as ugly as any man she had ever seen. As terrified as she was, she couldn't help but notice how far his nose extended from his face. It was big enough to be unnatural. When he lifted his dirt-stained right hand, he was missing his thumb and his middle finger.

"Well now, what does Skirv have here?" he asked.

She looked past his shoulder to Feeble, who was face-down on the ground with three other prisoners pressing their knees into his back. One of them covered Feeble's mouth with his hand.

Skirv's big nose came into her line of sight. "I'm talking to you, wife. I see you trying to keep near the barbarian, but that's foolish. He won't protect you." He grabbed her shoulders, indenting her flesh with his dirty nails. He pulled her to her feet, spun her around, and shoved her against the wall a few feet from Ugh's side.

"Don't hurt me," she warned him with a false bravado.

He touched her neck with his skinny, icy fingers, leaned in with his rank breath hot against her skin, and whispered, "My dear, Skirv is only the first one in here to hurt you. Like gentlemen, my friends are simply waiting their turn."

Makenna's eyes shot toward Ugh, but the barbarian was busy licking her bowl clean.

"I don't know why you keep looking at him. He's not going to help you." He cackled. "Are ya, Ugh?"

Ugh grunted.

"See. I told ya. He's a barbarian. He cares about no one but himself. Well, and your sick friend over there for some reason that escapes me."

Makenna pushed her god at him. "You will leave me alone."

"What did you say?" He released her shoulders. "You know, darlin', Skirv thinks we'll just leave you alone." He started to back away.

One of the men who had previously been holding Feeble down pushed past Skirv. Before Makenna could react, he smacked her temple, sending her sprawling to the floor. He shouted, "What are you doing, Skirv? Get back over here and finish this."

Skirv shook his head. Makenna pushed her god at the other man. "Look at Skirv."

The man turned his head. Then she kicked as hard as she could. The top of her foot met his groin with such force that it hurt her. He grabbed himself, doubled over, and fell beside her. A high-pitched squeak trickled from his gaping mouth. Ugh stood a little straighter and looked over.

Makenna thought of Samuel and what he would do if he were in her place. The one thing she knew he would never do was give up. She bounced to her feet, vowing to fight until they killed her rather than surrender to whatever sick plans they had for her.

Skirv looked into her eyes. "Feisty," he said through clenched teeth. While his friend with screaming balls dry-heaved on the ground, his other two friends left Feeble coughing on the floor and joined him. By now, everyone in the prison was watching, including the guards. Makenna looked for something to use as a weapon. Finding nothing, she realized her nails and teeth were all she had.

Slobber trickled over Skirv's bottom lip. He wagged his finger in front of her face. "Tst, tst, tst. Calm down, darlin'. This will allll be over soon enough." He nodded, and his two friends moved past him to grab her.

"Hit Skirv," she cried, but in her panic couldn't focus on either of them so neither caught her Influence. She swung at them with all she had, but they grabbed her arms and wrestled them to her sides.

"Stop fighting," Skirv ordered. You're only making it worse."

He grabbed her throat. She gasped for breath, finding none. Though she begged with her eyes for mercy, Skirv only smiled in return. She tried to kick him, but he squeezed her throat.

If only Samuel were there, he'd never allow anyone to hurt her like that. Her eyes blurred. The world slowed. Skirv tilted his head with pleasure. She clawed at his arm, drawing trails of blood with her nails. Why didn't anyone help her? Her lips tingled. Then a wall moved behind the bastard. *Oh. That's why.*

Skirv didn't notice he was in danger until Ugh's shadow engulfed him from behind. His good eye widened. He loosened his grip and Makenna gasped for air.

Ugh's wide palm swallowed Skirv's head. Skirv's hands shot from Makenna's throat to Ugh's massive fingers. Makenna fell to her knees. She scurried backward until her back met the wall. Skirv's once-brave accomplices retreated across the floor, one of them limping and still holding his balls.

Ugh lifted Skirv from the ground by his head. His legs kicking the air, Skirv changed his tone. "Skirv's sorry, Ugh. Skirv didn't know she belonged to you."

Ugh carried Skirv to the wall. Skirv planted his feet against the wall and pushed, but his effort was worthless against such a powerful man.

"Please," Skirv cried.

Stone-faced, Ugh drove Skirv's face into the wall and his screams ended with a bone-cracking thud. His body stiffened briefly before going limp. Ugh dropped him in a heap on the floor next to Makenna. He looked down at his foe's quivering body for a few seconds and tilted his head. Once satisfied that the threat had been nullified, he turned and headed back toward the stairs that led to his cell, the other prisoners parting from his path.

A sea of eyes watched him, not a single person making a sound. When Makenna made eye contact with the other prisoners, they immediately looked away as though she was their superior. Kind of like how they looked at Feeble. The other barbarians turned their backs on the scene to finish their meals.

Feeble hobbled to Makenna's side and helped her to her feet. She looked at Skirv's still twitching body. His nose, once so prominent, was now smashed into nothing. A crack ran across his glass eye and two of his three teeth were gone. When she examined the wall, she found a bloody stain in the shape of his head with two white specks protruding from the stone.

Feeble grabbed her hand. "Come on. We's better get back."

She nodded and followed him through the courtyard and up the stairs to their cell. Though she was quivering like a bowl of slop, no one dared cross their paths.

Chapter 14

Samuel's Quest

S amuel paced along the riverbank, nightmare visions of what could be happening to Makenna crushing his soul. He had been ready to go to the prison the moment he learned of her arrest, but Ian—that crafty Ian—had convinced him to wait until a strategy could be finalized. Samuel now regretted listening to him.

He wasn't waiting any longer. Makenna was in the worst hell he could imagine, and nothing could stop him from finding her.

"Are you sure I can't talk you out of this, Samuel?" Ian asked for the twentieth time.

"Not a chance."

"You really want to go before we have a plan to free you and Makenna once you get in there? This is madness."

"I don't care. Just get me across the river. Every minute we waste talking is another minute I can't protect Makenna. I gave you a whole day to plan. I won't give you another minute."

Ian touched Samuel's shoulder. "I will figure something out and come for you."

Samuel glared at his hand. "Do not touch me, stealth boy. If you and Tristin hadn't allowed her to join you in the first place, she wouldn't be stuck in the prison now."

Ian slowly withdrew his hand. "Samuel, I know I'm not without blame, but I'm pretty damn sure she used a god on us. Otherwise, we never would have—"

"It doesn't matter anymore. Makenna needs me and I'm going." His lifemask chirped and he shoved it against his face without taking his determined eyes from Ian. After his lifebreath, he fearlessly waded into the Slaybyrne. The grinderfish swarmed, forcing Ian to charge in behind him. The grinderfish quickly scattered.

Soldiers patrolled the bank, so Samuel and Ian crouched in the water with only their eyes and the tops of their heads remaining above the surface. It took every ounce of restraint for Samuel not to burst from the water and go to work on the soldiers. Going to war with all the Angel's men wouldn't do Makenna any good. The three-man squad eventually passed by. Before another squad approached, Samuel climbed onto the bank.

Ian whispered, "Be strong, warrior," but that was like telling the river to be wet or a mountain to be tall. Samuel wiped the slime from his arms and slung it into the dirt. Without looking back at Ian, he sprinted up the bank and raced through back alleys until he reached Madson's District. He was hardly winded. Tristin wasn't the only Slummer who was good at sneaking through the kingdom. Samuel travelled with only his clothes, his mask, and a bag of gold that was his entire life savings. He carried no knives or swords; only fists would serve him inside the prison.

He reached an old abandoned pub that had a sign above the door with an arrow through the "P" of the word "Pub." He pried up a rotted floorboard from the porch and shoved the gold in the space beneath. After replacing the floorboard, he continued his journey.

He found the perfect spot to stay hidden from soldiers while he waited until the town started to stir. Then Samuel stepped out of the shadows, standing out like a dirt stain on a piece of the rarest, whitest silk.

The Madsons gave him a wide berth, raking him with curious and condescending eyes. It was the kind of attitude of arrogance and superiority that he would normally take pleasure in beating out of their elitist skulls. It wasn't lost on him that he had likely looked at people in the same way earlier in his life, but he'd worked hard to become a different person since then. Seeing it now only made him as angry at himself as he was at them.

Samuel leaned against the wall of a barbershop close to Robert's watering hole. He hated to cause trouble near his friend's place, but there was a particular patron he hoped to run into.

The foot traffic increased. Even with other Terdicts coming and going on their way to work, Samuel still stood out. A Madson woman went out of her way to move to his side of the street just so she could lift her nose at him as she passed. He blew her a kiss. Her face contorted like she'd bitten into a grinderfish. He wouldn't object to being arrested for harassment, but that wouldn't be as satisfying as what he had in mind.

It wasn't long before Samuel was rewarded for his patience. The corners of his mouth crept upward upon seeing his prize. The man walked toward the tavern, oblivious to Samuel's piercing stare. Samuel thanked his god that the man was such an alcoholic that he started drinking so early in the day. Before the man reached the door, Samuel started across the street.

All he needed now were witnesses—preferably soldiers. Samuel scanned the morning shoppers. He found two soldiers chatting in front of a local eatery a few doors down. He grinned and reminded himself not to look too eager to be arrested. It was time to start the show.

"You," he shouted in a tone menacing enough to catch everyone's attention.

Everyone within shouting distance turned with a start, including Samuel's unsuspecting victim. When the man saw Samuel cutting the distance between them, he scoffed.

His judgmental eyes started at Samuel's tattered shoes and then worked their way up from there. "Is there a reason you have approached me in all of your ..." He pointed at Samuel's blouse and twirled his finger in a circle to encompass all of Samuel's attire. "... filth?" he finally concluded.

Samuel thought the man was awfully conceited for someone who burgled shops to support his drinking habit. "You don't remember me, do you?" he snarled.

The man squinted at him. "Vaguely. Aren't you the beggar whom I gave a bit to the other day?"

Samuel shook his head.

"Then, no."

"Remember when you robbed that store over there and tried to blame me?"

Samuel showed the devil in his eyes. The color drained from the man's face.

He swung his fist. A collective gasp went up from the spectators at the sound of flesh striking flesh. The man wobbled but didn't immediately fall. Maybe Samuel had taken a little too much off the punch. He launched into the air and thrust his knee into the man's jaw. The man dropped like a horseshoe thrown from a roof.

Samuel dove onto the man and straddled his chest. "This is for blaming me for your criminality," he growled, grabbing a fistful of the man's fine shirt. He pummeled his face with two jarring blows before the soldiers swarmed him.

Samuel immediately relaxed in their grips. The last thing he wanted to do was assault one of them. That could get him banishment if he wasn't careful. They bound his wrists and hoisted him to his feet. He glanced back to the semiconscious man moaning on the ground. Though he had hoped to dole out more punishment before he was stopped, finding Makenna took precedence over vengeance. Nonetheless, he was satisfied with how much damage he had done with only a few strikes.

Before the senior soldier led him away, he said to his junior, "Get this man a physician." He stopped and glanced down at a few white specks in the pooling blood and added, "He's gonna need a tooth man as well."

Samuel smiled. All was working to plan. The soldier led him to an empty lot near the northern outskirts of the wealthy district where several more soldiers stood guard over three men whose hands were also bound.

"Long night last night," one of the waiting soldiers called out. "The Angel will be busy this morning."

One of the waiting prisoners wore an expensive shirt, a pair of meticulously pressed slacks, and shoes that appeared to have never seen a dirty day until that one. His shoulders bobbed with uncontrolled sobs. The soldiers forced Samuel to his knees beside him. The man's sobbing ground at Samuel's nerves until he couldn't bear it any longer. "Shut your crying hole," he growled, which caused the man to sob even louder.

Samuel's lifemask chirped. A soldier removed it from his waist and tossed it onto the cobblestones. With his hands still bound behind his back, Samuel leaned into the mask, pinned it between his face and the ground, and inhaled.

It was late afternoon before the Angel of Justice rode into view, his chains jingling against his metal chest plate. Samuel wasn't impressed.

"On your feet," a soldier shouted to the first prisoner in line. The man was obviously a Terdict by the looks of his oversized hand-me-down clothes and dirty, wild hair.

The soldier saluted the Angel. "Sir, three men witnessed this man stealing a loaf of bread from a Madson market."

The Angel's stare burned through the Terdict until the man lowered his head.

"We have determined that the three witnesses are credible and in good standing," the soldier continued.

The Angel nodded and said without pause, "Two years."

The man lifted his head with desperate eyes. "But my family is starving," he cried. The soldier dragged the bread thief away from the group. "I was only trying to feed them," the man shouted.

The Angel flicked his wrist. "Next."

Samuel looked away with disgust. As far as he was concerned, feeding a family was a just cause for thievery regardless of what the law said.

The second man in line wore a long-sleeved shirt stained with blood. The soldier at his side said, "We found this man next to his murdered wife with this in his hand." He tossed a bloody dinner knife onto the ground.

From his perch on his horse, the Angel stared into the man's eyes. The man tried to turn away, but the soldier grabbed his head.

"Did you kill your wife?" the Angel asked.

"No, sir," the man answered, though his darting eyes betrayed him.

The Angel stroked his chin in thought. A speck of hope swelled in the man's worried eyes. Samuel knew that speck was about to be snuffed out.

The Angel answered, "Banishment outside the wall without his mask."

Samuel grinned.

The man dropped to his knees. "No. No. No. Please." The soldiers dragged him kicking and screaming to a different waiting area than the bread thief. His fate on the other side of the wall was already written. If the creatures rumored to live out there didn't kill him, the lack of his lifemask surely would.

Samuel had taken in all the spectacle he could stomach without speaking his piece. "Your justice is flawed, Angel. You think yourself righteous, but you're just the opposite."

The Angel tilted his head. "That man killed his wife. The evidence is overwhelming. Should he not be punished?"

Samuel smirked. "Sure, he should be punished. I'll even kill him for you if you'd like. But that's not why your justice is flawed."

"Go on, peasant. I am quite intrigued."

"I'm no peasant." Though he hadn't planned to draw so much attention to himself, Samuel was emboldened by the Angel appearing to give his words weight. This might be his only chance to talk some sense into that perfectly-shaped skull. "You claim to be just, yet you allow people to live as they do in Terdict's District while these men"—he nudged the weeping man beside him—"are allowed lives of privilege. Others suffer for no other reason than they weren't born into that privilege."

"Wealth is not a crime, nor is living in poverty. I do not contend that the world is fair, only that crimes committed against the king's laws must be punished."

"You call yourself just, but justice isn't only about the king's laws. It's about fairness. The weight of fairness is against the Terdicts, and they have to break the king's laws just to survive."

"I am just under the laws we are given. If you want the laws changed, you will need to petition the king."

"And how would I do that? When would one ever see him?"

"That is not my field."

"Hmph. Your thinking is too narrow," Samuel sneered. "You blame the fallen horse who has injured his rider. You don't take into account that the rider may have ridden the creature into the ground. This man stealing bread for his family did not create his own hardship any more than the horse chose to fall and throw its rider."

"I do not sentence men for how they live; I sentence them for the crimes they choose to engage in. This man is not an animal. He did not make that bread. It was not his. He knew this. I have never sentenced an innocent person."

"What constitutes fairness, then?"

"Everyone knows the king's laws. Agree with them or not, it is not for you to say which ones you will follow."

"That's what you don't understand. Those very laws protect the Madsons at the expense of the Terdicts."

"I do not hold allegiance to any class. There are people of all classes receiving judgments around you. Tell me the crime and who committed it, and I will investigate without bias."

"The king commits crimes with his lopsided governance."

"Your words are treason."

"You are naïve."

"You have no evidence to accuse our king of anything."

"Why don't you go beyond the prison and investigate him for yourself, Angel? I think it's because somewhere deep down you know I am right."

The Angel chuckled. "I doubt very much that you are right about most things, Samuel. And you know my authority stops at the prison walls. You were a soldier, after all."

"So, you do remember me?"

"The Angel never forgets."

Samuel wondered how a man who had lived so long could be so dense. "Believe me or not, our king is a criminal."

The Angel rolled his eyes. "Again, you speak with no proof. Any more treasonous talk without sufficient evidence, and I will add to your sentence."

"Tell me, Angel. Why do Madsons get replacement masks when theirs fail and Terdicts do not?

"That is not in my purview."

"But how is that just?"

"They are the king's masks. He can distribute them to whomever he chooses. If you had two loaves of bread, you could certainly choose to give one to that bread thief if you so desired."

Samuel shook his head.

"We all have a place in this world, Samuel. Yours will soon be in the prison. Crimes against the king's laws are not worthy of justification, only justice." The Angel seemed suddenly weary of the debate. "You Slummers are growing bolder every day. Pillaging trash for scraps is one thing, and I chose to look the other way. But stealing masks must stop. And stop it I will."

His words struck Samuel's heart. How did he know about the Slummers? "Wait. What do you mean?"

The Angel ignored his question and turned to the soldier beside Samuel. "What is Samuel's crime today?"

"No," Samuel interrupted. "Answer me. What do you mean?"

The soldier described the altercation outside Robert's tavern in vivid detail.

The Angel turned back to Samuel. "Why did you attack that man?"

Though Samuel feared for Makenna, all of the Slummers were now threatened. Somehow, he needed to get back to Ian and warn him, and then find another way to protect her. In a less defiant tone, he pleaded, "Sir, that man robbed a store and then blamed it on me. I was almost arrested, and he escaped. I was only giving him justice. You of all people must understand that and let me go."

"If this is true, why did I not meet you that night? Why did you break young Charlie's jaw and render two other soldiers unconscious?" His eyes burned through Samuel. "And what happened to the men who allegedly murdered your wife and child so many years ago? Did they unexpectedly meet the grinderfish, maybe?" He smiled and searched for a hint of guilt in Samuel's eyes. Samuel didn't falter.

The Angel added, "I suspect that you were indeed responsible for their disappearance, but no bodies were found and I cannot prove it. And though you were not well described by poor Charlie, I recognized your handiwork."

Samuel felt his god getting restless and pushed it down with all his might. Though he longed to show the Angel his "handiwork," now was not the time. "Sir, I don't know what you're talking about in regards to broken jaws or dead murder suspects, but as for the crime I am here for today, I believe I was justified in my actions."

The Angel stared at him for a moment, contemplating his decision. Then he nodded once and said, "Your mistake is in your lack of faith in the king's laws. Obey them and you will have no quarrel with me. That is how it is and how it's always been." He paused and then said, "I believe you, Samuel. The man you assaulted will be detained and questioned. If he is guilty, he will pay. As for you, I sentence you to ten years: two years for each man you assaulted, one for breaking curfew, and one for fleeing the scene of a crime. The laws are to be obeyed without condition. There will be no more treasonous ramblings from you or you will serve your time without your tongue."

The Angel turned to the soldier who had escorted Samuel. "Bring Samuel's victim to me. I will deliver justice as I always have. Now …" He pointed to the pudgy man next to Samuel, the fourth and last prisoner he had to deal with that day. "What's this man's crime?"

The soldier answered, "Tax evasion."

The Angel sentenced him to five years. The man sobbed even louder than before. The Angel turned his back; his decisions were always final.

Chapter 15

A Plan

The patrols along the river had increased since Tristin and Ian had been separated by the soldiers. Though Tristin had made multiple attempts to reach the bank and find Ian, they had so far been unable to get their timing right. Three days had passed with Tristin living in the cobbler's shop. He grew more and more anxious with each passing minute, desperately needing to warn his friends about the Angel invading the Slums. Every day he was unable to reach Ian was a day less that they had to prepare.

On the third night, Tristin finally made it to the islet where he and Makenna had hidden before meeting Ian. It was near midnight when he heard Ian swimming across.

"Ian," he quietly called and waved his hands. Ian made a beeline to the islet.

"Tristin. Thank the gods I found you. Are you all right?"

"The Angel's coming," Tristin blurted.

Ian looked to the bank. "Now?"

"No. I mean, he said he's coming for the Slums."

"That's impossible."

"I know. But he said it, so he must have found a way. We need to get back and tell Samuel."

"Samuel's gone."

Tristin's stomach sank. "What?"

"He went to the prison to protect your sister. I brought him across the night after we were separated."

Tristin deflated like a waterskin full of holes as his hope leaked out. "Oh no." A burning sensation crawled up his throat and he choked it back with a hard swallow. "Please tell me you didn't."

"I had no choice."

Tristin panicked. "But you don't understand. We need Samuel here. He's our best warrior. You shouldn't have let him go until we talked. There's more you don't know."

Ian's voice turned harsh. "Talk? I don't have to talk to you. I run the Slums, remember?"

"Yeah. You're going to run it right into the prison … or worse."

"And whose fault is that, Tristin?"

"You blame me for this?"

"The Angel never so much as glanced across the river before you started stealing masks, even with Samuel busting heads on a regular basis. You're the reason Makenna's in the prison. You're the reason Samuel's not here when we need him."

Tristin felt the sting of Ian's words, but he didn't know what else he could have done. "You'd have me let everyone die when their masks went bad?"

Ian looked back at the bank again and sighed. "I don't think what you did was wrong, but you never even considered that the consequences would affect everyone, not just you."

Tristin glared at him.

Ian shook his head. "Come on. We should head back. We need to figure something out." He stepped into the water. "You coming?"

Tristin stepped in behind him. He had more to say, but he bit his tongue.

As they waded across, Ian said, "What is it that I don't know yet?"

"Makenna's mask is failing. That's why she used her god to make us to take her over."

Ian stopped and turned a horrified stare on Tristin. "Oh no."

"Why did you take Samuel over so soon?"

"You know Makenna's like his own daughter."

"Yeah, but he couldn't have gone without your help."

"Would you have told him no?"

Tristin would like to think he would have, but he knew deep down he'd have done the same as Ian.

They swam for a bit and then started wading again. Ian put his hand on Tristin's shoulder. "Did the Angel sentence you?"

Tristin nodded without looking at his friend.

"Death by banishment without your mask?"

Tristin nodded again.

"Oh well. You knew what would happen if you were ever to meet him."

That didn't make it any easier.

They reached the Slummer bank and dried off. Tristin spent a few extra seconds digging at his irritated skin. Then he caught up to Ian. "We need to figure this out. And fast."

Ian's mind was turning; Tristin could see it in his eyes. "First, we have to figure out how he will get across."

"That's what I've been struggling with. He'll have to have a person like you, right?"

Ian bobbed his head. "Yes."

"Then that's who we have to focus on. What if we killed that someone before they got across?"

"That's probably our best chance."

"Do we have anyone good with sling shots?"

Ian scratched his head. "Can't get enough range with a sling shot. I know a couple people who have dabbled in archery, though."

"Seriously? Who could afford that?"

"Madsons. Marshall and Maddy both went to the same archery club. I don't know how good they are, but they have to be better than anyone else we have."

"If we kill their stealth man before the Angel gets across, then the Angel will be overrun with the grinderfish, right?"

Ian nodded. "If Marshall and Maddy are okay with killing people, that may not be a bad strategy."

Tristin's gut twisted. He was asking a lot of his friends.

Ian put his arm around Tristin's shoulders. "They'll come through once they know what's at stake. We just need bows and arrows now. Do you think you can get them?"

"I'll get directions to the archery club from Maddy. You can take me back tonight."

Ian nodded. "We'll get through this, kid. Get some sleep. We need to prepare our people."

Tristin headed home and threw himself onto his pallet. He couldn't sleep because his mind wouldn't stop spinning. What if his idea worked? What if there was no longer an Angel of Justice to enforce the king's laws?

Chapter 16

The True Cost of Resistance

During his long walk to the prison, Samuel repeatedly cursed himself for not trying to kill the Angel when he had his chance. He may have failed, especially with his hands bound, but it might have been his only hope to help all his friends at once. Now a new plan was needed, and one quickly evolved in his mind. First, free Makenna and find a way out of the prison. That would take time. Next, send her to the Slaybyrne to wait for Ian. Have her tell Ian of the Angel's plans so he can prepare for war. Finally, and this was the part he most looked forward to, find the Angel and kill him before he got a chance to start the war.

After cresting yet another hill, the blur of the prison appeared through the green fog. Seeing the prison didn't make Samuel nervous because his God of Killing made him excited when the threat of violence was near. The anticipation carried him to the gates.

Several prison guards met with the soldiers and received their report. When they spoke of Samuel, all the guards looked up at once. Then they shook hands and the soldiers left.

Samuel followed the line to where a bulky imbecile stood with a club. One of the guards whispered something to the man and his eyes shifted to Samuel.

He cleared his throat and spat green gunk to the side. "Use yer god and I'll hurted you."

Samuel glowered at him. "How 'bout you free my hands and I use it on you?"

The man's awkward face twisted. He stepped forward and lifted his club slightly. Two guards intervened. The man lowered his club.

When Samuel's turn in line came, he followed the others into the first room without hesitation. The clang of the lock on the metal door echoed in the room. They freed his hands and ordered him out of his clothes and into one of the rags hanging from a clothesline that stretched across the middle of the room. He wanted to be difficult, if for no other reason than it would be fun to give them a hard time, but he needed a favor and figured his chances of getting one would improve with an obliging attitude.

The guards escorted the man in front of him into the next room, momentarily leaving Samuel alone with a single guard. While Samuel shuffled through the rags for something that appeared likely to fit, he whispered, "I have a proposition for you."

"Excuse me?" the guard asked.

"I'd like to give you gold. A lot of gold, actually."

"Hmph." The guard didn't even lift his head. Samuel continued searching for something to wear. After a few seconds, the guard said, "Stolen, no doubt."

Samuel grinned; he had him now. "Gold is gold, is it not?"

That man wasn't very big for a guard, quite scrawny in fact, and definitely not someone who would give Samuel much of a problem. But it wasn't a fight that Samuel was seeking. Not yet, anyway. The guard made eye contact after looking him up and down. "Forgive me, but you don't look the type who has much gold."

"Oh, but I do."

"If you have gold with you, I don't want to know where it's hidden."

Samuel slipped his garment over his head. "Of course I don't have it with me."

"Then your offer is worthless." The skinny guard brushed Samuel off with a wave.

"Very well. I will offer it to the next guard I see."

The guard's hand hung in the air near the doorknob. Then he rubbed the back of his neck and grimaced. "Hold on. You've piqued my curiosity a bit. Though you must know before you go any farther that no matter how much gold you say you have, you aren't getting out of here before your twelve-year sentence is up."

"My sentence is ten years."

"That was before you tried to bribe a guard."

Ten years, twelve years, or a hundred years, it mattered little. Samuel nodded. "I wouldn't think of trying to leave early."

"So, where is it? The gold, I mean."

"Favor first."

The guard puffed out his puny chest and stepped away from the door. "How 'bout you tell me anyway and I don't hurt you?"

Samuel's voice turned suddenly deep and dangerous through clenched teeth. "You could try, but I wouldn't recommend it."

The guard's eyes darted nervously around the room as if he'd just realized how alone with Samuel he was. After a hard swallow, he asked, "What are you wanting me to do?"

"Simple. I hear you have a young girl inside the prison."

"We have several girls. Well, heh-heh, several still alive." He continued chuckling without any clue of how close he was to having his neck snapped.

Samuel stepped toward him, his obliging attitude evaporating. The guard's chest deflated.

Samuel inhaled a deep, calming breath that ended with him choking on the stale air. Once his cough subsided, he said, "This girl I'm looking for was brought here recently, probably for attempted theft. She should be housed in the nonviolent section. I need to get to her immediately."

"Ah, yes. You little devil. You want I should give you a few minutes alone with her? That's easy enough."

Samuel wanted to kill him as much as he wanted to make a deal. "No. I want in her cell. Permanently."

The guard studied his face, specifically his angry eyes, before answering, "Why? She do something to you? Are you looking to get a little payback where the Angel can't see you?"

Samuel's angry snarl nearly drowned out the guard's voice. "You are disgusting. She's just a child."

"All right. Calm down. What do you want me to do?"

"I need you to ignore my violent status and put me in with her."

"Oh. Is that all? That won't be necessary."

"Why not?"

"She's not in the nonviolent section."

Samuel's face blanched. "What?"

"Yeah. She pissed off your friend out front and he had her put into A-wing with the degenerates. Since that's where you're headed already, you can just tell me where to get that gold now."

"Not yet. You need to get me in her cell. Immediately." His blood boiled. He knew he should have killed that bastard out front.

"I would if I could, but she has already been spoken for."

"Spoken for? By whom?"

"A barbarian we call Ugh."

"I'll deal with this barbarian. Just put me in with him."

The guard chuckled again, followed by another nervous swallow. "I don't think I can do that. I don't know what arrangement they have, and I'm definitely not one to cross Ugh."

"You just get me to him. I'll take care of the rest."

The guard studied him again. "The soldiers told us about you. Are you really as good as they say?"

Samuel sneered. "I don't know. Depends on what they said."

"They said to be careful with you. You used to be a soldier and you have a god or something that makes you a handful."

Samuel shrugged.

The guard nodded as if he'd made a decision. "You know what? I've changed my mind. I don't need your gold after all."

"No? Why not?"

"I've got a better idea." The guard grabbed a whistle dangling from a cord around his neck and gave it a hard blow. Half a dozen guards poured into the room.

Samuel eyed them as they surrounded him with clubs raised. "What's this about?"

The guard ignored him and spoke to his colleagues instead. "Take this man to the basement." He grinned. "Tell Malvic I get fifty percent of whatever he earns."

Samuel gritted his teeth. Before the guards could close in, he lunged for the skinny man's throat. They were on him in a flash. The closest two guards went down immediately and stopped moving. Samuel plowed two more across the room. When one of them smacked his head on the stone wall, Samuel let him drop unconscious to the floor.

He heard more guards coming from the next room. As two guards grabbed his arms, he wondered if killing all of them would be easier.

The guards buried him beneath their weight as more and more filled the room. He snapped someone's wrist before a club bashed his temple. The first blow only stunned him. It was the second one that put him to sleep.

The world was black when Samuel came to again. He heard two men talking in muffled whispers nearby. He was naked and cold. His back brushed the ground as he hung suspended by chains that dug into the flesh of his wrists and ankles. It was going to be a long day. As he gathered his wits, he realized the darkness was caused by a hood over his head.

When the two men noticed him stirring, they stopped talking and their footsteps approached him. Though Samuel had an idea that what was coming wouldn't be pleasant, he was eager to get started. The sooner he figured out what the basement was, the sooner he could find a way out of it.

One of the men grabbed his hood and ripped it away. Samuel squinted, his eyes adjusting to the dim light. The man was wrinkled and scarred and wore a maniacal smile on his weathered face. A lumpy blob of flesh replaced part of his second finger. His gray hair was dirty, stringy, and grew in patches, matching the wiry tufts sticking out of his shirt collar and brushing the top of his black apron. "Good day," he said with a creaky voice.

Samuel grunted in return.

"What is your name?" the man asked.

Samuel looked away.

"I am Malvic," the old man said proudly, as if he thought Samuel should recognize the name. "That is my friend Coffer." He nodded toward a large man standing at the door. He was about Samuel's size, but with a belly that hung over his belt. He was shirtless. A full head of coal-black hair touched equally black eyebrows that met in the center. The shadow on his chin indicated he hadn't shaved that day.

Malvic continued. "We are happy to meet you, despite you being so rude as to not tell us your name. I so hoped we could be open with each other. Maybe you're just shy. If you're not going to tell me your name, I will simply call you friend until you change your mind. Is that all right, friend?"

Samuel didn't answer.

"I see from the markings on your arm that you have been given ten years in this prison." He cringed. "With the way we're starting out, I don't think you're going to make it."

Samuel lifted his eyes to his forearm where his sentence had been inked into his skin while he was unconscious.

"You should feel fortunate to be here. Not many prisoners get chosen for a job down here." Malvic motioned Coffer to the adjacent wall. There was a large, square stove with a pipe running into the ceiling. Coffer opened the front, revealing glowing orange coals and long iron brands. He grabbed a thick glove that was hanging beside the stove and slid it onto his right hand.

Malvic turned back to Samuel. "Oh, I hate to have to do this so soon after meeting you. Burning flesh gives off such a pungent stink as to be uncomfortable for everyone in the room." Coffer handed Malvic a glove and then passed him the red-glowing brand.

Samuel had been burned once before sneaking little cakes from his mother's oven, and he remembered it as one of the worst pains he'd ever felt. He'd been ten at the time. The next few minutes were going to be difficult at best. He looked into Malvic's eyes again. "What are you going to do?" he asked.

Malvic grinned. "Well, at least now we know you can talk." He thrust the brand toward Samuel's chest. Samuel's restraints rattled as he tried to squirm away, but there was nowhere to go. The scorching pain trailed the sizzling sound by a fraction of a second. Despite his determination to not make a sound, Samuel couldn't hold back a groan.

The room filled with the putrid stink Malvic had spoken of. He pulled the brand away and handed it back to Coffer. Gently, he touched Samuel's cheek. Samuel lunged to bite him, but Malvic pulled back, barely saving his finger.

"Feisty. I like that. Save it for the game. Now tell me, friend. Is there anything you'd like to say before we continue?"

Weakly, Samuel nodded.

"Wonderful." Malvic leaned in, but not close enough that he might lose his ear. "Are you going to tell me your name now?"

Despite the pain, Samuel chuckled and shook his head. "What does it say?" he whispered.

"Excuse me?"

Samuel paused to catch his breath. "The brand. What does the brand say?"

Malvic burst into laughter and smacked Samuel's bare chest. "You, my friend, are going to be fun." He glanced to Coffer and said, "Feed him well tonight. We need him strong for tomorrow." As Samuel's chest blistered and throbbed, his lifemask chirped on the floor. Malvic retrieved it and pressed it to his face. "We can't have you dying from toxic blood before we have our fun, now can we?"

Samuel took as deep a breath as he could. He wanted to be as strong as possible for whatever "fun" was in store.

"Try and get some rest. Tomorrow's gonna be a big day for you." Malvic took several steps toward the door before turning back one last time. "My name," he said. Seeing Samuel's confusion, he added, "The brand on your chest is my name. Malvic. We can't put you in the cage without everyone knowing who you belong to." With that, he left the room, whistling an unfamiliar song. His whistle had faded down the hall by the time Coffer released the pulley on Samuel's chains. Samuel's back slammed onto the cold, hard floor. When Coffer left, he shut the wood and steel door firmly behind him.

Though Malvic likely believed branding his name on Samuel's chest was a good idea, he couldn't have been more wrong. The brand would help keep him and his god focused throughout the coming "games" while reminding him of who he wanted to kill first when he got free. No matter what, he'd stay alive until he found Makenna.

Soon, the single torch on the farthest wall burned out and took his light. He began to shiver despite the stove. The complete darkness and silence felt like a tomb.

Coffer tossed an apple through the barred window in the door. Samuel scarfed it down. If that was their idea of feeding him well, then he was in trouble. Within a few minutes, he started feeling woozy and struggled to keep his eyes open. *Damn them. Those bastards drugged the apple.* He was barely able to complete the thought before he shivered himself to sleep.

Chapter 17

The Basement

S amuel heard a crowd cheering and slowly opened his eyes. He
sat up, still woozy from the drugs, and squinted in the
torchlight. He was in a fighting cage. He tried to rub away the
ache behind his temples.

Malvic, that dirty bastard, knelt outside the bars. He tossed a
waterskin into the cage and it landed next to Samuel's foot. "Drink
up. Get your strength."

Samuel worried the water would be drugged too, but his mouth
couldn't produce even enough saliva to spit in Malvic's face. He
took a chance. Though the water was warm, it was more than
refreshing.

The crowd beyond the cage roared. Samuel's eyes were drawn to
a staircase behind the cheering prison guards. Two men were
coming down the stairs and strutting down the aisle to the cage while
the crowd patted their backs and wished them luck. The cage door
opened so the two men could step inside.

Malvic shouted, "These two prisoners are quite violent. They
killed the last guy within a few seconds."

Trying to scare Samuel with the threat of violence was like trying to scare a grinderfish with the threat of drowning.

As Malvic made his way to his seat, Samuel heard him say, "Two bits on the Ferris brothers."

One of the brothers was a forehead taller than Samuel and quite a bit beefier. His upper lip was mostly chewed away, and the left side of his face bore scars like he had been burned. His bulging upper arms told stories of his strength. The other one was wiry and thin. Samuel moved toward them.

One of the earliest lessons his father had taught him was to strike first when the numbers weren't in his favor. Distracting his opponents was another. Samuel decided to use both. "I should warn the two of you. I have the Killing God with me."

The brothers smiled at each other. The beefier brother laughed out loud. "Do you have any idea how many times we've heard something like th—"

Samuel was on him in a flash, arms wrapped tight around his head. He used his momentum and weight to drive the man to the ground while twisting at the same time. The man grunted when his neck snapped. Samuel bounced back to his feet while the man pissed himself and quivered on the floor.

The cheering crowd went silent.

The other Ferris brother's sick grin seemed hours gone, replaced by the realization that it was his turn in the grinder. He stumbled backward.

Samuel charged. The surviving brother threw his fist and Samuel ate the punch with pleasure. Samuel swarmed him, ripping out the man's throat before they hit the ground. Blood sprayed his face. From his knees, he rolled his eyes back and took in a quivering breath. *Is that all they've got?*

The crowd erupted in shouts and boos, gold and silver changing hands.

Samuel wiped the blood from his face and then wiped his hand on the dying man's prison garb. He shrugged at Malvic. Deep inside, he felt his god celebrating. It was a euphoria that he hadn't felt in a while. He needed to be careful. Once his god got a taste, it would be difficult to push him back down. Just like the last time. Though he often welcomed his god's help, sustained violence brought out nastiness that Samuel couldn't always control.

Malvic waved him over to the bars. "The crowd's not happy. They want more of a show."

Samuel shook his head. In battle, Samuel could keep his god's bloodlust in check. But gratuitous violence emboldened his god in undesirable ways. The God of Killing was already enjoying the game too much.

Malvic grinned. "I'll never bet against you again, friend. That was phenomenal. They're bringing one of their champions down next. His name is Elemar."

Samuel shook his head. "I'm not fighting anymore today."

Malvic winced. "Then the next few minutes aren't going to turn out well for you." His eyes drifted toward the stairs.

Samuel followed them to where the biggest man he had ever seen walked through the crowd, head and shoulders above everyone else. Samuel could feel his god's excitement growing. He had always wanted to try a barbarian. He stepped away from the bars. His god warmed his blood.

Samuel closed his eyes and took a deep breath. There was no way he could survive against a barbarian without letting his god loose at least a little, and damn Malvic for making him do it. He would be wise to end the fight as quickly as possible.

Elemar ducked through the cage door and then straightened to his full intimidating height. He tilted his head and grunted. The cage door slammed shut. He charged. Samuel dove out of the way of his massive fist, nearly losing his head in the process. Elemar was faster than his size suggested. As quick as Samuel was in getting back to his feet, Elemar was already beside him. Samuel threw his arms up just in time to catch Elemar's fist on his forearms. The force tumbled him against the bars.

Elemar's next punch caught Samuel in the ribs, taking his breath. Samuel's god masked the pain long enough for him to drive a foot against Elemar's knee. It hardly fazed the behemoth.

With one hand, Elemar grabbed Samuel by the head and lifted him from the ground. Samuel's back met the bars next to one of the torches. Elemar drew back his fist.

Samuel grabbed the torch and jammed it into Elemar's face. The barbarian recoiled, dropping Samuel to his rear. Samuel bounced up and leaped at Elemar, planting his feet against Elemar's hips and wrapping his hands tight in Elemar's collar. Samuel shifted his weight to pull his foe off balance. When they thudded to the ground, Samuel scrambled onto Elemar's chest.

Before Elemar could recover, Samuel drove a fist at the barbarian's cheek. His god gave it extra pop and Elemar's eyes briefly went glassy. Samuel reacted without thought. He drove fist after fist into Elemar's face until the barbarian stopped struggling and his legs jolted spasmodically with each blow. And then his legs stopped, too. Samuel kept pounding.

By the time he reclaimed control over his god, his fists were striking mush and bits of broken bone. He pulled himself back, appalled at how easily he had given in to the rage … to his god. How easily his god had taken over. Memories of Makenna smiling as she ate the custard helped him fight the urge to kill everyone in the room. As he looked around, the crowd of guards applauded and cheered.

"I'll kill you all," he screamed. His breaths came in rapid bursts.

The guards paid him no heed as they collected their winnings and moved toward the stairs. Their parting chatter was electric over what they had just witnessed. As Samuel watched them file up the stairwell, his eyes landed on Malvic standing beside the cage. He burned a glare through him.

Malvic smiled. "Get some rest, friend. Your next opponent has a god of his own."

That meant nothing to Samuel.

"See you in three days." He tossed Samuel's lifemask into the cage. Then he turned and followed the line of guards up the stairs.

Samuel turned back to the three dead bodies. Seeing Elemar with his head nearly gone made him sick to his stomach. Not because violence bothered him—it didn't—but because it was a reminder of what would happen if his god ever gained control again.

The bigger Ferris brother stared back with fixed, empty eyes. His jaw was frozen open as if his soul had left through his mouth. His brother's blood that had pooled around him gave off a strong metallic stench.

Samuel sat against the bars, his every emotion rising to the surface. "I won't let him win again," he whispered to the ghost of his wife in case she might be watching. Though he had regained control this time, if the fighting continued for too long, he feared he wouldn't be able to regain control next time. And if that happened, he would never be able to help Makenna. He hated his god.

When guards returned to cart off the corpses, they threatened to starve Samuel if he didn't let them bind his hands to the bars first. He grudgingly complied; his stomach had been rumbling all day. After removing the bodies, they freed one of his hands and offered him an apple. He side-eyed it.

"Sure, it's drugged," one of the guards said. "But it's the only way you're going back to your cell where you can eat a real meal."

Samuel weighed his options and then hesitantly took a bite. When he woke again, he was in his cell. Though his hands and feet were chained again, Coffer was there to feed him and help him take lifebreaths. Two monotonous days passed this way, punctuated by Malvic dropping by periodically to assess his condition and ask his name. During the last such visit, Samuel's food was drugged again. Then he woke up in the cage once more.

"Damn it."

Malvic strolled down the stairs, his stupid cheerful whistling setting Samuel's teeth on edge. "Good, you're awake. You know, friend, if you were a bit more cooperative we wouldn't have to resort to such measures. How's my little champion today?" he asked.

"Why don't you come in here and find out?"

"Still feisty. That's good. You'll need that. I feel I should tell you a little about today's opponent."

Samuel turned away.

"You don't have to look at me to listen." He stood just out of arm's reach for good reason. "Your opponent's name is Zakaira."

Samuel lifted a brow.

"Oh, so you've heard of him?"

Samuel nodded. It had been so many years he'd figured Zakaira was long dead, but he knew the name.

"Then you also know he carries the God of Fury?"

Samuel nodded again.

"He's been fighting here for years and he's never been close to being defeated. In fact, I'd never seen anyone who even deserved to be in the same cage as him, quite frankly … That is, until you graced us with your presence. We always thought Elemar might have the best shot one day, but his handlers never wanted to risk their champion. There's a lot of politics in these fights down here. Let me ask you. Do you think *you* can beat him?"

Samuel gave him a sidelong look but didn't answer.

Malvic rubbed his hands together. "I can hardly wait. Rest up, friend. I'll see you in a little while."

The crowd filled the arena so full that every guard in the prison must be in attendance. They were almost getting too close to the cage, those in the back pushing to get a better view. Samuel stretched his muscles and warmed up with an invisible opponent until he broke out in a nice sweat. He was ready for anything. Though he didn't want to be Malvic's plaything, his only chance to save Makenna was to bide his time and stay alive.

The raucous crowd quieted and all eyes turned to the stairwell. The silence was so sharp that he could hear people breathing. And then he heard a door slam shut at the top of the stairwell. The slapping of bare feet on stone raced down the stairs. That's when he first saw Zakaira, buzzed blond hair and shirtless with an athletic build strikingly similar to his own. He was covered in scars.

Zakaira didn't slow as he reached the bottom of the stairs, sprinted past the crowd, and plowed through the open cage entrance. He shot across the floor toward Samuel. Samuel prepared to meet him head-on.

Zakaira faked high and dove at Samuel's waist. Samuel tried to slough him to the side, but Zakaira was stronger than expected.

Zakaira drove forward and to the left, knocking Samuel off balance. They tumbled to the ground. Zakaira rose up and rained punches on Samuel's face. The first one broke a tooth. The second crushed his nose. Before Samuel could react, Zakaira leaned down. Furious pain exploded in the side of Samuel's head. Zakaira pulled back and spit out Samuel's right ear. He started punching again, opening a cut over Samuel's right eye. Samuel reached out and Zakaira snapped two of his fingers.

Samuel couldn't catch a breath. As much as he didn't want his god before, he desperately needed him now.

When Zakaira's weight shifted momentarily, Samuel bucked his hips with all he had. Zakaira tumbled over, scurried back to his feet, and charged again. But Samuel was no slouch and had also gotten to his feet. And, more importantly, he had learned.

When Zakaira dove at his waist again, Samuel dropped an elbow to the back of his neck, sending him sprawling to the ground. As Zakaira scrambled to get up, Samuel kicked him in the jaw. It was the kind of kick that would kill a normal man, but it only spun Zakaira around. Samuel stumbled backward to catch his breath and assess the damage. The side of his head was on fire. Samuel had no choice. If he wanted to live through this, he had to unleash the very darkness he had vowed to never let loose again. He reached for his god.

Zakaira charged again. But this time Samuel's god gave him the strength to stay on his feet. Zakaira howled in rage. Samuel bit a chunk of flesh from the side of his neck. Zakaira didn't flinch. When Zakaira kicked him in the balls, Samuel didn't stop. He had lost himself in his god's wrath.

Zakaira punched Samuel's chest with ungodly strength. The impact drove Samuel backward all the way to the cage bars nearly a dozen steps behind him. He had never felt such power. Zakaira came at him.

Samuel jumped, his god lifting him over Zakaira's head. Samuel had forgotten what it felt like to embrace the God of Killing's true strength. Zakaira collided with the bars, opening a gash on his forehead to match Samuel's. He spun as Samuel landed behind him. When he roared again, Samuel jammed his thumbs into his mouth.

He fish-hooked Zakaira's cheeks and pulled until the corners of his lips ripped apart.

Blood sprayed his face. He licked it from his lips. His god was in ecstasy.

Zakaira howled.

Samuel knew he had him. As long as his body held together. The two tumbled to the ground again, both men giving and taking until they were gasping for air through blood-filled mouths. The crowd was in a frenzy. Samuel bounced up and climbed onto his opponent's exposed back. Zakaira stood up despite Samuel's weight and drove him hard against the bars. Samuel ignored the impact and wedged his forearm under Zakaira's chin. He grabbed his own hand to squeeze tighter. Zakaira flailed and bucked, but Samuel held strong. Zakaira clawed streaks across Samuel's face, but Samuel's god ate the pain.

The strength ebbed from Zakaira and he dropped to his knees. Samuel squeezed harder. As the bones in Zakaira's neck popped and snapped, Samuel kept squeezing. Even when Zakaira started twitching, Samuel couldn't stop. Zakaira's head popped upward when his spine gave way to the pressure. His body stiffened then went limp, yet Samuel still squeezed, unable to wrestle control back from his bloodthirsty god.

Inside Samuel's mind it was like he was watching someone else through a long, dark cave, and he was too small and powerless to stop it. *Let go,* he pleaded, but his body wasn't his anymore. He tried to concentrate on an image of Makenna's face, but it melted. The last time his god took control like this, it had taken months of isolation just to keep from killing everyone he saw. The fight to keep his sanity threatened to be even worse this time.

Samuel dropped Zakaira to the floor and readied himself for the next fight. Makenna screamed into the darkening cave, "No, Sam. It's over."

Samuel roared to the heavens. And then something gave way in his brain and he collapsed to his face.

Part Three
Breaking the Slums

Chapter 18

Curiosity

A nervous calm settled over the Slums in the days after Ian and Tristin broke the news of the Angel's threat. On the first day, the Slummers gathered table legs and window poles and whatever other scraps of wood they could find that could be turned into clubs or spears. They were as ready as they could be. All that was left was the nerve-wracking wait.

Jackson wasn't Ian's first choice to watch over the Slaybyrne River at night, but he'd begged for a chance to be useful and Lowen had promised to keep him from wondering off. Lowen was a crass older man, fit and powerful from a lifetime of labor on the other side. Despite walking with a limp, he was still one of the hardest workers in the Slums. Rumor had it he got his limp from fighting the three soldiers who had come to arrest him for speaking ill of King Searle, but he didn't talk much about it.

Jackson sat atop Lowen's roof at the edge of town facing the bank. As exciting as the job had sounded at first, sitting on the roof night after night quickly proved to be a boring task, and boredom was Jackson's greatest foe. Late into his third night on the roof, he picked at a splintered shingle, wondering if he pulled on it whether it would unravel the entire roof like pulling a string on a Richie's scarf. Though he knew it wouldn't, he still enjoyed the silly image it gave him.

When his lifemask chirped, it reminded him of a dangerous game he occasionally played. He had a theory that he could increase his tolerance of the green air by only using his mask when he couldn't wait any longer, and thereby one day he'd be able to go an entire cycle without using it at all. Just think of the sick people he could help if he could find a way to share one of his lifebreaths with them.

His previous attempts had been unsuccessful, but he wasn't discouraged. Lack of success was no reason to quit trying as far as he was concerned. He set the mask on the roof, knelt before it, and looked around to make sure no one was watching from the ground. Then he waited. The next chirp rang out. And then another soon after.

His fingers got tingly and he started to feel dizzy, but he'd gone way past that before. The longer he waited the more tired and cramped his muscles grew, which only meant it was working. His stomach turned. His eyes watered. Still, he wasn't ready to give in. The air burned his throat.

The length of chirps grew longer and longer until they blended together into one constant high-pitched squeal. It wasn't that he enjoyed feeling his blood turn toxic, or that he wanted to die, he was just curious. The other Slummers often called him a fool and insisted his game would eventually kill him, but Jackson felt not knowing his limits would be so much worse.

Staring at his blurry mask, he realized this was the longest he'd ever waited. As his eyelids grew heavier and the muscles in his arms turned to stone, he decided he'd gone far enough. He leaned forward, aiming for his mask, but missed, his face striking the roof. In hindsight, maybe he shouldn't have played his dangerous game alone.

Panic clenched his gut. He tried to call out for help, but there wasn't enough strength behind his voice for anyone to hear. His mask was inches away, antagonizing him with its squeal. Inches might as well have been miles.

Fire coursed through his veins. The world faded around him. Jackson had always wondered what thoughts go through a person's mind when they're near death. For him, it was flashes of Tristin with an ornery grin teasing him about having the God of Curiosity. If he really did have a god, it was just his luck that it was going to kill him.

He didn't particularly want to die, but death wasn't as scary for him as it was for most. On the other side there might be answers to questions no one alive had even thought to ask. That was the ultimate curiosity of all. Despite his impending death, he smiled at how far he had gone.

The suns crested the horizon as if to lead him through the darkness. His only regret was failing his Slummer friends in the job they'd trusted him with. His eyes grew heavier until he couldn't hold them open any longer. It wouldn't be long now. Death was more peaceful than he'd dreamed it could be.

"Jackson, use your mask already," someone shouted. They sounded very far away. Maybe it came from the other side. Maybe they were waiting for him. "Jackson," the voice shouted again. It sounded like Lowen. Had he died too? He sounded closer when he said, "You're making me crazy with that rack—"

Someone grabbed his arm. And then everything went quiet. Was he dead? He didn't feel dead, not that he had any idea how dead should feel. A mask whistled in the blackness far away. He heard breathing and realized it was his own. Not dead after all. He rolled to his side, a violent coughing fit grabbing hold of his chest. Once the coughing subsided, he opened his eyes. If not for Lowen's strong arm catching him, he'd have rolled off the roof completely.

Lowen sighed an annoyed breath. "Calm down, Jack. Just breathe."

Jackson opened his eyes. The glow from the suns gave Lowen a halo. "You're one ugly angel."

Lowen pushed him away, almost sending him over the very edge he had just saved him from. "You're not dead, Jack, but you should be."

Though the fuzziness faded, a blistering headache remained. Jackson sat up and dangled his legs over the edge. He tried to rub the pain from his temples. Lowen sat beside him. "I keep telling you to stop playing with that mask or you're going to get yourself killed, but you never listen."

Jackson rolled his eyes and rested his forehead in his palm. "Please, not now. My head's killing me."

"It won't last long. Once your blood adjusts and returns to your half-a-brain, you'll feel better. You gotta be smarter than this, Jack."

"I know. I'm sorry."

"Don't be sorry; just be more careful from now on." Lowen reached for the ladder.

Jackson tried to coax a smile from his old friend with one of his own.

"I'm not smiling, Jack. Not t—" He stopped, staring past Jackson at the Slaybyrne. "Oh my gods," he whispered.

Jackson followed his eyes. A chill ran through his body as if winter had suddenly fallen. The opposite bank hid behind an army of at least two- to three-hundred soldiers. He painfully realized that the sixty or so defenders in the Slums hadn't a chance. Sitting at the head of the army upon a magnificent stallion was a god of a man wearing bright armor. Though Jackson had never seen the Angel of Justice in person, he had no doubt it was him.

For a moment he couldn't breathe again, and it had nothing to do with his mask game. As if the Angel had summoned a storm for the coming battle, dark, angry clouds formed overhead.

Half on the roof and half on the ladder, Lowen's knee gave out and he almost tumbled off the side. The two men stared in awe, unable to move at first. The Angel and those who were likely his commanders marched their horses to the river's edge where a single soldier stood holding a torch above his head.

The gentle whistle of the cold breeze died as if the world was near its end. The clouds banged together, breaking the silence with an eerie rumble. The soldier holding the torch looked to the Angel and, when the Angel nodded, tossed the torch into the oily green water. The river erupted into a flaming wall that kissed the sky.

The fire parted around the torchbearer as he stepped into the Slaybyrne first. The Angel marched his horse into the water behind him. The fire formed a wall around them as the first line of soldiers stepped forward. The Angel, with the torchbearer at his side, led the soldiers through the muck.

The brilliant light of the blaze made the fog fluoresce. Enthralled, Jackson momentarily lost sight of his mission. Lowen was shouting at him to raise the alarm, but what was the point? Surely the whole Slums could see this. The Angel waded deeper into the Slaybyrne until Jackson couldn't see him past the flames anymore.

Ian arrived with the two archers, Maddy and Marshall. From the ground he shouted, "Jackson."

The awe over the Angel's protecting flames twisted Jackson's tongue. The two archers ascended the ladder as Lowen climbed back onto the roof and out of their way.

Maddy stopped at the top of the ladder and tied her hair back in a tail. Her bow was slung on her back with the bowstring between her breasts. She slipped past Jackson to the edge of the roof next to Marshall.

When Jackson made eye contact with him and nodded, Marshall quickly lowered his head and looked away. The two archers knelt and nocked their arrows as the army plodded across the flaming Slaybyrne. Maddy relaxed the tension on her bowstring and looked over the edge at Ian. "Is it time?" she asked.

"As soon as he's in range," Ian shouted.

Maddy waited until the Angel crossed the midpoint of the river. She nodded. "On three, Marshall. You aim for the Angel; I'll aim for the fire tamer."

He nodded.

"One ..." She drew her arrow back again. "Two ..." With her tongue peeking from the corner of her mouth and one eye squinted shut, she aimed. "Three." She took in a deep breath and held it, as did Marshall. Together, they released their arrows.

The fire tamer never saw it coming. Maddy's arrow struck true in his chest. He stiffened and fell, disappearing below the surface. Marshall's arrow sailed toward the Angel's head. It was the perfect shot. Without looking up, the Angel swatted it away as one would an annoying strand of hair.

"Did your arrows hit their marks?" Ian shouted, unable to see past the flames from his vantage point on the ground.

"Mine did, but Marshall's didn't," Maddy shouted back.

Without the fire tamer, the blaze slowly died around the army as though the man's god had been the only thing keeping the flames alive. It was the moment of truth. The Angel had two choices. He could retreat before the flames were completely extinguished and save his army, or he could continue forward and lose countless men to the grinderfish.

The Angel's army froze in place waiting for new orders as the flames shrank. The Angel looked to his left and right. If the man could know fear, Jackson was sure this would be the time one would see it.

No one moved, a tense silence covering both sides of the river. Thunder rumbled in the distance. Then, a single ripple broke the surface near the Angel's leg. He leaned over his horse's neck and shoved his hand into the water. After a moment, he yanked out a single squirming grinderfish. He held the creature above his head, squeezed the life from it with an angry grimace, and then dropped its limp body back into the water.

Another ripple broke the surface as the flames completely died. The Angel turned toward his nervous men, but before he could give his new orders, churning turbulence exploded around them. Soldiers panicked as the grinderfish attacked their legs. Others were dragged screaming beneath the surface. They wailed and died by the dozens. Their leather armor was no match for grinderfish teeth.

Unwavering, the Angel cupped his hands around his mouth and screamed, "We move forward. If anyone dares retreat, you will be punished severely for cowardice. Push forward, damn you. The only safety is on the other bank."

His commanders on horseback led the way. The Angel's horse screamed and reared back, sending the Angel tumbling from its back. The Angel disappeared beneath the surface. Then he bounced up in time to watch his thrashing horse get dragged under.

The Angel continued forward without pause. His army followed his lead. As the river sludge swirled with blood and rose to his chest, he drew two long blades and held them above the muck. Dozens more of his men fell by the second, but he continued forward, undaunted.

The turbulent water splashed around him as more and more men succumbed to the deadly fish. The Angel miraculously escaped their teeth as if the grinderfish were afraid of him. Occasionally, he'd wince and then drive his blades into the water until the offending creatures around him were dead. And still he pushed forward.

Maddy and Marshall emptied their quivers into the soldiers, but they only had seven arrows each and it didn't take long to exhaust their supply. After that, all they could do was sit and watch with Jackson.

As the Angel neared the bank, the water level dropped back to his waist. He appeared unconcerned about his falling men behind him. A yellow swarm attacked and pulled him under. The water splashed violently.

Jackson watched in awe. It wasn't possible. Had Tristin and Ian's plan worked? Could it be?

After what seemed like an eternity, the Angel's head burst from the surface with a grinderfish between his teeth and one latched on to his cheek. He spit the dead creature into the water and ripped the other one from his bloody face. Countless more dead grinderfish floated around him. His chest rose and fell in angry pants. His face distorted in rage. One of his two swords was missing, the other sporting a grinderfish impaled on the thin blade.

His men continued dying around him, their screams muffled as they were jerked beneath the surface. Despite losing a fifth of his men, the Angel didn't slow. The soldiers fought back, stabbing grinderfish with blades and crushing them with their bare hands, but there were far too many of the creatures to repel.

Ian scanned the crowd of Slummers before shouting up at Jackson. "Where's Tristin? Have you seen Tristin?"

Jackson shook his head. He couldn't believe the Angel had happily sacrificed so many men. The soldiers continued falling, but the rate at which they died seemed to be slowing. The Angel's plan—if it was indeed his plan—was working; for perhaps the first time ever, the insatiable grinderfish appeared to be getting full.

Jackson tried to count the surviving soldiers and realized how deadly the coming fight was going to be. There was no chance the Slummers could win.

Ian waved his hands over his head. "Set the signal fire," he shouted. "Warn everyone that the Angel is coming."

Jackson did as he was told, though he still couldn't imagine how anyone could have missed the river being on fire. Now was not the time to argue.

War was upon the Slums. Jackson said a silent prayer.

Chapter 19

The Battle of Slaybyrne

Tristin knelt near the wall beyond the japsy weed fields. Preparing for battle had mentally exhausted him, and waiting for the Angel to make his move had become unbearable. He needed a few minutes to himself. He used it to properly say goodbye to Shelly at the outer wall where he'd carried her ashes in a cloth-covered porcelain bowl.

Angry clouds had formed overhead, bringing a gentle breeze. Anxious to finish before the irritating rain moved in, he took the cover off the bowl. "Be free for the first time in your life, Shelly. May you find peace in the world you now walk within."

When the breeze picked up, he dumped the ashes into the air. He watched the cloud of ash swirl toward the top of the wall, like her ghost was really seeking freedom. The shifting wind carried some of the ashes back toward the Slums. As Tristin turned to watch, his eyes widened. Shelly's bowl dropped from his hand.

By the gods.

The river was on fire. Tristin called upon his god and blazed toward town. Before he made it to the first line of houses, the flames died and the signal fire was lit. He put on an extra burst of speed, and within minutes he met Ian at Lowen's house.

"Where have you been?" Ian shouted.

Tristin ignored him, trying to get a good look at the river. The Angel and his soldiers were already near the Slummers' bank. "How did they get so far? Did the Angel have someone with a Stealth God like you?"

"No. He had someone with a Fire God to hold off the grinderfish."

Tristin's heartbeat doubled, and not from the run. He watched as his Slummer friends scrambled into a ragtag formation. He hid his trembling hands at his sides, but Ian's subtle glance revealed he hadn't fooled him. Ian held out his own shaky hand to show Tristin that he wasn't alone.

Lowen limped toward the front line without a word. He carried a sword that no one except probably Ian had known he possessed. When he glanced back and saw Tristin staring, he nodded and kept walking.

Tristin's shoulders slouched and his head bowed. "We can't win, Ian."

Ian grabbed his arm. "Don't do that, Tristin. Stand tall. These men are about to go into battle. Don't let them see you already defeated."

"But I'm scared."

"We're all scared. You must stand strong at my side now. Hold your head up high. If we show courage, it will spread amongst our friends. If we show weakness, it'll be equally contagious. Even if we ultimately lose, the alternative is much worse." He released Tristin's arm. "You need to fight alongside us. We need everybody. Use your speed, Tristin. Use your god to his fullest potential."

Maddy climbed down from the roof and stood next to Jackson. She reached down and took his hand. Tristin had never felt as lost as he did staring into their anxious eyes. They needed words of encouragement, but he was afraid anything he said would be wrong.

"Do you remember what you told me your father said on the day he was taken away?" Ian asked.

Tristin nodded, never looking away from the passing men.

"He said you need to take care of Makenna. She could still be alive. If you give up now, she'll surely die. So you have to live today. If things get bad, you run. Run as fast and as far as you can, do you hear me? Don't let the Angel catch you."

He nodded again, slowly this time. Ian was right. Tristin looked to the edge of the Slaybyrne where the Angel approached the bank. A wave of anger replaced his fear.

Ian patted Tristin's shoulder and then marched behind the Slummer defenders. He shouted, "When they make land, push them back into the water. Let the grinderfish be our allies. When the Angel falls, we win."

The first of the Angel's men reached the bank with swords drawn. The Slummers attacked with makeshift spears, clubs, and slings swinging above their heads.

The Angel of Justice stood tall and proud at the edge of the bank as he watched his men engage the Slummers. Soldiers continued pouring from the river.

Tristin drew his knife from his waistband, wishing it were a sword. He gritted his teeth, searching for courage. Then he sprinted toward the enemy.

As he zipped past the first soldier, he sliced the man's sword arm with his knife. It wasn't a fatal wound by any measure, but it sent the stunned soldier's sword to the ground as intended. Tristin shoved his knife back into his waistband and snatched up the sword in a flash. With the sword in hand, he stopped face-to-face with another soldier. Though terrified of feeling the soldier's blade rake his flesh, he stood strong just in case any of the Slummers were watching.

"What are you going to do with that, boy?" the soldier asked.

Tristin held his sword out with trembling hands. The soldier swung his sword. Out of sheer reflex and luck, Tristin deflected it by thrusting his stolen blade in front of his face. Steel met steel, painfully jarring Tristin's sword from his hands. Tristin backed away and pulled out his knife again. The soldier laughed at him.

A chirp from the soldier's mask gave Tristin a nasty idea. Samuel had once told him that a warrior should use his greatest gift when in battle. "No use in saving it for after you're dead," he'd said.

Tristin feinted with his knife as if he was going to throw it. The soldier lifted his sword in defense. Tristin shot past him and snagged the mask from his waist. The metal clasp snapped with ease. Once out of reach, Tristin turned back with the lifemask clutched in his fist. The soldier looked down and then back at Tristin.

"Wait a minute, kid. What are you doing?"

Tristin didn't owe him an answer. With a heave, he hurled the mask into the Slaybyrne and watched just long enough to see it sink between two of the many soldiers still trying to get onto land. The soldier dropped his sword and sprinted after his mask. It was probably already grinderfish food.

Dirt flew into the air behind Tristin's feet as he weaved in and out of the fighting men, snatching mask after mask and hurling them into the Slaybyrne. After eight more men helplessly watched their masks sink into the river, Tristin raced back toward the Slums for a breather.

His first glimpse at how his friends were doing was as horrible as he could have imagined. Slummers either fell with hardly a fight or surrendered in the face of such overwhelming odds. The more soldiers who made it to the bank, the more the odds stacked against them. Anyone who stopped for a lifebreath was quickly overrun and killed. Those refusing to stop for lifebreaths grew too dizzy and ultimately fell to their tainted blood. The fight wouldn't last much longer if something didn't drastically change.

As Tristin stood with his hands on his knees, he saw the Angel towering above the fray. Now, that was a mask worth snagging. The Angel's blade danced and plunged into Slummers, beautifully flawless in its movements and deadly in its aim. No one in his path stood a chance, and he gave them no quarter. As Tristin watched him, he effortlessly unhooked his mask and took a breath without slowing. It was magical how he moved. No one in the world stood a chance against him. No one except Samuel. If only he was still there.

Some of the wounded Slummers moaned while their lifemasks chirped at their impotent sides. Any who stopped to help them met their own painful defeat at the soldiers' blades.

Though Lowen fought valiantly, he fell to his knees beneath the swarm. Tristin took off toward him. Lowen looked over, resignation crossing his face. A soldier shoved a blade into Lowen's back.

Tristin staggered to a stop, his heart breaking for his friends. It was a massacre. He scowled at the Angel's back. He'd never hated anyone as much as he hated him. He saw a path to him. With blistering speed, he charged. It was the fastest he'd ever run.

The Angel's mask dangled from his waist, begging Tristin to take it. Tristin reached out as he cut past the soldiers in a blur. By the time they felt him pass, he was already out of reach. He focused, knowing he would only get one chance. The golden mask was in his sights. He lunged for it.

Gotcha.

The Angel's lifemask was heavy in his grip, but only for a second. The Angel whipped around impossibly fast and grabbed Tristin's wrist. Tristin stopped with a jolt, his arm nearly coming out of the socket. There was no man in the world fast enough to catch Tristin when he used his gift, yet somehow the Angel had done just that. In one fluid motion, the Angel spun Tristin around, forced him to his knees, and grabbed his throat.

"You dare assault the Angel of Justice?" he snarled, anger carving deep ravines in his handsome face. His soldiers circled them in tight formation, removing any hope Tristin might have had of using his gift to escape.

The Angel leaned close, his breath hot in Tristin's face. "Restrain this boy," he said with a creaking voice. Two soldiers grabbed Tristin's arms and jerked him to his feet. The Angel stood up straight, hardly winded, and sheathed his sword.

The battle was over. The remaining Slummers surrendered. One by one, the soldiers lined them up on their knees along the bank.

The Angel sauntered to the first in line and addressed him without taking his eyes from Tristin. "What is your name?" he demanded.

The man hesitated. *Just tell the truth, Cibel,* Tristin pleaded. The Angel waited with patience that came from a lifetime of practice.

"F-F-Franklin," Cibel stuttered.

Tristin cringed. *Damn it, Cibel.*

The Angel tilted his head and studied Cibel's deceitful face. "That is a lie. I saw you steal a sword and use it to strike one of my men. I find you guilty of assaulting a soldier. Since he is not likely to die from his wounds, I sentence you to seventeen years hard labor in the king's prison. In addition, you are to receive ten more years for lying about your name." He paused before adding, "There will always be justice."

Cibel locked his gaze onto the Angel's boots. "I'm sorry, Angel. I didn't mean to lie. I was afraid."

"You should only fear justice if you have aligned against it."

"My name's Cibel. Please, have mercy." Cibel reached for the Angel's boots to grovel, but the Angel stepped away and Cibel's face met the dirt.

The Angel breathed in deep and rubbed his chin. "I believe you this time, Cibel." His eyes lightened. "I've heard your name before. You are wanted for crimes against the king's supply chain. Is that correct?"

Cibel reluctantly nodded.

"Justice never forgets crimes against it, no matter how many years have passed since those crimes were committed. I hereby amend your sentence to life in prison, as it has become obvious that deceit and immorality course through the darkness of your heart in place of blood."

Cibel sobbed into his hands until two soldiers pulled him to his feet and led him toward the edge of the water to start a fresh line.

The Angel moved to the next Slummer. "Your name?" the Angel asked.

"Potius, sir," the man answered.

The Angel searched for truth in the worry lines on his burly face. "I believe you. I do not know of any crimes you have committed, and I did not witness you killing any of my men here today. Though lifting your hand against my men is the same as lifting your hand against justice, I am suspending judgment on that offense. Also, I do not believe you are in command here. Therefore, I do not charge you with harboring the criminals who reside here." He turned to his commanding officers. "Have any of you witnessed anything to conflict with my findings?"

None of them spoke.

"Very well, Potius. You may have indeed committed crimes, but I cannot prove them here today. You will be freed once we cross the Slaybyrne."

Potius hung his head. Freedom under King Searle's rule was no better than prison. Potius was taken aside to start a second line next to Cibel.

Then it was Ian's turn. His left eye was blackened and swollen, and his upper lip was twice its normal size. He knelt as ordered.

The Angel cocked his head. "What is your na—"

"Ian," Ian snapped.

"Oh, yes. You are the one who can cross the Slaybyrne with your god? Very impressive."

Ian glared up at him.

"If not for you, none of these so-called Slummers could have evaded justice for so long. In a way, you have had a hand in every crime committed by these people, including the stealing of masks by this boy." He nodded toward Tristin. "Therefore, Ian, I have a special sentence for you. Instead of death, which is what you deserve, I sentence you to a lifetime of servitude in my army." The Angel's upper lip curled before he spoke again. "You will protect us from the grinderfish or I will kill you and all of your friends. Is that understood?"

Ian turned away.

"Answer me. You can serve me just the same with or without legs. It is your choice."

Ian looked back at the Angel and reluctantly nodded.

"Did any of the horses survive the journey?" the Angel asked one of his commanders.

"Two, sir."

"Prepare one of them for me and tether this man to the other."

As the soldiers pulled Ian up, Tristin whispered, "I'm so sorry, my friend."

Ian's shoulders sagged. "I told you to run and not let him catch you."

The soldiers yanked him away.

The Angel made Tristin watch as he judged every man and woman of the Slums. Some of Tristin's closest friends were sentenced to death, others to prison. Jakodi was one of those sentenced to prison; Maddy was one of those sentenced to death.

When Maddy was sentenced, Jackson hurled a rock at the Angel's head. He missed, but it still got the Angel's attention. "Banish me, too," Jackson shouted.

Maddy hissed, "Stop," but she was too late.

The Angel pondered Jackson's demand. "Very well, if that is your wish. Put him behind his lady friend. They can make the long march together."

Though they took Jackson's freedom, they couldn't take his defiant smile as they led him to the line of condemned. He'd always wondered what was beyond the wall.

Soon, it was Tristin's turn to face the Angel.

"So, we meet again as I promised," the Angel said.

Tristin turned away. What more could the Angel possibly do to him?

"Young Tristin, you have previously been sentenced to death by banishment without your mask. Is there anything I should hear before I carry out that sentence?"

Tristin spoke, but not to the Angel. Instead, he shouted to the Slummers watching from the bank. "I'm sorry, my friends. I only wanted us to be free. Please forgive me and remember me as someone who cared about you all. When you make it to the prison, tell my sister how much I love her and miss her. Tell her how sorry I am to have failed."

The Angel allowed him to finish before asking, "Is that all, boy?"

Tristin nodded.

"Very well. Take this thief of masks away from me."

A soldier jerked Tristin from his knees, jarring Jakodi's watch from his pocket. No one else noticed as it landed in the dirt. Tristin lunged for it, but the soldier yanked him away. It was the only material thing he'd ever valued, and he'd give anything to take it with him to the great beyond.

The soldiers led Tristin to the back of the short line of the condemned, behind Jackson. Each of the six faces looking back at him was like a claw raking his back. The Angel didn't bother binding his hands; there was nowhere left for him to run.

Maddy didn't cry, but her eyes were red. She grinned sadly at Tristin as if to say, "It's not your fault." But that didn't relieve any of his guilt. It *was* his fault. It was all his fault.

The Angel mounted one horse while his second-in-command mounted the other with Ian tethered to its saddle by a long leather strap. "How wide is your god's influence?" the Angel asked.

"I can protect twenty or so people at a time," Ian answered.

"Make it fifty." There wasn't room for arguing in his tone.

With that, the Angel's second-in-command rode to the edge of the water.

"Come back for me when you're done," the Angel ordered.

As the prison-bound Slummers were herded down the bank, a soldier near the rear of the line grew frustrated with Cibel's pace. He shouted, "Hurry up, scum," and slammed Cibel's back with the hilt of his sword. Cibel collapsed with a thud and a grunt. All eyes shot toward them. The soldier froze, instantly realizing what he had just done. He lifted his wide, fearful eyes to the Angel.

The Angel didn't say a word, only studying his man with disappointment.

Two other soldiers hurried over and restrained the offending soldier. He pleaded, "I'm so sorry. I didn't mean it. It'll never happen again. I promise. He was just moving so slow and he gave me a look."

The Angel nodded as though he understood and sympathized. Then he said one word with venom dripping from his tone: "Lashings."

The soldier fell to his knees and the color drained from his face. "No. Please," he begged.

"How many?" the soldier holding his left arm asked.

The Angel shook his hair from his eyes. "Seven. And immediate termination from my service. I do not need men who cannot control their tempers."

Tristin had never seen someone actually become a Terdict.

The offending soldier begged for forgiveness even as the other two soldiers—his friends only seconds before—stripped away his leather armor and clothing to reveal his bare back. They held his arms while a third soldier uncoiled a whip from his kit bag.

Lashings instead of prison was obviously the Angel's way of showing mercy and keeping his soldiers away from the very people they had incarcerated. Still, it didn't seem as though the man was getting off easy. The former soldier wailed with each blow that cut into his flesh. Though the man had been Tristin's enemy only minutes before, Tristin still cringed. He didn't believe anyone should suffer like that.

The Angel spoke again. "There will be only justice."

Tristin was sick of hearing about justice. The former soldier's back was bloody and purple and raw by the end of the seventh lash. Too weak to stand on his own, the other soldiers had to help him into the slimy river behind Ian. His blood sizzled when it hit the water.

The Angel nodded to the soldiers standing behind the prisoners. A dark hood swooped over Tristin's head.

Chapter 20

The Outside

The wind had picked up as Tristin marched toward certain death. The hood's stitching was thin enough that he could see his feet, but thick enough that the cloth sucked against his sweaty face with each breath. Though he couldn't see the Angel, he could hear the constant clop of hooves and jingle of chains behind him. Through all the walking, they never crossed the Slaybyrne which meant they hadn't left the Slums. Were the legendary Gates of Exilium in the Slums all along? That couldn't be.

Eventually, they stopped, and the only sound was the howl of the wind. Tristin's hood was ripped from his head. He winced, his eyes struggling to adjust in the sudden brightness.

The Angel dismounted and stood with the stone wall at his back. He turned to kneel at the base and pressed his palm against it. He closed his eyes, puckering his lips as though he was about to whistle. His voice was like heaven's breath, soothing and hypnotic, a song in a foreign tongue flowing like gentle waves over a mighty ocean. Each effortless word hung in the air, joining the others as though weaving a magical cloth. There was no word that didn't belong with the next and, despite Tristin not knowing the meaning of any of them, they resonated in his bones. Dim light etched a faint outline in the shape of barbarian-sized gates in the face of the wall. The Angel stood up and backed away.

Tristin had heard tales of the Gates of Exilium for most of his young life, though he had never spoken to anyone who had seen them. They were breathtaking.

"The Gates were in the Slums the whole time?" Maddy whispered.

Tristin leaned close. "I don't think so. I think they're wherever the Angel wants them to be."

The faint outline grew so brilliant that Tristin had to squint to keep from going blind. The stones within the outlines faded to reveal a barren stretch of land sick with green fog. Above the magical gates, a beam of light carved innate filigree as though someone were drawing it from inside the stone.

The Angel addressed the prisoners. "For your crimes against King Searle's people, you have been banished to the Outside without your masks. I predict you will not survive the fog creatures long enough to die from the growing toxicity of your blood, but your fate is your fate.

"All who oppose the king's law are given justice. As a demonstration of my mercy I will allow each of you one last lifebreath before you begin your final journey. When your masks chirp, take the deepest breath you are able and then depart these lands forever."

Tristin considered not taking his lifebreath just to spite the Angel's "mercy." He had long ago promised himself he wouldn't beg for his life when his time came, and he was proud of how well he'd held true to his word.

The Angel stood stoically beside the gates and waited as, one by one, the Slummers' lifemasks chirped and they began their journey. A few of them sobbed, a few of them begged, but all of them passed through the gates.

Last was Tristin. He shoved his mask against his face, glared at the Angel with hateful eyes, and took a cleansing breath. Determined not to show the Angel fear, he handed over his mask and stepped through the gates into the wind-swept Outside. The other Slummers had waited for him. The grit pelting his face halved his already poor field of vision to only ten or twenty feet at most.

He looked back to see the brilliant outline of Exilium fade and disappear, leaving only the solid, smooth wall behind. Maddy and Jackson crowded close to Tristin. Jackson wore an unexpected smile.

"Aren't you afraid?" Maddy asked.

His wide eyes took in everything around him. "Not really. Just curious." Calm acceptance masked any fear in his voice.

The Slummers looked to each other for some kind of plan. Their eyes settled on Tristin. He had no idea what to do. He lifted his shirt collar over his mouth and nose and used his forearm to shield his face from the stinging wind. Maddy touched his shoulder.

His sad eyes met hers. "I'm sorry, Maddy. I'm sorry for everything."

"Don't be sorry, Tristin. We made our own decisions. Now we just need to figure out what to do next." She glanced at the wall. "Do you think we could climb it?"

Tristin ran a hand along its smooth, flawless face. He shook his head.

"What about finding another way in?"

"I don't know, Maddy. The only openings are on the river and the sea cliffs, and they're both too far away. I've never heard of any other way through other than the Gates. I didn't even know if *that* was true until today. We could look forever and never find one."

"What abou—"

A low, rumbling hiss lifted above the wind.

"The fog creatures have already found us," Maddy said in a quivering whisper.

As the stories went, the fog creatures weren't troubled by the toxic green fog and had a hunger that rivaled that of the grinderfish. With no swords or masks, Tristin and his friends had few options.

"We have to run," he said.

A Slummer named Reeves stared at him with terror-rounded eyes. "But, Tristin, we can't keep up with you."

"I won't leave you behind. We must stay together. Everyone grab hands. Hurry." They did as he said. Maddy grabbed his hand and Jackson grabbed hers. "Are you ready?" he asked.

Maddy squeezed his hand.

Tristin began to jog, and the others stayed with him stride for stride. The distant hiss turned into grunts and growls that quickly surrounded them, keeping up with them as they ran. Tristin led his friends in one direction until he heard a growl up ahead, and then he darted in another direction.

The last Slummer in line fell to his knees, dragging the group to a halt. Tristin turned back. "Why are you stopping?"

The Slummer lifted his head. "I can't feel my legs." A slimy black blob slithered up his cheek.

Tristin shouted, "It's that creature. Pull it off his face."

As the Slummer closest to him reached for the slithering blob, an eight-legged beast with an upward-curving tail sprang from the fog. The creature's face was round and flat with long, droopy whiskers. It hissed and latched on to the paralyzed Slummer. He screamed as it dragged him into the fog. His cries faded and died. Maddy's sweaty hand tightened around Tristin's.

"Keep running," Tristin shouted, and they started again. He cut left and the others followed. As he ran, he wondered what would be worse—dying from toxic blood or being eaten alive. He immediately concluded he didn't want to be eaten alive. Another Slummer screamed and dropped from the group. Tristin wanted to turn back for him, but another fog creature was already dragging the poor man away.

Tristin shouted, "Don't look back. Just keep running."

An eight-legged shadow shot across Tristin's path and then disappeared. Tristin cut right, away from where it had gone. Another black blob slapped Maddy's arm. Jackson ripped it away and threw it.

With his friends being picked off at will, it was obvious running wasn't the answer. He slowed to a stop.

"Why are we stopping?" Maddy screamed.

"They're slaughtering us. Our only chance is to fight while there are enough of us left to fight."

"Fight?" she cried. "With what?"

"It's our only choice, Maddy. Quick. Everyone form a circle with your backs to the center."

The Slummers did as ordered.

Tristin's mind raced. How could one fight such monsters? "When a creature attacks, help the person next to you. Claw. Bite. Kick. Do whatever you can to protect them." He tried to sound confident even though his knees were shaking. For all he knew, there could be a thousand of them.

Together, they silently waited for the next attack. Maddy's hand trembled in his grip. Or maybe it was Tristin's hand trembling in hers. Jackson gently brushed her cheek with the back of his finger. Though the silence was agony, the sounds of approaching creatures that soon followed were much, much worse. They were everywhere.

Like a flash of black lightning, a mound of legs and scales exploded from the green fog. The creature was fast, almost as fast as Tristin, and it recklessly plowed into the circle. The Slummers fought back, beating and kicking the creature as it latched on to Reeves's shoulder with its teeth. Its tail swatted another Slummer away. Reeves cried out and thrashed as the creature dragged him into the abyss. Tristin released Maddy's hand.

Another creature shot from the fog. Tristin spun toward it and called upon his god. The world seemed to slow between them. Their eyes met. The beast had the eyes of a demon—sunken, black, and soulless. Its head sat snug on its powerful shoulders as though it had no neck.

The creature lunged at Jackson, plowing through the Slummers between them. Maddy grabbed his shoulders and yanked him from its path, but its claw still raked his arm. The creature swung its sharp tail at Maddy. Tristin reached out to shield his friend and blood sprayed from his own forearm. It wasn't a deep wound, but it hurt like fire.

Maddy stumbled from its path. The creature pounced again, smothering her. Snot and spit sprayed through the air. Tristin leaped onto its muscular back and dug his fingers deep into its thick, coarse mane. The creature ignored him and latched on to Maddy's shoulder and neck. She cried out. The creature bucked, flipping Tristin over its head. It whipped a squirmy blob at him from its tail. Tristin rolled out of the blob's path. He turned back in time to see the fog creature violently shaking the life from Maddy.

Jackson cried futilely for the beast to stop. The creature dropped Maddy and rounded on Tristin just as he got to his feet, coming so close he could count its bloodstained teeth. It roared into his face, its breath hot and rank. It swiped its dagger claws at him, but Tristin zipped out of the way. The creature turned back toward Jackson and leaped.

Oh no. Tristin raced toward his friend, but the creature got there first. Jackson grunted and grabbed his stomach. Tristin caught him against his chest as the beast circled around for another pass. He pulled Jackson close while locking eyes with the monster's cruel black orbs. The creature lifted its front two legs. Fresh blood— Jackson's blood—dripped from its black claws and formed globs in the dirt.

Behind Tristin, two more creatures burst from the fog and barreled into the panicking Slummers.

Jackson's strength seeped away with his lifeblood while he struggled to hold his head upright. Despite Tristin's arms around him, he slid to the ground.

"Be strong, Jackson," Tristin whispered as he dropped to his knees. The world erupted into screaming death around him as the others fell to the creatures. The beast that had wounded Jackson so gravely licked the edge of one claw with its colorless forked tongue. And then it backed into the fog and out of sight.

"Come on, Jackson. You gotta stay with me. We gotta run." Helpless, with all his friends being slaughtered around him, *because of* him, he saw saving Jackson as his last chance to redeem himself for all the death he had caused. "Please, please, please," he begged. His eyes blurred with tears.

"You have to run, Tristin," Jackson choked out, his throat filling with blood.

Tristin shook his head. "No, no, no. I can't leave you like this."

"You have to," he whispered so faintly he almost didn't make a sound.

One of the fog creatures scurried closer and Tristin jerked his head around to see the beast drag the last of his dying friends away. He and Jackson were alone now—he, Jackson, and a pack of the deadliest creatures on land.

Jackson whispered, "They're coming, Tristin. You don't have much time."

"No. I'm staying with you."

"You can't. You must use your gift and get away." The pink of his lips slowly faded to a pale bluish hue.

Tristin vowed to stay with him until the creatures came back and finished them both. While he cradled his friend on his lap, Jackson's arms slid off his belly to the ground. "I'm so cold, Tristin."

"I know." He wished he had a blanket to cover him.

"Promise me you'll get away."

He didn't want to get away; he wanted to stay with his friends. To comfort Jackson, he relented. "I will, Jackson. I will."

Jackson's breathing slowed. He stared up as every wonderful thing that made Jackson Jackson slowly faded from his eyes. Before he took his last breath, he smiled as though he had seen something special in the end. Maybe he saw the ultimate unknown that he had always dreamed of seeing. He closed his eyes and breathed out one last breath before his body stiffened and then went limp. Tristin pulled Jackson's face against his chest and sobbed.

He wanted to sit with him forever, the monsters surrounding him be damned. Hidden within the fog, the sounds of their feasting struck Tristin like the cruelest of daggers in his heart. Why hadn't they killed him yet? What were they waiting for? Was it the sport of a chase only Tristin could give?

Two fog creatures stepped from the gloom and flanked him, though they didn't immediately attack. Anger gave his legs renewed strength. He gently lowered Jackson to the dirt and rose to his feet. If they wanted a chase, he would give them one.

The creature on his left snarled, blood-tinged slobber dripping from its jowls. It was close enough to grab him. It sniffed the air. Tristin called for his god as the beast pounced. He dove from the creature's path—straight into the path of the second one. They were proving to be skilled hunters. But Tristin was no ordinary prey. The second creature swiped at his face. He pulled out of reach and felt the wind from its strike whiff past his nose. As he fell to the ground, the creature clamped its teeth on to Jackson's leg. The bones cracked.

Tristin's stomach turned. "Get away from him, you bastard," he screamed, and dove for his friend's hand. "Leave him be." The creature ripped Jackson from Tristin's grip with ease. Tristin lunged for him again, but he was gone in a flash.

Three more creatures burst from the fog, hurling paralyzing black blobs from their tails. Tristin bobbed and spun away. He wanted to fight them all, if for no other reason than revenge, but he had promised Jackson he would run. He didn't know where he would run to, but anywhere was better than there.

He picked a direction and sprinted into the unknown. The fog creatures gave chase. At the start of their pursuit, he didn't know if he *would* be faster, but the more he pushed himself, the more distant their grunts sounded.

Even when he couldn't hear them anymore, he ran. Even as his blood turned toxic in his veins and dizziness assailed him in waves, he ran. Even though he was unable to see where he was going or whether there was ground beneath his next step, he ran. He was determined to keep running until he died from the poisoned air or fell off the edge of the world. He'd never run so far or so fast in his life.

When his fingers started to tingle, his only surprise was in how long it had taken to happen. His last lifebreath seemed a lifetime ago. His thighs cramped, almost sending him sprawling, but he pushed through the pain. He felt as though he waded through porridge. Or the sludge of the Slaybyrne.

Though the creatures had fallen too far behind to catch him, he didn't slow. As he ran, a peculiar thing started to happen. The green fog thinned. Instead of ten or twenty feet, he could see almost as far as he could throw a rock. Maybe he was dying and the toxicity of his blood was playing tricks on his eyes. Or maybe he was already dead. A sharp pain gripped the right side of his chest. He wondered if he had blown out his lung.

His vision flashed black and he stumbled, but he regained his footing and continued on. He pushed his cramped legs past the point of fatigue, past the point of failure. If he was going to die, maybe dying on his own terms would give him solace.

The stabbing pain in his chest ripped into his back with such force it threw him face-first to the dirt. The unforgiving ground scraped his flesh raw before he finally slid to a stop. He tried to push himself up, but his arms quivered and gave out. With his mouth full of grit and his bloody chest and arms burning with raw, exposed nerves, he rolled to his back and stared up at the sky. He had no more fight left to give. He accepted death with an uncomfortable laugh. As he lay staring up at the clouds, he wondered if dying changed how a person saw the world. What else could explain white clouds in a blue sky?

Is this the afterworld? he wondered as his eyelids grew heavy. He licked his desert-dry lips. *Where did the green fog go?*

His vision faded and the world blurred. The darkness overtook him. He heard the sound of teeth clattering and realized it was his own. Shivers rode the waves of cold air across his skin. Sweat drenched his hair. He rolled to his side and curled into a ball. He closed his eyes.

Part Four
A New World

Chapter 21

The Barbarian Kingdom

Days or even weeks could have passed for all Tristin knew. He could not tell the waking world from the sleeping one. While his body waged a war against fever, a vision replaced the darkness in his mind. He saw Makenna, but it wasn't the Makenna he knew. Her face was gaunt and pale and weighted with sadness. She sat by herself in the corner of a lonely gray room with her knees pulled up to her chest. Tristin waved at her, but she didn't see him. It started raining inside the room. She shivered and looked around, her drenched hair matted to her face.

The Angel stepped through the only door and the downpour washed over his smooth skin as he moved effortlessly through the room. Tristin filled with rage at seeing his foe. He squeezed his fists as his eyes pierced the bastard's soul. The Angel drew his fancy sword from its sheath. Then he turned to Tristin with murder in his eyes. Tristin tried to shout, "Leave her be," but his mouth didn't work. Neither did his legs.

Makenna stood up as if in a trance. She walked to the Angel's side and reached for his hand. He lowered his sword. Makenna looked over her shoulder, finally seeing Tristin. She gave him the saddest smile. "Goodbye," she said.

The Angel glowered at him. "There's nothing you can do for her now," He whispered, though his lips didn't move.

He drew his sword back. Makenna lowered her head, defeated. "Look what you've done to me, Tristin."

Tristin sat up as though a fire had been lit beneath him, his eyes wide. Torrential rain pelted him, yet he welcomed the sting because it told him he'd been dreaming. The empty pit in his stomach lingered, reminding him of the nightmare he had just had. He quietly vowed to return to Altenbyrne to free Makenna.

The skin on his arms and right shoulder was tight, stinging, and scabbed over from his fall. He sat in the middle of a vast field, shivering and rubbing his arms. He needed cover before he froze to death. Or drowned. He struggled to his feet, shielded his eyes with his hand, and looked around.

A dull blue glow shone through the downpour in the distance. He stumbled toward it. Each staggering step forward better revealed the source.

A cave.

Shelter.

Warmth.

Tristin reached the cave mouth, the blue glow making his wet skin glisten. He stumbled inside and fell forward. His eyes were heavy.

Tristin rubbed his face and stretched away the kinks from sleeping on the hard cave floor. He sat up. Though his clothes were still damp, he was no longer shivering. He got to his feet and staggered to the mouth of the cave. The two suns had chased away the rain with welcomed heat. He had never seen the suns shining so bright.

He turned around to examine the cave. Hundreds of tiny blue specks peppered the walls, each dimly glowing with the same blue light that emanated from his mask.

His mask.

His hand shot to his empty belt clip. Dread filled his gut and his breaths quickened. How would he live without his mask? He wobbled and put a hand against the wall for balance. *Calm down,* he told himself, but the tingling fingers had already started. He pressed his back to the wall and slid to his rear. He closed his eyes, repeatedly telling himself to be calm.

It could have been mere minutes or even hours before the dizziness subsided. Tristin had no idea. As he sat up and slowly opened his eyes, he pumped his fists to rid himself of the lingering tingle. Once he finally felt close to being himself again, he pushed to his feet and turned back to the crystals.

Mesmerized, he touched one of them. It was coarse and porous. He searched the ground for something to dig them out with and began prying one of them free. He studied it. Could it possibly be the very crystal that lived inside the masks? He squeezed it in his hand. Only days before, such a find would have been worth more than gold. Now it was useless. He stepped back and stared at the glowing wall. If only he could show Jakodi what he had found.

A terrifying howl drifted in the breeze. Tristin rushed to the cave mouth. In the distance, near where he had collapsed, a single fog creature stood before the biggest man he had ever seen. The man had stacks of boulders for arms and stood as tall as the fog creature when it reared back with its four front legs lifted in the air. *A barbarian?*

The behemoth held a sword twice as big as Samuel's. With eyes trained on the creature, the barbarian circled to his left. When he stepped aside, Tristin saw another figure lying face-down and motionless in the dirt. The other figure also appeared to be a barbarian, though far smaller than the swordsman. Tristin wondered if the smaller one was a barbarian child.

The fog creature lunged. The barbarian swung his sword. The creature swatted the blade away and whipped its tail forward, throwing one of its paralyzing blobs. The barbarian's sword plunged into the ground. With his open hand, he swiped at the blob, but missed. It smacked his neck and quickly scuttled under his shirt. He wobbled, turned with a fear-stricken expression, and raced for the barbarian child still flat on the ground. The fog creature crouched. Watching. Waiting.

Two strides away from the child, the barbarian dropped to his knees, his legs no longer working. The fog creature stalked closer.

Panic rose like bile in Tristin's throat. It was no longer an interesting battle he was witnessing, but a budding massacre. He couldn't simply stand by and watch, but he didn't know what he could do against such a lethal beast.

Unless ...

Tristin scanned the field for any other fog creatures. Not seeing any, he called upon his god and tore across the field as the creature stalked closer to its paralyzed prey. Tristin closed the distance fast. Before he reached the barbarians, the creature lifted its head and sniffed the air. Tristin ignored it, focused on the barbarians' only chance to survive. As Tristin neared the child, possibly a boy, he saw the black blob pulsating on the boy's arm. He had one chance. He grabbed the slimy blob as he zipped past and ripped it away. Before it could sink its tiny teeth into his palm, he hurled it as far as he could. The fog creature took notice.

Without slowing, Tristin circled around and sped toward the adult. The fog creature tried to intercept him, but he zagged just out of reach. He was at the barbarian's side as the beast closed in. Blindly, he jammed his hand up the barbarian's shirt and felt around. By luck, he found the blob and ripped it free.

The fog creature pounced. Tristin tossed the blob to the side and dove out of reach. Confused, it turned back toward the stirring barbarian.

Tristin shouted, "Hey," and waved his arms above his head. The beast refocused on him. White froth bubbled from its mouth. *Come get me.* Tristin turned and ran. The creature gave chase. Tristin sprinted across the field and circled back to see if the barbarians had escaped. The child was now standing behind the bigger one, who was once again holding his sword. The barbarian warrior waved Tristin toward him with his blade cocked over his shoulder.

Tristin darted toward him, the hyper-focused fog creature on his heels. At the last second, the barbarian signaled for him to duck. Tristin dropped and slid past on his knees. The barbarian swung his sword just above Tristin's head. A clunk rang out followed by a shriek. The beast hit the ground, the barbarian's sword embedded in its throat. It tumbled violently before settling with its dead eyes trained on Tristin.

The barbarian extended his hand. Tristin's hand disappeared in his massive grasp. With an effortless pull, the barbarian yanked Tristin to his feet. Tristin lifted his eyes to the barbarian's hairy chin. He didn't mean to stare, but he'd never seen such an imposing figure. The barbarian's eyes sat deep beneath his jutting brow. Rough facial hair covered both his top and bottom lip. He licked it into his mouth and played with it for a moment before he spoke. "I am Tolk. Who are you?" His voice was deep and intimidating.

Tristin almost couldn't speak. Finally, he squeaked out his name.

"Are you from the walled kingdom, Tristin?"

Tristin nodded.

"You saved us here today. I thank you."

Tristin bowed his head shyly. Inside, he smiled.

The younger barbarian came forward. He stood as tall as Tristin and was nearly twice as thick. His smooth, childlike face and blue eyes were full of innocence and curiosity. "I'm Darragh Gaal, son of King Oskari Gaal." In his enthusiasm he nearly broke Tristin's hand when he shook it. He turned to Tolk. "Why do you think that creature came out during the day?"

Tolk braced his foot against the creature's body and jerked his sword free. "An outcast, probably. Driven out of the pack. They do that now and again. The hungrier they are, the more reckless they get." His hard, weathered face turned to Tristin. "Where are you staying, boy?"

"I have nowhere to stay."

Darragh piped in, "He can come with us, huh, Tolk?"

Tolk grunted and looked toward the fog. Then he looked in the opposite direction and nodded. "We should go back. It's a little more dangerous out here than I had expected this morning."

Darragh nodded. "Getting killed on my birthday would really irk my father."

"It's your birthday?" Tristin asked.

Darragh smiled. "Yes. Tolk took me exploring west of the fog as a gift." He fished in a waist pouch and held out a brightly colored purplish-and-blue rock. "We found this."

Tristin examined it. "Very nice."

"I have a whole pouch of them. You wanna see?"

He reached for his pouch again, but Tolk interrupted. "You can show him later, Darragh. For now, let's head back."

"How old do you think I am today?" Darragh asked as they walked.

While he appeared large enough to be twenty, Tristin decided to guess a little younger. "Seventeen?"

Darragh snorted. "I wish. I'm thirteen."

Thirteen?

Darragh tripped and stumbled to his hands and knees, just like a gangly human child. Tolk continued walking as if it was a common occurrence. Tristin reached for Darragh's arm. "Are you all right?"

Darragh bounced up and dusted himself off. A slight shade of red colored his cheeks. He answered, "I'm a bit clumsy sometimes. My mother says it's because I'm growing too fast and my coordination can't keep up with my body."

The barbarians' surprising kindness emboldened Tristin to ask the question that had been eating at him since he'd woken up in the cave. "Why don't we need masks out here?"

Darragh gave him a playful shove that nearly knocked him over. "Look around, silly. Do you see any green fog?"

Tristin shook his head.

"The fog doesn't come this far. This air is clean. Fresh."

That seemed impossible. "But I thought the whole world was covered in fog."

Darragh chuckled. As he and Tolk led Tristin across the open land, the ground changed from dirt to patches of thin, green, finger-like plants that reached as high as his knees. There were countless millions of them covering the ground.

Tristin asked, "What are these plants? They don't look like japsy weeds."

"It's called grass," Darragh answered.

"Grass?"

Darragh looked back with a grin. Tolk grunted.

Tristin stepped gingerly into it and it tickled his legs. "Well, I think I like grass." But as interesting as the grass was, Tristin couldn't keep his eyes from drifting up to the sky.

Darragh asked, "Why do you keep looking up there?"

"The clouds. They're so white."

"Of course. That's how they're supposed to look."

The pretty blue sky met the bright green grass at the top of a hill in the distance. Darragh pointed. "That's where we're going."

Tristin had a million questions, but held his tongue. Once at the crest of the hill, Darragh stepped aside, proudly pointing to a sprawling village spanning an area as big as two Slums combined. The village sat within a crater surrounded by a hilly ridge. People as big as Tolk walked the streets.

"We're going down there?" Tristin asked, trying unsuccessfully to hide the nervous squeak in his voice.

Darragh grinned. "We didn't bring you all this way just to look. Come on." Tolk waited at the top of the hill, scanning the field they had just left.

A ten-foot-tall wooden fence wrapped around the entire village. At the bottom of the hill, Darragh led Tristin to a gate where a single barbarian stood guard. His gaze was fixed forward as if Tristin was too inconsequential to warrant his concern or even curiosity. He held a battle axe across his chest, gripped tight in two powerful fists. A sword as long and wide as Tristin's leg hung from his waist. A history of violence was etched into the scars of his weathered face.

He studied the barbarian guard. The skin on his forearms stretched tightly around his rock-hard muscles, his bulging veins like raised trails to his heart. Beneath his broad nose a scar split his upper lip and revealed a gap where a tooth should have been. Once Tristin stood before him, the barbarian guard finally regarded him. Tristin immediately guided his gaze to the ground so as to not appear disrespectful.

"Step aside, Croate," Darragh said, as though he was the behemoth's master.

"Who is this boy with you?"

"He is a friend. He needs shelter and we're going to give it to him. Now, step aside."

Croate did as he was told. Tristin followed Darragh through the gate, giving the barbarian guard a wide berth.

They passed barbarian men, women, and children as they walked through the village. The adults mostly went about their business, but the children stopped whatever games they were playing to gawk.

"Where are we going?" Tristin whispered.

"We're going to meet my father. I wouldn't be much of a host if I didn't introduce you to the king, now would I?"

A barbarian man marched toward them carrying a large covered barrel on his shoulder. Tristin stepped out of his path.

"Good day, Darragh," the barbarian said as he marched past.

"Good day to you, too, Callan."

Callan didn't slow. Darragh called out after him, "Do you know where my father is this morning?"

Without looking back, he answered, "In the fields."

Tristin leaned in. "I can't believe no one's tried to kill me yet."

"What? Why?"

"Because … you're barbarians. I've always been taught barbarians were savage and could never be trusted."

Darragh smiled. "You should already be realizing that not everything you learned in your kingdom is true. In fact, I'd say most of what you know about the world is wrong. You have a lot to learn, Tristin. If the king lets you stay, maybe one day he'll tell you the real history of our banishment from the walled kingdom."

"And if he doesn't accept me?"

Darragh cringed and Tristin's eyes widened. Darragh gave him an ornery grin. "I'm just teasing, Tristin. I'm sure he'll like you just fine."

Though his heart was pounding, Tristin tried to play it off with a forced smile. "I just thought of something. Do you mind being called barbarians? It's not insulting, is it?"

Darragh gave him a funny look. "Why would we mind? Do you mind being called human?"

Tristin shook his head.

"Well, there you go."

On their way to the fields, a strange four-legged creature much smaller and rounder than a horse ran squealing past Tristin's feet. Tristin jumped out of the way. Three giggling children raced by after it.

"What was that?" Tristin cried.

Darragh laughed. "That was a pig. They're playing a game called chase the ghost. They'll never catch him."

"What's a pig?"

"That thing that just ran by."

"No. I mean, what's it do?"

"It makes something delicious called bacon."

"How's it make bacon?"

Darragh patted his shoulder. "You don't wanna know."

Tristin tried to get another look at the pig before it ran out of sight, but it was already too late. He could still hear the children laughing.

Darragh and Tristin arrived at the field soon after. The plants in the field were similar to japsy weed in size and shape, but the leaves were thinner and appeared much more delicate. They sprouted in meticulously managed rows in the dirt.

Barbarians pushed carts between the rows and dug out the roots of the plants. The roots were orange and oddly shaped. As Tristin looked closer, he realized they were actually carrots—large, plump carrots. Though he had eaten carrots many times, he'd never seen them growing from the ground.

The barbarians filled the carts with more carrots than Tristin could eat in a week. Once a cart couldn't hold anymore, they pushed it along the path toward Tristin and Darragh.

"Why were the carrots in the ground?" Tristin whispered.

"Because that's where they grow," Darragh answered.

"But nothing grows in the ground but japsy weed."

"Again, not everything you think you know is true. Remember the grass? All sorts of stuff grows in the ground, just not where you're from."

"Then how do the Richies have them?"

"Richies?"

"The rich people in Altenbyrne. They get all kinds of food."

"There'll be plenty of time for questions later. Just take a deep breath and relax." As a barbarian with a cart passed, Darragh reached in and snatched one of the carrots. "You have a lot to learn, Tristin." He wiped the dirt off with his shirt and then handed the carrot to him.

Tristin took a big, crunchy bite. It wasn't wrinkled like every other carrot he'd ever eaten. "What else grows out here?" he asked with his mouth full.

"You have no idea." Darragh surveyed the field again until he saw who he was looking for. "There," he said, and pointed toward a couple of men bending over a row of carrots. "Come on."

Tristin followed him along one of the paths between the knee-high plants. He finished his carrot, already craving another.

Darragh stopped him with a hand on his chest. "Wait here. I'll fetch my father."

Tristin looked around, expecting to see one of the barbarians sitting on a throne being carried by his subjects or overseeing the day's work in a fancy robe, but there was no one like that. Instead, Darragh approached one of the dirt-stained, sweat-drenched workers. The man stopped digging and rested his shovel against his hip when he saw Darragh. A thick braid hung down to the small of his back. Two smaller braids hung from both sides of his square chin to his chest. His fists were anvils. He leaned down to Darragh and smiled while he spoke. Tristin was too far away to hear what was said, but he had an idea when they both looked at him. Tristin fidgeted while nerves gnawed at his insides. After a moment, the man stood up straight and waved for Tristin to come to him.

Tristin bowed his head and complied.

Darragh said, "Tristin, I'd like you to meet my father, King Gaal." Tristin felt the king's narrow eyes studying him. "Father, this is Tristin."

King Gaal wiped his calloused hand on his pants and extended an offer for a shake. Not knowing if he should bow or kneel before taking the king's hand, Tristin froze.

Darragh continued, "I found him near the fog. Well, he found us, really. He's from the walled kingdom."

"Is that so?"

Tristin nodded. "Yes, sir," he answered, barely loud enough to be heard over the sound of his own beating heart.

"Well, Tristin, you don't carry a lifemask. How is it that you escaped the fog alive?"

Still staring at the ground, Tristin answered, "I just ran, sir."

"You ran?"

Darragh blurted, "He's fast. I mean, reeeally fast. I think he could beat our horses in a race, even."

"Is that so? How are you so fast, Tristin?"

Tristin shrugged. "I … I have a god that gives me great speed."

"A god, huh?" Gaal stroked his chin. "Those are rare."

Tristin didn't know if he should say anything, so he stood quietly.

Darragh's face brightened. "He saved my life. Tolk's, too."

Gaal's brow creased. His eyes fell back on Tristin. "You saved my son's life?"

Tristin wilted under his stare. He felt he should answer, but didn't want to sound boastful. "I mean … Your Majesty … I guess I just tried to help."

"He did more than help, Father. We got surprised by a fog creature. He ripped the leeches off us just before the creature got us. Then he led the creature into Tolk's sword like this. Blam." He enthusiastically re-enacted the whole story as he spoke. "It was incredible."

The king tilted his head slightly. "You did that, Tristin?"

Tristin nodded.

"Well, I am in your debt, young one." He bowed slightly.

Tristin bowed in return.

Gaal paused, twisting one of his beard braids. Then he said, "Welcome to my little kingdom, young Tristin. Have your travels built you an appetite?"

Tristin nodded.

"Very well. Darragh, show Tristin to a place he can stay and get cleaned up. Then get him something to tide him over until dinner. Tristin, I would like for you to join me tonight. I'd love to hear how the walled kingdom is faring these days."

"Of course, Your Majesty."

"Call me Oskari. We're all friends here."

Tristin imagined he'd never call him anything other than King or Your Majesty.

Gaal straightened and looked to the other workers in the field. "Now, if you'll excuse me, I have much work still to accomplish today."

Tristin swallowed hard before speaking again. "Is there anything I can help with, Your Majesty?"

Gaal cracked a grin. "No, thank you, Tristin. I'm sure there is a lot that Darragh would like to show you." With that, he turned and went back to digging up carrots.

Tristin looked at Darragh.

His smile glowed. "He likes you," he said.

For the first time since entering the barbarian village, Tristin could breathe again.

Chapter 22

The Lies of the "Truth"

As Tristin and Darragh shared some leathery meat the barbarian kid called "jerky," they made their way to where Tristin would stay. The jerky was tough but quite tasty. It left him terribly thirsty, though.

Darragh led him to the door of an empty house. "This is yours for as long as you choose to stay. Go inside and get cleaned up. I'll be out here when you're done."

The house was clean and sparsely furnished. A water pump stood next to a wash sink large enough for him to bathe in. The water that gushed into the sink was so clear he cupped his hands and took a sip to wash down the jerky. He grabbed a towel hanging from a hook and scrubbed his face. A piece of reflective metal over the sink helped him get all the dirt and grime. He was surprised to see his jawline sported a poor, patchy excuse of a beard and his upper lip was partially hidden by a narrow line of soft blond whiskers. He desperately needed a shave, but he would need a blade first. And someone to show him how, since his father never had the chance.

His ratted, wild hair also needed work. He dunked his head into the chilly water. Using his fingers, he worked out some of the tangles, though getting all of them would probably take a month. Eventually, he gave up on what was left and flattened his hair to his head with his palms. He parted the straggly strands over his eyes like his mother used to do when he was little.

As he worked, he caught a glimpse of his overgrown, green-stained fingernails. They were almost as long as Makenna liked to keep her nails. He grabbed the wet cloth from the sink and scrubbed at his nails until the skin along the edges grew raw. No matter how hard he scrubbed, he couldn't clean away the stains. Maybe they were permanent. He lowered his hands back to the sink and looked into the reflective metal again. This time, instead of seeing his own reflection, he saw Makenna's. He touched the reflection and whispered, "I'll find a way back to you even if I have to fight the Angel myself. I swear."

The door opened and Darragh stood in the doorway. "How are you doing?" he asked.

Tristin ducked his head. "I'm all right." Not wanting Darragh to see his wet eyes, he didn't turn around. "I'll be out soon."

Darragh backed out and pulled the door shut.

Tristin took a deep breath, wiped his eyes with the towel, and then joined Darragh outside. The barbarian prince sat beside the door on a large rock that had been chiseled into a seat. "You look sad," he said.

"I *am* sad."

"Why? You're free of the walled kingdom now."

"No, not really."

"What do you mean?"

"My sister, my father … if he's still alive … all my friends are in King Searle's prison. And it's all because of me."

"What did you do to put them there?"

"I was stupid. I angered the Angel of Justice. And I practically presented my sister to him."

"I'm sure you didn't mean to do any of that."

Tristin looked up. "Of course not."

"Then, why are you so hard on yourself?"

"Because it's all my fault."

"I'm sure your sister and friends don't blame you."

"It doesn't change how stupid I've been."

"All you can do is try not to make the same mistakes again. Try not to be stupid."

"That's what my sister used to tell me."

He grinned. "She sounds smart. Tell me about her."

"Where to start?" The first image that came to mind was Makenna smiling. "Well, she's my twin, so she's stunningly good-looking." He smirked at his own joke, though Darragh didn't laugh. "She is kind and gentle. And a bit sarcastic. Sometimes she drives me insane. But if there's anything good in me, my sister has it ten-fold. Everything I've gone through in this world, I've had her by my side. She's not only my sister, but my best friend." As he talked about her, a long-forgotten memory crept into his thoughts. "When we were little, I used to hide her things to tease her. But this one time I took it too far. She had this pendant on a chain that our mom had given her. It was the most god-awful shiny brown stone with puke-green gems around it. My mom said it had been passed down in her family for generations, but that didn't mean much to an eight-year-old boy. I mean, it was hideous. Anyway, it was Makenna's most precious treasure that she made me promise to never touch. Of course, that's the first thing I did."

As the rest of the memory played out in his mind, he stopped talking and looked up to the sky. Darragh sat quietly.

Tristin finally continued, "You know, I had forgotten about that pendant until just now. I hid that damn thing so well that when she finally noticed it was gone weeks later, I had forgotten where I had put it." He chuckled to keep from crying. "I remember she was so mad at me. She told our father and he reddened my rear but good. I don't know how she forgave me, but she did. That's why she's a better person than I'll ever be. I don't think I could have forgiven her so soon if she had done the same thing to me."

Darragh stood up and patted Tristin's back. His hand was as heavy as Samuel's. As Tristin stood, something amazing happened. He saw that ugly pendant sitting in a knothole in the rear wall of the general store near his home. He shook his head. "It's in the store," he mumbled.

"What?" Darragh asked.

"The pendant. I just remembered where I hid it. After all these years. I wonder if it could possibly still be there …" He trailed off. After a pause, he said, "I'll have to look for it when I go back for her."

Darragh frowned and cocked his head. "I'm sorry, but you can't go back. There's no way without a lifemask. And even if there was, the Angel would kill you. My father told me about him. Even the greatest barbarian warriors couldn't defeat him during the Battle of Slaybyrne River."

Tristin just shook his head. Darragh didn't know about Samuel.

"You're free now, Tristin. I know it's hard to see right now, but you have to accept that sometimes people are lost to us."

"No. I'll never accept that."

"You don't have to accept it for it to be true."

Tristin started to argue, but he was interrupted by a barbarian he hadn't yet met limping around the corner of the house. Darragh greeted him. "Baird. Welcome back."

The barbarian grunted. They seemed to like grunting for answers. Not being as large as Croate or Gaal did nothing to lessen Baird's intimidating effect. His face hid behind savagely overgrown blond whiskers and big, bushy blond eyebrows. His mane was nearly as yellow as the grinderfish and hid the tops of his shoulders.

"How were your travels?" Darragh asked.

He poked his lower lip out slightly and blew feathered bangs from his eyes. "Productive. I finally made it around the fog to the southern shore." His voice was smooth and surprisingly soft.

"Could you see the land spoken of by the foreign travelers?"

"I'm afraid not. All I could see was water."

Baird regarded Tristin. "Who is this? He looks like an Altenbyrne lad."

"He is. His name is Tristin."

Tristin stood with his eyes level with Baird's chest.

Baird sneered. Ignoring Tristin, he said, "King Gaal sent me to retrieve you. He is ready for your birthday feast. You shouldn't keep him waiting."

"Are you joining us tonight?"

He shook his head. "I have not seen my wife or son in more than three weeks. I will spend this evening with them."

After their goodbyes, Darragh led Tristin to his home.

By outward appearances, the house wasn't much different than any of the others, except twice as big. Above the oversized doorway was a carving of a crooked battle axe flanked by three small circles on each side.

Darragh burst through the door.

Tristin followed him. Gaal stood next to a table covered with nearly every kind of fruit imaginable. Decorating the wall behind him was a broadsword hanging from a hook next to a shield that stood as tall as Tristin. Both were dusty.

The king held a hand toward the table. "Tristin. Welcome. Have a seat."

Tristin looked to Darragh for guidance as to which chair he should choose. Gaal answered for him. "Your seat is at the head of the table, Tristin. You are my guest, after all."

Tristin felt awkward taking the seat at the head of the table, but he didn't want to offend the king. With an encouraging nudge from Darragh, he climbed into the oversized wooden chair.

"Is our guest here?" a woman's voice called from one of the other rooms.

"Yes, dear," Gaal replied.

A barbarian woman waddled into the room. She was short by barbarian standards, round, and full of life. She almost glowed as she hurried to the table. "Well, hello there, young man," she said. Her face brightened as though meeting new people was the rarest and sweetest of treats. Three wild hairs grew from her chin and several more from a mole on her upper lip.

Tristin scrambled from his chair to greet her. Though she was smaller than the other barbarians, she was still bigger than he. "My name is Merletta. It's nice to meet you." She sat in a chair next to the king's. A younger girl hurried in behind her. Her auburn hair was tied into twin tails on either side of her head. She stood as high as Tristin's chest.

"Are you from the walled kingdom?" she asked.

Tristin nodded.

"What's your name?"

"Tristin. What's yours?"

Darragh answered before she could. "This is my annoying little sister, Aoife. Ignore her."

She glowered at her brother.

"How old are you, Aoife?" Tristin asked.

"Ten."

Woah. She's nearly as tall as me.

Gaal tapped her shoulder. "Take your seat. You can visit with Tristin later. Right now I'm hungry."

"But, Daaad …"

Gaal's face hardened, shadowy eyes darkening beneath his creased brow. She knew the look. She bowed her head and mumbled something under her breath as she took her seat. Gaal carried a steaming platter from a smaller table and placed it among the fruits. The platter held what appeared to be a horse's hind leg.

"Have you ever tasted cooked animal meat before, Tristin?" Gaal asked.

"Only what Darragh gave me earlier. Jerky, I think he called it. It hurt my stomach a little."

"That's because your stomach isn't used it. I imagine you'll grow to appreciate it."

Tristin studied the platter. "Is this from a horse?"

Gaal chuckled. "No, no. We don't eat horse meat. We find the creatures too majestic and useful for slaughtering."

Reasoning that a creature could be eaten based on its attractiveness seemed odd to Tristin, but who was he to argue?

Gaal continued. "Actually, this is meat from a fog creature." Tristin didn't realize he'd made a sour face until the king added with another chuckle, "Hold your judgment. I know it sounds disgusting, but those creatures are very nourishing once you cook the toxins out of them. If you know how to prepare one just right, the taste can be exquisite."

Darragh sat next to his mother and tore off a piece of meat. He set it on Tristin's plate before grabbing a chunk for himself. With all eyes on him, Tristin hesitantly raised it to his nose and sniffed. Though he was uncomfortable being watched, he gingerly took a bite. Gaal, Merletta, and Darragh all waited for his reaction while Aoife shoved a piece into her own mouth, unconcerned with him. Though he was reluctant to admit it, the taste was incredible.

Gaal asked, "Is it too salty?"

Tristin took another bite, hardly waiting for the first to clear his throat. "It isn't too anything. It's perfect." Rich, succulent juices oozed over his tongue to mix in his saliva with every bite. He'd be in danger of drooling were he not so acutely aware of his manners.

Gaal grabbed a meaty bone and ripped away a piece of meat with his teeth, far less cautious than Tristin. With his mouth full, he started the dinner conversation.

"Tristin, this time is yours. What would you like to know about our life here outside the walled kingdom?"

Without hesitation, Tristin asked, "Is there any way back?"

The king stopped chewing and squinted with one eye. "You have just reached freedom. Why would you want to go back?"

Tristin stuffed another chunk of meat into his mouth before answering. "My sister is still there. As is my father and all my friends. They're locked away in the prison and I fear for their safety."

Gaal held his fist in front of his mouth while he finished chewing. His previously jovial expression faltered slightly. In a more considered tone, he said, "There's no way into the kingdom without new lifemasks and an army. Neither of which you have, young man."

Tristin wasn't deterred. Though the king's mood had suddenly turned serious, Tristin didn't get the sense that there was anger behind it. "Didn't your people live in the kingdom once?"

"Aye," Gaal answered with a nod.

"And you've never wanted to return?"

Gaal grunted and shoved another bite into his mouth.

As far as Tristin was concerned, a grunt wasn't a "no." He decided to press his luck. "Your Majesty, I have heard that some of your people might still be alive in the prison where my sister is now." He cringed, praying he hadn't offended his host with his forwardness.

"That is true. But even if there was a way to return, we couldn't defeat the Angel and his army. They're too powerful."

The flow of the conversation, as well as the king's openness to engage in it, gave Tristin the courage to broach a topic he'd planned to reserve until he had better earned his welcome. A barbarian army was just what he needed to help his sister and his friends, but he needed to play it smart. *Don't be too aggressive,* he told himself. Asking a king to potentially sacrifice his entire kingdom for someone he'd just met was foolish at best. That didn't mean he couldn't plant a seed, though. "How do you know you couldn't win?"

"Because the Angel defeated my people once when we were driven out of Altenbyrne, and we were much stronger back then."

"The Angel really was in that battle? He's been around that long?"

"Aye. He is beyond natural."

"May I ask how old you are, King?"

"I'm 117 years old." He paused and scratched his head. A tiny black creature about half the size of Tristin's pinky nail scrambled away from Gaal's fingers, but he chased it and picked it from his hair. "Damn bloodsuckers," he mumbled before squashing it against the table with his thumb.

Tristin had never seen a creature so small.

"We were forced from our homes," Gaal continued, wiping his thumb on his trousers. "I—"

"Did you live in the Slums west of Slaybyrne?" Tristin blurted, too excited to stop himself.

"I do not know 'Slums,' but our home was indeed west of the Slaybyrne."

"How was it that you lived there? I mean, what did you eat? Japsy weed?"

"We ate all kinds of food. Fish from the river and the ocean. Eggs from our chickens. Meat from our animals. But mostly we ate what we grew."

"I don't understand."

"What don't you understand?"

"Everything. How did you grow food in the fog?"

Trying to cut his potato, Darragh somehow managed to push it off his plate. It thudded onto the floor and rolled under Tristin's chair.

Aoife shook her head and mumbled, "Muggins."

"Aoife," Gaal snapped.

"What? He's always dropping things."

Gaal sighed. He looked to his wife. "Maybe I should just start at the beginning. I think he'll better understand, don't you?"

Merletta nodded. Tristin sat quietly, all but forgetting his meal.

Gaal cleared his throat. "When I was very young, before the fog came, we had a thriving relationship with the king of your people. There was an old stone bridge that spanned the river and we crossed it at will, sometimes living as much with your people as we did with our own. When I was about Aoife's age, I used to swim in the river with the human children. That was before it was green and infested with those cursed grinderfish."

Tristin had a hard time imagining anyone playing in the Slaybyrne.

"Our warriors even helped your people to push back foreign invaders long ago. We don't know where they were from, but they came to conquer us."

"The ones whose wizard created the fog?"

Gaal snorted. "Well, someone started the fog."

Tristin cocked his head. "But not a wizard?"

Gaal waved off the question and continued his story. "It was during that war that the Angel first appeared. He slaughtered the enemy soldiers almost single-handedly and probably saved the kingdom. I was maybe nine.

"When our warriors returned, the Slaybyrne had already turned green. I remember the gritty bitterness that constantly coated my tongue after the fog arrived. It didn't leave until I reached this place. My grandfather, who was our village leader at the time, banned everyone from the water until the intellectuals could determine the cause. Soon after, the fish started dying and floating to the surface. The fish that didn't die were … changed. They became what you know as the grinderfish. This vicious new breed seemed to thrive in the very gunk that had so potently killed everything else.

"The fog got worse and worse. All our crops except the japsy weed died, slowly at first. Next was our chickens, followed by our horses and cows. Our elders repeatedly met with the king to offer assistance, but he insisted finding a solution was his responsibility and our intellectuals would only get in his way. That was when my grandfather grew ill. He would be the first of many. With his breathing growing more and more labored every day, and his strength steadily waning, my father took me across the bridge to see if there were any doctors east of the Slaybyrne who could help him.

"That was the first time I saw what came to be known as a lifemask dangling from some of the rich people's belts. There were people lying dead or dying on the streets and it saddened me. That's also when I saw my first grinderfish funeral. The doctors said there was nothing they could do. Nothing helped but the lifemasks, and those were still in short supply.

"With more and more of our people growing ill, my grandfather invited the king to a meeting in our village. Using all his remaining strength, my grandfather negotiated a deal. The king would supply our people with lifemasks in exchange for our free labor.

"With those masks, the sick quickly improved, and even those of us who hadn't fallen ill could feel a difference. And from that moment on, we, as your people still are, were slaves to the king's masks."

Tristin leaned forward, immersed in the story. "Is that when your war with the king started?"

"Not quite. At that point, our animals were dead, the Slaybyrne was completely devoid of edible fish, and our fields were barren of all but japsy weed. Plus, we had accepted a labor agreement that was too strict for us to possibly honor to the king's satisfaction. We had no choice but to start relying on the king to keep us fed. Yet we no longer had anything to trade. We were so hungry and scared that we never questioned where *he* got the food.

"The king was not as generous with his food as he had been with his masks. If not for the japsy weed, we would have starved before the end of the first winter. The adults of my village began taking additional jobs working for the rich people, but even twenty-hour workdays weren't enough. Payment was thin, to say the least. To this day, I remember the pain in my father's eyes when he returned home each night with less and less food."

Images of Tristin's own father crowded his thoughts and lingered.

Gaal drank from a large tankard, spilling some of the brown, sudsy contents onto his beard. He wiped it away with his forearm. "My grandfather repeatedly met with the king in hopes of improving our food supply, but the king grew increasingly agitated and obstinate until he stopped meeting with us altogether.

"We lived like that until my grandfather's lifemask started acting strange and he grew ill again. Our elders appealed to the king for one more meeting. To our surprise, he agreed. Though my grandfather was too weak to attend, he hand-picked the delegation that would represent us. My older brother and several other young ones went with them as pages.

"At that meeting, the king accused our representatives of treachery and locked them in his prison without a trial. When we protested, he declared our people terrorists and severed all aid to us.

"The men of our village were angry, wanting to invade the kingdom and take whatever we needed to survive, but my grandfather restrained them with words of peace and patience. It wasn't until his mask failed completely and he died that my people had had enough."

"Our leaders sent our small army over the bridge to meet the king's soldiers on the eastern bank. They were waiting for us as though they had been planning a fight for a long time. Though we were under-equipped and outnumbered, our warriors battled hard and drove the king's army into the town. The bloody battle lasted six days and six nights and our victory seemed certain. Our leaders vowed not to stop until we reached the prison and freed every barbarian the king had taken, including my brother.

"We were so close to breaking them when *he* arrived."

Darragh fidgeted in his chair as if he'd heard the story a thousand times.

Tristin said, "The Angel."

"Yes. But he wasn't the same young, promising soldier who had annihilated the invaders. He was different. Detached. Deadly. He slaughtered many of our best fighters with ease.

"Despite the wrongs the king had already committed against our people, he called us the aggressors. With our soldiers falling in droves, they had no choice but to lay down their weapons else we all would have been run down and slaughtered. With the war ended so abruptly, the king's soldiers marched into our village and rounded up the rest of us.

"The Angel sentenced my people to banishment. He opened the Gates of Exilium, proclaimed himself merciful for allowing us to keep our masks, and banished us into the harsh Outside. I was terrified. The last thing I heard the Angel say was to destroy the bridge after the last of them crossed the Slaybyrne.

"The Outside was almost as horrible as the battle with the Angel had been. We were immediately attacked by the fog creatures. They killed many of my people, including my father, before we managed to fight our way out of the fog."

Gaal seemed to take an extra bit of pleasure in chewing a fresh mouthful of fog creature meat. After a satisfying swallow, he added, "We were not all that surprised to discover the king had been lying about the fog covering the whole world, but after the way the people of Altenbyrne treated us, we had no desire to even attempt to expose him. In the end, we simply started walking and eventually settled here where we live free to this day."

Tristin spoke up. "You say free, but your brother and the others from your village may still be in the prison."

"As you are already learning, Tristin, freedom has a price."

Tristin refused to accept that his sister's life was the price he'd pay for freedom. Nothing in the world was worth that. As a thousand thoughts rushed through his mind, one in particular came to the fore. "You said the old king lied about the fog covering the world. Does that mean the current king knows it's not true?"

Gaal smiled grimly. "Yes. I imagine your king does know how far his fog reaches."

Tristin scowled. "I don't understand. Why wouldn't he lead his people away from the fog if he knew?"

"To preserve his dominion like his father and grandfather before him. Though the wall was originally built to protect the kingdom from outside invaders, it now serves to keep you in. Your people cannot leave, and they dare not rebel. People of fear, my friend, will never rise up, while people of truth will never remain slaves."

Tristin took a moment to process this new information, staring blankly at his plate. Then he had a thought. "Do you still have the masks?"

Gaal shrugged as he refilled his tankard from a pitcher. "We have a few."

"Do they still work?"

"Well, that I don't know. Ever since we left the fog, they haven't made a sound, so I don't imagine they do. Why do you ask?"

"I was just curious," he said a little too quickly.

The king drained his tankard, letting a good bit dribble into his beard again. Then he pushed away from the table and stood up. "Just curious, huh?"

Tristin climbed from his chair and knelt beside the table.

"That is not necessary here."

Tristin slowly stood. The sheer size of Gaal still startled him. He looked up into the king's shadowy eyes. The king smiled.

Chapter 23

Small Tastes of a New World

For the first time in Tristin's life, he slept in a bed like a Richie. Darragh said the bed was stuffed with feathers. Though Tristin had never felt "feathers" before, he now knew they were soft and wonderful. He must have been more exhausted than he realized because when he'd gone to bed it was evening and when he opened his eyes again the suns were shining bright through the window.

For the briefest of moments, he forgot where he was, convinced his family was waiting for him in the next room. He stretched with a groan and sat up, his reality painfully returning.

A strange smell piqued his interest and pulled him from the bed, still in his clothes from the night before.

In the main room, Darragh had lit a cooking fire and was holding a skillet full of yellow and white mush over the flames. "Good morning, Tristin," he said.

"Good morning."

"Are you hungry?"

He was in fact starving.

"I'm cooking eggs. Have you had them before?"

Tristin shook his head.

"Well, they come from chickens. They're quite tasty." He handed him a bowl and a fork.

Tristin had yet to see a chicken and had no idea how the fluffy mush could "come from" one. Thinking back on the pigs and bacon question, he decided not to ask.

"Eat up. We have a busy day today. I have a lot to show you."

If where the barbarians kept their old masks was part of the tour, Tristin couldn't wait. Darragh sat across from him and watched him eat. Like everything the barbarians had fed him, the eggs were delicious. He finished and set the empty bowl on the table. Unbelievably, for the second time in two days his hunger was more than satisfied.

"Are you ready to go?" Darragh asked.

Tristin nodded and followed Darragh outside.

Two barbarian children were playing a game of tag out front. When they saw Tristin, they stopped and stared. Tristin gave them a slight wave. The children shyly waved back and then ran off, giggling.

As Darragh and Tristin walked through the village, some of the barbarian men nodded and a few even said "good morning" as though Tristin had lived there all his life.

Croate was guarding the main gate like he had been when Tristin first arrived. He smiled with crooked, gapped teeth when he saw Darragh. Everyone seemed to smile when they saw the future king.

"Where are you off to today?" Croate asked.

"We're headed to the forest. If you see Tolk, will you let him know so he can join us?"

"I most certainly will."

Tristin politely nodded as he passed. The barbarian's smile soured, and he grunted and turned away. Tristin was determined to be as nice to Croate as possible until the grumpy guard had no other choice but to be cordial in return.

"What's a forest, by the way?" Tristin asked as he and Darragh climbed the hill.

"It's where the trees grow."

Tristin's school lessons had told of trees, but short of crude drawings passed down from an earlier generation, he'd never seen one. "Do you think your friend will join us?"

"Tolk? Oh, yes. Of course he will. It can be dangerous in the forest and my father doesn't like for me to travel far from the village on my own."

Tristin looked over his shoulder at the village, but there wasn't anyone coming that he could see.

"Don't worry. We probably won't even know he's with us. He'll stay back for the most part."

Tristin wondered how inconspicuous someone as large as Tolk could be.

They walked along the top of the hill until Tristin saw a distant, seemingly endless line of trees that vaguely resembled the drawings that his teachers had shown him.

"That's a forest," Darragh said.

Tristin glanced back at the barbarian village and then over the vast field that led to the forest. "It'll take us a day to get there."

"Nonsense. It's not as far as it looks. Especially if we run." When Darragh said "run," he pushed Tristin backward and started down the hill as if in a race. He'd have better luck racing the wind.

Tristin gave chase, careful not to use his god since that would be cheating. Well, not all his god. Just like with the other Terdict children when he was growing up, he balanced not cheating with not losing. Tristin had never run down such a steep hill before and his feet moved faster on the uneven ground than his balance could keep up with. Unable to slow his momentum, his foot landed awkwardly and he tumbled end-over-end. His breath grunted from his chest with each painful impact until he slid to a stop on his face near the bottom. He spat out dirt and grass and rolled onto his back.

Darragh landed on his face beside him. Tristin sat up. "You are clumsy, aren't you?"

Darragh shrugged. "You're lying next to me. What's your excuse?"

"I've never run down a hill like that before."

"Hmph."

Tristin assessed whether he was injured or not, ultimately deciding he was fine. As he started to get up, he let his hand linger in the soft grass. He couldn't get enough of it. "Is grass alive like japsy weed?" he asked.

"Of course. Things are alive all around you. Those trees, the creatures living in the forest. Everything. There are even creatures smaller than your fingernails living in the ground under your feet."

Tristin lifted his foot for a look. He didn't see anything.

"Unlike where you're from, this world is more about life than death." Darragh looked toward the forest. "Can you still run?"

"Faster than you."

"Really?" Darragh gave Tristin another shove backward and took off for the trees. He was a good cheater.

Since Darragh had cheated twice, Tristin decided using his god wouldn't be such a bad thing. He raced past his barbarian friend and tapped his shoulder as he zipped by.

"No fair," Darragh shouted.

Tristin didn't slow until he reached the edge of the forest. By the time Darragh caught up, he had already regained his breath and was studying the closest tree. He dragged his fingers across the rough grooves and then pressed his cheek to them just to see how it felt against his face. "It's amazing."

"It's just a tree," Darragh answered.

"What does it do?"

"What do you mean, 'what does it do'? It grows."

"But for what?"

Darragh leaned against the tree, facing him. "In this world, things just live for no reason."

Tristin picked up a leaf and took a bite before Darragh could stop him. As he chewed, he made a sour face.

"Not every plant is edible like the japsy weed," Darragh said. "If it's not on the dinner table, you'd better ask if it's okay before you eat it. You haven't eaten any grass, have you?"

Tristin spat the chewed-up leaf out of his mouth and shook his head.

"Good. Don't. It probably won't hurt you, but it's only good for grazing animals." Darragh retrieved something from the ground.

"See this?" He held out a green, fist-sized fruit and gave it a slight squeeze. "Study it good. This is a costa fruit. Never eat one. They're poisonous. Especially the root." Darragh tossed it aside.

As the barbarian prince gave an impromptu lecture on which plants and creatures were safe to eat, Tristin stared in awe at the unending world of trees. He had trouble keeping his breathing even. It was as if he stood on the precipice of heaven and Darragh was his Angel of Guidance.

Something darted behind them and Tristin spun in time to see a small creature with a bushy tail scurry up a tree. "What was that?" he asked.

Darragh chuckled. "It's just a squirrel."

Tristin watched the squirrel disappear within the leaves toward the top. "Is it dangerous?"

Darragh shook his head.

"Could I touch it if I caught it?"

"Don't go trying to catch any wild animals on your own. Squirrels might not look dangerous, but they bite and sometimes carry diseases."

"Can we go farther?" he asked.

"As far as you want. We are free."

Tristin walked into the forest until he reached a shallow ditch where the clearest, purest water flowed past. He turned excitedly to Darragh.

Darragh nodded. "Thirsty? Go ahead. It's safe."

Tristin dropped to his knees and slurped the water into his mouth. It wasn't bitter like Slaybyrne water. As he drank, a black, finger-length creature swam past. He froze, water dripping from his cupped hands.

"Darragh," he whispered, hoping not to scare the creature away. "What's that?"

Darragh leaned past his shoulder for a better look. "Oh. That's a tadpole."

"A tadpole?"

"One day it'll grow into a frog."

"A frog?"

Darragh snorted.

"Does it bite?"

"No, silly. It's just one of the many fantastic creatures living out here for no reason."

"This world is amazing. Every person alive should witness this before they die. My sister would love it."

Darragh turned away from the stream. "Come on. There's so much more to see." He led Tristin deeper into the forest. "Maybe, if we're really quiet, we'll see a deer this morning."

"A deer?"

Darragh smiled.

"I love it here."

Chapter 24

The Labor Field

The cell door clanged open, startling Makenna from her sleep with a jolt. She was on her feet before her eyes even focused. Two prison guards rushed in with batons raised. Feeble stood up beside Makenna, groggy and confused. A guard slammed his baton against Feeble's head with a terrifying thunk. Feeble dropped, unconscious and bleeding.

Ugh groaned as he struggled to his hands and knees, but his bad knees slowed him terribly. Several more guards poured into the cell, also carrying weapons. They wore black handkerchiefs over their noses and mouths. Makenna backed against the wall beside Ugh.

One of the guards drew back his weapon. Makenna shouted, "Don't hit him," and he lowered it. Two other guards shoved him aside as Ugh straightened to his full intimidating height. They swarmed him. One of them swung a baton at Ugh's head. Makenna shrieked. Ugh wobbled but didn't go down. The second joined in, and soon a bloody curtain covered Ugh's face. Instead of cowering away from the blows, Ugh roared at his attackers.

"What are you doing?" Makenna screamed.

Ugh stumbled sideways. With blood flowing into his eyes, he reached out blindly and grabbed the guard Makenna had swayed. Without effort, he snapped the guard's neck and tossed him aside. More guards swarmed the crowded cell. Ugh swung his mighty fists, but his aim was flawed because of the dizziness and the blood.

There wasn't enough room for Ugh to fight so many men. One guard struck Ugh's ribs while another struck his arm. Ugh didn't surrender or give ground. He blindly shoved the closest guard into the cell wall with the force of a horse kick. The guard collapsed to his knees with only the wall holding him up.

Ugh swiped his forearm across his eyes as another baton bashed his spine. Makenna used her god to its fullest, screaming at guards to stop, but there were too many of them filling the cell. Ugh ignored each blow while swinging his fists like war hammers.

With a guard plastered to his back, Ugh plowed past the others and out the cell door where more guards were waiting. Makenna tried to follow, but two of the guards grabbed her arms.

"Use your god again and we won't just beat him, we'll kill him," one of them hissed.

Each blow against Ugh's body jolted through Makenna as if she'd absorbed it herself. Ugh broke one guard's arm and sent another guard over the rail to his death, but they kept coming. After a vicious blow to his weakened knees, Ugh dropped. He looked past the swarming guards to Makenna and roared loud enough to wake the rest of the prison. With his eyes fixed on hers, he shouted, "Makenna, I'll find you."

She cried out as blows rained down on his skull. He crumpled to his face. The guards stood around him, winded and assessing their losses. Two guards were dead, and several others had injuries that they may never recover from. It took five guards and plenty of curses, but they managed to drag Ugh's limp body back into the cell.

One of them looked to another and asked, "You ever heard that big bastard talk before?"

The other guard shook his head. "I didn't know he could."

The guards escorted Makenna past Feeble and the growing pool of blood from his head. Feeble's wheezing breaths came in short, sporadic spurts. Makenna helplessly watched a guard shove a cloth over Feeble's face and hold it until he stopped struggling. How could anyone be so cruel?

The guards led her down the stairs, through several halls and doors, and into the brisk outside air. All she could think about was poor Feeble and Ugh, praying that the former would find peace in the afterworld and the latter would survive the day. She fought back tears.

The rough stone floor of the prison became packed dirt beneath her bare feet. Shivering from both terror and cold, she entered another building. Inside, it smelled sweaty and sour. There were no windows. The only light came from torches and lanterns. A guard met them near the entrance. Everywhere his skin was exposed was stained with a greenish tint. "Welcome to the factory," he said. He shook hands with the guards escorting Makenna.

Makenna looked past him to a knee-high stone wall that encircled a dozen or so prisoners. They held their heads bowed and wearily marched in unending circles, stomping with each tired step. Other prisoners carried woven baskets and dumped the contents into the pit. Two prisoners trudged past pushing a cart full of fine green powder.

Makenna's mask made a sound halfway between a chirp and a clunk. The green-skinned guard's eyes shot toward it. "Is her mask failing?" he asked. His demeanor had hardened.

One of Makenna's guards stammered, "Well … uh … I guess. Does it matter?"

The green-tinted man brushed his hand limply at her. "I can't use her here. Look how weak she is. She couldn't crush a single costa root."

"Well, where do you want us to take her? She keeps using her god. We have to make an example of her."

"I don't care. Take her to the slave fields. Anywhere but here." He flicked his hand toward them. "Be gone. And don't ever bring me someone with a failing mask again." He turned back to his prisoners.

The guards led Makenna back outside. One of them helped her use her mask. After a brief walk past dozens of carts coming and going on the factory road, she stood before the gate of a nearly ten-foot-high iron fence that surrounded a sea of tents.

While one guard waited outside, the other escorted her through the gate to another guard who sat at a table. His heavy, disinterested eyes examined her. He brushed a hand toward the camp. "Find an empty tent. There are plenty available."

Makenna wheezed in a sickly breath. The green fog was even thicker here than it was in the prison.

Her escort handed over her mask. "Get some rest. You've got a busy day tomorrow." He smirked. "Actually, you've got a busy day for the rest of your short life." He shoved her closer to the table and then closed the gate as he left.

The guard at the table bobbed his head, fighting boredom and sleep. The table was empty except for his mask and a half-full tankard. She licked her dry lips. His sword leaned against his chair as if daring her to grab it. She imagined what Samuel could do with such a weapon, but Samuel wasn't there. The guard lifted his heavy eyes and mumbled, "Keep moving, girl. It'll be morning soon. You'll need your rest." His head bowed and almost immediately he started to snore. A thin, stringy line of drool dripped from the corner of his lips.

The only sign of life Makenna noticed within the fence was the guards patrolling the tents. One of them watched her to make sure she didn't flee. With her head bowed, she trudged down the closest row of tents, careful not to make eye contact with any of the guards she passed. Most of them ignored her anyway.

She walked along two more rows before she found a tent that had an open flap and no one inside. She ducked under the flap to enter. The stink of piss punched her in the face. Trenches running along the paths carried streams of urine downhill from the camp. She shoved her nose into the crook of her elbow and crawled into the empty tent. The thin gray blanket on the ground stank of sweat, so she wadded it up and shoved it outside. Maybe in the morning the guards would give her a new one, or at least let her wash the nasty one.

Curled in a ball on the dirt, she closed her eyes and tried to sleep. Visions of Ugh and Feeble taking their beatings played out across the insides of her eyelids. Despite what the guard had said about sleeping, her spinning thoughts made it impossible.

A few hours of sleepless shivering passed before a pair of muddy boots approached the mouth of her open tent. "Time for work," the owner of the boots said. Then he shuffled to the next tent.

Makenna peeked outside. A line of prisoners had already formed. Her mask gave off a sickly chirp and she took a breath from it.

There was no sign of the sunrise, and she wondered how the guards defined "morning." She watched the line, hoping that somehow she might see her brother or her friends looking back. But only strangers filed past. She climbed out and searched for somewhere to join in.

"Hey," one of the prisoners whispered from the closest line. Though he appeared younger than her father, the hunched curve to his back was more common in men twice his age. His cheeks were sunken and tight. Like a lot of other men in line, it appeared he hadn't shaved in years and his beard touched the top of his chest. His eyes darted around. "Get in line." He subtly waved her over and moved back a step to make room. Makenna hurried over and squeezed in front of him.

"Thank you," she whispered, hoping he had made the room for compassionate reasons and not something sinister.

"Shh. Just keep your voice low. We're not supposed to be talking."

Glancing at the guards, she nodded.

"You're new here," he whispered. When she looked back at him, he snapped, "Face forward. Are you crazy?"

She jerked her head back around. She had no reason to trust him, but no better option. At least he was willing to talk to her.

"Whatever you do, don't look at any of the guards while we're walking. And don't act like you're new here, either. Just pretend you've been working the slave fields for years. When we get to where we're going, you stay near me. If I lift a basket, you lift a basket. If I grab a shovel, you grab a shovel. Understand?"

With her eyes fixed forward, she nodded.

"I know you're scared, but consider yourself lucky that you're not in the factories. People rot alive in there. I think some of them eat the powder on purpose just to end it."

"Thank you," she answered.

"What's your name?"

She wasn't sure she should tell him, but she didn't want to offend him either. After a moment's hesitation, she whispered, "Makenna."

"Nice to meet you, Makenna. My name's Joseph."

The line moved and then stopped. Moved and then stopped. When she accidentally fell out of step, one of the guards snapped her back with a stinging switch to her shoulder. Eventually they neared a tent in the center of the camp that was twice as big as the house she'd grown up in. The line snaked into the tent and led to a long table where she was given a bowl of slop, a single japsy weed, and a dirty cup of water.

"Eat fast," Joseph whispered. The line continued moving and quickly approached another table where the laborers set their empty bowls and cups. Makenna choked down as much of the bitter soup as she could and all her water before setting her bowl and cup on the table with the others. She ate the japsy weed as she walked.

The line continued through the main gate. They marched until she could see the prison to her left. She thought about Samuel and hoped he was all right. Another line of laborers approached from the opposite direction.

"That's the night shift," Joseph explained. "They're headed back to the camp." As the other laborers passed, Makenna studied each of their gaunt, tired faces and saw her desolate future in them. Each man and woman in line stared vacantly forward. They looked like they were returning from war, each face blending into an endless montage of exhaustion and sacrifice. Near the end of the line, one man in particular caught her eye. Though he was painfully thin and broken like the others, there was something familiar about him. She studied him like she would a tricky math problem. When he lifted his head a little, Makenna's heart skipped. She saw Tristin in his eyes. Though he had lost most of his girth and his cheeks pressed tight against his skull, she had no doubt who it was. As the man passed close enough to touch, she whispered, "Dad?"

He jerked his head around and his thick eyebrows dipped into a confused frown. His mouth dropped open. He stumbled, his legs momentarily forgetting how to work. The man behind him grabbed his arm. As she and he continued in opposite directions, he watched her over his bony shoulder, and she watched him.

He mouthed, "Makenna."

Her heart shattered. She wanted to run to him and hug him and never let go.

"Forward, Makenna," Joseph snapped.

"But that's my father."

"That's great, but keep walking. A guard's coming."

She turned back toward the front just in time for the guard to pass. He glared at her and continued along the line. For the rest of the walk Makenna replayed the encounter over and over in her mind. She couldn't believe he was still alive. Seeing him gave her renewed strength.

The line moved toward several tarp-covered mounds in wooden enclosures. One of the mounds was uncovered, revealing a pile of the same fine green powder she'd seen in the factory carts.

The suns peeked over the southern horizon. One of the guards walked along the line, his lips softly moving as if he was talking to himself. "What's he doing, Joseph?" she whispered after the guard passed.

"He's counting us. If his count comes back even one person shy, we'll all pay until that person is found."

"What do you mean 'pay'?"

"Let's just hope no one fell out of line."

While waiting for their next orders, Makenna's gaze drifted to the faint outline of a mountain in the distance beyond the slave camps.

Joseph caught her looking and nudged her with his elbow. "Never look at the king's castle. It's forbidden."

Makenna turned away before any guards took notice.

The line of prisoners began moving, some walking straight ahead and some marching toward the uncovered green powder. Makenna started to panic. "Joseph? Which way do I go?"

"Stay calm. Just grab a shovel and walk straight ahead; that's where I'm going."

To the river?

Makenna, Joseph, and some of the other prisoners picked up the shovels left by the night shift and approached the banks of the Slaybyrne. The water was magically clear and brilliant, somehow free of green muck. She asked, "How is it so clean?"

He pointed back to the powder that some prisoners were already shoveling into carts. "Because we haven't done our jobs yet today."

Chapter 25

Respect

Tristin's dreams varied night to night from pleasant memories of his childhood to horrible nightmares of losing his family. Tonight it was a nightmare. He tossed and turned in his bed. Somehow he knew he was sleeping, yet he couldn't wake himself up. He was in the same room as his last dream, only this time there was a window instead of a door. Through the cloudy glass, he saw Makenna kneeling in the grass in front of the Angel. Tristin tried to get closer to the window, but his feet wouldn't move.

The Angel locked eyes with him through the pane and gave him a twisted smile that deadened when he turned his attention back to Makenna. Tristin felt helpless. *Work, damn you,* he silently screamed at his legs. Makenna bowed her head and sobbed into her hands. Full of malice and hate, the Angel lifted his sword. Tristin reached for his sister. He called for his god, but his god had abandoned him.

The Angel swung his sword. Tristin screamed at the top of his lungs as the blade met the flesh below Makenna's left ear. Tristin closed his eyes and flinched away. When he opened them again, the Angel was gone and only Makenna remained, still kneeling, her lifeblood spurting into the air. A gaping mortal wound stretched from the back of her ear to the opposite side of her chest. She turned toward Tristin, her eyes hollow and cold. "Why did you do this to me," she cried.

Tristin sprang from his bed with a jolt, sweat sticking his shirt to his back and matting his hair to his face. Panicked, he scrambled for his lifemask, but found the same emptiness that now filled his broken heart. Images of his sister's violent death etched themselves into his soul with the permanency of an artist chiseling a picture into stone.

"Makenna," Tristin cried out, clutching his chest. "I'm so sorry." His sweaty back met the cold wall. He shivered.

Even as his eyes adjusted to the room, he saw the Angel's "justice" repeated endlessly in his mind. The nightmares were coming more frequently, and he was starting to feel like sleeping meant drowning.

Tristin rubbed his eyes. The suns peeked through the window. He panicked, late to the fields where he had promised to help for another day in order to earn his keep. Though he had a quarter of the strength of the barbarians, if not less, he had received a few compliments on his work ethic and didn't want to disappoint.

He got up and dressed in the work clothes Queen Gaal had sewn for him after his second day of helping. Though they were only Darragh's hand-me-downs altered to fit him, he thought they were the nicest clothes he'd ever owned. After downing a glass of fruit juice, once an unimaginable luxury, he blazed to the field where Gaal and several other barbarians were already gathered near a boulder that seemed nearly as large as a Terdict house.

"Good Morning, Tristin," Gaal said.

"Morning, King. What are we doing today?"

He pointed to the perimeter fence about fifty paces away. "We are moving this boulder from here to there. We plan to farm this land next and the boulder is in the way."

"And how are we going to accomplish this?" Tristin asked.

"We're going to roll it, of course."

Of course. Tristin regarded the boulder dubiously. It seemed an impossible task. He moved sideways to get a better idea of the boulder's actual size and accidentally bumped into Kearney, one of the stronger barbarians. The impact with Kearney's rock-hard muscles nearly dislocated Tristin's shoulder. Tristin realized he was thinking like a regular person. "Excuse me, Kearney."

Kearney looked down in mild surprise as though he hadn't noticed the collision.

While Kearney, Tristin, and most of the other barbarians lined up at the back of the boulder, two more barbarians lined up on each side. When the men started pushing, Tristin pushed as well, though he suspected he wasn't much help. The boulder barely moved. Per Gaal's instructions, they relaxed enough for the boulder to rock back toward them and then shoved again. After three more heaves, the boulder finally rolled a few feet. For the next hour they worked nonstop, flattening the ground ahead of the boulder and then rolling it a few more feet.

When Darragh finally arrived to help, Gaal didn't appear pleased with his son's tardiness. Darragh didn't seem concerned. "Morning, Tristin," he said.

Tristin nodded with a smile.

The same kind of tiny, winged bug that had been annoying Tristin and the others all morning hovered near Darragh's cheek. Darragh swatted at it, somehow managing to poke himself in the eye. He winced and his hand shot over the stinging eye. Gaal shook his head and went back to work.

On their next break, Tristin leaned his back against the boulder and wiped his sweaty brow. The suns were brutal in the late morning. As the barbarians joked with each other over who was the weakest, Tristin's eyes fell on three storage sheds that he hadn't noticed before. "King?" he asked after taking a drink from his waterskin.

Gaal lifted his head.

"What's in the sheds over there?"

Gaal's eyes followed Tristin's finger. He hesitated before answering. "Let's just say they house some useless relics from another time."

Tristin fought to remain stone-faced. "Oh, lifemasks," he said, as though he already knew.

Gaal's head tilted. He squinted like he was trying to read something small written on Tristin's face. "Perhaps."

"Any chance I could see those relics one day?"

Gaal shrugged. "Possibly. You haven't seen enough lifemasks in your life?"

"Not any that would fit a barbarian."

"They're not much different except a bit bigger, I suppose." Gaal stood up, signaling an end to the break. The others immediately returned to their places.

Tristin turned away and smiled, careful not to let Gaal see.

They spent hours moving the boulder and readying the field for planting. Throughout the day, Tristin couldn't get the three sheds out of his mind. After he and the others had put in a good day's work, Gaal announced an evening feast in the village green. Tristin hurried home to clean himself up, his muscles sore from the hard work. The soreness made him feel good. Useful.

There were places called greens in Altenbyrne, but this one was actually green, and not from fog. Darragh explained that they used the grass-covered area for meetings and celebrations during fine weather. When Tristin arrived, cooks were roasting two fog creatures over huge fire pits. Gaal insisted he sit at the "warriors' table" as they called it, which was simply the same table as Kearney.

The barbarians feasted while telling stories of lore and making jokes at the expense of Tristin's skinny arms. Tristin let them laugh and concentrated on stuffing his face. The food was glorious. His favorite was a stew of cooked carrots and succulent meat seeping with real flavor, unlike Ian's japsy weed and water concoction. Just when he thought he couldn't take another bite, Merletta presented the table with something she called apple pastry. When he smelled the pastry, he suddenly found he had room for dessert after all. Somewhere in his feet, he imagined. Or a special hidden dessert stomach that he hadn't needed until now. He could barely push himself from the table once he finished. His belly had never felt so sated.

The children began washing and drying the dinnerware at a large trough of water. Seeing them work, Tristin excused himself from the table and joined them. It did no favors for his tired muscles, but it was a nice break from the barbarians' teasing. The children made room and gave him a rag. Soon, the other dishwashers peeled away and left him as the only one washing the dishes. Though he found it strange, he continued anyway. He never minded hard work. Each dish they handed him, he washed and then passed to the child beside him to dry. The number of dirty dishes seemed unending. While he worked, the children watched and giggled and pointed. A few of the adults chuckled as well. But he kept washing.

He took yet another dish, washed it, and passed it on. And the children laughed again.

Eventually, the sheer number of dishes convinced Tristin there was something afoot. He took another bowl, washed it, and passed it on. Then he spun around and caught the child who was supposed to be drying the bowl passing it to another child who put it in the stack to be washed again. With their game foiled, they burst into laughter. Darragh, laughing so hard there were tears in his eyes, put his thick arm around Tristin's shoulder. It was still hard to believe Tristin was three years older than the young giant.

Tristin leaned close to his ear. "How many times did I wash the same dishes?" he whispered.

"Enough that they'll never need washing again."

Tristin turned to the laughing crowd and took a good-natured bow. So much for escaping the razzing.

Gaal joined him and patted his back. "Have a seat, Tristin." He lightly pinched one of Tristin's biceps and added, "Rest those massive arms for a bit." Everyone laughed again.

Once they settled down, Gaal told the story of how Tristin had heroically saved Darragh's and Tolk's lives. Ashamed by his failure to protect the prince, Tolk looked down at the table while his friends on either side patted his shoulders. At the end of the story, Gaal assured Tristin that he owed him the world. Tristin took his words to heart.

When the partygoers started to disperse, Tristin decided to take a stroll instead of going home. On his way, he picked up one of the lit torches that lit the green. He would be sure to replace it when he was finished.

The three secluded sheds along the perimeter fence stood unguarded in the dark. Though a single barbarian stood watch near the field far from them, he only waved as Tristin walked toward the sheds. Tristin was earning their trust.

The door to the first shed opened to a sticky, stringy wall of white from floor to ceiling. Darragh had called it spider webs after Tristin had gotten tangled in one while they were in the forest. Tristin swiped a hand through the silky wall. "How big of a spider must it be to create such a thick wall of webs?" he whispered. He hoped not to meet it.

He toyed with the sticky substance between his fingers before trying to wipe it onto his pant leg without much success. Then he looked to see what was beyond the webs and gawked at a jackpot worth far more than gold: huge crates full of countless barbarian-sized lifemasks.

He reached for the closest one. It was covered in dust and webs. Though it was larger than his old mask, it wasn't much different in design than all the masks he'd ever seen. He wiped it clean and held it to his face. It was at least twice as big as what he would need. Setting it aside, he searched the crate until he found one that appeared to be sized for a barbarian child. It wasn't a perfect fit, but it would do.

He took the mask with him and closed the shed door. The next part of his plan would be the dangerous part. After all, the mask wouldn't do him any good if it didn't work.

Chapter 26

Crystals

Tristin hurried from the sheds with his "borrowed" mask, careful that no one noticed what he carried. As he walked, he searched the ground for a flattened rock with a sharp edge that could be used as a tool. At the edge of the village he found the perfect one.

Croate stood guard at the main entrance. Tristin kept the mask out of sight, though it wasn't necessary as Croate barely looked at him.

"Good evening, Croate," he said.

"Hmph," Croate grunted.

"May I pass?"

"Where are you going at such a late hour?"

"For a walk. I need some alone time."

"Does the king know?"

"I didn't think I had to tell him every time I left."

Croate raised an eyebrow, but still didn't look at him. "Dangerous out there, you know. Especially at night."

"I understand. It's just for a while. I won't go very far."

To Tristin's surprise, Croate stepped aside. "Go on, then."

As Tristin scooted past with a torch in one hand and the mask in the other, Croate added, "You're free to come and go as you wish. You're not a prisoner here." And then, though it seemed to pain him, he added, "Be careful, young one."

Hiding a smile, Tristin headed up the hill. After a glance back at the village, he continued to the same field he had met Darragh in.

By nothing more than luck, he had chosen a night when the moon was bright and the sky was cloudless. He jogged across the open land with his head on a swivel, reserving his god's speed for when he might truly need it.

The moon had crept to its peak before Tristin finally found the cave he was looking for. Almost subconsciously, his finger caressed the nosecone of the barbarian mask.

As soon as he stepped into the cave, he rested the torch against the side wall and sat with the mask in his lap. Using his flattened rock, he unscrewed the fasteners, loosened the nosecone, and worked the cover free just like he'd watched Jakodi do so many times. The filter cloth inside was off-white with just a hint of yellow staining on the edges. He was deadly careful not to touch it as he focused on the dimly glowing crystal alongside it.

The crystal was snug in its cavity, but after some careful prying he wriggled it free. If Jakodi was right and the crystal, not the filter, was the key, a new crystal was all he needed. He set the mask on the ground and scooted over to the cave wall. He dug out a crystal and compared it to the one from the mask. They seemed identical, even down to the tiny pores, except the new crystal was far too small. Tristin kept digging until he found one that was close in size. The crystal was a little misshapen, but he still managed to cram it into the slot.

While fiddling with the cover, he accidentally kicked one of the three fasteners that he'd set on the floor. Tristin scrambled for it as it rolled into a crack. *Damn.* He crammed his fingers into the crack in the floor, but they were too fat. Frustrated, he reassembled the mask with just two fasteners. Though it held together, there was a tiny gap where the third fastener should have been.

It'll have to do, he figured. He'd just have to be very careful not to get it wet. He collapsed to his back with his hands over his face and laughed out loud. It was an uncontrollable, gut-cramping laugh that brought tears to his eyes. He'd readily admit it wasn't the most appropriate way to express his relief, but it sure felt good.

After he gathered his composure, he sat up and stared at the mask. It was time for the final test. As lucky as finding the crystals had been, it was only half the battle. Now came the dangerous part.

He stepped out into the moonlight, his torch in one hand and the mask in the other. His feet carried him south as though they knew the way. Before long, the all-too-familiar chalky film of the green fog coated his tongue. He had already forgotten how bad it tasted, or maybe it simply tasted worse after having relished such goodness in the barbarian kingdom.

The safe bet would have been to stay at the edge of the fog and hope it was enough for his experiment to work, but it was important that he didn't leave any doubt. He walked until the fog thickened enough to halve his visibility. That's where he squatted with his ears perked to watch the mask. The glowing vents stared silently back. Though the wait was torture, the silence was worse. Not knowing how fog creatures sensed their prey added to his anxiety.

An agonizing hour passed and still the glow didn't pulsate. That's when an awful snort came from deep in the fog. He slowly stood with the mask held tight in his fist.

"Chirp, damn you," he whispered.

More grunts answered the first. They were surrounding him. He turned in circles, searching for some hint as to where they might attack from. The mask taunted him with its silence. He was out of time. It wasn't working. Maybe he was wrong. Using the moon as a beacon back to the barbarian kingdom, he prepared to run. He'd have to find another way to make the masks work.

His fingers started to tingle. Was it from the fog or nerves? Maybe they weren't the same crystals after all. He was ready to throw the damn mask when a black blob slapped the back of his hand. He dropped the mask, chased the blob up his arm, snatched it, and ripped it free. Tristin turned to run, but in his panic his feet tangled together and he fell, hitting his forehead on a jagged rock. His vision flashed white. The torch flew from his grip. He sat up and the world spun beneath him. A warm drop trickled down his temple and onto his cheek. He swiped his hand clumsily across his forehead, smearing blood over his fingers.

Despite death surrounding him and closing in, he could only think about finding the mask he had wanted to throw away just seconds before. He still needed it, even if the crystal didn't work. He spun around until he saw its faint blue glow. Almost forgetting about the creatures stalking him, he looked down at the worthless mask and cursed it.

What made the other masks work? What was so different about them? As he prayed for the mask to whistle or pulsate or anything that would change his fortune, a drop of his blood fell onto the nosecone and slipped into the gap beside the missing fastener. He cocked his head as the faint blue glow began to pulsate in sync with his nervous breaths.

The missing piece that even Jakodi hadn't been able to decipher hit him like a horse kick. At that moment, sitting in the fog waiting for claws to rake his back or teeth to rip out his throat, he understood it all. Blood was the key to making new crystals work.

The mask off-gassed a beautiful life-changing chirp. He pressed it snug against his tingling face, breathed out once, and then sucked in a wonderful whistling breath. He didn't care how loud it was because those creatures would never catch him. His fingers stopped tingling. Nothing could stop him from going back for his sister now.

Tristin found the moon, snatched up his torch, and heaved it into the fog. When the fog creature shadows skittered away from the flame, Tristin exploded into motion. A creature pounced and sliced a claw at his chest. Tristin shifted sideways and the claw grazed his shoulder. It was not enough to slow him, but the blow steered him into the path of another beast.

If not for his reflexes and speed, he'd have lost his guts. He batted the creature's claw away as he dodged its attack. His momentum threw him into the dirt. He scurried back to his feet. Two creatures stalked him from the fore. More closed in from behind. They were everywhere. How many could there possibly be?

Drool hung from the closest creature's jowls as it tilted its head from one side to the other. It was baiting him to run into the others.

When it stalked closer, it dropped back onto its rear legs, coiled to spring. Tristin's only hope was to make sure it missed him.

The creature sprang. Tristin contorted past its thrashing claws and under its swinging tail before somersaulting out of reach. He was back on his feet in a flash and sprinting toward the moon. Within seconds, he burst out of the fog. Looking over his shoulder for fog creatures, he slammed into a wall and crashed to the ground. He looked up. It wasn't a wall—it was Croate.

"I told you it was dangerous, young one. Let's get out of here," Croate said. Together they jogged across the open land, both watching over their shoulders for pursuers.

At the top of the distant hill, a group of barbarian warriors had assembled. Gaal and Tolk were at their head. Gaal wore a leather chest plate and a dented helmet a size too small that sat too high on his head and squashed his cheeks.

Seeing Croate and Tristin returning safely, all of the warriors except Tolk and Gaal started back down the hill to the village. Tristin approached with his head bowed.

Gaal worked his tight helmet from his head and tossed it to the ground. "I guess it's been a few birthdays since I've had need to wear this get-up."

"And a few meals," Tolk added with a chuckle.

"Good evening, Your Majesty," Tristin said, and looked away.

Gaal nodded. "And what were you doing out here, Tristin?"

Tristin knew honesty was the only way to keep from making things worse. "I wanted to test a theory."

"And this theory was worth risking your life?"

Tristin looked up. "Actually, yes."

"You need to be honest with me, Tristin. I don't like secrets in my village."

"Of course, King."

"Why were you in the fog?"

"I borrowed one of your lifemasks for an experiment."

Gaal's forehead wrinkled. "Why were you borrowing a mask?"

"I needed to know how to make them work again."

The king sat quietly for a moment and nibbled on his lower lip. Finally, he asked, "Did it?"

"Did it what?"

"Did the mask work?"

Tristin nodded.

Gaal rubbed his braided beard. "Interesting." He looked around. "You can tell me later why you think you needed to fix the mask in the first place, though I have a guess."

"Your guess is probably accurate."

Gaal, Tolk, and Tristin headed back to the village. Tristin hid his smile.

Chapter 27

Broken

S amuel woke up in the cell with the stove. He looked down at his shackled hands and feet. A voice he had only heard once before whispered in his head. *We will kill them all. Every one of them.*

He shook his head. His mind hummed.

The light at the mouth of the cave was all that kept his mind from the blackness. He was stuck in that place deep within his soul—that dark, nasty, hateful place that lived only in men like him. Because of Malvic and the guards, his god had gotten loose again, and he feared if the light went dark he would never be able to return. Despite fighting his god with every hopeful memory he had, he felt somehow different. He *was* different. Out of everything he would lose if the light extinguished, it was compassion that he would miss the most. A lot of people were going to die. And maybe he would start with the stranger hiding in the corner behind him.

"Who are you?" Samuel asked, his voice harsh and gravelly.

The stranger stuttered, "M-m-my name is Arthur. I was a doctor. I've been salting your wounds while you were unconscious."

Samuel glowered up at him. *Kill him.* "No," Samuel snapped. In his mind he crawled toward the light at the mouth of the cave, but it stayed just as far out of reach. It was crucial that he kept it going. He coughed up blood and let it leak past his lips. The cave dimmed as the light shrank a little. He thought about Makenna and the light struggled to stay shining. Only focusing on saving her could keep his god at bay. The ice-cold ground beneath his chest felt soothing to his feverish skin, though the oozing burn from Malvic's brand felt like thousands of dirty needles. His teeth chattered. As much as he longed to meet Malvic again, he feared Zakaira had done too much damage and his body would fail him before he made it to the next round.

Arthur shuffled closer, his chains jingling along the floor. "You have been through quite a lot." He spoke with a kindness in his voice that only those who were accustomed to helping people had. "They allow me to keep salt in here to help their victims, though I'd understand if you'd rather I didn't treat your wounds at all. May I continue to help you?"

He nodded. Of course he wanted his wounds treated. How else would he be strong enough to get his vengeance?

The man shuffled across the room and then back again. He helped Samuel roll to his back and touched the brand with a rag that felt like a hot poker. Samuel flinched, but the man followed him, keeping the rag pressed against his flesh.

"It's infected. I know this hurts, but the salt will help to fight the infection." He pressed the back of his hand to Samuel's forehead. "You're still fighting a fever."

That explained why Samuel felt so tired.

After the first round of agonizing treatment, Arthur stopped and allowed Samuel to catch his breath. Samuel dug deep to find the strength to talk. With a cracked and broken voice, he said, "Free my hands."

Arthur leaned closer and Samuel saw him for the first time. His face was long and narrow, marred by a scar covering his left cheek. His hairline showed more of his forehead than it probably had when he was younger, and he wore crooked spectacles with one of the lenses missing. His breath was as rotten as his teeth. "I'm sorry?" Arthur asked.

Samuel struggled to say it again. "Free my hands."

"I don't know if I can, sir. Besides, even if I did, Malvic would just shackle you again when he returns. And he'll be angry."

"Please," Samuel whispered.

"Nonsense. Why would you want to defy them by removing your shackles? You know what they'll do to you."

"Because I'm going to kill them," Samuel said. He didn't care who knew.

"Oh?" Arthur's tone implied he didn't give much weight to the threat. He returned to treating Samuel's wounds.

"I'm having trouble breathing through my nose. Can you straighten it?"

Arthur winced. "That'll hurt."

Of course it would hurt. What in the world didn't? "Just do it."

Arthur pinched Samuel's nose between two of his knuckles. He closed his eyes and then jerked it out and to the side. The pain was sudden and breathtaking. The light at the mouth of the cave dimmed briefly, but Samuel fought to keep it burning with Makenna's smile. The pain faded. Blood trickled down Samuel's upper lip. He inhaled a wonderful breath through his nose. "Thanks. Now get these shackles off."

"I don't think I can do that."

Samuel was too tired to argue. He needed more rest. Maybe after a nap. He rolled to his side and closed his eyes.

He had no idea how long he slept, but when he woke Arthur sat next to him holding a bowl of slop. "They brought lunch. I saved it for you."

Arthur held up Samuel's head and poured the cold slop into his mouth. Some of it stayed down, but most of it came back up. Samuel's ribs ached terribly with each movement. Elemar's fist had done more damage than he had realized.

Arthur persisted. "The most important part of healing is keeping up your strength. You must drink all of this."

"What about you?" Samuel mumbled.

"Nonsense. I don't have to eat *every* day."

After choking down as much of the slop as he could, Samuel again insisted that Arthur find a way to free his hands. That was crucial, even more so than treating wounds that wouldn't kill him right away. Arthur brushed off his request once more, and Samuel was still too weak to press.

Sometime later, Samuel awoke to find Arthur sleeping curled up in the corner. Samuel lifted his head enough to see the cell door and prayed Malvic would give him more time to recover before the next fight. It wouldn't take much strength to do what he needed to do— Malvic was skinny and weak—but it would take more than he had in his current state. He lay awake on his side, his hands and feet still shackled, and waited for Arthur to wake up again. He fell asleep two more times before Arthur finally sat up and scooted across the cell toward him.

"My hands," he said, while Arthur started with the stinging salt again.

Arthur breathed a frustrated sigh. "I've told you. I don't think I can."

"If you dislocate my thumbs, you should be able to slide the shackles off my wrists."

Arthur balked at the idea—he was a doctor, after all—but then he sighed again. "If I do this for you, you know it will be extremely painful."

Samuel snorted at the thought that something might hurt any worse than what he had already been through. He rolled to his back and asked, "How long do you think it'll be till they come back for me?"

"Oh, I don't know. It varies from fighter to fighter. Judging by the extent of your wounds, I think you have some time still. They can be very patient."

"Perfect." Samuel struggled to lift his hands from his stomach. "My hands now, if you please."

Arthur studied the shackles and then looked into Samuel's unwavering eyes. "Are you sure about this?" he asked.

There was nothing Samuel wanted more. He grinned.

Arthur set his rag down and took one of Samuel's hands into his. "I can't believe you're asking me to do this."

Samuel nodded.

"I can't believe I'm actually doing this."

Samuel stared, stone-faced.

"Would you like to close your eyes?"

Samuel shook his head.

"On three. Is that all right?"

Samuel didn't answer. The sooner the better, as far as he was concerned.

"One ..." Arthur looked away. "Two ..." He closed his own eyes. "Three." With a cringe and a single jerk, he sent a wave of agony up Samuel's arm.

Samuel didn't pull away, though he bit his lip until it bled. Arthur dabbed a warm, wet cloth against Samuel's feverish forehead; however, he didn't remove the shackles. "Your thumb is dislocated, but ..." His words hung in the air.

"What is it?"

"It's just ... Well, there's another problem. I'm afraid the skin around your shackles is quite swollen. There's no easy way to do this. I'll have to practically skin part of your wrists. It'll be most uncomfortable."

Samuel knew "uncomfortable" was a doctor's polite way of saying "hurt like hell." Samuel closed his eyes. "Just get on with it," he whispered. To shut out some of the pain and keep his god from slaughtering the good doctor, he imagined Makenna standing in the light outside the cave again. Strangely, Tristin stood next to her this time.

Arthur twisted and pulled at the shackles in delicate tugs until the one around Samuel's left wrist tore free, taking plenty of skin with it. He shoved a salted rag over the wound before getting to work on the other hand. Makenna wanted to leave and Samuel fought to keep her there. At some point, he passed out again.

When he opened his eyes, his bloody shackles were lying on the floor. Both of his wrists were wrapped in strips of salty rag. Arthur sat on the other side of the room.

"Thank you," Samuel whispered.

Arthur looked up with glossy eyes. "I can't believe what you've just endured. I've never seen any man absorb so much. And willingly at that."

Samuel knew he was no ordinary man.

"I reset your thumbs while you were asleep and dressed the wounds on your wrists. As for the restraints around your ankles, well, I have no idea how to get those off and I don't particularly want to try."

That was fine. The shackles on Samuel's legs were unimportant. Once the killing began there'd be plenty of keys lying around.

Arthur shook his head. "Samuel, you are the toughest man I've ever met."

Samuel swallowed hard. "You haven't seen anything yet."

Chapter 28

The Crystal Mines

Tristin worked in the fields daily, slowly earning the trust and respect of Gaal and the others. He was a hard worker, a trait learned from his father. Though he did all that was asked, it was difficult to keep his mind on his work. Each day began and ended with thoughts of Makenna. It was past time to have a serious talk with the king. He stood on Gaal's porch and took a deep breath before knocking.

The king himself opened the door. He had mashed potato in his beard; he always seemed to have food in there.

"Tristin? What brings you by?"

Tristin rubbed his damp palms together. "King, I was wondering if we could … uh … have a talk."

"Of course. Come on in." Gaal lifted a pitcher from the table. "Juice?"

Tristin shook his head. "No, thank you."

Gaal sat in his favorite wooden chair and gestured toward the chair across from him. "What is it you'd like to discuss?"

Tristin climbed into the chair. "For one, is there any chance to get a few chairs made that I don't need a rope or ladder to get into?"

Gaal snorted. "I think we could arrange that. Now, why are you really here? Not to talk furniture, I assume."

Tristin hesitated, worried he hadn't yet earned the right to ask. With Gaal's kind yet serious eyes trained on him, he blurted, "I want to return to Altenbyrne for my sister and my friends. I want to help them before it's too late."

Gaal's gaze lifted. "Is that what this is about? I wondered when you'd build up the courage to come see me."

"You knew I was going to ask?"

"Of course. You have spoken of nothing but your sister since you arrived. I'm not stupid."

"Then you'll help me?"

"I didn't say that. While I understand your desire, returning to the walled kingdom would be nothing short of suicidal."

"I'm willing to take that risk."

"It's more than a risk. It's an absolute."

"With all due respect, Your Majesty, I'm going to Altenbyrne one way or another."

"As I have said before, you are free here. That means you do not need my permission to leave. But going into the walled kingdom is impossible. What about the fog?"

"I told you I made a mask work."

"And what about the fog creatures?"

"I'm faster." Tristin leaned forward intently as he spoke.

Gaal smirked and held his hands out in front of his chest. "Calm down, my friend. Let's think this through for a moment. Let's say you made it all the way to the wall. How would you breech it?"

"That's why I came to you. If you and your men escort me to the wall and help me through or over it, I will do the rest."

Gaal rubbed his chin and studied Tristin's determined face. "I would like to discuss this matter with the elders. Will you allow me the night to make a decision?"

Tristin nodded. It was more than he could have hoped for.

Gaal reached for a stack of papers and rifled through them. Tristin sat motionless, unsure whether he'd been dismissed and not wanting to get up before he was. After a few seconds of uncomfortable silence, Gaal lifted his eyes from his papers. He flicked his hand at Tristin with a kind grin.

"Oh. Right. Thank you." Tristin climbed down from the chair, said goodbye, and hurried back to his home. He spent most of the night watching the ceiling until he eventually gave up on sleeping altogether. He figured a stroll might help his nerves. He made his way to the main gate where Croate was standing guard.

"What are you doing out so late?" the barbarian asked.

"I don't know. Just thinking, I guess. Maybe I'll watch the sunrise from the top of the hill."

"After your last experience, you want to leave the village again?"

"No, no. Just to the top of the hill. I won't go any farther."

Croate stepped aside.

Tristin climbed the hill. There was something uniquely pleasant about watching the sunrise away from King Searle's smothering fog. While sitting and waiting for the fantastic colors of the predawn sky, he thought about Makenna and Ian and Jakodi and hoped they were doing as well as could be expected. He feared for Samuel, praying his fight inside the prison hadn't been too difficult. And he wondered what he would do if Gaal rejected his request.

He didn't notice Darragh's approach until he spoke. "Hi, Tristin," he said.

Tristin spun around, startled. "Oh. Good morning, Darragh."

Darragh had a fresh scuff on his chin and Tristin pointed to his own chin with a curious nod. Darragh's shoulders slouched. "I'm sure you can guess."

"Fell again?"

"Aoife left her pail in the hall. I didn't see it." He stretched and yawned. "Couldn't sleep either, huh?"

Tristin shook his head. "I was just thinking about my friends."

"You miss your sister?"

"Wouldn't you?"

Darragh gave him a mischievous grin. "Welll ... I'm just teasing. Of course I would."

"Then you understand?"

"Yes. I spoke to my father before I came out here and told him exactly that."

"You did? Did you get any sense of which way he was leaning?" Darragh shook his head.

"I appreciate you doing that." Tristin looked out over the horizon. "Sometimes I think it might be easier to simply walk to the edge of the world and jump off. Do you think you could get there if you tried?"

"I used to think that, but my father said no matter how far you go, the edge of the world continues to remain just as far out of reach. He said if you traveled far enough, you'd end up right back where you started."

"That's impossible."

"That's what he says."

"Is he just guessing? I mean, how would he know? Has he traveled that far?"

"I don't think so."

"Then how?"

"There have been a few explorers who have passed through over the years. Some of them said the world is round."

"Round? That's silly. We'd fall off."

Croate shouted from the bottom of the hill that King Gaal had his answer. A tightening lump formed in Tristin's gut. He stood up and looked to his friend.

Darragh patted his back. "Well, what are you waiting for? Go see what he says."

Tristin blazed down the hill and all the way to Gaal's home.

Seven barbarians stood with the king around the table inside. Four of them were young—apparently old age wasn't a requirement to be an elder—while the other three were as old as the king himself. Tristin recognized Kearney among them. Their faces were blank, devoid of any emotion that might hint at their answer.

Gaal cleared his throat. "Good morning, Tristin."

Tristin bowed and waited in nervous silence. His chest felt heavy and full.

"The elders have weighed your request, and with their advice I have come to a conclusion. We will not lead you to the wall and your certain death. There is no scenario in which you can infiltrate the prison and free your sister and your friends on your own."

Tristin opened his mouth to protest, but something made him hold his tongue.

"In your short time here, you have proven yourself as a boy of great character. You even saved my son and Tolk from a fog creature when they were strangers to you, which I can never repay. But that is not all that has gone into our decision. I feel the need to thank you."

"Thank me?"

"Yes, Tristin. For far too long I have viewed protecting my people here as my role as their king. Because of you and your dedication to your sister and friends, I realize that belief was wrong. My duty is to keep all my people safe. You have opened my eyes. When my brother was taken to prison, I was but a young boy. If he still draws breath, he deserves to breathe the same free air we enjoy here. All the barbarians in King Searle's prison deserve as much. Tristin, if you have indeed solved the mystery of the masks, you may have given us a way back in. We shall leave as soon as we are ready."

The mountain lifted from Tristin's chest. He felt woozy, but in a good way. "I don't know what to say."

"You needn't say anything. Since I do not believe the prisoners can be liberated without declaring war on the Angel's army, this order I am preparing to give is one I do not take lightly. Are you sure you can fix the masks?"

"Positive. But before we free the prisoners, we need to free my friend Ian. The gods only know what they're doing to him."

"He's not locked away?"

"I don't think so. He has a god that the Angel finds useful. He was sentenced to a life of servitude."

"What is this god that the Angel needs?"

"Ian can protect people from the grinderfish and take them across Slaybyrne."

Gaal stroked his beard. "Is that so? Let's say we drew the Angel's men west of the Slaybyrne. Would your friend help us across?"

"I'm sure he would. If he's able."

Gaal grinned. "That means we wouldn't have to risk crossing upriver. Which leaves just one other major hurtle."

Tristin smiled. "The Angel?" Tristin asked.

Gaal nodded.

"I actually may have a solution for that as well."

Gaal tilted his head.

"One of my friends in the prison is a man who can kill the Angel. His name is Samuel."

"You say that with much confidence."

"I am confident. Samuel carries the God of Killing within him. He cannot be defeated in battle."

"Then why is he in the prison now?"

"He chose to go to protect my sister."

"Hmm." Gaal glanced at Kearney, who shrugged. "If this Samuel does indeed carry the God of Killing and can defeat the Angel, why hasn't he yet?"

"Because he can't defeat an army."

Gaal rubbed the back of his neck. "Do you believe you can repair enough masks for my men?"

"If I can get enough crystals."

"Crystals?"

"Yes. Glowing blue ones."

"Can we just use the ones already in the masks?"

"I don't think they'll work. Once they're linked to a person, I don't believe they can be reawakened with someone new."

Tristin dug into his pocket and retrieved one of the crystals from the cave. "I need a lot of these, but bigger." He tossed it to Gaal. "The cave I found has hardly any the right size."

The king squinted one eye and examined it. "How do you even know there *are* more?"

"Because King Searle seems to have an unlimited supply."

A grin cracked Gaal's hardened face. He tossed the crystal to Tolk. "What do you think? Is this what they're carting out of the mines up north?"

Tolk examined the crystal and then tossed it back. "I imagine so."

Tristin raised an eyebrow. "Mines?"

"Tolk, take Tristin with you and your team to the northern mines. Gather enough crystals for our army. I will prepare a strategy while you're gone. Thank you, Tristin. Now, if you'll excuse us, we have a lot of planning to do."

When Tolk opened the door, Darragh was standing on the other side. He immediately blurted, "I'm going with you, Tolk."

Tolk turned to Gaal with raised hands.

Gaal nodded. "Let him go. It'll be good for him to see. Let him show Tristin the fields as well."

"I'll protect him with my life, King."

"I know you will, Tolk."

It took an entire day for Tolk, Tristin, Darragh, and twelve other barbarians to travel through the forest to where it touched a sprawling field to the east.

Tolk ordered a break. Then he said to Darragh, "You can show Tristin now."

Darragh nodded. "Come on, Tristin." He led Tristin to the edge of the thick, knee-high grass while Tolk and the others waited within the tree line. Darragh pulled Tristin down to his belly. "Stay low," he said. Together they crawled deep into the field. For the tenth time Tristin asked what Darragh wanted to show him, and for the tenth time Darragh shushed him in return. Tristin was ready to ask for an eleventh time when Darragh stopped him with a finger to his lips. He slowly lifted his head above the grass and then jerked it back down. He looked back to Tristin and pointed ahead.

Curious, Tristin slowly lifted his eyes above the top of the grass. It took him a few seconds to make out what he was looking at. Then he jerked his head back down. He turned to Darragh with wide eyes. "Soldiers," he whispered.

"Not just soldiers. Take another look."

Tristin lifted his head again. At least a hundred soldiers lined the nearby banks of a flowing river. He looked to Darragh. "Is that Slaybyrne?"

"Yes."

"How can that be? The water's so clear."

"Of course it is. That's how water is supposed to look. Did you see the boats?"

"What's a boat?"

"Floating on the water. Look again."

He raised his head above the grass for a third time and scanned the water. Two wooden structures floated downstream toward a pier on the opposite bank.

Darragh lifted his head beside Tristin.

The boats towed a floating tree that was stripped bare of its branches. Guards barked orders and swung switches at a line of laborers who waded out to the tree and guided it to the bank where they wrapped chains around it. Two pairs of muscular four-legged animals Darragh called oxen dragged the tree onto land. Once the tree was clear of the water, another set of boats approached towing another tree.

Darragh tapped Tristin's shoulder and pointed downriver where green fog obscured Altenbyrne's walls. "That's where the costa root powder goes in. Remember the costa fruit I showed you?"

Tristin nodded, too stunned to speak as the pieces slowly fell into place.

"That's what poisons your kingdom. When powdered costa root is mixed with water, it produces a toxic gas." Darragh guided Tristin's chin toward another, much larger boat approaching from upriver. "See that?"

He nodded.

"That's how the supplies come in."

"What kind of supplies?"

"Everything from apples to animal meat to ..." He trailed off.

Tristin's wide eyes coaxed him to continue.

His lips curved upward. "... to magic crystals. Until you came along, we could never figure out what made them work." Still grinning, he reached over and gently pressed Tristin's gaping jaw closed.

"I can't believe what I'm seeing," Tristin said.

"Are you starting to understand now? Everything in the kingdom comes from the Outside. If you walked far enough northeast past the Slaybyrne you would see that the king has acres and acres of farmland protected by guards."

"By the gods. How many guards does he have?"

"A whole army."

"You mean the Angel's army?"

Darragh shook his head. "The guards in the prison and the ones out here have nothing to do with the Angel. They don't even live in the city."

"And the prisoners? How many slaves do they have?"

"Too many to count. That's why your king has such petty laws. He wants your people to break them. He needs a constant supply of slaves."

As Tristin looked back to the laborers—no, slaves—carrying crates from the boat, a thought simultaneously terrifying and hopeful crept into his mind. "Do you think my sister might be there?"

Darragh's forehead creased. "I suppose she could be."

Overwhelmed, Tristin started to stand up. "We have to find her."

Darragh yanked him back down. "Stop it. Are you crazy? If your sister is there, it won't do her any good for us to join her. We need to have patience. My father said he would help you, and he is a man of his word."

It pained him that Darragh was right.

"One last thing before we go. See that mountain? That's where the king's castle is."

From this angle, Tristin could see that the mountain was free of the fog. His hateful glower lingered on it while Darragh started crawling back toward the forest. He couldn't wait for Samuel to kill the Angel so they could meet the king in person. Filled with grim determination, he turned and followed Darragh back to the others.

Tristin peeked around a tree. The orange glow of torches radiated from the mine's entrance. Though they'd waited until armed guards escorted a line of exhausted slaves with carts full of crystals toward the river, shadows from within revealed someone was still there.

Tolk held up his hand. "Tristin and Darragh, you two wait here. We'll handle the guards and then we'll call for you. We'll need to hurry. The next shift of workers will be here soon."

Tristin didn't want to wait—he wanted to help—but the authority in Tolk's tone stopped him from arguing. Tolk nodded to the others. They separated and stalked the entrance from both sides. They were more deliberate than stealthy, though, and were quickly spotted. Four guards ran out of the mine. Seeing their barbarian foes, three of them threw up their hands and dropped to their knees. The fourth guard decided to flee. As the barbarians attempted to close off his escape, he slipped past Tolk's lunging hands and sprinted toward the river. Tolk hurriedly waved Tristin and Darragh over.

Tristin streaked to his side. "You're just going to let him escape?" he cried.

"We can't worry about him now."

"But he'll tell the others and they'll come with more soldiers."

"I know. That's why we must grab what we can."

Tristin didn't like that plan. He called on his god and shot toward the fleeing guard. Tolk called for him to stop, but Tristin had already gotten going. Though he didn't know what he was going to do once he caught the man, he knew he had to do something. The guard slowed as if he had run out of breath. Tristin drew back a fist as the soldier turned his head and reached for his sword. Tristin threw the luckiest punch in the history of punches as he zipped past. Pain exploded in his knuckles. The guard dropped in a heap, a fresh laceration painting his cheek with blood.

Tristin raced back to the mine. Tolk nodded his thanks and ordered Kearney to retrieve the unconscious man. Tristin followed Tolk into the mine. The air was warm and stale. The only way to go was down a tunnel lit with torches. Two barbarians ventured ahead to assure no surprises would be waiting.

The tunnel floor made a long downward pitch until it eventually led to a second opening with the same orange glow beyond it. At the end of the tunnel, Tristin stood in awe of a sprawling cavern that spanned farther than the entire barbarian village. Looking up at the staggeringly high ceiling, he wondered how far underground he had actually travelled.

Instead of torches, the cavern was lit by stone columns glistening with some oily substance that sheathed the columns in flames. The fiery glow blended with the light of countless blue crystals to cast a breathtaking muted orange throughout the cave that rivaled the most awe-inspiring sunrises. It immediately became Tristin's favorite color in the world. The columns were spaced generously throughout the far-reaching cavern. The smoke appeared to ventilate through many vents carved into the ceiling.

Tolk passed out canvas bags to everyone. "Fill them," he ordered. "We don't know how long before the next shift of slaves arrives."

Piles of crystals already littered the cave floor. Darragh started for the closest pile, but Tristin didn't move. "What's wrong?" Darragh asked.

"My mom didn't need to die," he whispered.

Darragh's usually jovial face saddened. "I know, my friend. I know."

Tristin pried a crystal from the wall and squeezed it in his fist. "What happened to my mom won't happen to my sister. Not as long as I'm still alive." He kissed the crystal and stuffed it into a pouch tied to his waist. Then he and Darragh opened their canvas bags and filled them with crystals roughly the appropriate size.

Though his full bag was far too heavy for Tristin to carry, the barbarians tossed theirs over their shoulders with ease. Even Darragh didn't appear to have much trouble. Tolk hefted Tristin's bag along with his own and they set off back through the tunnel. Outside, the four bound guards sat under Kearney's watchful eye.

Kearney nodded at the guards. "We have to kill them, you know."

The guards' faces paled; their eyes pleaded.

Tolk sighed and set down his canvas bags.

Tristin couldn't hold his tongue. "You can't kill them, Tolk. It's not right."

"I'm afraid we have no other choice, Tristin."

Tristin snapped, "Why don't we have a choice?"

"They'll report what they've seen."

"And what have they seen?"

"They've seen you and your speed for one. How long do you think before the king realizes why we're stealing crystals? How safe will your sister be then?" He turned and nodded to Kearney.

Tristin looked to the guards' wide eyes as Kearney marched toward them. "We can take them with us," Tristin blurted.

Kearney glanced back, a dagger already in his grip. Darragh watched quietly.

Tolk shook his head. "I'm sorry, Tristin." He nodded to Kearney again. Tristin sprinted between Kearney and the guards. Kearney moved to shove him out of the way. Tristin cringed.

"Wait," Darragh shouted.

Everyone paused and looked at him.

"You will not kill those men, Kearney," Darragh said. "And you will never strike Tristin."

Kearney's upper lip curled as he reluctantly stepped back.

Tolk sighed. "Kearney, bring them along."

Tristin exhaled. He was surprised Darragh carried such power. He'd never seen the young boy assert it before. Kearney tethered the guards together and led them into the forest.

Tristin said, "Thank you, Darragh."

Darragh nodded.

Gaal was visiting with Croate at the main gate when the party finally arrived home a few days after they had left. He was a bit surprised to have four prisoners, but Tolk explained Tristin's bleeding heart and Darragh's insistence. Gaal rubbed his forehead like he'd suddenly acquired a headache. "Take them ... I don't know ... somewhere. Keep watch over them until we leave. You can free them then, as it won't matter where they go."

The guard Tristin had knocked out spoke. "Thank you for your kindness, sir. When you free us, we won't go back and tell them. I promise."

Kearney yanked them through the gate by their tether.

Gaal and Tolk stepped aside for a brief conversation. Then Tolk and the others continued into the village with the bags of crystals while Gaal joined Darragh and Tristin for a stroll. "Tolk says you did well."

Tristin didn't know how to answer.

"The plan is moving along nicely."

"That's good to hear, King."

"After you get some rest, I need another favor."

"Anything."

"I need you to fix nine masks, and while you do that, I want you to teach a few of my men how to fix the rest."

"Why only nine?"

"My army will go to war against the king's guards at the Slaybyrne near where you just were."

"They won't need masks back there," Darragh said.

"No. Not there. But if they push the guards far enough, they'll need masks later. Anyway, once King Searle feels threatened, he will call for his Angel. After the Angel and his soldiers pass through the prison to the battle, we will sneak in and free your friends. If Samuel chooses to help us, he will be able to meet the Angel on the battlefield."

And that was why Gaal was planning the attack and not Tristin.

"Get plenty of rest tonight. Fix the masks in the morning. I'd like to leave when the suns set tomorrow."

"Yes, Your Majesty."

Part Five
The War of Altenbyrne

Chapter 29

Forbidden Talk

Makenna's fingers were raw and oozing blood—had been for days. The ache in her lower back had become so persistent that she wondered if it had always been there. The guards only allowed her to sleep for a few hours each night, starting each new day before the next sunrise, and she was exhausted to a degree she'd never thought possible.

Endless carts carried an infinite amount of powder from the factory. She struggled to carry the next shovelful of green powder to the river while Joseph quietly encouraged her from behind. Adding to her exhaustion was her wheezing, which had grown worse. Though Joseph sometimes gave her a sad look when he heard her mask clunk, he never spoke about it.

Makenna could no longer work for more than a few minutes without stopping to catch her breath. Lately even that didn't help. If not for Joseph pushing her and picking up her slack, she would have been lashed many times over already.

When a guard passed on horseback, Makenna wondered if the animal's specially fitted lifemask would be replaced if it failed. Was she less valuable than a horse? Since she'd never seen a dead one, she concluded she probably was.

The green powder irritated her skin, like the Slaybyrne did to Tristin's. Despite the maddening itch, she didn't scratch anymore because it only made it worse. She was carrying yet another shovelful when her head started spinning and the ground wobbled beneath her feet. She dropped her shovel and fell to her knees.

Joseph knelt in front of her. "Makenna? Your eyes. They're so red and swollen. Can you even see?"

Her wheezing almost drowned out his words. "A little."

He removed a rag from his pocket and dabbed her eyes. "I've seen this before. Your eyes are having trouble with the powder. Just stay close to me. It won't last. I promise."

She felt around for her shovel, found it, and scooped the powder back up. As she followed Joseph to the river, a blister on her left foot popped and stung like someone was carving the flesh from her sole when the powder seeped into the wound.

Seeing her limp, Joseph said, "Your feet will callous soon. They'll feel better. I promise."

He keeps promising everything will get better, but everything keeps getting worse.

With Joseph's help, she suffered through her work shift until it was time to head back to camp. Once away from the powder piles her eyesight improved slightly, though the irritation and itching didn't. While she waited behind Joseph in the gradually forming line of prisoners, she gathered the courage to ask him something that had been on her mind since she'd first arrived. "Joseph?" she whispered.

"What is it?"

"Have you ever thought about running?"

His head jerked around. "Don't say that, Makenna," he snapped, his eyes tracing the nearby prisoners. "Someone will hear."

"Just answer me. Have you?"

He bit his lower lip with his eyes locked on the passing guards. "When I first got here I did. But I saw someone else try once and he was hanged in front of everyone."

"What if we jumped in the river? I can swim."

"Makenna, stop it."

She stared at him, refusing to let it rest without an answer.

He shook his head. "They would chase you down with their boats. Besides, the current flows toward the city."

"What if we went with it? The current, I mean?"

"And deal with the grinderfish? No thanks. Don't you get it, Makenna? Don't you get what we're doing with this powder? It's poison. That's why no one ever leaves the slave fields or the factory alive."

"But I wasn't given a death sentence."

"Most of us here weren't." He looked nervously around. "We shouldn't even be talking about this."

Makenna ignored his warning and pressed on. "I have a god, Joseph."

Joseph crossed his arms and turned around. "This is no time for jokes."

"I'm serious. I can make people do what I want."

He cocked his head. "Is that so? Well, excuse me if I don't believe you."

She wheezed in another breath and staggered slightly. He steadied her.

She looked around to make sure no guards were watching. "I'll prove it to you." She called upon her god. "Joseph, put your thumb in your mouth like a baby."

Joseph snorted and tried to protest even as his words jumbled around his thumb. He yanked his thumb from his mouth. The line started forward. Wide-eyed, he snapped, "Just stop this nonsense, Makenna."

As they walked, they passed another line of powder carts. She wasn't done. "I'm not staying here forever, Joseph. If I get any strength ba—"

Joseph groaned. "Damn it, Makenna. You know if anyone besides me hears you talking like this we'll both be killed on the spot."

With her eyes trained on the ground, she whispered, "Maybe that wouldn't be so bad." Then she looked up in time to see him glare back at her over his shoulder.

"You're too trusting, Makenna." His compassionate voice hardened. "There are people here who would sell you out for an extra meal. In fact, they would be forced to tell the guards what you've said else they'd be executed for not reporting." He talked into his shoulder as he walked. "As your friend, believe me when I tell you escape is impossible. You'll be killed if you try. There are guards everywhere. Even if you made it past their perimeter, which is impossible, they have trackers who will follow you and catch you. There is nowhere to go. Promise me, Makenna. Promise me you won't try anything, and you'll stop this foolish talk before it's too late."

"I'm dying, Joseph. What's it matter how it happens?"

"Don't say that. Your body just needs to adjust to the strength of the powder here."

"I've already been here a while."

"I know. It affects everyone differently. You'll get better."

Why did he lie? Everyone who heard her mask knew what it meant. She was tired of arguing. "Why do you help me, anyway?"

He took a deep breath as if the question pained him. "You remind me of my daughter," he answered.

"You have a daughter?"

"Yes. But I haven't seen her in many years. Now hush before you get me lashed."

She stumbled forward and fell against his back. He spun to catch her, but her outstretched hand slipped through his grasp. She fell from the line. Despite the threat of a lashing, he stopped to help her.

"Hold the line," a guard shouted. "You two there. What's going on?"

As Joseph hoisted Makenna to her feet, he answered, "She's very sick, sir. Her mask is failing." The guard closed the distance with a curled upper lip and his baton raised. Joseph winced, but instead of striking him, the guard used his baton to pry him away from her.

Makenna fell to her knees, gasping for air.

"Get back in line," the guard shouted, his mouth inches from Joseph's face.

"Just let me help her—"

The guard threatened him with his raised baton again. More guards rushed in and surrounded them. Joseph returned to the line of prisoners. Makenna tried desperately to get up again. She looked to Joseph for strength.

"Get up," he mouthed.

She didn't think she could.

Three guards surrounded her. "Get up, girlie," one of them said.

"She can't," Joseph shouted.

The guard sneered over his shoulder. "Mind your business. Either she gets up on her own or she dies out here."

Makenna strained to see Joseph past the guards. He willed her up with determined, hopeful eyes. She begged her lungs to give her legs the strength to stand. With quivering arms, she pushed against the ground. Her maladroit breaths came almost as rapidly as the beat of her heart. Though it seemed to take a lifetime, she staggered back to her wobbly feet.

"Now fall in line," one of the other guards snapped.

She stumbled to Joseph. He reached out to steady her, but another guard swatted his hand away. "You will not touch her again. Face forward, prisoner, or you will work with bound hands from now on."

Reluctantly, Joseph did as he was told. Makenna leaned her forehead against his back for support.

Despite the threat of a lashing, he whispered, "It's all right, Makenna. Just lean on me and we'll make it to the tents."

Her mask clunked and she struggled to hold it to her face for another nearly worthless breath. It wasn't much, but it gave her the strength to continue.

Once the guards released them into the tent city, Joseph helped Makenna to her tent. "I'll be back in the morning," he whispered.

Makenna was already fast asleep.

"Wake up," a man shouted outside Makenna's tent. Her eyes fluttered. He shouted again. "Wake up. It's time for work."

Makenna felt like she had slept for less than a minute. She could only open her eyes enough to see a hunched-over guard peering through the tent opening. She pictured herself getting up as ordered, but her body didn't respond. Her mask gurgled beside her. She tried to reach for it, but didn't have the strength.

The guard reached over and lifted it to her face. While she inhaled a tiny breath, he shouted to someone outside, "This one's not gonna last much longer. Go ask the supervisor if he wants to replace her mask."

She was unable to hold her eyes open. She heard Joseph's voice outside as he pleaded to stay with her to help her with her mask. The guard threatened him with joining her in the afterworld if he didn't keep moving.

"Stay strong, Makenna," he shouted. She heard him grunt as if he'd been struck.

The other guard returned. She heard his cold words. "The supervisor said to let her go. She wasn't one of the stronger workers anyway. We'll replace her tomorrow."

"Very well."

Makenna felt a hand pat her foot. "Good luck on your journey to the other side, young lady." The guard joined his partner outside. As they walked away, she heard the second guard ask, "How long does she have?"

"I don't know. A day. Two, tops."

"It's a shame."

Makenna dozed off again.

As Makenna slept, a gentle finger traced her cheek down to her jaw and then back up again. It was the first morsel of peace she had felt in a long time. She leaned into the warm touch and smiled, momentarily forgetting how sick she was. Maybe she was dreaming.

"Makenna?" someone said with a soft and caring voice. "It's me. Your dad. Can you open your eyes?"

She didn't want to open her eyes in case she was dreaming. It had been too long since she had felt her father's touch, and she wasn't ready to lose that feeling again so soon.

He shook her gently. "Honey? It's all right. Open your eyes if you can." He kissed her forehead.

She fought her heavy eyelids. He was blurry at first, but slowly his face came into focus. "Dad? How?"

Rhett dipped a cloth into a bucket of warm water and dabbed it beneath her eyes. "This'll help the irritation. It's clean water from the fresh side of Slaybyrne."

She still hadn't discerned whether she was alive, dead, or dreaming, but decided seeing her father's face and feeling his touch again was worth it in any case.

He pressed his forehead to hers and closed his eyes. "I've missed you so much."

"I've missed you, too, Dad."

"I'm so sorry I had to leave you, honey. I wanted to protect you and your brother. Not a minute went by that I didn't think about you two and pray that you were safe."

Though even whispering took so much strength, it was worth the effort. "How did you know where I was?" she asked.

"Your friend Joseph. When our paths crossed this morning, he earned himself a beating telling me where you were and how sick you had gotten. Is Tristin ...?" He trailed off, unable to finish.

She didn't want to answer. "I don't know. I think the Angel got to him." She had to rest before continuing. "I think he was banished."

"Without his mask?"

She nodded.

Rhett bowed his head.

"You would have been so proud of him, Dad. He was becoming so much like you."

He swallowed hard. She saw in his eyes and the quiver of his lower lip that his already broken heart had broken again. While he sat with her, holding her hand and dabbing her forehead with the damp cloth, she dozed on and off, too weak to stay awake for long. If her mask clunked, he helped her take a lifebreath. If she needed a drink, he helped her sip the freshest water she'd ever tasted. Every time she woke up he was there, and he didn't leave her side for the entire morning. But even as he sat with her, they both knew his work shift was fast approaching. That unspoken inevitability weighed on her heart like an anvil.

And then she woke up and he wasn't holding her hand anymore. She panicked, fearing he had left and that she would never see him again. Then she saw him, standing near the tent opening.

"I don't want you to go," she cried.

"I know. I don't want to go. But I'll come back in the morning. I promise." With the back of his finger, he wiped a tear from her cheek and then wiped one from his own. "I love you, honey. More than you could ever know."

"I love you, too."

"Your friend Joseph will be here soon." He kissed her forehead again, stood up, and backed out of the tent. Makenna cried herself back to sleep.

When she woke up again, Joseph was by her side. His left eye was swollen and discolored. "Did you have a good visit?" he asked with a grin.

"Oh, Joseph. Thank you."

"It was the right thing to do."

She stared at his wounded eye.

"Don't worry. It wasn't as bad as it could have been. I think they took it easy on me."

He held her gurgling mask to her face. "Just relax. I'm going to sit with you tonight. If you need anything, I'll be here."

Chapter 30

Journey into the Green

The masks were ready. Gaal's army had started north. And Tristin could barely control his nerves. It was just before sunsdown when Gaal, Tristin, and a group of Gaal's men reached the outer edge of the green fog. The barbarians wore hardened leather armor over their vulnerable parts, swords at their hips, and war hammers strapped to their backs. Each man had a small bag of supplies draped over their shoulders, a pouch of spare crystals at their waists, and a lifemask.

A branchless tree with handholds notched into each side rested at their feet. One end of the tree had been carved into a dull point and capped with thick, hardened metal. Three of the barbarians stood along each side, ready to hoist it on command. Gaal had called it a battering ram.

Tristin eyed the fog warily and fidgeted with his lifemask, praying all the masks would work.

"Have faith in yourself, boy," Gaal said, as if reading Tristin's mind. "We have faith in you."

Carrying lit torches and the battering ram, the small band ventured into the fog. Tristin walked at the front alongside Tolk and Gaal. It wouldn't be long before the fog creatures sensed them.

Tristin licked his chalky lips. After walking for nearly an hour, Gaal's mask chirped and startled them. Everyone stopped. With the ram resting on the ground, they gathered around. Gaal pressed the mask to his face and took a beautiful whistling breath. Everyone stood silent.

"How do you feel?" Tolk finally asked.

Gaal took another deep breath. "I feel ... good. I never had a doubt."

Tristin's shoulders relaxed. That was the first of many trials. The next one would be getting past the fog creatures. As if on cue, a hiss broke their celebratory mood.

"It's about time," Tolk said, and clenched his fist.

A second hiss followed the first, only closer and from behind them. Tolk squeezed his sword hilt, leaned down to Tristin's ear, and whispered, "Won't be long now." He flashed him an inappropriate grin.

And you're smiling about it? Tristin's quivering lower lip told Tolk how he felt.

Three fog creatures closed in. Hisses and grunts surrounded them. "Form a circle and watch for leeches," Gaal ordered. "We're in for a fight, boys."

Darragh had told Tristin that "leech" was the name for the black blobs the fog creatures flicked at their prey. He wondered how many leeches a pack would have. It was a big pack. Tristin counted thirteen now.

Fourteen.

Fifteen.

Tristin felt the growing tension in the group. Their swords were already drawn. Kearney opened his mouth to shout something just as a black leech slapped his neck. Egan ripped the leech away before it could crawl beneath his collar. Kearney shook himself and stood firm. Another leech struck Gaal's forearm. Tristin swatted it to the ground and squished it beneath his foot. They were coming from all directions.

The barbarian behind Tristin fell backward into the circle, paralyzed. Tristin frantically searched him until he found the leech on his back beneath his leather armor. He pinched it and pulled it free, careful to avoid its tiny, toxin-injecting teeth. The man thanked him and struggled back to his feet.

The hisses were everywhere now. Sixteen. Seventeen. The creature facing Tolk pounced. Tolk caught him and both went to the ground.

"Hold the circle," Gaal shouted.

One of the creature's rear claws swiped across Tolk's gut. Though the claw missed his flesh, it ripped open his pouch, spilling crystals to the ground. Tolk disengaged and bounded back to his feet.

The creature righted itself with ease. Instead of attacking again, the creature tilted its head at the glowing crystals. When it looked up again, it seemed to look right through Tolk. It gave an angry hiss.

Slowly, Tolk retrieved one of the crystals and held it out toward the confused creature. He stepped to the side and waved his hand in front of the creature's face. The creature' nostrils flared. Tolk stepped closer. Even touching the top of its head only made it flinch and twitch its ears. Tolk peered back at Gaal. "I don't think it can see me anymore."

Gaal shrugged. He reached into his own pouch and removed a crystal. Tristin and the others followed his lead. Once everyone's hands were glowing blue, the rest of the creatures hesitated and looked around. They sniffed the air in search of lost prey. It was like the barbarians had become invisible. Gaal watched with a growing smile as the creatures lost interest and ambled away.

Only the one beside Tolk remained, still confused and licking its lips. Tolk asked, "What about this one?" The creature perked its ears as though it had heard him but couldn't locate the source.

Gaal answered, "Kill it. We could use the meat."

With that, Tolk plunged his sword into the creature's heart. It squealed and stiffened and collapsed.

Egan, the youngest of the barbarian party, crowded past Tolk with his crystal extended and his eyes fixed on the roaming beasts. Hovering over the dead one, he asked, "Should we dress it here?"

Gaal nodded.

Egan opened the creature from crotch to neck and then dug out its entrails. Tristin watched, curious despite the gruesome work turning his stomach a bit.

Once finished, Egan stood up with his hands stained red and slung the creature over his shoulder. He said, "I'll deal with the scales later."

A barbarian named Paedar asked, "Should we get another one? Looks like easy pickins."

Gaal shook his head. "There's plenty of meat on one for what we need." He examined his crystal. "Tristin, did you know these things blinded the fog creatures when you had us bring extra?"

Tristin shook his head. "Since we don't know how to tell a good crystal from a bad one, I just thought we should have extra in case we got any duds."

After they'd watched the fog creatures for a little longer, Gaal announced it was time to go. "We will feast once the wall is at our backs."

The other barbarians stuffed their crystals into the tops of their chest plates and lifted the battering ram from the ground. Croate led the way through the milling creatures, even bumping into one of them as he passed. The creature simply snarled and continued on its way. Tristin stayed at Gaal's side. Before long, they left the creatures searching aimlessly behind them.

Tristin moved in front of Gaal and behind Egan. The dead fog creature hung over Egan's shoulder with its face dangling at Tristin's eye level. Thick, bloody slobber swayed from the creature's lower jaw, threatening to drip with each bouncing step yet hanging on by some kind of magic. Tristin wondered if touching the creature might dispel the fearful hold it had over him. He reached out nervously, his gaze locked on the beast's cold, black eyes. He was so focused that he didn't see Paedar walk up next to him. With his fingers timidly hovering inches away from the beast, Paedar grabbed his arm and shouted, "Look out." Tristin yanked back his hand and yelped.

The barbarians roared with laughter. Tristin glared at Paedar. "I nearly wet myself," he said, which made the barbarians laugh even harder.

"I'm sorry, I just couldn't resist." Paedar nodded toward the carcass. "If you want to touch him, go ahead. I won't mess with you again. I promise."

Not wanting it to seem as though Paedar had gotten the best of him, Tristin reached out and touched the dead creature's neck. Its coarse, black mane protruded through thick, dark-gray scales. His fingers traced three parallel slits in the scales along the side of the creature's neck.

"Gills," Paedar said.

Tristin's hand moved past the gills to the creature's upper jaw and across its deadly teeth. As silly as it was, he wanted to punch the dead thing. He didn't because, among other reasons, his hand was still sore from punching the guard at the mine.

Paedar playfully slapped his shoulder, nearly knocking him over. Then he pointed ahead. The stone wall of the kingdom loomed out of the fog. Tristin couldn't believe he was back.

Gaal dragged his finger along the stone surface. He closed his eyes and pressed his forehead to it. "I've wanted to come back here for many years. Thank you, Tristin, for helping me see that."

Tristin touched the wall. "No. Thank *you*, King. I wouldn't have made it this far if I'd had to go alone, despite what I said earlier."

Gaal rested his heavy hand on Tristin's shoulder. "Do not fear the coming fight, my friend. We are on the side of good and we will be protected."

Since Tristin's memory of the Angel in battle was much fresher than the king's, he wasn't so confident. He tapped curiously on the wall. "Are you worried the Angel might have guards patrolling the other side?"

"If that's the case, there's nothing I can do to prevent it. Although, I believe that's unlikely. The wall spans far too many miles for the Angel to adequately patrol all of it. Besides, he has no reason to suspect anyone is coming."

Fog creatures howled their songs deep in the fog, but they weren't creeping any closer. Gaal gave the breaching order. The six barbarians who carried the battering ram took up position behind where Croate stood with a hammer. Unlike the dual blunt sides of the other war hammers, Croate's had chiseled points. He drew it back with both hands, and then swung at the wall with all his considerable might. Two tiny chips of rock exploded into the air. He did it fifteen times before a fist-sized dent had been chipped away. Winded, he let his weapon dangle at his side and glanced back at Gaal. The king nodded and Croate backed away.

The other barbarians charged forward with the ram. The two at the front turned their heads just before impact. The metal point crashed into the stone, jolting the barbarians violently forward. They repositioned their grips, backed away, and charged again. Their powerful muscles rippled with each bone-jarring strike. A tiny crack spidered outward from the center of the impact.

The flattening point of the ram sank deeper and deeper with each charge until it finally burst through the wall like a sword through flesh. Stone and mortar crumbled onto the ram.

The barbarians wriggled the ram free and more stone broke loose. They set the ram aside and took up their war hammers. As if they had practiced a thousand times, two of them at a time alternated strikes until the hole had widened considerably. When it was wide enough for one barbarian to squeeze through, Gaal went first, followed by Tristin and the others.

Tristin instantly recognized the japsy weed fields on the other side. In a strange way, it felt good to be home. After everyone was through they walked along one of the japsy weed rows toward the Slums.

When Gaal reached the edge of the Slums, he paused to take it in. Conflicting emotions were written across his forehead in deep wrinkles. None of the others were old enough to have lived there. They stood beside him, silent.

Gaal pointed to the first row of houses and said, "I used to play in that one as a boy." Tristin recognized it as Jackson's. Gaal went to it and stepped through the open doorway.

Tristin and the others waited quietly while the king relived his earliest memories. After a few minutes, Gaal returned with resolve in his dark eyes. "Tolk, we shall proceed near dawn. Send three men on patrol and make sure none of the Angel's soldiers are still lingering. And then start the fire. We shall eat while we wait."

Tolk and Croate tore apart one of the houses and stacked the old wood in a towering pile. Tolk said, "Bigger is better. We want to make sure those bastards see it." He rubbed two japsy leaves between his palms as though he was trying to keep warm. Nothing happened at first, but then a wisp of smoke lifted from his hands.

Tolk put the smoking leaves under a piece of wood and blew on them. Soon a small flame took hold. He laid smaller pieces of wood on the pile. Once they began to char, he added them to the woodpile. It took a while to get going, but once it did it grew into a magnificent inferno.

While Tolk worked on the fire, Egan worked on the fog creature. Once all the scales and bristly hair had been removed, Egan ripped off the legs and roasted them in the flames. Everyone got a portion when they were cooked. After it cooled a little, Tristin took a bite. A pungent blast sprayed the back of his throat and gagged him.

Gaal smirked. "Bite into a bursac, did ya?"

Tristin didn't know what a bursac was, but nodded just the same.

Egan looked up from his meal. "Sorry, I thought I got all of them. Must have missed one." He tossed his waterskin over. "Drink some of this whiskey. It'll help get rid of the nasty taste. Go slow, though. It's a bit harsh."

Tristin took a cautious sip, remembering his experience with Samuel's ale. He winced. Egan was right—it was harsh. But it did as advertised and he quickly forgot the nastiness of the bursac.

Egan took back his waterskin.

From then on, Tristin examined each bite before cramming it into his mouth.

Two of the three patrolling barbarians returned, leaving one to keep watch at the river. Once they were finished eating, Gaal announced, "We've been here long enough. They should have seen the flames by now."

Tristin's memories of losing so decisively to the Angel flooded back at the first sight of the riverbank. He hardly noticed when the lookouts joined them and Gaal called the party to a halt.

Gaal said, "Now we hide and wait. If all goes well, they'll come to investigate soon."

Tristin asked, "And what if they send the Angel?"

"They won't."
Tristin hoped the king was right.

Chapter 31

Ian

The light of the bonfire danced across the bow of an approaching boat. Judging by the size, it couldn't hold more than a half-dozen soldiers, which bode well for Tristin's barbarian friends.

As the boat crossed the midpoint of the river, Tristin caught sight of Ian. His friend was bound by leather straps to the ship's bow with his legs dipping into the water. He was shirtless and his flesh was stretched tight over protruding ribs. His arms dangled at his sides and his head drooped.

Before the boat reached the bank, a soldier reached over the edge and held a chirping mask to Ian's face for a lifebreath. After Ian took it, the soldier held an apple to Ian's mouth. Ian defiantly turned his head away. The soldier said something, laughed, and took a bite of the apple. Tristin wondered why Ian wouldn't eat it.

Gaal whispered, "You're up, Tristin. Don't let that boat leave." Croate handed Tristin a piece of wood whittled into a club. Tristin would have preferred a war hammer instead if he thought he could lift it. Then the barbarians melted into the shadows.

Tristin ducked behind the house nearest the bank where he could still see the boat. Five of the Angel's soldiers climbed out with their swords already drawn. One stayed with Ian, while the other four marched toward the fire.

When the soldiers disappeared over the crest of the hill, it was Tristin's turn. He locked eyes on the boat and called upon his god. After a deep breath, he zipped toward the river with blistering speed.

He was upon Ian's guard in a flash. He swung the club at the soldier's head as he whipped by. The man dropped like a rock from a roof.

Tristin's momentum carried him all the way into the Slaybyrne. His eyes widened as he realized what he had done. The bank was only four steps away, but it was already four steps too many. He jerked away from the yellow blurs that crowded his feet and cut off his escape. But instead of attacking, the grinderfish parted and swam past him as if he wasn't there. Tristin lifted his eyes to the boat.

Ian struggled to hold his head up and gave Tristin a weak smile. Tristin hurried back to the bank. He cupped his friend's gaunt face with both hands. "I promised I'd come back. I can't wait to show you what I've seen."

Ian looked past him to the crest of the hill where the barbarians stood with four kneeling prisoners.

"They're with me," Tristin said with a proud grin. "I brought them to rescue you. We're going to save all our friends."

Tristin cut away the straps binding Ian and lowered him to the ground. Ian coughed and winced. Tristin gave him a sip of water from his waterskin and he choked it down.

"Why didn't you eat that apple the soldier gave you?"

"I wasn't eating anything they gave me. It's called a hunger strike."

Tristin climbed into the boat. "I'll get you something." After a quick search, he found the apple stash. This time Ian happily ate one. As soon as he was finished Tristin blurted, "I need a favor. I know you're tired, but it's the last thing you'll need to do for a while."

"Anything."

"Are you strong enough to make one more trip across Slaybyrne?"

Ian smiled weakly. "Just help me into the boat."

Gaal approached with Tolk and started to introduce himself.

Tristin interrupted the pleasantries. "He said he would help."

"Very good. That will be much appreciated, Ian."

Tolk gently lifted Ian into the boat. With the Angel's five soldiers bound together, the other barbarians joined Gaal.

Gaal ordered two of his men to stay behind and guard the captives. The rest climbed into the boat. Ian cast his stealthy net around them as they rowed across the river to the eastern bank.

Before climbing out, Gaal knelt beside Ian and whispered, "You've done well. I will have one of my men return to the other side with you. He will see to your needs. Your ordeal is over." He turned to Egan. "Take care of this man as if he were your own brother."

Egan nodded.

"Wait for us on the other bank. If we are forced to retreat before the battle has been won, we will light a fire here and hold them off until you can come back for us." He turned to Tristin. "Lead the way."

Considering the barbarians' size and overall clumsiness, Tristin decided they should go around rather than sneak through the city as he had done many times. Though he had a plan firmly in mind, a sudden thought made him hesitate.

"Is there something else?" Gaal asked.

"Actually, yes. I have something I need to do before we make the journey. It will only take a couple minutes."

Gaal pursed his lips and looked around.

"Please?"

Gaal sighed and nodded.

Tristin smiled. He raced into the sleeping city in a blur. To his relief, the old store was still standing and still had its knothole in the back wall. Tristin retrieved Makenna's godawful yet beautiful pendant and held it against his chest. He closed his eyes. "This is for you, Makenna."

"Everything good?" Gaal asked on his return.

Tristin nodded. "Everything's perfect."

"Then let's head out."

Tristin led the barbarians north around the outer edge of the city and then west past the affluent side of town to the road leading to the prison. The tiring walk took hours, but they reached it undetected. By late afternoon they were far enough away to not worry about meeting soldiers. And with the Angel's army likely already engaged in battle beyond the prison, it was time for Gaal's party to step up their pace.

As they travelled, Tristin repeatedly thought of Makenna making the same lonely journey. He wondered how scared she had been and whether the Angel's men had treated her fairly. He pictured her looking over her shoulder for him or Samuel, and it broke his heart to know her every glance back had met with disappointment.

The cracked and broken cobblestone road eventually led up a hill. At the crest, Tristin noticed two things. First, he saw the prison—a sprawling compound behind a wall. What was it with King Searle and walls? And second, he saw the faint shadow of the mountain Darragh had pointed out.

The prison grew more intimidating with every step. A water stain on one dark and dreary wall formed the face of a demon if Tristin looked at it just right. He tried to shake off his uneasiness. The plan was simple: walk through the main gates and kill anyone who tried to stop them.

Only one man stood on guard. He was a large man with no neck, sitting in a chair with a blood-stained club across his lap. He looked confused to see barbarians outside the prison. He sat motionless, watching their approach.

Tolk and Gaal stopped within a few feet of him. The guard peered up as if he'd seen enough barbarians to be unimpressed. Tolk's knuckles cracked around his sword's hilt.

Gaal broke the heavy silence. "We're here to free the prisoners."

The guard asked, "Which pritiners?"

Gaal rubbed his fist. "A lot of them."

The guard stood up. "I duntin' fear barbarians. Now bugger off."

Tolk swarmed him in a flash, taking him violently to the ground. After a half-dozen punches, Tolk stood up. The guard stayed down, his body quivering.

Gaal glanced back at Tristin. "Let's go find your sister and this Samuel fella."

Chapter 32

No Turning Back

Samuel lay in wait on the cold stone floor for Malvic to return. He longed to bathe in the blood of that bastard. Every day, every minute, every second that passed gave him more time to heal. It would be Malvic's second biggest mistake. His first was ever crossing Samuel.

Now that his wounds had healed, his god burned with such hunger for violence that nothing short of a massacre could sate. If not for his need to help Makenna, he wouldn't have been able to resist unleashing his mounting need for violence on Arthur.

Each morning brought renewed hope that Malvic would return, and that morning was no different. Arthur paced and jabbered away about the life he'd once had. Samuel leered unflinchingly at the door and didn't hear a word Arthur said.

When the heavy iron doors at the end of the hall finally clanked open and he heard Malvic's sick whistle, it felt like a blessing. Samuel couldn't wait. His ribs were still sore when he moved, but pain didn't matter anymore.

Arthur whispered, "Please don't do what you're planning, Samuel. They'll only hurt you for it. Malvic likes his torture."

"All the more reason to kill him," Samuel growled back. There was nothing in the world that could stop him now. The anticipation was almost more than he could stand. He held his finger to his lips. "Shhh."

Then he picked up his discarded shackles and held them so it would look like they still bound his wrists. Coffer peeked through the grate in the door. Samuel lifted his head to glare at him. It was all a game now.

"You're looking better," Coffer said as his keys rattled against the door. "That's good. We've been quite bored lately."

Before the door swung open, Samuel whispered one last warning to Arthur. "You might not want to watch."

Arthur turned away. Samuel whispered a prayer to his god, not for any kind of strength, but to beg him for restraint. He wasn't needed for this one.

The door swung open. Coffer and Malvic stood like presents in the doorway. The only thing missing was a bow. Coffer approached first and hovered over Samuel.

"Please," Samuel moaned. "I can't fight today."

Coffer looked to Malvic, chuckled, and then looked back to Samuel. "Sorry about your luck. This time we were thinking about giving your opponents swords."

Samuel hated bullies almost more than he hated predators, and these two men were both. "Can we talk first? I have something to tell you."

Like unwitting prey, Malvic fully stepped into the cell and gestured for Samuel to continue. His confidence was comical.

Perfect. Samuel nodded. Everyone should know the name of their murderer. "My name is Samuel." Fixing a blood-red glower on Malvic, he added, "And *I AM* the God of Killing."

"Really, now?" Coffer started to laugh, but his jaw shattered before the first guffaw left his mouth. He dropped like a stone.

Samuel stood over him, playfully swinging the shackle he'd used to strike him, and looked over his shoulder at Malvic. Fear filled the space between them, and it wasn't Samuel's. Coffer quivered at his feet. Malvic's face paled. He tried to retreat through the open door, but Samuel was on him in an instant, dragging him back into the cell. His panicked screams brought charging footsteps farther down the hall, but that was merely an inconvenience. Samuel snapped Malvic's left leg with a well-placed stomp to his knee. "Wait here."

Malvic screamed louder.

The violence came suddenly, like thunder on a clear night. The mouth of the cave in Samuel's mind went almost completely dark with only a sliver of hope shining through. When it brightened again, the walls of the hallway were painted with blood and half a dozen guards lay dead at his feet.

Samuel turned back to Malvic. He dragged a guard's body into the doorway to prevent it from closing while he worked. Malvic sobbed against the farthest wall, holding his shattered leg while Arthur knelt over Coffer, who had started to stir.

Samuel growled, "Get away from him, Arthur. There's nothing you can do for these men. The Angel himself couldn't save them now."

Fearful, and rightfully so, Arthur gently touched Coffer's shoulder before scooting over to Malvic. He whispered something sympathetic into the man's ear. It was more compassion than either of the men deserved. Samuel took a set of keys from Coffer's belt and freed his shackled ankles.

Coffer tried to speak through his fractured jaw, but Samuel couldn't understand him over the constant hum of his own rage. It was important that Coffer died first so Malvic could watch, but since Coffer hadn't personally harmed him, Samuel wouldn't drag it out. Besides, he was anxious to get to Malvic. He reached for Coffer's throat, but Coffer grabbed his wrists. Samuel snapped one of his forearms across his knee and then snapped the other just for fun. He reached for Coffer's throat again. While squeezing the life out of the big man, he watched Malvic try to drag himself to the door out of the corner of his eye. He laughed.

Coffer's eyes bulged and pleaded for mercy. It was the first bit of pleasure Samuel had felt in a while. Once Coffer's body went limp, Samuel left him and turned to Malvic. Unable to escape, Malvic rolled to his back. "I'm not going to beg," he said.

Samuel straddled his chest. "Good. It'll make things much quieter." He started with Malvic's fingers, snapping them one by one. When he scooped out Malvic's left eye with his finger, he wondered if he had crossed the line from vengeance to evil and then laughed because it didn't matter anymore. His god was hungry. And he would feed him.

It turned out Malvic had lied about not begging.

Over the dull hum filling his head, he heard other prisoners cheering from their cells. He glanced over his shoulder to the door across the hallway. The prisoner inside narrated the scene for the others down the hall. It had become a show. Samuel wouldn't disappoint. As he tested whether he could rip the broken bone from Malvic's leg, he realized he could never be himself again.

Malvic passed out. Samuel sat with his back against the wall and waited for him to wake. It was so dark in the cave of his mind that he couldn't think straight. When Malvic woke up Samuel set to work with the dirty, rusty key to the shackles. It made a surprisingly good tool for carving Malvic's skin in deep, jagged lines. He carved his name into Malvic's chest and then again across his forehead. At one point he got clumsy and wedged the key between two of Malvic's ribs where it got stuck. The other keys on the ring dangled like wind chimes. It made a great handle for dragging the bastard into the hall for everyone to see.

The God of Killing would have played for hours, but a gentle hand on Samuel's shoulder stopped him. He looked up and smiled. Makenna stood behind him. "That's enough, Sam."

Though he knew she wasn't really there, he could see a tiny light in the raging dark again. He nodded. "I'm coming, Makenna."

He stood over the dying man with drool dripping from his lower lip. The life in Malvic's remaining eye slowly faded. The rise and fall of his chest slowed. It was time for Samuel's mercy, not his god's.

Samuel stomped on Malvic's face with his heel one bone-shattering time. He wrenched the keyring free and then returned to the cell to retrieve his chirping lifemask.

Arthur flinched when Samuel handed him the bloody keys to the shackles. Samuel searched Coffer's pockets until he found the door keys. Leaving the door open so Arthur could escape if he chose, Samuel charged through the hall, unconcerned that other guards might have been alerted. In fact, he hoped they'd come. More killing now meant less killing later.

It took Samuel a little over an hour to navigate the vast corridors of the prison, killing several more guards along the way. The last guard gave him directions to Ugh's cell where Makenna was supposed to be.

He peeked into the mess hall to see what awaited him. A horde of guards gathered for some kind of meeting at the far end. Samuel raced to the second level unnoticed. As he ran along the row of cells, prisoners whispered, "Free us. Please."

Samuel ignored them. He searched every cell until he found one with a barbarian sitting against the back wall. "Are you Ugh?" he snarled.

Ugh lifted his head.

"Where's Makenna? Did you hurt her?"

Ugh shook his head and struggled to his feet. "They took her to the slave fields. I couldn't stop them."

Samuel grasped the bars in a white-knuckled grip. "Which way are the fields?"

Ugh pointed toward a set of double doors on the first floor.

"Why are the guards gathered down there?"

"The Angel and his army passed through earlier this morning. They said the king called them out. There's some sort of army attacking behind the prison."

Samuel started to leave, but Ugh called him back. "Free me. I'll help you against them."

Samuel didn't need help, especially not from a barbarian, but the more chaos he could create the better. Samuel crammed Coffer's key into the lock and twisted.

"Thank you." Ugh held out his hand.

Samuel turned away.

The main doors to the mess hall clanked open and Samuel hurried to the rail to see why. The crowd of guards turned toward the commotion. Several barbarians poured through the doors. The guards turned to flee, but the barbarians ran them down to the exultant roar of the watching prisoners.

To Samuel's shock, Tristin came through the doorway. Tristin waved when he looked up and saw him. Samuel turned away. Before he reached the stairs, Tristin was already there. "Samuel. Your ear. What ha—"

Samuel shoved him aside and kept walking.

Tristin shouted, "Where's Makenna?"

Samuel ignored him. He raced through the doors and searched for a way outside. Eventually, he found one.

Two guards stood oblivious outside the exit. Samuel killed the first guard and crippled the second in a flash. With both legs broken, the guard begged for mercy. Samuel gave him a choice. "Tell me where to find the slave fields and I won't bring you any more pain before I kill you."

"Which ones?"

"Let's start with the closest."

The soldier pointed to a distant wall across a sprawling expanse of dirt. Ever a man of his word, Samuel took the guard's sword and delivered an instantly fatal blow to his neck. He took in a deep, quivering breath and released it. His god was happy. He raced across the field toward the wall.

"I'm coming, Makenna."

Chapter 33

A Brother's Love

Tristin stood in the narrow walkway watching Samuel disappear through the door. A voice from behind broke his trance.

"Hey, kid."

Tristin turned. Though the two had never met, the barbarian's face was strangely familiar. His deep-set eyes settled on Tristin with an equally puzzled gaze. "Are you Tristin?" he asked.

Tristin nodded.

"I know your sister. She is my friend."

Tristin studied his face. "And what is your name?"

"They call me Ugh."

"No. What's your given name?"

Ugh paused as if he had to think about it. Then his eyes brightened with pride. "Gareth. Gareth Gaal."

"Gaal?"

"That's correct. Is that strange to you, boy?"

"Not at all. Gareth, you have no idea how happy I am to meet you. You're not going to believe who's with me …"

Gareth's gaze lifted past him to the stairs where Gaal stood at the landing. "Excuse me for a moment, kid." Gareth nudged past Tristin.

The barbarian king met him halfway. "You look old, brother."

"Me?" Gareth reached out and squeezed the king's biceps. "Freedom has made you soft." Then he rubbed the king's extended gut and Gaal sucked it in as much as he could. "Over all these years, have you lifted anything heavier than a fork?"

Gaal rolled his eyes.

"Where have you been? I've been locked in this shithole for more years than I can count."

"That's probably because you can only count to ten."

"A caring brother would have seen to it that I would have no need to count any higher."

"I was a child. However much I longed to come for you, such a journey through the green fog was impossible. We lost many men trying to return in the early days. I had given up hope until …," he paused and nodded toward Tristin, "… this boy showed us a way."

Tristin tugged at Gaal's forearm. "I'm sorry to interrupt, King, but we need to find Makenna."

Gareth gasped. "Did he just call you 'King'?"

Gaal nodded.

"You've decided to call yourself king? That's rich. What, did 'Almighty Emperor' not come to mind fast enough?"

Gaal scoffed and rolled his eyes again. "Tristin's right. We need to get moving."

Tristin followed Gaal and Gareth down the stairs to Tolk and the other barbarians. Gareth asked, "How many men did you bring to fight the Angel's men, Oskari?"

"All of them."

Using keys from fallen guards, Tristin helped free the rest of the barbarian prisoners. On Gareth's instructions they didn't free anyone else—he said this wing was for violent offenders—with one exception. One barbarian was sharing a cell with none other than Jakodi. Tristin couldn't open it fast enough.

Jakodi embraced him with as much shock as relief. With a proud hand on Tristin's shoulder, he said, "You never cease to amaze me, Tristin."

Tristin grinned at him. "I'm so sorry I lost your watch."

Jakodi scoffed. "No need to be sorry. It was only a watch."

Tristin handed him the keys. "Free all our Slummer friends and get out of here."

Gaal, Tristin, and Gareth led the other barbarians through the corridors until they reached an open door at the rear of the prison. Two guards lay dead outside. The only obvious path to take led to a gated wall in the distance.

Tristin said, "I can get there faster without you. I'll go find my sister."

Gaal nodded. "Don't fight anyone if you don't absolutely have to. I'll be there as soon as I can. Be careful."

As if the king's words had released a coiled spring in Tristin's legs, Tristin shot across the field and barreled through the open gate. He slowed to get his bearings on the other side. Distant battle cries and a din of clashing weapons drifted from the northwest. The fight was going strong. When he looked east, a familiar voice startled him from behind. "Hey, kid."

Tristin spun to see Samuel leaning against the wall beside the gate. He held a bloody sword over a dead prison guard. "I've been waiting for you." He stepped away from the wall.

"I thought maybe you were going for Makenna."

"I was. But I can't hold him back anymore."

"Who?"

"You need to find your sister now."

"Why?"

"I let one of the soldiers escape to bring me the Angel. I can barely see out of the cave now. It's too dark."

"What are you talking about?"

"My calling is right here. Makenna won't truly be free until I kill the Angel anyway."

"Where is she?"

"This guard said she's down there." Samuel pointed to a path that led away from the sounds of war.

Tristin turned toward the path, but Samuel stopped him. "There'll be guards at the camp. How do you plan on getting past them?" His head twitched to the side in a way Tristin found unnerving.

"I thought she'd be inside. I didn't plan for this."

Samuel looked to the side as if listening to someone next to him. "All right already. Hold on. I'm going."

Tristin's uneasiness intensified.

"Come 'ere, kid. Take my clothes." He started to disrobe.

"What?"

"Take my clothes. If you look like a prisoner, you can convince the guards to let you into the camp. Then you can find your sister."

He tossed Tristin his robe and started stripping the guard. The word "Malvic" was branded across Samuel's chest. Tristin wanted to ask what it meant, but decided now wasn't the time. "Come with me," he said. "We can find the Angel later."

Samuel shook his head as he put on the dead man's trousers. "Not this time, kid. I can't let Makenna see what I've become."

"She won't care about the scars."

"It's not the scars you can see that I'm worried about."

Tristin felt that uneasiness again. When he looked Samuel in the eyes, something dark looked back.

Samuel leaned in and whispered something into Tristin's ear.

Tristin leaned back. "You can tell her yourself when you're done. Or you can show her."

Samuel grimaced. "Not this time, kid. It's even getting harder and harder to push back the rage."

Tristin gave him a crooked look.

"You should go now. It's not safe for you to be near me anymore."

"I don't believe that."

Samuel's lip curled in an expression Tristin had never seen on his face before, as though something else had control of it. "I know you don't, kid. You'd better get moving." He traced the sharp edge of his bloody sword with one finger. "It won't be long now."

Tristin donned the prison robe over his pouch, hoping no one would notice the bulge. Then he looked past his friend to where the Angel approached on his steed in the distance. When Samuel saw the Angel, his head jerked to the side in that unnerving way and an ugly hatred contorted his face.

Tristin took a step backward. "Samuel?"

Samuel answered with a sneer. There was nothing left of the man Tristin had known in his glaring eyes. He licked his lips and let out a primal growl.

As Tristin watched Samuel march toward the Angel, he whispered, "The gods be with you, Samuel." He started for the camp, picking up a sharp-edged rock as he ran. He dragged the rock across his temple, gouging his flesh. It wasn't a deep cut, but enough to draw blood. He smeared it across his face, dropped the rock, and wiped his hands on his clothes.

The sprawling camp was surrounded by an iron fence. He slowed to what he hoped was a convincing stagger and then fell to his knees as soon as the guards at the gate looked his way.

Three of the guards ventured out to investigate. One of them prodded Tristin with his sheathed sword. "You, there. What are you doing out here?"

Tristin kept his head down. "I-I-I got left behind. I need to get back to the camp before I get in any more trouble."

With the sole of his boot, the guard shoved Tristin to his back. "Why didn't you return with your group?"

"I don't know what happened. One moment I was relieving myself, and then the next thing I knew I was waking up with a terrible headache. I think somebody hit me."

The guard studied him and the smeared blood on his face. "Take this boy inside," he finally ordered the others.

The two other guards grabbed him beneath his arms and yanked him up. He let his feet drag, forcing them to practically carry him back to the camp.

Once they passed through the heavily guarded entrance, one guard asked, "Which one's your tent?"

Tristin limply pointed across the campsite to no tent in particular. "I think I can make it from here," he said.

They released his arms. He pretended to almost fall before steadying himself and shuffling in the direction he'd pointed. The two guards turned and marched back to the front gate. Tristin wondered why so many guarded the same gate. There were at least a dozen of them that he could see, and they all seemed to be waiting for something. Tristin wondered if they had any idea that what they were waiting for was a barbarian army. He'd love to see their faces when they figured it out.

But first things first. He needed to find his sister. A few prisoners milled around the camp, but most of them stayed in their tents. Tristin grabbed one man's arm as he passed. "Do you know Makenna?" he asked.

The man scowled at him.

"Makenna? Do you know her?" Tristin said more forcefully.

The man scrunched his nose, wrinkled his brow, and shook his head.

Tristin hurried to the next row of tents, asking several more prisoners along the way. Each one shrugged their shoulders and blew him off. While pleading with a small group of men, two other passing prisoners stopped. "Excuse me," one of them asked. "Who are you looking for?" His thick, wild eyebrows met in the center. He was thin, but with the look of a man who used to be plenty strong.

"I'm looking for a girl named Makenna. Do you know her?"

The man squinted and studied Tristin's face. "Would she be a young girl who remarkably shares your likeness?"

"Yes."

The man looked to his partner and then back to Tristin. "I think the girl you're looking for is …" He scanned the tents nearest the fence. "Yeah. Over there in one of those."

He pointed to a line of tents that looked like all the other tents.

Tristin thanked him and ran to where he had pointed, careful not to use his god. After looking into three tents and finding only sleeping prisoners, the scene in the fourth tent nearly stopped his heart.

Makenna lay motionless on her back with someone else squatting over her. The man was holding a mask to her face. Then he turned toward Tristin, and suddenly Tristin couldn't breathe.

"Dad?" he whispered.

Rhett stared back, equally speechless.

Tristin dropped to his knees. His father lowered Makenna's head gently onto a rolled-up blanket and crawled to Tristin. He grabbed him so tightly that he almost broke Tristin's ribs. "By the gods, son.

How is this possible?" He pulled Tristin's head against his chest and kissed the top of it again and again.

"I came to free you, Dad. And I brought a barbarian army with me."

Rhett pulled away. "Let me look at you, boy." He regarded his son up and down. "I can't believe you're actually here in front of me. I don't know what to say." Makenna wheezed in a breath, cutting short the father-son reunion. "Your sister's very sick. Her mask is failing."

"I know. But I know how to fix them." Tristin dug into his pouch and retrieved the crystal he had brought specifically for Makenna. "This is what makes the masks work. I just need another working mask to change out the crystals because Makenna's filter is probably ruined."

"Crystals? Filters? What are you talking about?"

"No time to explain. I need a mask."

Rhett held out his own. "Take mine."

Tristin shoved it away. "No. You need yours. I'm not going to let you or Makenna die like I did Mom."

"You didn't let her die, son. King Searle did. What do you need me to do?"

"Find another mask." With a grin he added, "Preferably one from a guard."

Rhett's proud gaze morphed into focused resolve. "I'll be right back." He backed out of the tent and closed the flap.

Tristin took Rhett's place next to Makenna and watched her chest flutter in time with her wheezing breaths. Her face was thin, pale, and tired, and her eyes were mere slits between swollen, reddened lids. He whispered, "Makenna? It's me. Tristin. Can you hear me?"

Her eyelids fluttered.

"Just rest. I'm going to help you." He held her hand while he waited for Rhett to return. "Be strong for just a little longer."

Rhett was winded when he ripped open the tent flap. He had four fresh scratches on the side of his neck. He also held a mask clenched in his fist. He handed it over. Tristin noticed that two of his knuckles were scraped and swelling into one nasty lump.

Tristin grabbed the mask and dug into the nosecone with the special tool one of the barbarian blacksmiths had made him. Carefully, he exchanged the crystal from the soldier's mask with the new one from his pouch. Then he gently took Makenna's thin, calloused hand again. "I'm sorry for this," he whispered. He swiped the sharp edge of his tool across the pad of her index finger. She was too weak to flinch. He held her finger over the mask and squeezed it until a drop of blood fell onto the crystal. Tristin quickly replaced the cover and looked up into his father's concerned eyes.

"Now, we wait for it to chirp," he said.

"That's it?"

Tristin nodded.

Neither of them spoke while they watched the lifemask. An eternity passed before the blue glow flared a single time in the nosecone. Tristin held his breath. And then, like a newborn baby's first cry, the mask chirped and the blue glow pulsed with Makenna's rapid breaths. Tristin shoved it over her mouth and nose and held it until the tiniest whistle accompanied her next gasp.

"Did it work?" Rhett asked.

"I don't know. It'll take time."

Chapter 34

Of Gods and Angels

The noisome odor of death from the battlefield filled the air. Samuel breathed it in with a grin. The clanging of swords and wailing of men sang a shrill song of war that Samuel longed to join. But before he could do that, he had one other matter to attend to.

The Angel dismounted from his stallion. To any normal man, seeing the Angel approach with the promise of violence in his eyes would bring fear. For Samuel it brought delicious anticipation. He stood firm, ready to free his god completely. It was the only way he could win.

The Angel stopped less than ten feet away. Tension crackled between them. "We should have done this when I sentenced you," he said.

Samuel nodded. "Yes, we should have."

The Angel cocked his head. "There's something different about you today, Samuel. Though I can't quite place what. I mean, besides your missing ear and fresh scars."

Samuel knew exactly what it was. It was the rage filling his eyes with red. Any true warrior should be able to see it. He playfully twirled his sword at his side; the Angel scoffed in return.

The Angel invited Samuel forward with a subtle wave. Samuel didn't need the invite. This was the reason he had lived his life.

The Angel spoke as Samuel sauntered closer. "I sentence you to death for your crimes here today."

"Your sentences mean nothing to me. You're a fraud. You don't serve justice. You serve a corrupt king."

"Heh. You truly are one of a kind, I'll give you that."

"You'll give me your head." The air blistered between them.

Samuel had always found that killing a strong opponent was best done suddenly. He launched himself at the Angel, covering the ten feet between them as if it were two. The Angel barely deflected Samuel's initial attack. Samuel spun around with another strike, his god increasing his speed. But whatever god the Angel harbored granted him speed as well. To anyone watching, it would seem that the Angel's defense was effortless, but Samuel saw the strain in his enemy's creased forehead. He decided sheer relentlessness like Zakaira's style was the best way to end this fight quickly.

Though it was subtle, the Angel gave ground, giving Samuel confidence that his unyielding assault was effective. Samuel lunged again, and again the Angel defended.

Samuel had never met a man who could match his god. He moved closer with a series of relentless strikes and drove his heel into the top of the Angel's kneecap. The Angel staggered backward. The two warriors locked eyes and Samuel searched the Angel's for surprise. He saw none.

It was the Angel's turn to show what he had. He was fast and deadly, taking flesh from Samuel's right shoulder and left thigh before Samuel could even react.

In Samuel's mind, the tiny dot of light at the mouth of the cave snuffed completely, leaving only blackness … Blackness and the Angel. Ignoring the fresh wounds, Samuel feigned a strike, spun around, and sank his blade into the Angel's arm just below the leather shoulder guard. The Angel winced and jerked away. A trickle of blood dripped from his elbow. Samuel grinned.

The Angel lashed out with his sword almost too quickly for Samuel to see. Almost. Despite the Angel's skill and speed, Samuel adjusted and defended well.

The Angel swung his sword at Samuel's neck. To escape the would-be fatal blow, Samuel tumbled to the ground. The Angel was on him in a flash. Samuel rolled away as the next deadly plunge embedded the Angel's sword in the dirt beside his head. He kicked the Angel's chest plate with such unnatural force that the Angel left the ground and landed on his back at least a dozen feet away. Samuel bounced to his feet with the grace of a dancer.

The Angel stood up and wiped dirt off his dented chest plate. He nodded respectfully; Samuel spat at him in return. The two warriors studied each other as they circled. The Angel squinted and tilted his head. Then he smiled as though he had solved a riddle.

Samuel lunged again. Though he moved faster and more precisely than any man should be able to, the Angel somehow countered. Samuel tried to avoid the next blow, but the Angel took the top of his other ear. Ignoring the burning pain and the distant thought that he needed to stop losing ears, Samuel thrust his sword again.

The Angel's swordplay remained flawless while Samuel felt suddenly sloppy. It was as if the Angel's speed had doubled. He had thrown Samuel off his game, and it was a feeling Samuel had never experienced before. But like any good warrior, he adapted. He just needed to stop giving so much flesh and blood beforehand. The two attacked and counterattacked, bouncing around like drops of water thrown on a sizzling skillet.

It was becoming increasingly obvious that the Angel's swordplay matched the Killing God's. Another approach was needed. Since Samuel had killed just as many men with his bare hands as he had with his blade, he figured a change in tactics might be what was needed now.

He swung his weapon again, offering it up in a way that only the most skilled warriors would be able to recognize. Though he knew it was risky and would quite possibly hurt something fierce, he also knew if the Angel took the bait it would open him up for the second part of Samuel's attack. As expected, the Angel's blade met Samuel's.

The Angel flicked his wrist in a half-circle and his blade slid along Samuel's to the hilt. Samuel tried to let loose without revealing his plan or sacrificing his hand. He failed on both counts. He'd never witnessed such speed and skill. The Angel's sword severed Samuel's pinky, the remaining nub of his ring finger, and continued through his palm to the wrist. It was more of a sacrifice than Samuel wanted to make, but it gave him his shot.

He punched the wrist of the Angel's sword hand, knocking the weapon away. In the same fluid motion, Samuel spun and slammed his heel against the side of the Angel's helmet, knocking it askew on his pretty head.

The Angel stumbled out of reach. He straightened, removed his dented helmet, and tossed it to the ground. Blood trickled from his lower lip.

"Is that surprise I see on your face?" Samuel asked.

The Angel shook his head. He was a liar. He glanced at his sword lying a few feet away.

"Go for it," Samuel said.

The Angel was too experienced to fall for such an amateurish trap. If he lunged for his weapon, Samuel would be on his back before his fingers ever touched his blade, like he had killed Zakaira. But Samuel didn't become so skilled by relying solely on the mistakes of his opponent. He charged headlong. The Angel shuffled backward out of reach while pummeling Samuel's face bloody with his fists. Samuel plowed forward undeterred, fresh blood from a cut on his brow blinding one of his eyes. He grabbed for something—anything—on the Angel's body to pull him close. He snagged one of the Angel's decorative chains with his two remaining fingers. Despite the pounding he was taking to his increasingly battered face, he held on for dear life and yanked the Angel to the dirt with a thud and a grunt. By as much luck as skill, he landed straddling the Angel's chest. He rained punches designed to maim onto the Angel's soft, unscarred face. The ground shook beneath each blow to the Angel's head. Blood sprayed from the Angel's nose and above his left eye.

"Do you see?" Samuel cried in the midst of his bloodlust. "You're no angel. You bleed like all others."

Despite the relentless beating, the Angel never panicked, never stopped searching for an out. Calmly, he grabbed for Samuel's right arm as Samuel threw another punch. Before Samuel could pull free, the Angel snapped his arm at the elbow. Samuel hesitated for only a second, trying to process how badly he was injured. That second was all the Angel needed. He bucked Samuel from his chest. Samuel landed next to the Angel's sword.

Samuel grabbed the hilt with his left hand. He strained to lift it, but the sword weighed a ton, nearly yanking his shoulder from the socket. His god gave him the strength to pick it up, but its weight made wielding it impractical.

The Angel sprang to his feet with an air of victory oozing from his cocky, blood-tinged smile. He dragged his forearm across his upper lip, smearing gore from his nose across his cheek as if it were a badge of honor. His chin-length blond bangs were plastered to his face with a combination of sweat and blood.

Samuel dropped the Angel's sword. His right arm hung awkwardly at his side, blood pouring from where his two fingers used to be. "Do you know why you bleed at my hands?" he screamed.

The Angel smirked. He wasn't even winded.

"Because you are, and have always been, a perversion of the justice you claim to deliver. You're a puppet." Not waiting for a rebuttal, Samuel charged, scooping his own sword from the ground with his left hand.

The Angel staggered backward. Samuel spun like a flash of lightning. The Angel's eyes widened. Many years of a civilization living in fear beneath the Angel's rule was about to end with one final, beautiful act of violence. Samuel felt the victory long before landing his killing blow. His god gave it all he had. The blade drove toward the Angel's neck with blazing speed and precision. He saw nothing the Angel could do to stop him. It was as good as over.

And then the Angel shifted so slightly that it seemed he didn't move at all. With Samuel's blade inches from his throat, Samuel's left forearm shattered. His sword whiffed past the Angel's cheek before the pain even registered. The Angel's soft face turned dark and angry in an instant. His upper lip curled over bloody teeth. At that moment, Samuel realized what he'd never allowed himself to believe: The Killing God had met his equal.

The Angel snatched Samuel's sword from the air and swung it. Samuel dodged the first attack, but the Angel trailed him with the blade dancing between them. Samuel bounced away from the Angel's next lunge, and again the Angel followed him like a shadow. The sword plunged toward Samuel's head once more, and Samuel barely slipped away.

Worse than his injuries and the Angel's relentless attack was the boisterous grin plastered across the Angel's face. Samuel shifted away from the next blow and instantly realized his mistake. His god was a fool. The Angel had lured him to the exact spot where his next blow would land. It was the same tactic Samuel had used to great effect many times before, yet he had never met anyone skilled enough to do it to him.

The Angel dropped the sword and grabbed the back of Samuel's neck. His grip was as strong as Samuel's hatred. With his piercing eyes devoid of mercy, he drew a shorter blade from his waist and jammed it upward into Samuel's gut. Samuel's body knew it was over before his brain accepted that he had been bested.

With an angry grimace, the Angel twisted the blade. Samuel almost nodded in appreciation; it's what he would have done. The Angel's mouth was close enough to his nose that Samuel smelled his stale breath when he whispered, "I am unbeatable."

Samuel locked eyes with him, not yet willing to concede victory. The Angel yanked the blade free and let Samuel drop to his knees. He backed away. The wound was mortal. He knew it. Samuel knew it.

"Your god doesn't work on me, Samuel. My justice cannot be denied."

The Angel casually retrieved his sword from the ground.

Samuel lifted his eyes, the red haze of rage fading. He cursed his god for his failure. "Will you give me a warrior's death?" he asked.

The Angel nodded. "You have been the greatest foe I have ever faced, Samuel. You should know that before you die."

Samuel spat blood into the dirt. He looked toward the tents where he hoped he had given Tristin enough time to save Makenna. Thinking of her again sparked a small sliver of light in his mind.

"I will kill your friends now," the Angel said.

Samuel knew that was probably inevitable, and the pain of that realization was worse than any physical pain that currently wracked his body.

The Angel raised his sword. "I rather enjoy killing gods. Goodbye, Samuel."

Samuel whispered a prayer for Tristin and Makenna and the light in his mind brightened like a sun. For the first time in his violent life he felt warm and at peace. He saw his wife and daughter waiting for him. He smiled. The Angel took his head.

Chapter 35

In Search of a King

Makenna's condition had improved at least a little, but she still hadn't woken up. While waiting, Tristin told Rhett everything he'd missed since his arrest, from living in the Slums to his banishment Outside. He described the barbarian kingdom in vivid detail and proudly related how he had learned to repair lifemasks. Rhett sat quietly and listened, a mix of amazement and fatherly pride on his face.

Tristin had just gotten to his meeting with Samuel outside the prison when Makenna croaked, "Your voice is so annoying."

Though her eyes were still slits in her swollen face, their customary brightness was returning. The corners of her lips struggled to touch her dimples. Rhett helped her sit up and draped his thin arms around her from behind. She gave Tristin a what-took-you-so-long sort of look.

Tristin scowled back. "Tell me the truth, sis. You swayed me to take you to the Mask Exchange, didn't you?"

She nodded miserably. "I am so sorry. Believe me, I've had plenty of time to think about how wrong it was. I felt like I had no choice."

"You know, Samuel could have killed me for that."

"I know, I know. I'm a little surprised he didn't, actually." She leaned against Rhett, still too weak to sit up on her own. "Where is Samuel anyway?"

"He's killing the Angel. Probably already has."

"We should help him." She tried to get up, but her arms and legs weren't yet as strong as her will.

Rhett rubbed the back of her head. "Just relax, honey. You need to get your strength back."

Her shoulders squared. "I'm actually feeling better."

Tristin dug through his waist pouch. "I have something for you." He retrieved the ugly, dirt-brown pendant.

Makenna's eyes brightened. "Is that ...?"

Tristin nodded.

"How did you find it after all these years?"

"I was telling one of my new barbarian friends about when I hid it from you and how I couldn't remember where I had put it. Then it just came to me. When I went back to look, it was still there."

Makenna slowly took it from his hand. "It's as beautiful as I remembered."

Tristin wondered what *she* was looking at because he didn't see anything beautiful.

"Thank you, Tristin."

Tristin took it from her and fastened the chain around her neck. She put her hand over it and squeezed.

She started to say something else when someone outside shouted, "There's a fight at the gates." Prisoners ran toward the fence.

Tristin turned back to Makenna and Rhett. "I'll go check." He used his god to get to the gate in a flash. There were no guards left inside the fence that he could see. He fought through the crowd for a better look. Gaal and his brother stood in the center of ten fallen guards. They appeared winded but no worse for wear.

Tristin zipped to Gaal's side. "I've found them, King. I've found my sister and my dad. They're alive."

Gaal's head was on a swivel constantly monitoring the surroundings. "That's great, Tristin. But we need to go now. Gather your family and come with us before the Angel arrives."

"We don't have to worry about the Angel anymore. Samuel is taking care of him. He—"

The weight of a mountain was in the sad shake of Gaal's head. "I'm afraid your friend Samuel isn't part of this battle anymore."

"Wait. No. What do you mean?"

"He fell to the Angel's blade. I saw it with my own eyes. I'm sorry, Tristin. Samuel is dead."

A cold, hard knot replaced the bright hope in Tristin's heart. If the gods favored the Angel over someone as deadly as Samuel, who was left to stand against him? Tristin staggered and caught himself. "But ..."

Gaal grabbed his shoulders "Tristin," he snapped, his voice deep and commanding. "This battle has been lost. Gather your family and flee. We will try to hold off the Angel. You must escape."

"But—"

"Listen to me, Tristin. The Angel is coming. It's over. We failed. There's nothing you can do about it. Just get away from here and run as far as you can from this place."

"What about you? What about your people?"

"We will fight until none of us draw breath."

Bewildered, Tristin held his gaze. "Come with us. We'll fight again another day."

Gaal shook his head. "No. This was always going to be our final battle one way or another. When I agreed to come, I knew this was a possibility. Besides, I've always wanted a shot at the Angel." He winked. "With my brother at my side, no one can beat us." His smile didn't reach his eyes. "Now get going. There's no room for debate."

Tristin felt unworthy of such a sacrifice. As he looked helplessly at his big friend, his eyes drifted past him to a single horseman cantering across the open ground without a worry in the world. Gaal followed his gaze. Gareth took up a guard's sword and straightened to his full intimidating height.

Gaal pulled his war hammer from his back. He nodded. "Go now." He gave Tristin's shoulder a slight shove. "Goodbye, Tristin. I hope we will meet again, in this world or the next." With that, he and Gareth marched toward the waiting Angel.

The barbarian brothers stopped short of the Angel's horse and separated—Gaal to one side and Gareth to the other. The Angel dismounted and drew his sword. His perfect face was now marred by Samuel's work.

Instead of running as Gaal had ordered, Tristin stood and watched.

"Tristin," Rhett shouted from behind. Tristin glanced over his shoulder to see that another prisoner had joined his father and they were helping Makenna through the crowd. They hurried to him.

Tristin nodded to the stranger who Makenna introduced as Joseph. "Dad, take Makenna and go to the castle in the mountain." He pointed past the tent city.

"Why the castle?" Makenna asked.

"We have no other choice. We're going to meet the king and end all this one way or another."

Makenna's eyes widened. "Shouldn't we wait for Samuel?"

Tristin grimly shook his head.

"Why not? Samuel's our only chance. If we find him—"

"Makenna, Samuel's not coming. He can't help us now."

"Why not? Where is he?"

There was no way to soften the answer and no time to try. He held her gaze. "He's dead. The Angel killed him."

Her hands shot to her mouth. "What? No."

Tristin tried to hug her, but she pulled away.

"You're lying."

"I wish I was. I'm so sorry."

"No. He would never leave me behind."

"Look at me, Makenna." She wouldn't at first, but he gently guided her chin back and leaned into her view. "I saw Samuel just before he fought the Angel and he gave me a message for you."

She dragged in a breath and blinked back tears. "It's not true."

"He said, 'because of you, I'm smiling now.'"

Those words released all the sorrow she had held back in a single overwhelming squall. Tristin pulled her forehead to his chest and caressed her shorn hair. After a moment, he looked to Rhett and motioned for him to take her.

She repeated, "It's not possible," over and over as Rhett and Joseph guided her away along the path that led toward the mountain. Then they were too far away and all Tristin heard was her sobbing.

Once the three were out of sight, Tristin turned his attention back to the Angel and the barbarian brothers. The battle had already started.

Gaal swung his hammer with a grunt. What he lacked in grace, he made up for in brute power. Gareth attacked from the other side. The Angel ducked Gaal's powerful swing, spun, and defended against Gareth's sword with his own blade. The sheer strength of Gareth's blow knocked the Angel off balance. Gaal swung his hammer again, and again the Angel dodged, though he misjudged the king's wingspan. Gaal's hammer bashed his side below his left arm. The impact lifted the Angel from his feet and sent him sprawling face-first on the ground. Gareth pounced.

But the Angel bounced up and faced them again. He leaned to one side with his arm drawn tight against his ribs. His upper lip curled and his eyes seared through them. He attacked.

With speed matching Tristin's, in one fluid motion he shifted away from Gaal's next swing, ducked Gareth's sword, and plunged his blade up through Gareth's gut. Gareth dropped his sword and grabbed the Angel's hilt, but he couldn't stop the sword from bursting through his back. The Angel yanked his blade free and spun toward Gaal as the king swung his hammer again. The Angel ducked and swiped his sword across the small of Gaal's back before Gareth had even fallen to his knees. Gaal's chest jutted outward and he crashed to the ground. The Angel stood proud.

Tristin covered his mouth. He couldn't believe the battle had ended so quickly.

The Angel drew in short, angry breaths. He tilted his head and stared at his fallen foes as they writhed on the ground. Gaal rolled to his back and coughed blood into the air. The Angel clutched his sword hilt with both hands and twirled the blade so that it pointed downward.

"Nooo," Tristin shouted. He took a breath from his chirping mask and called upon his god. The Angel lifted his sword above his head for the killing blow. Gaal lay glowering helplessly up at him. Tristin sped toward them. Having no weapon, he lowered his shoulder, held his breath, and collided with the Angel with enough force to knock them both to the ground. The Angel's sword plunged into the dirt nearby. Tristin gasped, the wind knocked from his lungs.

The Angel rolled to his knees holding his left elbow close to his injured ribs. He stood up. Though an invisible chain seemed to be wrapped around Tristin's chest, he rolled to his hands and knees and struggled to his feet. His eyes met the Angel's.

"Your king is a liar," Tristin shouted.

The Angel tossed his hair from his eyes with a flick of his head. "You sound like Samuel before I took his head. Are you going to run again? I grow tired of chasing you. It is past time for you to meet justice."

"You mean King Searle's justice?"

"Is there any other kind?"

Tristin scoffed. "I've seen the world since we last met. You are a fool."

With Tristin-like speed, the Angel lunged and grabbed for Tristin's throat. Surprised, Tristin jerked backward, the Angel's fingernails grazing his neck. Tristin gathered his wits and ran, not toward the castle and his family, but toward the Slaybyrne. If the Angel was going to kill them all, he should do it knowing the fog was a lie.

Tristin blazed past the slave tents and the prison wall where he saw a headless body. He turned away, trying to convince himself it wasn't Samuel's, even though he knew it was. He wished he hadn't seen it. The sounds of battle grew louder from the north. He could almost see the water ahead when he heard something behind him. He had no time to react before a powerful hand grabbed the back of his neck, stopping him cold and yanking him from the ground. It was impossible; no one could catch him from behind.

The Angel turned Tristin to face him, Tristin's feet dangling helplessly above the ground. Tristin kicked, but the Angel didn't even flinch.

The Angel drew a bloody dagger from his waist. "This is what I killed your friend Samuel with. Now I'm going to use it to kill you and your friends." He pressed the point to the soft underside of

Tristin's chin. "I'm sick of you, boy. I have …" His eyes drifted over Tristin's shoulder. "I … I …"

Tristin tried to speak, but the Angel's grip on his throat was too tight. Wrinkles slowly creased the Angel's forehead. He lowered his arm and his grip loosened. Tristin dropped hard to his rear. The Angel stepped past him as if in a trance. Tristin rubbed his neck and followed the Angel's gaze to the river—to the slaves shoveling green powder into the clear water.

Tristin stood up behind him, massaging his throat. "Now do you see?" he rasped.

The Angel ignored him, his gaze locked on the water.

Tristin persisted. "You don't need these stupid masks outside Altenbyrne. Only here where King Searle rules."

The Angel's dagger clanged on the rocky ground. He whispered, "But the wizard?"

"There's no wizard. There's no curse. Just your crooked king poisoning us all. That's it. I may not be able to beat you, Angel, but you can't call yourself Justice anymore, either. Your whole life has been based on a lie."

He whispered a name Tristin had never heard before. It sounded like "Crighton." There was unbelievable sadness in it. Then he glared over his shoulder. His jaw muscles tightened. His mask chirped and he stared down at it. Then he unclipped it and slowly lifted it to his face. After he took his lifebreath, he dropped his mask in the dirt and lifted a baleful scowl toward the mountain castle.

Tristin stepped in front of him. "Do you finally see?"

The Angel shoved him aside and marched toward the castle.

Tristin followed from a distance. The Angel didn't say another word. When they passed Gaal and Gareth, Tristin stopped and knelt beside them. Gaal opened his eyes. "Guess I didn't do as well as I'd hoped, huh?" he said, weakly.

"You did fine. Where's Tolk and the others?"

"I sent them to the front line." Gaal grunted and winced. "I can't feel my legs, Tristin."

"I know. I'll bring help as soon as I can." He squeezed Gaal's hand and stood up. "I'll be back. I promise." A quick check on Gareth assured he was still breathing. Then Tristin caught up to the

Angel again and trailed him. The closer they got to the castle, the more the green fog thinned. The Angel looked around curiously. By the time they reached the castle stairs, the air was as clear as it was in the barbarian village.

Tristin took in the spectacle that was the castle. Deep, jagged ridges and jutting rock formations matched those in the mountain as if sculpted by the same gods. It was impossible to tell where the castle ended and the mountain began. Enormous double doors large enough to build a small house between stood at the top of the seemingly infinite stairs. Barbarian-sized statues of crowned men wearing robes flecked with bright, multicolored jewels lined the walls on each side of the doorway. Rhett, Joseph, and Makenna stood next to one of them.

At first Tristin was surprised there weren't guards posted at the double doors, but after a moment's thought it made perfect sense. The castle hadn't likely faced a single threat in over a hundred years. That was plenty of time for vigilance to grow into complacency.

The Angel started up the stairs with Tristin on his heels. When Rhett looked back by chance and saw the Angel marching up, his face filled with panic. Then he saw Tristin. Tristin shrugged and waved for him to move aside.

Rhett guided Makenna and Joseph behind him and shielded them as the Angel reached the last step. The Angel barely glanced at them before grabbing the hoop handles of the double doors. He flung them open effortlessly and marched inside.

Tristin ran to his family.

"What's going on?" Makenna asked.

"It's all right. I made sure the Angel saw the powder going in the river. Come on. It's time to finish this." He waved for them to follow.

Makenna grabbed his arm. "Did you see Samuel?"

Tristin swallowed and nodded.

"So, it's true?"

"I'm afraid so. I'm so sorry."

"And Ugh?" she whispered. "Is he dead, too?" Her voice quivered.

"He's alive. But his fight is over for today."

Tristin led them into the foyer where a blast of warm air met his cheeks. He quickly saw the source—a magnificent two-story stone fireplace in the center of the room with a decorative block chimney stretching to the ceiling seemingly miles above. Decorative iron rails rode winding stairways around each side of the fireplace to a landing and another colossal door behind it.

Plush carpet replaced the cold, hard stone beneath the thin soles of his shoes, the thick pile nearly swallowing his feet. Meticulously placed stone tables against each wall held elaborate vases, each bursting with vibrant flowers of lavender and maroon. They were far more stunning than any flowers Darragh had shown him in the forest. The walls were lined with gold-plated oil lamps burning bright enough to illuminate the entire room, even without the fireplace blazing.

Life-sized statues of half-naked women stood on each side of an entrance to a hallway beneath the stairs to the left. Two dead guards were lying there.

"Which way?" Makenna asked.

"I guess we follow the bodies," Tristin answered. As he pulled the double doors closed behind them he noticed spears large enough to have been made for barbarians were mounted on either side of the entry. He wondered if the spears were trophies from the first barbarian war.

They stepped over the dead guards on their way through the hall. At the farthest end, bright light poured through an open door. Behind it men shouted curses and swords clanged together. Rhett and Makenna stopped short of the doorway. Tristin and Joseph pressed against the wall next to them.

Makenna whispered, "What are we doing here? We should be running as far from this place as we can."

Tristin shook his head. "No. We've run long enough. Today we bring down a king."

She pulled him in for a hug. "I love you, Tristin."

"I love you, too, sis." He pulled away and slipped past Rhett and Joseph. He took a deep breath and stepped through the door onto a landing of the grandest staircase he'd ever seen overlooking a magnificent ballroom.

Chapter 36

The Great Lie

Tristin stood in awe on the landing. The ballroom stretched at least as far and wide as the prison mess hall. Candelabras and mirrors lined golden walls. Three huge golden chandeliers hung from the vaulted ceiling down the center of the room, each with at least a hundred candles burning bright and hot.

The floor was nearly hidden beneath exquisite rugs, gold coins and jewelry, and tables of food of every flavor. More flowers than Tristin could pick in a lifetime decorated seemingly every open space along the walls. The room stank of rotten flesh as though some of the cooked animals had been there for a while.

The Angel stood in the center of the room amid the bodies of six slaughtered guards. He lifted his eyes, taking in the enormity of the room as Tristin had. His gaze lingered on piles of unused masks heaped in one corner. His jaw hardened.

He glowered at a slob of a man nearly swallowed by the cushions of a gaudy, jewel-encrusted golden throne. The man's dark, curly hair poked from beneath an oversized crown that matched his hideous throne. A gaping purple robe allowed rolls of hairy fat to hang out over his waist. Bits of food rested in his wild beard and matted chest hair. His nose was as wide as the corners of his lips and his eyes were dark pebbles almost lost within his fat face. He fixed an imperious glare on the Angel and set his jeweled chalice aside.

"What are you doing in here?" he sneered.

The Angel stood silent.

Tristin cautiously descended the stairs, his eyes never leaving the king.

King Searle shouted, "Answer me. What is the meaning of this? Why are you in my castle? And why did you kill my guards?"

The Angel returned a death scowl.

Makenna, Joseph, and Rhett joined Tristin at the bottom of the stairs, gawking at the tableau before them. Tristin motioned for them to stay quiet.

King Searle grabbed his armrests and wiggled and scooted forward on his barbarian-sized throne. Then he dropped to his feet. He stood to the Angel's chest yet was nearly five times as wide. His open robe revealed the bottom of his urine-stained undergarments. "I asked you a question, Angel."

The Angel tilted his head. He didn't answer.

King Searle shouted again, "Angel, are you a mute? I'm speaking to you." Then he mumbled, "I don't know how my predecessors ever dealt with you. You know—"

The Angel snapped, "I will do the speaking now."

The king's shoulders drew back. "What did you say?"

"SILENCE," the Angel roared.

Another group of six soldiers raced in from a hidden door in the back of the room. When they saw the Angel surrounded by their fallen brethren, they lowered their swords and froze. The Angel ignored them.

"Why do you not carry a mask?" the Angel asked.

"I-I do.' The king pointed to one of the piles. His hand trembled. "It's over there somewhere." King Searle's tone softened. "Angel, you know how good my family has been to you. Why would you disobey my strictest edict by coming here?"

"I've already seen the powder. I've seen it put into the clear water of the Slaybyrne. You are causing the fog."

"No, I'm not. That powder you saw is to lessen the fog's potency. The wiza—"

The Angel shouted, "No more lies."

"I'm not lying. You must believe me. I am your master."

The Angel looked over his shoulder at Makenna. "Young one, make him tell me the truth. I must hear it."

Tristin stepped forward and shouted, "You've seen the truth. Are you dense?"

Makenna gently touched his arm. "It's all right, Tristin. He needs this." She stepped around him, suddenly full of confidence, and walked straight-backed toward the throne. Then she locked eyes with the king and said in the strongest voice she'd managed since waking, "King Searle, you will speak only truth from now on. Tell the Angel what the powder really does."

King Searle rolled his eyes. But even as he scoffed, he answered, "The powder is the poison, you fools. We control all of you with it. You're all idiots." His eyes widened and he clapped a pudgy hand over his mouth.

The Angel's expression withered. "Did the invaders even create the fog?"

"Of course they did," King Searle answered through his fingers.

"The fog killed my son. Did your family even try to stop it?"

"No, why would we? Then we wouldn't be able to control you all. My ancestor was a genius. He discovered a new use for the blue crystals and invented the masks, and then he found a way to make the poison even stronger so no one could live without one. He—"

The Angel's cold glower silenced the king. A stoic resolve washed over him as he ground his teeth. "I've heard all I need to hear. Your family killed my son. In a way, you also killed my wife." He bowed his head. "I know what needs to be done now."

The king opened his mouth to protest but the Angel roared, "ENOUGH," and it shook the golden chandeliers.

King Searle's imperiousness wilted before their eyes. He pulled his robe closed as if suddenly shy.

The Angel clenched his fists at his sides. King Searle looked around the room frantically. Seeing the guards at the back, he shouted, "Arrest this false Angel."

The guards took one look at the Angel and shook their heads in concert.

The Angel addressed them. "Go to the battlefield. Tell the commanders I have ordered a surrender. We have killed too many barbarians because of this lie. This war ends now."

All six guards nearly trampled each other to get to the stairs. Tristin and the others stepped out of their way as they raced past.

The Angel's fingers traced his sword hilt.

King Searle backed away until he bumped into his throne.

"Why did you call for me?" the Angel growled. "You must have known I'd see what you've done."

"I had no choice. I needed your men. I needed your skills. Without your army, the barbarians would overrun my guards. Besides, you have never questioned my family before. I thought I could smooth things over once the battle was won. I didn't even know about your family." The king clasped his hands together and pleaded, "Please, Angel. Have mercy. I'll do whatever I need to do to right the wrongs I've committed."

The Angel glared at him, his eyes so cold that Tristin shivered. "Can you bring back my wife and son?"

"You know I can't do that. Besides, that was my ancestor. Not me."

The Angel stepped toward him. The king's eyes danced around the room looking for somewhere to hide. Then they brightened. "Angel, I proclaim a new law."

The Angel shook his head. "It is too late for that. Your own laws require a sentence of death for the crime of murder. Killing your own subjects with poison fog is the very definition of murder on a massive scale. I hereby sentence you to death."

The king dropped to his knees and stretched a supplicating hand toward the Angel. In one lightning swipe, the Angel drew his sword and swung. Makenna covered her eyes; Tristin kept his open. King Searle's head landed on the throne, terror permanently frozen on his face. And then his body flopped over beside it.

The Angel lowered his sword and his head.

Tristin stepped forward. "What will you do with us, Angel?"

Looking more than a little dazed, the Angel wiped the blood from his blade onto his pant leg. He shook his head and paced across the room to the opposite wall. When he turned back, a tear crawled down his delicate bruised cheek.

Makenna called after him, "Angel? What are you doing?"

The Angel looked up. "I find you all innocent and rescind every sentence I have delivered." He smiled sadly. "I find myself to be unjust. I have nothing left. My role as the Angel of Justice is my entire life. That is now gone.

"I am no longer the Angel of Justice. My name is Keenan. I was married and I was a father. I loved my wife and son more than life. I believed the green fog was the work of an evil wizard. I believed the Searles were our saviors. I was wrong. And I've been wrong every day since. I hope you can forgive me."

He pressed the point of his blade to the soft underside of his chin and held the hilt with both hands.

Makenna covered her mouth. "Please, Tristin, use your speed. Stop him."

Tristin shook his head. "This is the only way it can end."

The Angel dropped to his rear. The hilt of his sword hit the ground between his legs and drove the blade through his chin and into his brain. His body stiffened briefly and then fell to the side.

Makenna turned away, tears blurring her eyes.

Though Tristin had hated the Angel for as long as he could remember, he felt a bit of sadness for him at that moment. He faced Makenna. "We should go."

"No. Not yet."

She went to the Angel's side and knelt. His chest slowly rose and fell as his blood stained the gold coins around him. Makenna lifted his hand onto her lap and held it. "No one should have to die alone," she said. And she sat with him until his breathing slowed and ultimately stopped. Then she gently laid his hand on his chest, stood up, and walked back to the others. Her swollen eyes were red and wet. "Now we can go." She went to Rhett, who enfolded her in his loving arms.

Tristin patted his sister's shoulder. "Things will be better now, I promise," he said. "I can't wait to show you what I've seen. This world is a beautiful place."

She smiled. "And I can't wait to see it."

Rhett grabbed Tristin's hand and pulled him in for a hug. Makenna joined them. Joseph picked up a gold coin and studied it. Then he tossed it back onto the pile.

Epilogue

A crowd had gathered at the Madson town square to hear an official announcement. Tristin stood in their midst with a hood pulled over his head. Since Searle had died without an heir, uncertainty within the kingdom now threatened to spill into unrest. Barbarians patrolled the streets just to keep the peace.

Ian made his way to the pretenders' stage. He had gained some weight back and was looking stronger. Kearney, Tolk, and Paedar flanked him. Seeing Ian climb onto stage quieted the crowd. Everyone was craving information, regardless of how they got it.

Ian smiled. "Good afternoon, my Madson brothers and sisters. My name is Ian. Over the weeks since the fall of King Searle and his Angel, the kingdom has grown fearful and uncertain. Fear of tomorrow is paralyzing you, but it doesn't have to be that way. I speak on behalf of all Terdicts when I say we seek an end to the division between our two districts. We seek a kingdom not where you have less, but where everyone has more. And we can do this. With your help, we can build the greatest, fairest, most prosperous kingdom the world has ever known.

"But we cannot do it without you. We have many plans and …"

Tristin turned and slipped out of the crowd while Ian continued to talk of peace and prosperity. There would be challenges, but his friends had gotten a good start.

Former prison guards had disclosed the location of a records room where everyone's crimes were written out. Already a large team of volunteers had headed to the prison to review them. As far as Ian and Tristin were concerned, the best way to give the kingdom a fresh start was to free everyone who hadn't been deemed too violent. Their sentences could be commuted to time served. The main problem they faced was identifying prisoners and matching them with their records with only tattoos and each individual's word to go on. Though it wasn't a perfect system, it was all they had to work with. Just sifting through the records and determining who was still alive versus who had already died threatened to take months.

Madson stores continued to receive supplies for free and keep their doors open until a better economy could be formed. Smarter people than Tristin would need to develop that, but Tristin knew one thing for sure: There would be no slave labor. There were plenty of people in need of jobs and plenty of gold in the castle to pay them.

While the anxious Madsons listened to Ian's speech, Tristin walked freely through the wealthy district without fear of being questioned for the first time in his life. He lowered his hood and looked around. It was a beautiful day, if a bit chilly.

A couple of Madson kids were playing chase on a side street. Tristin stopped to watch for a minute. One of them claimed to be a fog creature and started chasing the other.

"You'll never catch Tristin," the fleeing kid shouted.

Tristin grinned and continued his stroll. On the day before, he had heard how he'd stood up to the barbarian king and ordered him to free the people from King Searle's corrupt rule. One version even claimed that Tristin killed the Angel himself. It was all ridiculous, but the rumors still spread faster than level-headed rationale could douse them.

Tristin walked to the local medical clinic where some of the wounded had been taken for extended care. King Gaal was one of them. He sat in front of the clinic in a special wheeled chair Jakodi had built. His legs would never work again.

Tristin greeted the king with a smile. Gaal winced, though he tried to mask his obvious pain. "Tristin, ol' boy. How are you this fine day?"

"I'm fine, thanks. More importantly, how are you?"

"Good enough to dance," Gaal answered. He breathed in through his nose and let out his breath with a sigh. "Have you noticed how well the air is clearing?"

Tristin nodded. It had been days since he'd used his lifemask. He was fairly certain it would never chirp again.

He sat in a wicker chair next to Gaal. Neither of them said much—they didn't need to—as they watched the townspeople wander the streets, still trying to figure out what the new normal was going to be. Tristin didn't know how long he'd stayed there before Makenna approached.

"How's Ugh?" Makenna asked without saying hello.

Gaal chuckled at the nickname. "They say my brother should live, but it'll be a long road to recovery. I know you want to go see him, but I don't want anything taxing his recovery. He needs all his strength."

Makenna sighed and nodded. "Any word from the city wall today?"

Gaal answered, "Tolk says they're making slow but steady progress. Small sections have been razed and gates are being built. Once we eradicate the fog creatures we can consider demolishing it completely."

Tristin asked, "Are the crystals helpful in the hunts?"

"Immensely. The hunters have been able to follow them straight back to their nests. They'll find them all before long."

"And what are your plans, Your Majesty? After you get better, I mean."

"Will you please call me Oskari?"

"Never."

Gaal groaned. "Well, after my brother heals, I think we will do a bit of exploring."

"Oh?"

"Yes. I once met a traveler who talked of an incredible kingdom beyond the Infinite Sea. I think he called it Epertase."

"Hmph. That sounds dangerous."

"Oh no, my boy. That sounds exciting."

Makenna smiled. "Excuse my rudeness, but may I borrow my brother for a bit?"

Gaal bowed his head. "By all means."

She tugged Tristin's hand. "Will you go for a walk with me? I'd like to show you something."

Curious, Tristin rose from his seat. He patted Gaal's shoulder. "If you'll excuse me, *Oskari*." He let Makenna lead him away from the clinic.

"Are you going to come watch me tomorrow night?" Makenna asked.

"Are you really going to be on the stage?"

"Yes." She straightened her shoulders. "Emilia says I'm good enough already. I am officially a pretender now." Emilia was Joseph's daughter and a popular pretender. Ever since Joseph had introduced her to Makenna, the two had been almost inseparable. "I'm going to help tell the real story of the fall of King Searle. We've been working really hard in the evenings. We're almost ready."

"Then I wouldn't miss it." They continued walking west while Makenna talked about her new friends. Tristin listened quietly until his curiosity threatened to eat him alive. "Why are we going toward Slaybyrne?" he finally interrupted when she stopped for a wheeze-free breath.

"I want to visit our old home." She wore her mother's pendant proudly over her clean, tailored blouse. It was probably the nicest shirt she'd ever owned. Tristin still wouldn't admit that the brown stone was anything but ugly, but he had stopped razzing her about it.

They eventually reached their old neighborhood. When Tristin rounded the corner to where his parents' home had stood, his mouth dropped open. Makenna giggled. Instead of the rickety three-room shack with the broken door, he saw the skeletal frame of a new house being built. There were a dozen men working on it. A horse-drawn cart passed by full of new-cut wooden planks and boards. "What's going on, Makenna?"

"They're building a new house for you."

"For me? I don't understand."

"They want to thank you for what you've done for them."

He watched in awe as the workers planed wood and nailed up walls. Rhett caught his eye, waved, and then went back to his work. Even Clinton ran by with a bag of spikes.

"I … I can't believe this, Makenna. They're building us a house."

"Not *us*, Tristin. *You*. This is just for you." She tugged his hand. "Come on. That's not all I brought you to see."

He couldn't imagine anything topping what she had already shown him. She dragged him to the edge of town where the cobblestone street ended at the Slaybyrne's bank. With her hands covering his eyes, she led him down the bank and into the water. When it touched his feet, he leaped backward. "Makenna," he shouted, pulling her hands away from his eyes. "The grinderf—" He froze. Thousands of the lethal fish floated on the surface, some clearly dead while others wriggled in their death throes. Their eyes bulged with each feeble gasp as they floated by.

"They're dying, Tristin. They're all dying."

As Tristin stood stunned, unable to take his eyes from the yellow fish floating in the ever-clearing Slaybyrne, a crowd began to form behind him.

He slowly turned, almost paralyzed by their quiet, weighted gazes. It was as if they wanted him to say something, but he didn't know what to say. Instead, he looked down at his lifemask—that cursed and worthless reminder of King Searle's reign—hanging from his belt. They didn't need them anymore; they just needed someone to show them.

He undid the clasp, turned to the water again, and hurled his mask into the sea of dead and dying grinderfish. Makenna followed his lead, hurling her mask into the water as well.

The crowd stood in quiet shock until one man finally stepped forward, removed his own lifemask, and tossed it onto the bank. A woman stepped up and did the same, followed by a young boy. One by one, each person in the crowd dropped their masks.

Tristin silently vowed to help the people build a new world with fairness and equality. The people were on Tristin's side, and that was more powerful than any army. Together, he and Makenna stood and watched the death of the grinderfish usher in the birth of a bright new world. He thought about his mom and how badly he missed her. He pulled Makenna to his side and put his arm around her shoulders. She hugged his waist as they walked back to the city.

She bent down and plucked something from the dirt. "What's this?" she asked, and held out a thin, green sliver of a plant.

"Well, I'll be. That's called grass, sis."

"Grass? What's it do?"

"Heh." He put his arm around her again. "There's so much for you to see."

Makenna kissed his cheek.

END

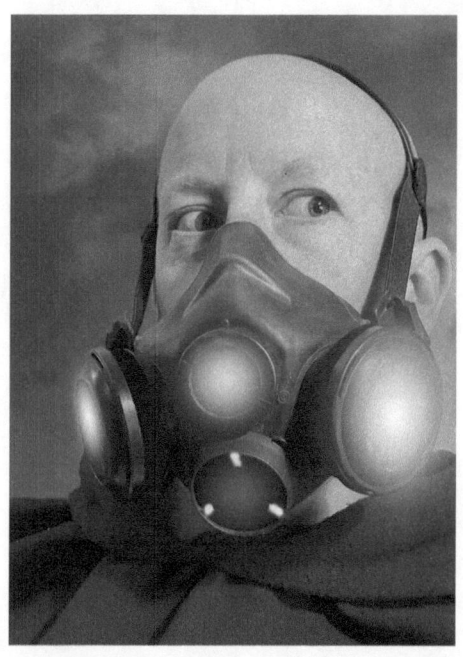

About the Author

Douglas R. Brown is a fantasy and horror writer living in Pataskala, Ohio. He began writing as a cathartic way of dealing with the day-to-day stresses of life as a firefighter/paramedic in Columbus, Ohio. Now he focuses his writing on fantasy and horror, where he can draw from his lifelong love of the genres. He has been married since 1996 and has a son. He has had four books published to date, including his werewolf tale with a twist, *Tamed*, and his fantasy series, *The Light of Epertase* trilogy. Though the publishing company ultimately closed its doors, Douglas has given his work a new home under his own imprint, Epertase Publishing, where he is proud to add his *Death of the Grinderfish* story to the catalogue. Visit Douglas at www.epertasepublishing.com or email him your thoughts at epertase@gmail.com.

Other Books By
Douglas R. Brown

Tamed

The Light of Epertase Trilogy
Including
Legends Reborn
A Kingdom's Fall
The Rise of Cridon

Coming Fall 2021
A Firefighter Christmas Carol